Bronzeville Books, LLC
269 S. Beverly Drive, #202
Beverly Hills, CA 90212
www.bronzevillebooks.com

Library of Congress Control Number: 2021949265

ISBN 978-1-952427-37-4 (hardcover)
ISBN 978-1-952427-38-1 (paperback)
ISBN 978-1-952427-39-8 (ebook)

First Edition

Cover Design: JT Lindroos
Book Design: Reggie Pulliam

TROY LOVE STORY

LIAM SWEENY

BRONZEVILLE™
— BOOKS —

*This story is dedicated to my father, Robert H. Sweeny,
and my good friend, Michelle Ward, two people who brought light
into the world that was darkened far too soon.*

Chapter One

Craig

Craig's eyes swam in tears as slivers of frigid, river-kissed wind found their way through the window frame. The bourbon was below the bottom of the label and the last of the pills sat on the coffee table, lonely, as their compatriots were fighting a war in his guts. Heavy metal music coursed through his laptop from a local internet radio station. The pounding of thrash riffs and double bass beats was no substitute for a spray of Naloxone and an AED. Craig trembled when he realized those last two would never come.

He didn't want to die. He wanted to get up in the morning and relish a warm shower, inhale Danielle's scrambled eggs on his way out the door. He wanted to stop at Tollsby's, like he did most mornings, a smile on his face as he laid down gridiron prophecies with his fellow grunts before they started their days in the cabs of F-150s. He wanted to get the house ready for Christmas as it neared. Tonight, he found himself wanting more.

He wanted his back not to spin acid-soaked webs through his muscles and bones. He wanted his shoulder to pick a spot he could press down on to get rid of that sickening feeling, if only for a few seconds. He wanted that good high he used to get when he'd come home after eight hours of pushing muscle on a road crew. He wanted his sacrifice to mean something other than new pain.

Downstairs, Danielle slept. It should have been him that took the couch, put in earplugs to keep the kids from waking him up at 6 a.m. in their battle for the last blueberry waffle. He was a man, and a man suffered the couch-cushions so their woman could rest in the bed. Hell, a real man didn't have to sleep somewhere else, because any time their wife tossed and turned, an alarm buzzer of fresh agony woke them up. His forty-three years congealed his blood. Or maybe it was the Vicodin.

Craig cried out. A creaky gasp disintegrated into the cold air. He couldn't call out. He couldn't move or lift his arms enough to plant them on the armrests and push himself up. He felt pinpricks of ice hit his wind-chapped cheek. He rolled his head to the side and noticed that the plastic had fallen off the window, and what little warmth it offered disappeared along with the sensation in the pads of his feet.

He wanted to chuckle at the irony, that part of the pain that drove him to feast on Vicodin that night came from his working overtime to pay for new windows, which were getting put in the following week. Every band-aid on their battered Victorian was a week of hours spent under balloon lights hoping some text-obsessed asshole didn't pop over the traffic cones. Every envelope in the mail might be the one he had to hide from his wife.

It wasn't supposed to end like this. Not slobbering on himself, not panicking beneath the collapse of his pulse when everyone he loved was in an early Tuesday night slumber. He was fading with a pocket full of hundred-dollar bills, each one earmarked for the upkeep of their good life. His vision tinted dark, and he fought to keep his mind on his hits more than his misses.

He married his best girl, the one he sat behind in math class freshman year, the one everyone assumed would take his last name one day, so they teased endlessly when he and Danielle began dating. They owned, didn't rent. They paid a loan officer who stayed the fuck home, not a landlord with an appetite for surprise inspections. They had kids that would grow up to go college and move past them on the social ladder.

Danielle joked about him getting a will, until it wasn't a joke. Then it wasn't in the budget to follow through with a lawyer. It was tomorrow's problem.

His sternum was taking on weight, pushing into his lungs, pressing his breath like a boa constrictor. Pins and needles mixed with ice crystals on his skin. So many things were tomorrow's problem. But what happened when it was your last today?

He was finding out. Craig's eyes were heavy, and it took a sheer force of will not to succumb to a permanent, midnight sleep. He started to breathe, really breathe. Heavier than he did even when he wasn't loaded with downers. He snapped his eyes open and planted his hands on the armrests, pushing the pain back into the place where he held the hard memories—of cockroaches in the cupboards when he was growing up in the projects; of his mother's heaping ashtray at the dinner table; his father's hard drinking and his harder belt buckle collection. He pushed the pain back and he launched himself off the chair.

He saw it all again, all the horror, all the hope. He planted his numb, wobbly legs on the shag carpet. It was only ten feet to the door, but so much farther to the stairway. Maybe if he got out into the hallway he could fall, and Danielle would hear him. She'd rush up. She'd save him; she was a nurse. She had Naloxone and she knew CPR. Just ten feet.

Jimi started singing "All Along the Watchtower" when he hit the five-foot mark and in a split half-second his focus was on the guitar and not on the shag. That soon changed. Another split half-second sent him flat, bashing his chest and chin, squeezing out whatever adrenaline his body could pump. His tear ducts had since dried up and the pins and needles had spread like a wet table through a paper towel. His vision became fuzzy. The sounds from the laptop slid into mud.

His mind drifted to a ride at the Adirondack Playworld, a round chamber that spun so fast, the force pinned people to the walls. As his flame began to eat the matchstick and the night overtook him, he bounced a mantra in his head, a token to whatever gate he'd find through the shadows.

I tried.

Danielle

Danielle started the worst day of her life with a broken shoelace. She fell apart when it snapped in her hand, almost sending her crashing to the ground. And saying her day started then was not altogether true, but it was the first thing she noticed when the sun came up. The shoelace breaking was the first real thing to happen since they turned the lights off on the ambulance, because the paramedics knew they were at least three hours past it being an emergency. She kept the lace in her balled-up fist until Marybeth's crying drew her hand to her child's cheek.

The neighbor's hellhound woke her up. That's how she found Craig crumpled on the ground in his study. He was soaked in his own piss when she turned him over, and a slick broth trailed off his mouth onto his shirt and the floor. It didn't look like throw up, but the paramedic said that's what it was. The look on their faces, the jaded stares off to the side—they'd seen it so many times. But it was different for her. Then again, she supposed it was always different when it was someone you loved.

She could still feel the weight of him when she turned him, when she shook him, when she pounded his chest in a futile attempt to keep her world right side up. Like a tough roast in the plastic. He'd just been having double helpings of mashed potatoes and then he was an unyielding slab. She screamed like she had words that would punish God, but her shrieks became molten sobs by the time her little boy Joey pried the door open, Marybeth in tow. They poked at him, but if there was a blessing, it was that Marybeth was too young to know that Daddy wasn't sleeping.

Danielle pulled her phone out of her pocket and stared at the lock screen. No one knew. Not her mother-in-law, who'd surely blame her. His friends would probably know more than she did, but the thought of them condescending to a witless widow turned her stomach. Her own mom would be happy to be rid of a guy she thought wasn't good enough for her daughter, a guy that brought her away from a major design firm to play commoner. Her mom would jeer, and then she wouldn't have a mom anymore.

She dialed the first number on the speed dial. Three rings and she heard house music and engine noise in the background.

"Whattup, babe?"

"Sandy, it's Craig," she said. Saying his name aloud brought everything into a focus that was quick to spin and blur.

"What happened? Is everything okay?"

"He's—" Danielle had a hard time finishing. "I found him last night."

"Found him what?"

"He wasn't moving… I tried to—" Danielle was crying. "He's dead." She held the phone away to keep Sandy's questions at bay.

"Honey, where are you?"

Danielle wiped her nose on a rag. "I'm home with the kids. The cops were here this morning asking me questions. They wanted to search the house for fucking drugs. They think he was a junkie."

"Oh God. Do you know what happened?"

"No. He had Vicodins for his back, and the bottle I got him for Christmas was up there. What if he—"

"No. No way he did that. He knows better." Sandy lowered her voice. "Who knows?"

"Nobody. Me, Marybeth, Joey… now you. I can't call anyone else yet. I'm having a real hard time dealing. I got Marybeth in daycare, got her home early an hour ago. Thought it'd be easier for some reason. Joey never went to school; I didn't even try. I couldn't even call the school myself. The cops said they'd do it."

"How are they?" Sandy asked.

Danielle wiped her face. "Joey's snapping at Marybeth. I don't think either of them fully realize yet. Beth is so little." She took a deep breath. "Sandy, what the fuck am I going to do?"

"You guys can stay here if you want."

Danielle heard a voice grumble in the background—probably Sandy's boyfriend, Mark, who didn't appreciate the idea.

"Yes, they fucking can," Sandy shot back, before returning to the call.

"Sorry about that," she said. "Seriously, don't stay in that house tonight. We got the couch bed, and we can have Billy and Jake stay at my sister's house so Joey and Marybeth can sleep on their bunks."

Danielle didn't want to start her first day alone being a burden to the people around her. There wasn't anything wrong with their house that wasn't already wrong with it. She knew that was a lie. The house might as well have been gutted from a sinkhole that opened up in the study. She knew she wouldn't get any sleep there that night.

"Thanks, Sandy. I'll call you later."

Maybe Danielle wouldn't sleep anywhere for the next few days, but at least at Sandy's, she'd have her night-owl friend for company and coffee.

The rain started coming down outside, washing the tire impressions off the blacktop. Craig had spent this past Saturday working on the driveway, a twelve pack of light beer in a red, white, and blue cooler on the porch and some local garage rock pumping out of the stereo system in his study, the speakers in the open window, aimed outside. He was over the moon because he'd just got back injections from his doctor, and despite the doc's warnings not to do too much, he felt industrious.

Danielle started making more calls. Telling Sandy was the first cut; the rest wouldn't hurt as bad.

By the time she got to her mother, she might as well have been reading a script.

"I'm not going to tell you what I really think, Dani," she said. "I love you and I know you loved him. But you have to think of the here and now."

"I know, Mom."

"Did you and Craig draw up a will?"

"Mom, I'm not even thinking of that right now."

She heard her mother letting out a breath of smoke. She could picture her on the landline, twirling the long, curly cable in her fingers.

"I've been through this. It's you and the state of New York. Only one of you feels like grieving. You're gonna have to shelve it and take care of your business. He left you holding a bunch of bags. They all have precious cargo." Another breath. "If you need to stay here, you can. I'll clean out your old room."

Danielle watched as lightning tore the gray sky white. The rain was cascading in torrents and the wind blew the oak branches like they were threaded with elastic.

"I gotta go, Mom." Danielle hung up and went to the front door. Walking out on the porch, she felt the spray of the storm and pondered an uncertain forecast.

Donny

Donny hung up the phone, walked over to the new plate-glass window they just installed, and put his fist through it. Harry asked him why he didn't smash the old one on the far wall before realizing that it wasn't time for jokes. That was about the same time the blood started seeping onto the hardwood floor, also just put in.

"What the fuck, Donny?" Harry pulled a drop cloth off the floor and rushed it over to wrap up his hand. "Meyer's gonna fucking kill you. Who was that?"

Donny ran his uninjured hand through his hair. "Danielle. Craig's dead."

Harry took a box cutter and sliced at the cloth, leaving enough to do a piss-poor job of soaking up blood. Donny knew he was going to have to go to the ER. Meyer had been gunning to fire him ever since he'd missed the last weekend bonus work. Meyer didn't care if you got high, drunk, robbed banks, or molested kids, but you started missing days, you were a rabid dog to him. Next time you called Meyer, he'd let you know he "didn't need anybody today." And that was that.

"C'mon, dude," Harry said. "We gotta clean this shit up."

"Did you fucking hear me? Craig's dead."

"Yeah. It's fucked up."

"That's what you got? It's *fucked up*? Craig vouched for you. You wouldn't have survived high school if he didn't vouch for you. Don't you even want to know how he died?"

"I want to keep my job. I'm barely treading water right now and I can't afford Meyer pulling one of his tantrums over a broken window. Let's get this shit cleaned up, and you can tell me about it on the way to the hospital before it's too late." Harry grabbed a broom and a dustpan from the closet and circled around the glass on the floor.

Meyer was a neurotic bedbug of a man. He could be in the middle of a brawl and not care about getting punched in the face fifty times, but if one of those shots broke his fifty-dollar glasses, that was unacceptable, and that meant everybody had to die. He was a big guy, mostly fat, but at his size it didn't matter. It didn't matter what a freight train was made of when it hit you.

Donny walked out of the room and made his way to the back patio. The walls were wrapped in Tyvek and the yard was filled with plastic-covered plywood and bare vinyl siding. Pushing his pack up through his shirt, he pulled out a bent cigarette. He didn't bother straightening it out before he lit it to draw in a moment's peace and clarity.

Craig's name was a roadblock to every thought. *I got to get the truck back to Craig— Craig was supposed to— What's going to happen to Craig's—* like his train of thought was a king in a chess stalemate. Donny's mental moves became so erratic, he zoned out and felt the big empty of his heart breaking.

Donny met Craig in the fourth grade, decked out on the first day of class in a plaid button-down under a gray sweater. Long before he got the laser surgery, he wore thick glasses, which made him an easy target. Donny didn't know then how rough he had it at home, but he knew the other kids' taunts were something that had to be answered for, and Craig didn't have it in him.

They made a pact back when words like that were magic, and they conquered the schoolyard and street in a city that tossed other kids around. They knew too many cops by face. One time, Craig busted a car window 'cause Donny got sent to six months of juvie and Craig needed to get in to help his buddy escape. The plan didn't work, leaving Craig a glass repair bill to work off over the summer.

Maybe if Craig had done the juvie time, he would've spent the past twenty years on the same rollercoaster Donny had. Maybe he wouldn't have married Danielle, been in that house—maybe he'd be alive, waking up at noon, gargling vodka and fishing stubs out of the ashtray. Or maybe he'd have been dead long before then, leaving Donny to fix his own messes. Donny's laugh came out bittersweet. He wasn't the philosophical one.

"Donny, you wanna tell me about the window?" Meyer stood in the doorway, looking away as he picked a fleck of paint from the frame.

"Sorry, Mr. Meyer," Donny said. "I got a really bad phone call. A friend just died."

"Sorry to hear about your friend. But I'm gonna have to charge you for the window, though. Not trying to be a hard-ass."

"I understand," Donny said. Meyer's calm unnerved him.

The rain was picking up, peppering shots off the plastic in the yard, rippling through the growing puddles, circles overtaking circles like art he saw in one of the River Street galleries. The cigarette's ember wrapped around the filter and he flicked it in the puddle. Let the landscaper deal with it.

Harry was putting up the last of the sheetrock when Donny got back upstairs. He looked at his hand, which had stopped bleeding before he went outside. But the shock was wearing off, and now the pain was crystalline and real. He knew he needed to go to the ER, or at least see his doctor. He didn't know how long it would be before stitches were pointless. He couldn't get away with having a fucked-up hand doing the shit he did.

Donny helped Harry do all the touch-up best he could, careful not to scrape his hand against any surfaces, both to avoid the pain and smearing blood. By the time lunch rolled around, Donny couldn't hide the agony any longer.

Meyer walked up to the truck as Donny and Harry chowed down on their sandwiches.

"Donny, you need to go to the hospital," he said. "Take care of that hand."

"I can get through the day, I'm good." It was a lie, but people expect lies.

Meyer looked out over the development, a cookie-cutter community across the river from the northern end of Troy. They had a view of the water, made murky by the mud and sewage drawn up in the previous day's downpour.

"Go and get yourself taken care of, Donny," he said. "Give me a call tomorrow. We'll be finished up here, but I'm sure we'll have something else for you."

Chapter Two

Rob

Rob crumpled the lakehouse in his rough hands as a fishing boat sailed past the overlook. He cursed the gods of fortune, whose favor fell on an office pool in Ohio. Two hundred and fifty-seven million. It surprised him that a rustic, three bedroom on a no-name lake and a passion project '57 Chevy were all he could dream up. Truth be told, with half of that jackpot, he could've named the lake after himself, and bought one of every car made in 1957. Perhaps a hard life had made him humble. Or maybe his ego would've grown to match the size of that check. The answer to that floated through a stiff breeze as Rob let it go.

His eyes rested on the dead grass on the shore below. Juliet used to fish from the edge of the water, sour gummy worms as bait. He'd like to think it was her innocence, but she knew she couldn't catch anything with candy. She'd gagged when Rob put her hook through the first and last nightcrawler she'd ever use. She cried as it was pierced. He raised his voice when he commanded she cast the line. He knew she had to be as strong and tough as the world would soon be for her.

Or maybe he was just an asshole too stupid to admire what she had.

He picked up the paper and scanned the classifieds. Until Hannigan's gave him the shove last week, he hadn't realized that the jobs section was losing column inches to opinion pages where talking heads worshipped mythical job creators. Welding was a good trade. He could've got a good-paying job anywhere, except for the place where he was, where his mother and father wouldn't leave. Back in the day around the five-one-eight they pitched welding school so hard, they had an army with self-darkening helmets and glowing blue-white arcs. But the war had left years ago.

Ken Hannigan was an affable guy who'd take the company pickup out to the job, in the middle of nowhere, with silver airpots full of dark roast and blue coolers of off-label spring water in the bed. Ken paid everybody out of his own pocket when he couldn't make payroll, but nobody expected him to survive that way. Rob choked back rage at the fact that he had to console the person taking his job. It wasn't right. Nothing lately was right.

Letting go of the lottery ticket, the only paper that mattered was the twelve dollars in his wallet. It was just enough to get what he needed to make his mother some eggplant parmesan. She'd taught him the recipe so many years ago, back when the pain wasn't so bad; back when she could stand in a kitchen for hours over a boiling pot, waving a sauce-covered spoon like a scepter over her culinary fiefdom.

But the pain had overtaken her, stealing so much. In weird way, though, that pain also kept her spirit burning, keeping it bright like an ember. Forcing her to be hopeful, passionate, about getting better. Rob couldn't show her the cost of the surgery. Neither could his father. They hoped it would work. She'd be able to get up more, to move with more freedom, and make plans around her desires instead of her limitations. But if his mother knew the cost, she'd never allow them to take on the debt. And Dad couldn't keep it from her forever. It would be written on his face in worrisome creases as he struggled to balance all the burning balls that kept the family afloat.

No, Rob needed a way out of this. Twenty-six-thousand, eight-hundred-and-forty-three dollars, and ninety-five cents, to be exact. That was the amount on the letter from the hospital. The ink might as well have been in high-def; it crowded out the rest. His mother might get her life back, but it would cost them close to thirty grand.

In the big picture, it wasn't bad, he supposed. That was a semester at a decent college or a new, mid-price sedan. Small price to pay, really. Hell of a deal. Something his dad said once stuck to him like a commandment: A dollar's a great deal for everyone but the guy with ninety-nine cents. The hospital letter was like the lottery ticket in reverse.

Rob crossed his arms, clenched his fists and twisted his torso left and right, waiting for his back to pop out the kinks. His body aches had become a living resume. He felt the dull throb in his shoulders from where he landed after falling from a ladder when he was a kid, painting garages and porches for his neighbors. His ribs had the tiniest sting in them from when he got hit by the swing arm of a backhoe, which was also the day he decided never to drink vodka on a weeknight. His arms were crisscrossed with burn marks brought about by itinerant kitchen work and the sparks that caught him through his PPE.

Rob got up and waited out his body's protest. He felt the sound of crunching leaves wash over him as he walked off the overlook and down the trail. Peebles Island State Park compensated for living across the river from Van Schaick Island, which connected to it by a steel one-way bridge that could've doubled as a railroad bridge if seen from afar. Peebles Island, and Van Schaick, for that matter, were the last line of defense for the continental army if General Burgoyne's troops had won in Saratoga.

Two hundred years later, earthen breastworks still existed from where the cannons would have been placed. Maybe that's why Rob liked it. It was the place of the last stand that wasn't needed, a monument to the reprieves of history. Rob dug in his pocket and pulled out his phone. He'd just paid the phone bill but the clock was ticking. They had and would turn it off if he was more than three days late. He pulled up his speed-dial panel. Why was she still there? He knew he wasn't on hers—he was lucky if he was even a contact in her phone anymore. He found himself pressing her number with his thumb as he reached for his flattened pack of menthols.

"What?"

"What do you mean, what? Is that how you answer your phone to strangers?"

"No, I might want to hear from a stranger."

"Did you hear I got laid off?"

"How could I?" she said. "I don't know your boss."

"I thought you'd want to know."

"You don't pay alimony, and Juliet—"

"Just stop," he said.

"No, you stop. You don't own our grief. I can talk about Jules too. And you've got to stop thinking what happened is some kind of chain binding us together. You have no right to use her like that."

"I don't know what to do. I'm having a hard time."

"You spent our whole marriage knowing what you were doing. You don't get to keep calling me every time you stub your toe now."

"Can we just stop?"

"When you stop calling me every day, maybe we can be civil. But I've got a fiancé now. And he's not screaming at me about you calling. But it's not fair to him. I won't lose him over you."

Rob glanced down the road before crossing, though there was never traffic into the park at that hour.

"I'm glad that you're happy, anyway."

"I wish you meant that, Rob. I have to go."

"Can you do me a favor—"

The call ended before he could finish.

Asher

His after-market sound system pumped neo-funk as his fingers pressed into the steering wheel in time to the pulses of a pipe organ blowing spectral grooves, its notes crunching in syncopation with a pristine crash cymbal. The block was quiet for ten in the morning. The fancy ladies were wearing hooded sweatshirts and pajama bottoms, walking to the bodega to buy formula and USA Gold 100s.

He knew he'd get dirty looks on his block if he didn't turn the music down. Between Frank Bilica sleeping off his second job and Freida Thomas, whose sole job it was to sip Irish coffee on her front porch year-round and stick her nose in everyone's business, he might as well have been driving into the main floor of the library. Asher lowered the volume as he turned on 118th Street. He was already working off back rent; he didn't need to give his landlord any reminders.

Asher locked his doors, then remembered he had to pop the trunk, and his key fob was dead on the keyring. He brought home his guitar and his effects rig, which amounted to a year's worth of scavenging at the local music shops. He'd DIY'd the pedal board from a shelving unit. These things worked, but they weren't glamorous. Sound was his lover and he was not monogamous.

He turned to see Freida approaching from across the street, waving her hand as her tortoiseshell cane guided her over the cracks.

"You can pull up a little bit to the next car, you know. Then there will be enough room for another car behind you."

"Hi, Freida. I love you too."

Either she was not affected by Asher's sentiment or she had her hearing aid in backward again.

"If we all do our part, no one has to park on the other street from where they live."

"I'll keep that in mind for next time, but I'm a little busy right now."

She wiped her glasses with one of her talons and moved them up her nose. "You're not going to play music this morning, are you? Because Frank is trying to sleep, and he really needs his sleep. He's got a job."

"I've got a job too, Freida," Asher said through breaths as he made his way to his front door, his arms full. "And if his job's so good, why's he livin' here?"

He shut the door on Freida. One good thing about her is that her memory wasn't good enough to realize what a dick he was to her most days. He freed a hand to check the mailbox. His downstairs neighbor had bought mailboxes for the inside hallway. He was cool enough to buy two.

Asher turned to the sound of the door creaking. Carl popped out in a blue flannel bathrobe, a veteran of many overindulgent nights.

"Hey, Asher, bro, you want a hand with that shit?"

"Sure." Asher handed him the part of the rig that wouldn't be impossible to replace, and they walked up the steps to the second-floor landing. Asher balanced the box of pedals on his hip as Carl reported the news of the neighborhood. In a way, he was like Freida, except that his business was closer to Asher's own. He told Asher about the apartment at a show last summer, so they were in the same orbits.

"You hear about Craig Hill?"

"Nah, what about him?"

"Dead, dude."

"Damn, that sucks," Asher said. "He was a good guy." Asher sat the box down on an open spot on his couch and rifled through the cushions for the remote.

"Yeah, and that Danielle… She's gonna need someone to be around."

"Oh, Carl, c'mon, man, don't be gross."

"I've had a thing for her since she used to lifeguard up at the South Troy Pool."

"When was that? Aren't you, like, forty?"

"This was the nineties. I wasn't forty then. And seriously, she was the hottest chick in South Troy."

"You snort pecker pills in your free time?" Asher found the remote and turned on one of the baby-daddy talk shows. He didn't give a shit who was screwing who, but Carl hated those shows.

"All right, buddy, I'm gonna head back down," Carl said. "Do me a favor, you know, what I said about Danielle…"

"Don't worry, I try not to remember half the shit that comes out of your mouth. But seriously though … bad dog."

"Ruff ruff." Carl let himself out. Asher turned the sound down on the television because, to be honest, he didn't like the baby-daddy drama either. He wouldn't tell Danielle what Carl said, not out of any loyalty, but out of the ridiculousness of the whole thing. Carl was a guy who used to be cool. He was in a hot band called Shift when the mall belonged to their crew, before the epicenter of all social activity was a cellphone. By current standards, they had a lackluster run. Hell, Asher's band played more shows than Carl's did. But there was something about musicians in the nineties. Gear wasn't so cheap, and the venues weren't so indifferent to who they booked, which today meant putting you on when your only draw was ten friends. 'Cause they used to pay for talent, and now bands like Asher's were giving it away for free exposure.

Asher walked out into the kitchen and pulled a soda out of the fridge. Too early for beer. He didn't have a show that night, but he promised himself he wouldn't waste whole days.

His need of a new sound coincided with the new place that had opened up down on the riverfront. It looked cool, like an old roadhouse in a pulp novel, red-and-blue neon proclaiming Sam Wilson's open for business.

He picked up their card from the bulletin board at the Beat Shop. Sam Wilson's sure did their homework, the Beat Shop being the one place in the Capital Region where every local band or act held lunchtime court on weekends. The card had the feel of black felt and purple satin. Troy was a junkie for concert venues, love at first sight with everyone.

Asher whipped out his phone and squinted at the number. He punched it in and stared out the window as it rang. Maybe Sam Wilson's would love Troy back.

Jordan

Crunchy guitar riffs invaded Jordan's ears, finding her nervous system and ringing up and down her spinal cord. The blast-beat pushed the sweet release through her sluggish muscles. Her feet chewed up cracked concrete and her ankles swiveled to counter the uneven blocks that made up the First Street sidewalk. She was battling the cold in a runner's outfit that fit a little too snug and a Baphomet T-shirt.

She didn't run when she lived in the city. She had a gym membership, and her neighborhood offered views of dumpsters, chained storefronts, and lumps in the ground under blankets that may or may not have been dead people. New York City was a tourist wonderland, but it had down-and-dirty guts, and she lived in the large intestines. But she never felt unsafe, even if she should've.

Troy was a hell of a lot quieter, but she didn't see it as much friendlier. When she moved into her apartment on Fifteenth Street, her neighbors welcomed her by shielding her driveway with their cars because her apartment had been vacant for so long and they were too lazy to back into their own driveways. It was a good thing her dog Mitzi liked pissing on SUVs.

Nearing downtown, she checked her watch, calculating she'd be able to meet her dad at the Bagel Shoppe on time, but only if she slowed her pace. Otherwise, she'd be there early, which meant she'd wander through the historic district and find some architectural feature that Sam Wilson's would have to have, and she only had so many doors to re-handle, or windows to re-frame.

She had a band for tomorrow night. Sounded like a jam band, which wasn't exactly her groove, but what she was learning, in fits and starts, was that it no longer mattered what she liked. It was all about audience and draw. She had to live with herself, probably wouldn't book country or gangster rap, but every act, every band that she put on that stage had to pull in a crowd, who, in turn, would order beer, whiskey, scotch, rum, keeping the cash flowing. She'd given birth to her very own scene when she signed the loan papers. So hopefully this Captain Pneuma would bring a thirsty Thursday night crowd.

Jordan was getting near Frear College, with a campus nestled over the Congress Street tunnel that brought Route 2 traffic into Troy. She was dodging guys in black ski jackets and skinny jeans with store-bought frayed edges and girls in billowy knit sweaters, matching scarves, and face-covering sunglasses. Everyone had a cup of coffee from The Beanery, which might as well have been yet another fashion accessory. Maybe Jordan was bitter, but nowhere near as bitter as that burnt Beanery roast.

She rounded the corner to the Bagel Shoppe and checked her watch. She'd have enough time to check her email before her dad showed up. He was punctual to a fault, being one of the few people that could plan a drive to see her in Manhattan and actually arrive, via car, on time. He worked in the railyard in Albany, which ensured that he would always catch dawn on the job.

"Hey, hon." His voice startled her from behind. She only heard it because she'd just turned off her MP3 player.

"Dad, you're early. That's weird."

"Not so much," he said. "I told you I'd meet you here at one. I didn't say I was coming to Troy at one."

"That's splitting hairs."

"Until I don't have many left." He hugged her with an arm that could wrench iron levers loose, and kissed the top of her head.

"I'm sweaty."

"You've peed on me before."

"Oh, Dad! That's gross. And you never changed me. Mom said she couldn't ever get you to."

"She couldn't ever get me to *again*." He pulled out his wallet. "C'mon, kiddo, let's grub up."

They walked into the Bagel Shoppe, which Jordan liked, but it wasn't really a bagel shop. There were five things people from the city were sentimental about, from her time as an upstate transplant: pizza, taxis, the subway, rats, and, last but certainly not least, bagels. There was not only a way they were supposed to be made and a way they were supposed to taste, but also a way they were supposed to be sold, an attitude.

Troy had plenty of attitude, but not for slinging dough. Jordan didn't mind, though. She didn't move back to Troy for bagels. Looking over the college crowd, hipsters to a last one, she felt a sinking in her gut that she hadn't come home to Troy. At least not the one she remembered, with the city pool summers and ice-skating winters. Every day brought new unsettling news. Someone she had known in the old crew was in jail now, or married and living in the suburbs, which Jordan didn't see as much different. And of course, the deaths, some that shocked her, and some that, sadly, didn't.

"You okay, kiddo?"

"Yeah." Jordan yawned. "A lot on my mind."

"Business picking up?"

"I have a slow trickle of people coming in, but I'm not expecting huge crowds on the weeknights. I am worried, though."

She pointed to the crowd around them. Her dad caught on. They had developed an almost sign language, which was how she communicated with him whenever she'd visit the railyards, because he never would've heard her otherwise.

"I came home expecting a roadhouse crowd waiting for rock-and-roll and metal, and it's looking a whole lot like house music or dubstep. I hope my crowd isn't in bed by the time I open the doors."

"So you got old. You can always open at noon to catch us geriatric folks. Make sure you mash up your lime wedges so we can chew 'em."

Jordan rapped on her dad's chest. "C'mon, now."

They ordered two bagels and two coffees, Jordan's dad a lot less finicky about it than his daughter. She settled on an onion bagel with smoked salmon cream cheese, which was a blasphemy, but she was wearing a Baphomet T-shirt, so she may as well offend her stomach too.

"I was listening to the radio this morning," her dad said. "Did they tell you about the Riverfront Renewal project?"

"Who's *they*?"

"I don't know, the city? Your bank?"

"No. What is it?"

Her dad took a bite, swiping his napkin. "They got a grant to revive the riverfront. They're talking about doing a bike trail all the way from the Waterford Bridge in Lansingburgh to the 378 Bridge. They have a park planned for the lot that Sam Wilson's is on. They really didn't tell you?"

"No?" Jordan put down her bagel. "Don't they have to?"

"I don't know, maybe they're going to work around your property?" He picked up his coffee. "I wouldn't worry about it. If they needed to move you out, you wouldn't have been able to secure a loan with the bank in the first place." He patted her hand. "Hey, it could be a good thing—people emptying out into your front yard."

Jordan's brow furrowed.

"Hey, now, you know the deal," he said. "Get your ass down to city hall and do your research before you assume the worst. And put it in God's hands." He glanced at her shirt. "…or, you know, whoever."

Chapter Three

Danielle

No amount of grief can press forever, lest it kill its host. It comes in waves, which can be broken by the simple rituals, like two young children stuck in the back seat of a cramped car.

"Mom, Joey's foot is in my spot." Marybeth punctuated the last word with a stuffed monkey shot across Joey's nose.

"Ow, mom!"

"Both of you, enough," Danielle said. "We'll be at Aunt Sandy's in a minute."

"I want to play *Creature Builder*."

"Only if the boys let you play their games. They're not going to be there all night."

"Where they going, Mom?" Marybeth said. "Are they going away too?"

Danielle's eyes dropped for a moment to check the dashboard. "No, they're going to their gram's house. They'll be back tomorrow, okay, honey?"

"Why can't they stay home? I want to play with the guitar."

"It's not a real guitar, Beth, it's plastic. And you stink at it—"

"Watch your mouth, Joey..."

Joey swung his foot to the side but stopped short of hitting Marybeth in the shins. He folded his arms and shut his eyes, pretending to sleep.

Danielle stared at the red light they were waiting under, piercing it with her stare, as if that could make transistors pop left instead of right and grant passage beneath the longest light in the South End. A cold gust of wind blew. She tore her eyes off the light to watch a page of the newspaper twist, contort, and sail through the fog that hung over the five-way intersection. It was the only movement on an empty street too cold for even the dealers and junkies.

Craig would've been out that day, working the on-ramp to the 378 Bridge from 787, the winner of a little New York State love. The governor issued a decree, granting funds for bridge repair, and showing a little love for the upstaters in the process.

Of course the governor couldn't care less about Route 378 or upstate New York. His chauffeur had taken the bridge as a shortcut on the way to a bed-and-breakfast in Vermont, which resulted in a flat tire and bent rim. An inconvenience. That was talk, anyway, which flowed on worksites like asphalt. Danielle wondered what the workers were saying when Craig didn't show up for work that morning.

They rounded the mural of the Burden Waterwheel that formed the corner of Mill Street, which went up the hill toward the college and away from South Troy. Sandy lived on the hill, in a nook that was, arguably, "deep South Troy," a point of Troy pride if someone agreed on what constituted good borders in Troy. Sandy didn't care for pride unless she had eight-and-a-half beers in her. Then the old South Troy hardcore came out.

Sandy's porchlight was on when they pulled up. A white picket fence and a garden yard. Almost magazine quality, except the picket fences were plastic and from the Dollar Friendly store. The garden had red, white, and blue winter bulbs, the names of which Danielle never remembered no matter how many times a drunken Sandy pointed them out. Sandy had a makeshift playground in the backyard, just visible from the front, where her youngest, Jake, played. It was old and breaking down, since at one point it had been her son Billy's, and he was five years older, but it had been a while since Billy played like that.

Danielle got the kids out of the back seat, counting her blessings that Marybeth was too tired to wriggle through her unbolting. Joey had released his harness and was on his way to the door by the time Danielle turned around. He was growing up so fast. Now he'd have to grow a different way. Queasiness washed over her.

"Hey, girl," Sandy said. "Hurry up, it's cold as my tits out here."

"Hey, mouth, kids."

"They've heard worse, Dani."

Danielle lugged Marybeth up the steps. Her exhaustion gave way to manic energy once they walked in the door and she heard the other kids' voices playing ping pong against the walls. She squirmed to be free, and Danielle set her down like a wind-up race car, before following Sandy into the kitchen, enticed by the smell of Rocket Fuel coffee, which she'd recognize anywhere. Mark worked for the company up in Glens Falls.

"Where's Mark?"

"He's putting in some overtime tonight," Sandy said.

"He doesn't like me very much, does he?"

"It's not that." Sandy pulled a Yankees mug out of the cupboard. "He's a private person. I mean, look at how we hooked up. He's still not over the way we had to go about things."

Sandy and Mark started their relationship in the shadow of her marriage to her former husband and father of her kids, Kyle, a loathsome piece of shit who broke Sandy's face with his fists and her heart with a steady diet of manipulation. Except in public, where Kyle pretended to be a great guy. Everyone thought they were the couple to beat. To those who knew Kyle, Mark was a homewrecker. Danielle knew better. But she had her own problems to worry about. And for that she'd earned Mark's scorn, which ate Danielle up as much as the Rocket Fuel now gnawing her empty gut.

"I got a letter for you," Sandy said. "It's from the pharmacy, but you know, it's heartfelt." Sandy pulled out the envelope and slid it in her pocket. "Open it whenever you feel ready."

"Thanks, Sandy." They sat at the table and drank coffee. They talked about Craig, but not the Craig on the floor the night before, or the Craig that came home and had to sit in a hot tub for an hour, or the Craig who couldn't lift his four-year-old daughter by the time he was forty.

They talked as sisters talked, about the wedding and the only good day Sandy had with Kyle. About the shows they used to have at the park, when every band that had the presence of mind to bring gear and plug into the park power could have a rip at some all-American glory, and Sandy and Danielle could have a rip at a flask of coconut-flavored rum mixed with a touch of grain alcohol. They talked about the kids, school, and what they'd do during the fast-approaching winter break. Danielle, after a fit of laughter preceded a long silence, said, "I don't know how I'm going to pull this off, sis."

Sandy placed her warm, plump hand on Danielle's, giving a gentle squeeze.

"Just know you won't have to do it alone."

Donny

The streetlights and the glow from thirty blocks of rowhouse windows were the stars and the nebulae that covered Troy from the cliffs of Oakwood Cemetery. Donny called up everyone he had in mind for pallbearers. Danielle hadn't asked him to, but it was the least he could do. She carried all the weight on her shoulders, not least of which was finding a casket big enough to fit that solid fuck. All Donny had was an ounce of Vermont-grown Sticky, and the shopping bag of forties he swiped from the 112st Street Market while the owner watched soccer instead of his cameras. He didn't need to steal them—Donny had a hundred in his pocket—but he and Craig had been robbing forties from that store since they were kids.

Donny gathered brush, illuminated by his keychain flashlight. Maybe he needed to steal something that night as much as he needed to drink, and for the same reason. He hoped the cops would find it too ass-numbingly cold to go up and fuck with them. And he was counting on only drinking with the toughest sons-of-bitches that could lift a pine box.

He got the fire going, small but still able to push some heat, when he heard arguing and laughing in the weeds.

"About damn time."

Terry Francis and Ollie Taylor emerged through the forest, followed by Rob Paulson.

"This fucker almost took us into the lake," Terry said. Ollie shrugged and took a sip of a Tollsby's coffee, which he would most assuredly chase with malt liquor. Terry and Ollie were the shortest and tallest guys in the zip code. Terry used to be a running back in high school, or so he said, because he didn't go to Troy High, but he could run when the cops showed up, which was frequent; they all ran wild downtown. He sold used cars out on Central Avenue in Albany, so aside from running to the breakroom to fish an undecided customer a doughnut, running from the police was the most action he saw.

An enormous guy, Ollie was six foot eight, and where his height stopped, he grew horizontal, making any attempt by him to dress fashionably futile. He would bulge out of any suit, but there he was tonight, braving sharp nipples and hypothermia with the rest of them, to honor Craig.

"Gary can't go, but Ginny May wants to do it," Rob said.

Donny wasn't surprised to see Rob. Of all of them, Rob just lost his kid, Juliet. In fact, that was the last time they were all together, last summer, for the funeral.

"I don't give a fuck," Donny said. "But she's gotta be up here. You know the rules."

"Isn't it terrible that we have rules for this?" Ollie said.

"Dude, not cool," Terry said. "You just make sure you don't take a wrong turn and fall off the cliff."

"You almost followed me into the lake, what's that say about you?"

"Your big, tall, fat ass blocked out the moon."

Ollie mocked laughter and squatted down by the fire, which didn't pan out, so he let himself fall on his ass. Terry and Rob joined him, albeit more gracefully, and Donny passed four of the five forties around, sad that they needed six people and didn't have them. Even if Ginny May showed up, they would be one short. When Rob's kid died, there were twenty guys up on the cliff playing feats of strength for a coveted spot. But that was in July.

The crunch behind them sounded loudly. Ginny was the drummer for an alternative band named Captain Pneuma, one of the best, Craig once told him. Heavyset with long, blond, wavy hair, she had an impish, devious smile.

She held out her hand. "Look what I found."

"What, in your car?"

"Nope, on a tombstone," she said. "There's gotta be like five bucks here."

Ollie groaned. "Tell me you didn't take it off Uncle Sam's grave."

"Might've been."

"What the hell are you doing at Uncle Sam's grave at night?"

"Getting rich, apparently."

"Nah, you gotta put that shit back," Terry said. "People put that money there. It's a tradition, you know, *paying Uncle Sam...*"

"I didn't get a refund this year, so I'm owed."

"Donny..."

"Ginny," Donny said. "Keep the fuckin' money. Are you in with this or what?" He lit a joint, one of the six he rolled after work, of which he had four left. He handed it to Ollie, who passed it along to Terry.

"I'm in," she said. "Craig was a cool cat, and let's just say there's debts owed."

"When's the funeral, Donny?" Rob said.

Out of all of them, Donny trusted Rob most. Since he lost his job welding, Rob had been doing odd jobs anywhere and everywhere. He did grimy shit jobs even Donny wouldn't touch. And, unlike Donny, Rob never bitched about the boss.

"I'm not sure, man," Donny said. He slammed out of one of the bottles. "Fuck, I don't even know what Danielle's doing with his, you know..."

"So we're out here, piss-freezing, and you don't even know if we're gonna be pallbearers?" Terry said.

"You want to fuckin' leave?" Donny stared at Terry dead eye. "Try not to fall in the lake on your way back."

"Whoa, chill, man..."

"Craig would be here for any one of you, even if you were getting spit through a damn woodchipper."

"I didn't mean to piss you off, dude."

"I think he meant—" Ollie said.

"He can speak for himself, Ollie. Don't jump in, I ain't in the mood." Donny stirred the newly formed embers and tossed some of the thicker branches on the fire. The tension was a thick blanket of silence, punctuated by the hiss, pop, and snap of wood.

"Craig was up here in July," Rob said. "I didn't know what we were doing with Juliet."

"Sorry, man," Terry said. "I'm with you to the end. You know that."

Donny handed him a fresh joint. "No worries. I'm not in a good head space." He held up the hand he'd put through the window, crisscrossed with stitches and fresh scabs. "I loved him. He was my brother, my best friend."

Ginny took his bandaged hand gently and held it by the firelight.

"Hate to see what happens to someone you hate," she said.

Rob

He made her breakfast while his father walked to Tollsby's to put in their numbers. They were a small offering on a Monday, a play for the entire week. But it was an offering nonetheless, with all the reverence, and all the sense of foreboding on the frequent occasions when the machine was down. He made sure to get down there early, since he'd been away for most of the week, and he knew the consequence of his absence.

"So what is the chef making this morning?" she asked.

"I got French toast on, Ma."

She rubbed her hands together and licked the corners of her mouth. "Oh, I'm getting the royal treatment today. So, what do you want?"

Rob chuckled. "Nothing. Thought I'd do breakfast today."

"You didn't wait for your father to get back."

"He wouldn't have wanted me to mess up all the dishes."

"You could wash them after."

"And you know he'll re-wash them," Rob said. "What's that they say about begging forgiveness instead of asking permission?"

Rob pressed the spatula down on the slices, provoking a hiss from the pan. He sliced off a couple of squares of the salted butter he brought down from his apartment and tossed them in, swirling them in between the bread.

"Rob, honey, I saw Jennifer at the craft store. She gave me a hug. Have you talked to her lately?"

"She doesn't want to talk to me, Ma."

"It's a shame, you two got along so well."

"A lot's gone down since then," Rob said. He pulled the French toast off the pan and slid the pieces on his mother's plate except for one, which he put on a saucer for himself, knowing she wouldn't eat alone. He put the rest of the mix in the fridge for his father once he got back.

"It's been a tough year for me," he said as he sat down. "And she just ran into a guy's arms and they're gonna go off and get married. I guess she's moved on from what we had."

"I saw her fiancé," his mother said. "I think she could do better." She used her fork to cut off a corner of her breakfast. "I think she already did once."

"Thanks, Ma." Rob poured himself some orange juice after taking a caution sip, which was a necessary thing at his parents' house, their being of a generation that never threw things out easily. "Are you all set to go to the doc's today?"

"Yup. You driving me, or am I driving myself?"

"I'll drive you today," he said. "I have to visit someone at the hospital, so I can do that while I'm waiting."

"Someone sick?"

"No. Well, sort of. A friend died, and his wife works at the hospital. She's a nurse. I figure I'll find her and give my condolences and all that."

"That's terrible, honey. Did I know him?"

"I don't think so. Maybe. If he was ever at the house, I would've been too drunk to remember."

"So probably," she smiled and patted Rob's hand. "I'm teasing."

"You may be right, though."

The creak of the door announced his father, bundled up in a Daytona 500 toque, Troy hoodie stuffed with layers of sweatshirts and tees, and a black-and-white checked shemagh.

"Are you guys getting ready to go?" he asked. "It's almost nine."

"Shit," Rob said. "Feel like bagging up breakfast for the ride, Ma?"

She slid her plate forward. "Doggy bags all around."

Lansingburgh was just past its rush hour and wasn't due for the jobless push until about noon, when dealers' hours commenced. Not that 'Burgh was any worse than any other place in Troy, or for that matter the Capital District itself, but it was struggling to hold on to a time before thumb-sized baggies and burnt spoons were given more consideration than leaf pickup. Second Avenue and, to a lesser degree, Fifth Avenue were the arteries that carried Troy proper into 'Burgh. They were crossed by side streets numbering in the hundreds, which confused the hell out of New York City tourists, who expected any city that had a 112th Street to also have a Forty-Second Street. Rob heard that when Troy annexed 'Burgh, they had to rename all of the 'Burgh streets and rather than give up their numbered streets they put a "one" in front of them.

Rob's mother was knitting in the passenger seat, telling him the history of her time growing up in the 'Burgh.

"Do you see that beige house?" she asked. "I lived there for a year. I remember your grandfather picked us up from school one day with everything we owned in his pickup truck and we moved down the street that night."

"Was he short on rent?"

"Are you kidding? He had plenty of money. He was a steelworker over in Watervliet." She counted out the row she was on, then put the soon-to-be scarf in her lap.

"He had his troubles," she said. "We moved a lot. He couldn't help it. I mean back then nobody knew about what war did to people."

They pulled up to the red light by the old garage that Rob swore by, where the biggest inconvenience was the owner's never-ending mouth.

"He spent so much time alone in his study, always had one room set as his study, even if it meant I slept in the living room." She squinted and grabbed Rob's hand as a young girl darted out in the road between cars.

"Good way to get killed, little girl," she said. "Where are her parents?"

"Why isn't she in school?" Rob said.

Rob took the next few blocks slowly. Lansingburgh didn't have much of a policy on crosswalks, formal or informal. He didn't know who else might be playing hooky.

Rob's mother nudged him and pointed to two houses to the left, side by side, one white and one green. One looked like it could've held a business at one time, but judging by the buildings' style, that time was probably the seventies.

"That was Aunt Leona's house," she said. Aunt Leona was his mother's unofficial guardian when her parents felt the house was too dysfunctional for her to live in. She'd spent a lot of time in the house to the left.

"I used to live there, many years," she said.

Rob, of course, had heard all of this, but he knew she needed to say it, as much as he needed to tell his friends about Juliet and the gummy worm. We tell our stories to keep them alive, lest the past untold become a hungry spirit to eat us up.

"I used to party all night at the Night Cap next door, after Aunt Leona went to bed." Rob flipped his signal as the approached the Collar City Bridge underpass, ready to turn on Hoosick Street, a Troy-specific artery that pumped motorists clear out to Vermont if they so choose.

"I used to have to sleep in my car, so I could go to work the next morning."

"How long ago was that?"

She scratched her head with one of her sewing needles.

"How old are you now?" she asked. They caught the light that opened up into the main bulk of Hoosick, where Alternate Route 7 took in and spit out commuters from across the Hudson River.

"Let's just say I stopped when you started," she said.

Chapter Four

Asher

The young trees that lined the sidewalks of Third Street were covered in strings of clear white lights that would cast a wintry peace from the freshly fallen snow.

Of course, snow hadn't fallen much since a quick dumping right after Thanksgiving. Asher had gotten to use the electric snow-thrower his landlord bought, bringing him a few extra twenties. At work, they only gave him salt to clear the sidewalks.

The Victorian Stroll was coming on Saturday. One of Troy's principal festivals, the Stroll transported downtown streets back to late nineteenth-century. Costumed revelry, gimmicky food trucks with hot apple cider next to modern standards like sausage burgers and fried ice cream, the whole deal.

The Beanery was bustling. College kids in trendsetting scarves and smart glasses came out to colonize the few tables that were set outside. Asher walked into the aroma of earth and cinnamon and patchouli. They were playing "Carol of the Bells" in what could've been pan flutes, if Asher knew the difference between different types of flutes. For a place that made most of its money slinging a stimulant, the ambiance was like snuggling inside a Quaalude.

"Asher," a voice came from a table up front.

Asher turned around to see a familiar face wrapped in tweed and soft wool. Ash waved and placed his order, set to join her, as his phone told him he had a half hour to kill before he was due at the hotel for his half-shift.

"What are you, camouflaging?" he asked.

"I'm hunting hipsters in the wild," Mena said.

Mena sang for Trachea, a death metal band. Asher got his start playing for her when they met at a Capital Region gear swap. She had pipes that could peel the chrome off an eighteen-wheeler and a growl like spun gravel. They'd still be rocking together if Asher's girlfriend at the time wasn't so jealous. It was a pointless worry—Mena would've been more interested in the girlfriend—but jealousy is blind.

"Don't you work?" Asher said.

"Don't you?"

"I'm not in yet."

She slid up her sleeve and tapped her watch. "Break."

Asher opened his coffee to get that first sip. He never put cream and sugar in until he knew how strong the brew was. He chose to burn his mouth instead.

"Dumbass," she said. "Still doing that, huh?"

"Shit is weak. I'm gonna drink it as is." Asher put the lid back on and blew through the tiny opening. "I heard you guys are playing The Chamber. You're opening for Death Market?"

"Yup, can't wait for that shit. Saw them in the city last year. You should've been there. They had an ambulance outside, on the ready."

"For the show? How big was it?"

"It was a small-ass club, like maybe a couple hundred people, if that. Turns out the ambulance was just two dudes that dug the bands. Never can be too careful though, y'know? Death Market rocks live."

"They rock on the CD too. I'm jealous."

"Show up, then. I'll get you backstage."

"Ain't no backstage, just the back alley."

"I'll get you there." She reached into a knapsack on the floor and pulled out a neon-yellow wristband. "Comes with a free drink."

Asher held the wristband up to the light of the front window. "For real, though, I gotta work that night. I would've already had a ticket."

Mena cracked a smile. "You still with what's-her-name?"

"You know her name, and no. We split."

"She was dumb as hell."

"I was dumb too, though."

"You were thinking with your dick," she said. "What was her excuse?"

"Man, she thought we were fucking nightly."

Mena took a sip of what Asher guessed was tea, if past tastes hadn't changed. "You told her I don't go that way, right?"

"Didn't matter. Her head was wrapped around your legs being wrapped around my head."

"Say that five times fast."

"Oh, yo, speaking of gigs, we're playing that new joint down on the old industrial lot in South Troy," Asher said. "Sam Wilson's."

"Troy's new tourist trap. No offense. I give it six months before the owner gives up. That place'll be luxury apartments nobody can afford in no time."

"Wow, you're really glass-half-full today."

"It's some girl from New York City. They come here, they make some cutesy business, like Troy's gonna be the next Brooklyn, and soon as the city gets all cozy with their taxes, they're building condos and we get tax hikes to pay for the shit. I'm tired of it."

"I don't know," Asher said. "I used to live up the hill from there. I would've loved a venue right on the river like that. I hope it lasts."

"It's carpetbagger shit," Mena said.

"Is there anything in Troy that wasn't carpetbagger shit at one point?"

Mena wiped her mouth with her scarf, absently tapping the napkin once she remembered it was there.

"No offense to you, Ash. You know, good luck tonight."

The Beanery was starting to pick up. Asher checked his phone and figured that it must have been a break time for the college kids up the hill. Troy had three colleges in city limits, and even though only two were four-year schools, students packed the city center's rivers of youth before, after, and in between classes.

Asher took off from the Beanery and walked down past the parking garage, a four-story brick structure that, as he had once read, replaced a large part of Fulton Street in the nineteen-sixties, when the city tried its hand at urban renewal. But he never knew Fulton Street like that. No one still living had, yet people in Troy could still muster up nostalgia for it.

He kept going toward the hotel. A quick shift and he'd be out in time for his gig at the Sam Wilson's opening. Despite Mena's sourness on the subject, he did hold out some hope that the venue would make it long enough to be a part of someone's nostalgia.

Jordan

Before the neon sign company installed the white-bearded, top-hatted symbol of America and the machine shed officially became "Sam Wilson's," Jordan had what anybody else would've called a money pit. She, however, in true South Troy fashion, rolled up her sleeves and started sweeping up bolts, screws, and nails off a floor that would, in time, be covered in polished oak planks, stained to look as well-worn as any bar off the highway, like the kind she visited often as a girl with her father on road trips.

She put in sixteen hours every day for nearly a year, passing out each night on an air mattress with a space heater or an oscillating fan or both, depending on the season. She kept a few shotguns lying around like they were pest control. Because they were. The county jail was a few blocks down the road, and every bum and lowlife knew the oilfields was where you went to avoid the police. Before the neon sign went up, Sam Wilson's was little more than an attractive nuisance.

She still had friends in the old neighborhood, people who'd never moved on, and some that had and, like her, bounced back. In true Troy fashion, people came down to the oilfields in moving trucks and pickups; even a rogue city garbage truck made its way to the big side doors that opened out to a concrete loading area.

Buster Hall grabbed a quick crew and took the bigger machine parts and the equipment that tooled them and hauled it all away for scrap. Marissa and her boyfriend and a few of his bandmates helped her insulate the walls. One by one, people came to do this or that little thing, like the old story, Stone Soup, pitching in what they could.

Jordan scavenged and traded the promise of future drink passes for help installing the perfectly good windows she found in an industrial dumpster outside the recently renovated Mortimer Building. She spent years in the theater district working with set designs, planting the seeds of her own place in her own mind and she could finally twirl around on a stool just like the ones she dreamed about in her cramped Brooklyn studio.

Jordan loved to work with her hands. What she didn't love—what nobody she trusted loved—was dealing with the politics. Jordan had no patience for people who made and broke promises, particularly the ones she only half-heartedly voted for. She navigated the Troy City website, looking for anything about the Riverfront Renewal Project, details of which they kept well hidden.

What she found was a news item about the grant, which was north of five million, and a whole lot of descriptive words and heart-tugging propaganda about the rich heritage of the Troy waterfront. Jordan knew the waterfront's heritage wasn't pastoral fields and pedestrian walkways, et al. It was horseshit and wagon tracks and boats docked, getting loaded up with whatever Troy could feed into to the Erie Canal. Commerce. Industry, not scenery.

Not that she was against some cool views. The park in the artist's conceptual drawing looked nice. But it was missing something, like some crucial piece of architecture. *That's right*, she thought. It was missing Sam Wilson's. She was sitting in the middle of the pond they had drawn up, and if she moved over one stool, the fake fountain would be spritzing her ass like the world's most ornate bidet.

She picked up the phone and went back to the home page.

"City of Troy," an older woman said. "How may I direct your call?"

Jordan had no idea, opting instead to spend five minutes telling the lady the short version of her past year and letting her decide where Jordan's time should be spent.

"I can send you to economic development, but I don't think they're back from lunch yet. You can leave a message, though."

"I don't know, is there anyone there that I can talk to, like you? I'm trying to hear from someone who knows more about this than I do, or what's on the website. I'm not always near the phone."

"I'm pretty sure there's no one here, honey." She wasn't helpful, but she was friendly. "You could try calling back around two. Most people are back by then." She shuffled papers and cleared her throat. "They're probably going to tell you to go to the public meeting on the eleventh. I'm assuming you already know about that."

"First I'm hearing of it."

"Do you have Facebook? The city has a Facebook page. I know it's on there." More shuffling. "I'm trying to find the time and room that they're— Oh! January the eleventh at six p.m., Room 309. That's the conference room on the third floor of this building. Do you want me to repeat that?"

#

As B.B. King sang "How Blue Can You Get," his moans floated through the air, Lucille's guitar licks tickled the windows and Jordan imagined that if she could concentrate hard, she could catch them vibrating.

She wasn't done with her mind's eye plans for the place. She owned the parcel all the way to the river's edge, to the concrete jetty. She'd explored the cost of expanding an outdoor stage to the water's edge, and though it was expensive, it was only a couple of good years' worth of expensive. It had promise, and she'd gotten this far.

She picked up a broom and started sweeping an already immaculate floor, trying to push down the prospect of having to defend Sam Wilson's from its city. She'd gathered half of the city to bring the place into shape. It had the look. Later that night, when they had a band and a few people for Thursday night's soft opening, they'd start giving it a name.

Danielle

The frame of Sandy's mirror was covered in pictures of Billy and Jake, wallet-sized ones of the day Jake graduated pre-K dressed in a Harry Potter costume, because Sandy got a late jump on clothes shopping and figured it wouldn't matter. Turned out it didn't, because according to her, nobody else bothered to dress their kids up in anything other than clean sweaters.

Danielle noticed that she had changed the model pic in the top right corner of the glass. Her hairstyle was called a "lazy side braid," if she remembered the magazines in the waiting room correctly. Sandy always put up her hair inspirations on her mirror, and she would work all the styles when her beauty school certificate hung on the wall. But it was off the wall that day—maybe the braid wasn't the only thing that was being lazy.

Danielle picked at her own hair. She felt like a zombie being shown her reflection for the first time, trying to figure out what it was seeing. She pulled at strands of loose hair that fell out of her ponytail until her scalp stung. It beat sipping cold coffee in the short term, but it wouldn't fly in an hour when she was at work.

She didn't have to go in. St. Francis Hospital wasn't generous with personal leave, but all the nurses in her unit agreed to cover her shifts for a few days. Who could blame her for taking the time to be with her kids, make arrangements, or simply wrap her head around losing her husband?

The light from above the mirror caught on a facet of her wedding ring. She rubbed the stone, a cubic zirconia that never fooled anyone. Her diamond wedding ring was still in the jeweler's box on her nightstand at home. She wore it only during the wedding and the reception. She didn't hate it—quite the opposite, she loved it too much to lose it down a drain, or in a sharps container at work. Plus, she couldn't wear *any* ring when she donned skintight nitrile gloves for poop patrol.

"Hurry up, Dani," Sandy called out from the kitchen. "Unless you decided you ain't going."

"I'm going, I'm going. Trying not to look like a wreck."

Sandy came in and gently pulled out Danielle's scrunchy, letting her auburn shoulder-length hair spill onto her scrubs. "Who cares? So what if you're a wreck? Own it."

"I don't want everybody asking me if I'm okay every five seconds. They mean well, but I could use a distraction, you know?"

"My marvelous company wasn't distracting enough?"

"Sandy, you're badass, but I got so much shit I gotta run through my head. I figure a twelve-hour day of cleaning colostomy bags and getting my ass pinched will help me focus."

"You are one strange chick."

Danielle stepped out in the kitchen and grabbed one of Mark's camouflaged thermoses—ensuring that her new presence in his life was even more burdensome. She made her way to Billy and Jake's room on padded feet as its new occupants slept soundly, hopefully free from nightmare reminders of their father that would haunt them for the rest of their lives. For now, they radiated innocence and bliss.

Danielle walked in the lobby of St. Francis Hospital smelling of rancid meat and rotten milk. She'd gotten caught behind a garbage truck on Fifteen Street, which had just popped a mystery bag in its teeth in front of the Sushi restaurant. She was smoking a cigarette while the kids weren't with her, windows down, which let the stink in.

From Helen's earnest expression behind the front desk, Danielle could tell she'd heard the news. Which means everyone had. How many times would she have to deal with well-intentioned condolences today?

"I'm okay, Helen," Danielle assured her. "The kids too, as well as they can be. How did you find out?"

Helen folded the newspaper and set it by her side next to the phone. "People walk by and they talk. I should get extra pay for keeping my mouth shut, but not from you, Danielle. You're a sweetheart."

"I hope I don't hear anybody saying anything today. I'm not going to be able to deal. Might hit somebody with a saline bag."

"Better than an open box of needles."

"Are they saying anything about Craig?" Danielle didn't want to know. The answer was a train wreck holding up traffic, and Danielle cursed herself for slowing down to rubberneck.

"Nothing you need to hear," Helen said. "Just talk. Nobody knows anything."

"You're not going to tell me, are you?"

"Not for the reasons you might think," Helen said. "I mean, I'm not protecting anyone but you."

"Why don't I feel better?"

"Hon, you're one of the few nurses that bothers to see if I want tea when it's your turn to do coffee runs. If there was anything that was floating around this hall that I thought you needed to know, I'd go up to your unit and leave a note in your jacket pocket."

Danielle didn't know if a callous, uncaring unit was preferable to a super-supportive "family" following her on rounds. But either option was preferrable to fellow nurses speculating and spreading gossip about her dead husband.

As she hopped on the elevator and took the ride up to the sixth floor, she saw her funhouse-mirror figure in the polished steel walls and it hit her that her husband, the love of her life, was downstairs in the morgue, and it was up to her where he went from there.

Chapter Five

Donny

The tinny pitch of Clapton's guitar crying "Layla" through Donny's radio alarm clock told him that the day was going to be a bad one—mainly because if he could hear it go off, it meant he was three hours late to work. He launched himself off the clothes-strewn bed and wiped his face with a hand towel that was hanging from the bedpost. He needed a shower, and that need would go unmet as he tore apart the living room looking for work clothes that could pass for clean.

He couldn't say he got too shit-faced at Oakwood last night—he'd argue that he didn't get shit-faced enough. If he marked his drink- and drug-addled all-nighters on a calendar, there wouldn't be any room for plans. Not that he did much else. He reserved his weekends to sleep like the dead. A SWAT team or house fire would be wise to strike on a Saturday or Sunday morning if either wanted to punch Donny's ticket.

He ran his head under the bathroom faucet and toweled off. He'd have to skip the coffee, and if he broke into his stash and did a thin line to wake up, Meyer would spot that shit quick, seeing as how Meyer's kid was a straight cokehead. If he still had a job when he got on site, he'd—

Shit, he thought. *On Site*. Meyer wanted him to call that day. They were done with the housing over in Cohoes. Donny couldn't even think of where they might've gone next. Meyer kept everything close to the vest, figuring if his workers didn't know where the next job was, they couldn't undercut him. Never mind that Meyer wasn't hiring the kind of people that had their shit together enough to snake a job from him.

He called out to Meyer a few times in the bathroom mirror, testing his voice, trying to thread the needle between sick and hungover. It took another ten minutes to find his phone, and a few seconds to realize he'd forgotten to charge it. He wanted to hurl it against the wall, but he couldn't afford replacing it in his mid-morning rage. He threw on his work clothes and his work coat and left everything in his apartment. His only blessing was that he lived on Fulton Street, a block up from Fourth Street News, the last stop in downtown Troy for bus folk going to all points north. It was always one of the few spots left with payphones.

"Who's this?"

"It's me, Donny, Sorry I'm not there,"

"You in jail?" Meyer said. "I'm not accepting charges."

"No, man, I'm at the payphone by my house. My phone's dead."

"Did you break it?"

"What? No, it's out of charge," Donny said. He rested his arm on the edge of the casing that held the phone. "My alarm went off late, I can get to you, just need to know where you are."

Meyer was quiet. Donny could hear seagulls, which didn't tell him much, being that Troy was on the Hudson river.

"Look, Donny, you need some time. We're good here for a little while. Why don't you take a couple days? I got a job coming up Monday, over in Watervliet. We'll need a few guys then."

"What am I gonna do till then? I'm broke, Meyer. I gotta get some money today."

"I don't know what to tell ya, kid. Wake up on time."

"Can I get an advance? I can drive to where you are."

"I don't do advances, you know that. I spend the upfronts on supplies and shit. And, honestly man, I don't know if you're gonna be back in a week. If I knew that, I might give you something out of pocket, but you worry me."

"What? I work my ass off for you. You know that. Name one time I didn't do the job you asked me to."

"You work like a dog, no doubt. But you're unreliable. I don't know some days whether you're coming or going. And you show up here stinking like liquor and weed—God forbid an OSHA inspector come on site and get a whiff of you. You don't have to worry about that shit. Your name's not on the LLC."

"So I'll come in sober."

"Call me Monday. I'll see what I got for you. It's only a few days from now. You're resourceful."

Donny grumbled okay and hung up the receiver, before pounding the side of the fiberglass with the flat of his palm.

Piece of shit. Donny figured Meyer would bring him back, if only to have to pay for the window he broke. But that was Monday, three days away. He had the rent in his pocket, and a whole weekend full of places to blow it. Craig would have to be buried. Donny had to talk to Danielle. The Victorian Stroll could be coasted through, but he was known for assembling the afterparty. Donny hung on the side of the bus stop, feeling the synapses throw switches in his brain, trains bouncing off tracks. His obligations and his means were a shell game.

The bus pulled up, letting weary commuters out to wait in the cold that Donny was just then starting to feel. He wondered if he had any weed left in his other pants. Meyer thought he was a druggie scumbag, no use proving him wrong while he still had a stash.

Donny walked into 4th Street News and asked for a pack of Marlboros from the North Korean shop owner who knew a lot more English that he let on.

"Ten seventy-eight," he said.

Donny pulled out the rent knot from his wallet and peeled away the first day.

Rob

Acrylic flowers courted crimson and teal lace ribbon around the hats, a gift from the studios of Theresa Paulson. Rob held the pile carefully with one hand and squeezed his mother's hand with the other, more to remind her that he was there to catch her. As much as he loved the creativity and effort she put into her craft, he would've preferred she paid more attention to where she was stepping. Her latest fall terrified him.

"Oh my, what do we have here?" The head nurse came around the station, a teacher set to receive polished apples.

"The nurses here were so nice to me last time," Teresa said. "I made these. Maybe they could go on the walls. I noticed the paintings look a little bit like they came from a hotel room."

The head nurse chuckled. She cocked her ear for the sound of one of the many room alarms.

"You work the upper floors, don't you?" Rob said.

She smiled with half of her face. "I'm sorry, do I know you?"

"Oh no, you had an ear out for the alarms, like you would if you worked upstairs. I mean, this is a testing floor, so, no alarms."

"Ah, sharp," she said.

"I've spent too much time in here." He held out the hats in his hand, and the head nurse cleared a spot off the counter, which became, in Rob's and his mother's opinion, the most beautiful spot in the wing.

"I'm Theresa," his mother said. "I'm here for pain management. They want to put me in a tube and leave me there."

"She's here for an MRI," Rob said.

"That's what I said, dear son."

The head nurse bobbed her head as she reached for a plastic clipboard decorated in a colorful drug insignia. "Well, Theresa, we're just going to have you fill this out and take a seat in the waiting room. Do you know where that is?"

"I should. I forward my mail there." Her joking was pretty much her own private rebellion from the blinding, mind-shearing pain she only spoke of when it ripped the civility out of her.

The head nurse was done with banter, walking off to another room.

"I don't think she's going to put those up," Theresa said.

"I'm sure they have a break room."

"I didn't make them to sit on a break room wall," she said. "This place is depressing. And I don't remember that woman. Don't you have a friend that works here?"

"That's Danielle. That's the one I have to visit."

"Oh, honey, I can wait if you want to go to see her. I'm sure she could use her friends to talk to."

"More than that. We're going to help her with the arrangements, for her husband Craig."

"Can we help?" Theresa said. "I have some money set aside from crafts. I can pitch in for some flowers."

"We'll see, Ma." Rob got up and searched the room for craft or cooking magazines. Coming up empty, he settled for a two-week-old news magazine.

"Here, Ma. Are you sure you're gonna be okay to go through this?"

"I'm not an invalid. I drive, I cook, clean, do all that stuff." She reached over and patted Rob's arm. "I'll be fine."

Rob got up to the sixth floor just in time for Danielle's having earned a half hour lunch, vomit stains on her scrubs serving as her receipt. They made hospital chatter on the way down, something Rob learned was an unspoken habit by hospital staff after hours of having to keep everything bottled up. People wound up becoming fluent in speaking nothing, and after spending so much time in the hospital with his mother, Rob was picking up the dialect.

They generally let their guards down in the cafeteria. Danielle and Rob sat in a back corner.

She pushed an escaped bang away from her face. "I wish I had time to visit your mom. I miss her. She always knew what to say and gave the best hugs."

"I'm sure she'll be around for a while." Rob stopped. "Sorry. Didn't mean to—"

"No. It needs to be talked about." Danielle swirled spaghetti on a white plastic fork. "I have to meet the Walsh's Funeral Home tomorrow. I would have had to take an extra shift, but Craig's parents are taking the financial part over."

"That's good of them, right?"

"Yes and no. I'm glad they're helping. Craig never made arrangements for his funeral. Who thinks of it at our age?" Danielle set down her fork, her mind was elsewhere.

"They don't think I could give Craig a good send-off, and they're right. If it was on me alone, I could barely afford a pine box."

"We wouldn't let that happen," Rob said. "We'd crowdsource that funeral."

"I thought of it. I did. But even if we raised the money overnight, it still takes days to get it. That stuff is good for covering expenses you couldn't afford to dole out, not for money you need right away and don't have."

Danielle took a sip of soda, reaching deep for the remaining liquid. "And what if we only got like a hundred bucks? I couldn't see that and not blow up. You know how Craig was to everyone."

"I think you'd get thousands, but…" Rob checked his watch. His mom would be in the MRI for a few more minutes. "When and where's the funeral?"

Danielle pulled out a business card, one of Craig's from when he tried his hand at contracting. "The wake is Saturday, from four till seven. The funeral's going to be at Saint Patrick's on Sunday at ten."

"I thought they had closed Saint Pat's."

"For church, yeah. But Craig was an altar boy there, and his old priest, he's retired now, but he offered to open it up and do the service."

Rob finished his coffee. "That's the day of the Victorian Stroll."

"Shit." Danielle's head dropped, her rogue bang hanging down. "Forgot about that."

"It's fine. Everyone will still show up. Me and Donny, we'll make sure of it."

"I hope so," she said.

Rob checked his watch again, but he knew he had to go.

"Hey, I gotta bolt, but Dani, don't worry about people being there. But plan on everybody being drunk. We may have to sell it as the ultimate pre-game."

Asher

People who said that they could always tell the difference b etween firecrackers a nd g unshots n ever l ived i n t he a mphitheater t hat w as t he Hudson Valley. Half of the time, Asher couldn't figure out if it was coming from Troy or from Watervliet, Green Island, or Cohoes, west of the river. He couldn't differentiate by sound, relying on reputation. If it came from the east, that most likely meant Greenville Heights, a housing project nestled in the woods behind the Tollsby's, near his bass player Annette's, house.

"Jesus, you gotta put up with that shit all year?" he said. "I figured it'd be too cold to beef outside."

"Probably some kids lighting off firecrackers," Annette muttered as she picked up a bib and a pair of socks and hovered around, looking for more grist for her washer. Her house was eerily calm for a single mother, the accoutrements of child raising—the red-and-white plastic walker decked out in geometric baubles and plastic-covered lights, toys in a box, and stuffed animals on the dining room chair nestled in a matrix—lacked the hairpulling disarray anyone would expect from a twenty-eight-year-old.

"They ain't no fi recrackers," Asher said, his eyes never leaving the the app on his phone.

"Until me and Jeffrey can afford to move out of here, they're firecrackers. Besides, didn't you have, like, two people get murdered over in 'Burgh this week?"

"They're not emptying clips."

"No, just hitting what they aim at."

"Point taken." Asher down put his phone. Annette had a sweet Fender bass tube head with a one-fifteen cabinet. A great bass amp with a sound that reminded Asher of a sweet, mellow bourbon.

Despite her neurotic impulses for personal order, her bass lines were an escape. They took long walks through the melodic forest, hypnotizing as she slapped, thumped and slid over the fretboard. It took Asher forever to catch her groove, but as he checked out her bass—a Fender Jaguar with a violin burst finish overlaid with a half-transparent image of a honeycomb on the body—he was glad he made the effort.

Asher's own guitar and amp were locked in his trunk. Annette and Asher were opposites when it came to gear. Annette polished her bass and made sure it had new strings on a regular basis. By contrast, she knew what kind of strings Asher liked because she brought a set to every gig, knowing his lazy ass would wait until a string burst onstage before he changed it.

Asher's guitar was the cheapest thing he could find that wasn't categorical junk. He spent his money on effects. But he could make anything sound good onstage. He had a sort of Zen thing coaxing sweet sounds from sour instruments. That's what he told himself—and Annette, Ginny, and anyone else who cared for an explanation as to why there were scorch marks on his guitar neck from where he rested burning cigarettes under the strings.

The bell rang. Asher got up to answer. He knew it would be their drummer, Ginny, who walked in with wet hair.

"Wow, someone got a later start than me," he said.

"I love you too." She set down her bag with her crash cymbal in it. She was particular about keeping hardware from the cold. Her hand slid into the outside pocket, pulling out a pint of Irish Whiskey. She offered it to Asher.

"A nip for the trip?"

"It's literally down the road," he said. Annette wandered over and took the bottle, giving her wrist a flit, enough to disinfect her mouth.

Ginny took the bottle and raised it over her head. "A nip for the trip."

Asher grabbed the twenty-two-ounce coffee he picked up from the Beanery down the street and opened it to cool it down. This was the last one he could have before the show if he didn't want jitters.

"I saw Mena," he said. "She told me the girl that owns Sam Wilson's is from New York City."

"New York City money spends fine here," Annette said. "So you hanging with Mena again?"

"Nah, I saw her at the coffee shop. Why, do you care?"

"You've mistaken my curiosity for giving a fuck."

"She never did nothing to you," he said.

"And she never did nothing *for* me either."

"Oh, give her a break," Ginny said. "You would've never been happy jamming out with her, 'Nette."

"I'm just saying, you know, women helping women, in this game… She ain't about it."

"Would you rather be playing bass for Trachea?" Asher asked.

"Nope."

He burned his mouth on a sip, surprised that the coffee was still hot after being in a car with third-class heat. "Mena doesn't fuck with many people. And she hates women. Except the ones she loves." Asher wiped his mouth. "Be thankful you never got with her playing. She'd have gotten you thrown in jail by now."

"You say so." Annette rocked her bass on its wheels. "You guys want to help me with this?"

"Hey, guys, did you get invited to Craig's funeral yet?" Ginny said.

"I heard he died," Asher said.

Annette shook her head.

"It's on Facebook. Danielle is inviting everyone to Saint Patrick's on Sunday morning. It says dress your best."

"Should we go?" Annette asked.

"I'm thinking it's for people who knew Craig." Asher turned to Ginny, whose eyes were on her screen. "Hey, isn't that the Victorian Stroll? Sunday?"

"Yeah," she said. "But I have to go. I'm the pallbearer. So that means you guys got to go."

"Why's that?"

Head unmoving, she lifted her eyes up, framed by her long, stringy curls.

"'Cause I can't drop Craig," she said. "And you're the only people I like sober."

"I didn't really know him," Annette said.

Ginny closed her phone case and rolled it around in her hands. "Craig was the kind of guy who would've protested your arrest just 'cause someone told him you were a good girl. He'd have been out there in front of the jail, selling T-shirts to pay your lawyers. The least we all can do is fill chairs and make his family feel loved."

Asher took another sip of coffee and wondered what he'd have to do to his Victorian-era costume to make it funeral worthy.

Chapter Six

Jordan

Thursday was the new Friday was the talk in the bar circles of Brooklyn, when Jordan spent night after night nursing free drinks and picking up the tricks of the trade. The people who said it were usually drunks who felt they needed to preface an extra night of getting hammered by making it a "thing."

Thursday was the new Friday, which made Friday the new Saturday, and the real Saturday a liver-busting holiday, leaving Sunday to forever be dedicated to hangovers and regret while Monday waggled a finger like a watchful nun.

Jordan preferred the intimate gatherings that had grown around Sam Wilson's in the afternoons and the weeknights, but the cash register was starving.

Sarah's Pekingese, Chewy, was on the bar with its snout in a nut bowl that Jordan had cleaned out and refilled with water.

"Thirsty little Chewy, yes she is!" Sarah put her nose in Chewy's fur and shook her head back and forth.

"I don't have any food for him," Jordan said. "Do you?"

Without looking up, Sarah reached into her purse and pulled out a sealed bag with packaging graphics of a spread of rice, meat, and vegetables looking better than anything Jordan had in the past month. People around here fed their dogs chef's fare.

"I have to walk him in a little bit. He likes to wee when he gets nervous. Which sucks 'cause he likes to drink when he's nervous too."

"Aren't those yapper dogs always nervous?"

Jordan's question was answered by a quick, sharp yap.

"Aww, did she call you a little yapper dog? Mean old Auntie Jordan's just mad 'cause her landlord won't let her have dogs."

"No, he won't let me have a Husky, which is the only kind of dog I like. I can have all the yappers I want."

"You should get a Husky for here. She could guard the place and have puppies and I could get one too."

"I'm sure the Department of Health would love that."

"Don't you mean the State Liquor Authority?" Sarah said. "You plan on serving food?"

"Not yet, but I have a kitchen, so I'm registered with the Department of Health, too. I don't think the liquor authority gives a shit unless I'm feeding her margaritas."

Sarah set Chewy on the floor, wrapping her leash up in the leg of her stool. Chewy ran around until she exhausted her slack and sniffed the floor as she retraced her steps.

"So first night with a band that isn't using this as a practice space," Sarah said.

Jordan chuckled and nodded. Half the reason people from bands helped her clean out the place, beyond neighborhood loyalty, was that she had a space in the middle of the oilfield with the power on, and a good practice room was expensive. They got to play if they cleaned up after themselves and the ghost of Rogers Die and Tool Company.

"It's a soft opening," Jordan said. "I didn't plan it that way, but I'm broke right now, so hopefully the bands bring people in."

"I've been inviting people on Facebook and Twitter," Sarah said. "Pretty sure I got about ten people coming, maybe more if Tessa cancels her makeup party."

"She's having a makeup party?" Jordan said. "Is she in one of those pyramid scheme cults?"

"Yuh huh." Sarah tugged once on the leash, enough to redirect Chewy away from behind the bar. "She's been all about it. You haven't seen her Facebook posts?"

"Nah, I'm not on there much. I check in and share memes. I never see her on my feed."

"She's all business now. You know I asked her if she wanted to go out to the mall and catch that new movie about the time traveler, you know which one?"

"I forget the name, but yeah. I saw the trailer."

"Badass movie, but she's all like, 'I got to check my day planner.' Bitch is home all day, her boyfriend got no job and he's the one that watches the kids anyway. Oh, she's Miss Business now, please."

"Hey, at least she's not sitting there watching *The Pauly Show* all day."

"She's *exactly* sitting around watching Pauly all day." She picked up her beer and tipped it skyward. "But, hey, maybe she'll show up and bring half that block with her. I gotta go walk my girl, be right back."

Sarah lifted the barstool, releasing the leash as she picked up Chewy and cuddled her furry face all the way out the front door. Jordan picked up the empty beer and wiped the bar down with a fresh rag. She'd gauge the night by how quickly that rag became so dirty it had to be traded out.

A few people started to show up, some she knew, and some, apparently, were friends with the bands that were coming. It was a general rule that the friends of a band showed up late, if at all, but in truth, there were always those friends that had nothing better to do.

Jordan made nice. She smiled, warm and inviting. She felt it even though her expressions were largely practiced. For a person who spent a decade of her life around performers, Jordan found it odd that she felt so out of place near a stage.

She had figured out a dance to do with the eleven customers that had shown up, and her barback, Samantha, was earning the pay she'd be getting, which would come out of her tips. She had finished a round with her black enamel serving tray when her first band showed up. She'd never met them, but the second band's drummer was her first best friend in the neighborhood.

She walked over and shook hands with them. The bassist was almost as tall as her, with a red bob haircut and glasses. Annette. Ginny, the drummer, seemed to have opened her bar tab at home. And the guitar player and singer, who she'd talked to on the phone, was mixed race, with brown frizzy hair in curls that shot up like uncooked rotini noodles. He too had glasses, but thick black frames.

He held out his hand, and Jordan shook it.

"Glad you guys could make it," she said. "Welcome."

"This is the coolest-looking place I've seen," he smiled. "It's got a great groove."

Jordan felt a small flush as she realized that this was what she'd spent a year picturing in her mind. Tonight, she'd have a scene. Her own first scene.

Danielle

Alerts from the hospital PA system preached over the choir of beeps and ticks from the monitors and machines that told the nurse's station all was well on Sixth Floor North. Being that there were only thirty beds on the entire sixth floor, separating them into North and South, always struck Danielle as idiotic. Didn't make much of a difference, s eeing h ow t he nurse's station was the only thing separating Sixth North from Sixth South.

She walked down the hall with her clipboard and peeked in to check on the guests that were assigned to her. Both sides of the sixth floor were what the more jaded hospital staff termed the cold case files. Most of the guests were return visitors, and they had complicated ailments. Doctors could do little but run tests and observe. Despite the TV shows with renegade geniuses sporting white coats and stethoscopes, the doctors Danielle knew didn't have the time to spend all shift with one patient on the blackboard.

Ingrid Porcenz was one such frequent flyer. She was lucky, all pain aside, in that her family visited every day. She had a garden on her dresser complete with a fruit basket. Danielle noticed it was a bit lopsided and asked her if she ate any fruit. Ingrid had, and for a person without a mystery bowel ailment, that would've been fine. Danielle managed to convince her to let them refrigerate it, which would piss off her other nurses, but it came with the job.

Patrick Lafferty, aka Smilin' Pat, was probably on the opposite end of the spectrum for their guests. He, too, was a regular. Sixth North was his home away from home, which made it his only home, because the other place he lived was beneath the Collar City bridge. His conundrum was infectious sores. Patrick made Danielle's heart hurt. She'd seen him covered in rat bites, and he was known throughout the floor for offering up half his plate to any nurse or doctor that looked hungry.

"Hey, Patrick, how are you this afternoon, hon?"
Patrick looked battered. He smiled wide, his top plate of false teeth cracked down the center. Was that glue holding the pieces together?

"Dani! Fancy meeting you here."

"Patrick, tell me you didn't glue your dentures together."

He closed his mouth some, but he didn't turn off the smile. "I broke 'em in a fight. It's fine."

"I'll take your word for it. Please try to get a new plate, okay?"

"If I had a thousand bucks, I'd have a bachelor pad with a full liquor cabinet. And I'd invite you over, but I know you're spoken for."

Danielle felt a wave of reality wash over her, one she'd been surfing for most of the afternoon.

"Thank you, Patrick." She pulled up his chart. "So, they want you to get a CT scan later on, and an MRI after that. Jeez, what the heck did you do?"

"They're covering all their bases," Patrick said. "And all their asses. They sent me out of the ER with some ibuprofen two days ago. I didn't make it to the front entrance before I passed out, fell on my face. Shit, they could've left me there, gave me a blanket. At least no one would steal my coat if I was bedding out on hospital grounds."

Patrick leaned up and took his clear plastic cup of apple juice and put a straw in it. "But hey, I'll take the room and board."

Danielle pulled the curtain and sat on the adjoining bed, her clipboard in both hands in front of her. "Patrick, why don't you go to a shelter? It's freezing outside."

"I ain't making it easy for them to rob me and beat me up," Patrick said. "I'm a friendly, hippie bum. Not everybody is, y'know?"

"Is it really that bad?"

"They pay those kids a smidge over minimum wage—you think they're funding cops and security to protect us? When they actually have cops, or rent-a-cops, it's to keep us from going over the desk for an extra damn muffin."

Danielle leaned forward and rubbed the side of Patrick's arm. "Okay, okay. Tell you what. You think about finding a way to replace that top plate, and I'll go get you a blueberry muffin from the cafeteria."

"What did I do to get an angel to smile on me?"

Danielle soldiered on through the day, relieved at how she didn't have a whole lot of time to think about Craig. She knew it was a temporary respite; she had to take the next day off, to tackle the even more difficult job of dealing with her mother-in-law. What she told Rob was half true; she didn't have much say over what was spent. But she did have the task of deciding what was bought for the wake and funeral, including the coffin, floral spray, and, most importantly, Craig's last wardrobe.

Anyone else, she figured, would be happy to have someone bankrolling such a moment. But Danielle knew that she was on a tight leash. She had to make Gloria Hill happy. Don Hill, she was sure, just wanted it to be over, but Gloria was the matron, not only of Craig, but of the family, and all of Craig's friends from before he and Danielle met, which admittedly weren't many. In any case, she would make her presence felt throughout the weekend. It wasn't just the loss of Craig that faced them both; it was the loss of the place where he put them. He was the center of both of their maps, and now they were lost.

Donny

The coat of arms shone through a layer of smoke that had risen above the front of McEntyre's, or Mackey's to most people after a few drinks. Old man Mack built a smokers' patio in the back, in what little land he had off the alley, but people got tired of crackheads drawn to the smell of free cigarettes. So the coat of arms, which Macky spent good coin making beautiful, would never be cleaned enough to reclaim its true colors.

Donny knew the coat of arms wasn't actually a McEntyre family thing— he looked up McEntyre on his phone one night he and the youngest Mack were doing shots, and Donny bet the kid he was a bastard on account of the family crest tattoo he'd just got. It made sense to both at the time to search heraldry sites to find out two things; one, that you can't tell who's a bastard with a search engine, and two, McEntyre had a completely different coat of arms than what was on the front sign and young Mack's arm. Old Mack later admitted that it was on a mug he bought at a flea market.

Donny was two drinks in and trying to pace himself. He wasn't trying to control his shitty mood; he was trying to budget his shitty paycheck. Since he'd called Meyer earlier, he was able to stay on the day's rent he peeled off his knot. He hit Burger Town and filled a bag with gut-stuffers that would last him a few days in the fridge if he nuked them. He planned on going to the bodega on Fifth across from the church to grab a pouch of roll-your-own, for which he had a few packs of rolling papers in his dresser drawer, on his coffee table, on his kitchen counter and in the medicine cabinet.

He pulled a cigarette to his mouth as the vibrant red, white, and blue neon beer signs cast reflections in the two front windows. Younger partygoers wrapped themselves in stylish, black quilted-down jackets, jeans, and leggings, no doubt holiday pickups from the stores on River Street that surrounded Monument Square. They smoked and vaped and released their fumes to the sky as they laughed and cajoled each other to pull out their wild sides and conquer the Troy night.

On any night, he would've pulled out the good clothes and passed. He might even have picked up a number or two, and, if any of his buddies' bands were doing sets, he'd be making room on his mattress that night. He wiped his free hand on faded black jeans scarred in primer and Robin's Egg paint. His other hand felt the heat of the cherry creep into the crisscrossed slashes that were fully crusted in scab. He should've been at the Underdog down by the river or caught a cab to one of the biker bars on Second Street.

He was trying to think of what he and Craig would be doing if Craig was still alive, but he knew he was kidding himself. It was Thursday. Craig would've been home, watching TV with Danielle, making sure the kids weren't using the computer to cheat on their homework and calling it an early night for that five a.m. alarm.

"He and Craig" was a memory of a time when Danielle worked at the Yarrow Tavern, the Wicca-themed bar three blocks up from where he was standing. It was a time when Joey was only a dream and they spent their nights getting free drinks or sneaking in bottles to keep Danielle from getting fired. They'd pretend they were bouncers and keep the peace no matter what curses some drunk witch or cosplay warlock threw at them.

Donny flicked his cigarette butt to the curb in time to nearly catch on Easy's pants. He nodded in lieu of an apology.

"Whattup, Donny?" Easy said. "What are you doing out on a work night?" He laughed. Donny never held back on work nights, and everyone knew it.

Donny rubbed his cut-up hand gently. "How's tricks, Easy-D?"

"You know, it's tricks. Everybody wants the go-go for the Stroll. I've been working more routes than the fuckin' mailman lately. C'mon, I got you on a beverage, what say?"

Donny said nothing. He went to the door and opened it for Easy as a reply.

The bar was packed, but Thursday nights were always like that at the bars the college kids frequented. Thursday was the new Friday. Donny and Easy deftly secured spots for themselves, not seats, but places the swamped bartenders would be sure to see them. Easy got a vodka tonic and Donny grabbed a bourbon double on the rocks. They opted for the patio, despite the sign on the wall that forbade taking drinks out there.

"Yo, I heard Craig died, man. What the fuck happened?"

"I don't know, he died at night," Donny said. "I don't really want to talk about that, no offense."

"Sorry, bro. I didn't mean to dig it up."

"It's cool. It just happened. I ain't really had time to process it is all."

"No, I get it. Can I ask if there's going to be a service?"

"You just did." Donny cracked a smirk. "Sunday, St. Pat's in North Troy."

Easy tapped into his drink. "I wonder if I should go. I didn't really know Craig. I mean, I knew him as a customer."

"Customer? What, weed?"

"Sometimes weed. Usually hydros and shit like that."

Donny felt colder than a body in November should feel. His shoulders and the back of his neck turned gooseflesh.

"You sold him that shit?"

"Yeah. I mean, he wasn't a junkie. He needed the pills, and his doctor was a piece of shit. Wouldn't give him nothing stronger than Naproxen. Half my customers are people who need pain relief. I'm like a street doctor."

"How many people you figure you killed, doc?"

Easy set his drink down. "Dude, what are you saying? Did Craig OD or something?"

"I told you I didn't want to talk about it."

"I don't want to be accused of killing folks, but here we are."

Donny pulled out another cigarette. His drink lay untouched from his first sips. "Maybe you should stick to weed, Easy-D," he said. Easy picked up his drink and flicked his half-smoked cig over the patio gate into the alley.

"Maybe you should chill out, Donny, cut up a fentanyl or some—"

Donny heard the squish of his fist pulping Easy's nose through a rage-soaked tunnel.

Chapter Seven

Rob

His skin was flush and a sheen of sweat made his forehead sensitive to the kitchen breeze that got carried to their table every time a server opened the door. His tie was tight because he didn't see the point of wearing it sloppy and loose, and the pictures on her profile, the ones of her life at leisure, were filled with guys who wore jackets and ties.

He wanted a cigarette. He wanted to get out of there, go home, blast punk, and claim victory over loneliness, like the simple act of being there was a symbol that could ward off reality, that she might not choose to share photos of the meal they had coming.

They met at Hudson Market, in the aisle that held not a thing under seven dollars. The aisle even looked different than the others, accents colored like grain to offset the pale beige of the rest of the aisles' trim. If there was one splurge Rob made, it was on extra-virgin olive oil.

Her name was Cheryl. She worked in the bank housed in a storefront past the registers. She was dressed in sleek black business attire. Her long blond hair was blended shades of honey flowing over her shoulders. She needed quinoa, and neither of them could find what they needed, and in the spirit of cooperation, they helped each other look.

Rob knew where the olive oil was all along, and it felt like the beginning of Rob pretending.

He lifted his napkin and unfolded it, arranging it as deftly as he could, as if he would fold it into a raven, or better yet, an appetizer.

"I'm not normally this nervous," he said. "I'm afraid if I say something funny, it's gonna come out as a pick-up line."

"You already picked me up, so I wouldn't worry about it."

"Good." He took up the napkin and wiped his brow. "Is it hot in here, or is it you?"

"On second thought…" She smiled.

"See? I really am hot, though. I don't know if it's nerves, or if I'm getting a special screw you draft from the oven back there."

"I think the oven's cock-blocking you."

"I don't need much help there," he said. "So, okay, full confession, I checked out your profile."

"You did, did you? What part?"

"All of it." Her eyebrow raised in what Rob took for jest. "No, not all of it. You know, the basics. The about, the pics, you know, the ones up top. I wasn't going full stalker or anything."

"So only half stalker."

"Only half." He wiped his mouth and reached for a glass of water. He'd asked them to put a lemon wedge in it because he saw that at a five-star hotel he got to stay at on a job, so it must have been highbrow.

"So I saw all your party pictures. You know, fancy dress, suits and ties. Is that what you like, or were those special-occasion pics?"

Cheryl set her forearms on the table just below her elbows and clasped her porcelain hands.

"People treat you different depending on how you're dressed," she said. "Someone told me that the best disguise is a completely different wardrobe."

She sipped from her water glass. "When we go out all dressed up, we can get in places that we couldn't if we were in our street clothes."

"So you have street clothes."

"Oh, I can rock a pair of jeans. It doesn't hurt to dress up. Maybe an extra couple minutes every day?" She pointed at Rob's neck. "I can tell you I know at least one guy that got a ten-thousand-dollar loan because he knew how to tie a tie." She smiled.

The waiter brought out appetizers and took their dinner order. Rob and Cheryl had a lively discussion about vegan cooking. It was one-sided, with Cheryl the consummate home-kitchen chef and Rob the eager student whose culinary accomplishment was making a mushroom burger that could fill a meaty hunger. He didn't mind; he knew that he could make more of an impression with fewer words.

Their dinner arrived, and they interspersed their eating with comments on the food like it was their baby. Then they were down to the sprigs of kale and the gristle of steak, the ordering of which had incidentally spawned all prior vegan talk. Cheryl swirled wine subtly in her hand.

"I'm having a good time," Cheryl said. "This was fun."

"So maybe we can do round two sometime?" Rob said. "Maybe I could cook a mushroom burger for you. You know, for science."

"For science. It might be fun, but we'll have to see."

"So you think maybe another date?"

Cheryl cleared her throat. "Rob, you're a nice guy. You're funny... I don't know if this is what I'm looking for right now."

Rob picked up the napkin and checked his shirt for stains, successfully, he hoped, concealing the disappointment on his face.

"Gotta admit, that sounds like what someone would say on a bad date to be nice."

"No, no it's not," she said. "It's just that I'm..." She paused and put a finger to her lips. "...I'm only twenty-six. I'm in a space right now where I want to meet people, and yeah, guys too. I'm not trying to settle down, and we might not be looking for the same thing."

Rob felt his face become a heat sink and wished he knew some Zen technique to cool it down. He wanted to be ice, to be thinking about what episode of *Donner Party* he had waiting at home on the DVR, because rejection hurt no matter how pure and logical the cause. There were plenty of fish in the sea, but when you swam alone, the ocean was vast.

"Say something, Rob. C'mon. It's not you, you know?"

"I'm trying to figure why you said yes to me in the first place," he said.

"'Cause I do like you. And I enjoyed our time. Didn't you?"

"Sure. I liked it so much I want to do it again."

Cheryl wiped her mouth. She was compacting herself in, like she was tucking in to go. Rob was mad, but he wasn't trying to scare her, so he relaxed himself and loosened his posture.

"I can't," she said. "You were married before. You've had kids."

"One," he said. "I had one."

Cheryl let out a breath. Rob picked up the dessert menu and glanced at all the epicurean delights that would be enjoyed by people having better nights.

Asher

Asher held the sparse crowd captive with his left hand, navigating the spaces between frets with acrobatic attention. He strummed each note as if his pick was a scalpel, lining up flush to slice a tendon. His guitar was both weapon, shield and helmet, and the small polished wooden stage was Thermopylae that Thursday night.

Annette found the place last week, when they shut down the Toga because the county upped the smoking age to twenty-one and the jam kids figured a concert hall that made its history on the smoking patio couldn't compete with the county legislature. Not that kids smoked much these days. Maybe the Toga was on life support the past few years and was looking to find a killer because it couldn't face its own passive suicide.

But Sam Wilson's was something else. Rustic wooden walls drained of grain color held onto framed prints and memorabilia like keepsakes. Stage lights oozed red and blue haze through pale-yellow table lamps that held court over round black walnut tabletops. Jordan Wilson, the owner, worked the bar and laughed with the few seatholders while she polished the brass rail.

"We'd like to thank Sam Wilson's for having us tonight," Asher said, feeling a tingle as the ungrounded microphone nipped his sweaty lips with a lick of voltage. "This next song is a new one. We're excited about it." He backed up and his gaze across the room caught the new arrivals. "Hope you like it."

Tom Filmore had shown up, which was promising. He wouldn't bring anybody to this show, it being a Thursday night, but Tom's orbital pull on the weekends made Jupiter look like space junk. Tom was an "it guy" in the local scene. He was a big deal in a big band back when the scene was twenty years younger and the kids mobbed the venues instead of making dank memes on their favorite fuckery apps. But he had the right look; he'd been to Europe, so he even made cleaning the blue plastic shitters on the side of the road look like the job to beat.

Annette started popping a bass line that formed the embryo of their new groove, and Asher chicken-scratched the spaces in between, pressing the wah like a gas pedal to flood the rhythm points with fuel. Ginny rolled on the snare and let her right-hand stick bounce on the hi-hat. Ginny had so much control over that kit Asher wondered how she ever let so much chaos into the rest of her life.

Tom's shape moved in the corner of Asher's eye, and that shape took a spot on a booth by the wall, one of the many that lined the two shorter sides of Sam's. Asher grew up in a deep and profoundly quiet state of envy toward Tom. In time, it became a demon that tripped him at every inopportune moment. And demons don't die, but they grow weary of hating the blessed. Whatever happened in the glory days, he and Tom both knew that they weren't ever leaving the valley as anything but urn filling.

The band sailed through the movement of their new baby. Asher sung lyrics he had taken days to craft in every quiet place he found, not to mention the practices during which he held Annette and Ginny hostage to the same groove and the same beat, the same thump pumping through the warmth of Annette's vacuum tubes so he could find the perfect word wrapping. But he'd found it, and on that small hardwood stage, the thin supper crowd found it too.

Tom walked up after their set, as Asher was rolling the power cord into the back of his amp.

"Not bad, not bad," he said, his hand out.

"Thanks." Asher slow-walked his rig over to the wall that butted against the back office behind the bar. The owner told him that was where the house band lined up their gear during open mics. They didn't land the gig yet, but Asher figured you should dress for the job you wanted, not the one you had.

"Hey, Tom, good to see you out." Annette packed up her own rig. "How're things with … Sarah?"

"Who's that?"

"You know, the one you were telling me about at the Merry Go Round.

You'd just broken up with her."

Asher snuck a peek at Tom, who, even in the red-and-blue haze, couldn't push the pink out of his face.

Tom laughed. "Oh, yeah, Sarah," he said. "She's good, I guess."

This time it was Asher who laughed. Annette shot him dagger eyes.

"What's so funny?" Tom said.

"What did Angie say when you told her about Sarah and the 'break-up?'"

"You're saying I'm a liar?" Tom folded his arms. Asher wondered how much he dare shave the nerve he was on.

"Nah," Asher said. "I'm positive you have plenty of girls."

"Whatever, dude." Tom turned to Annette. "Don't listen to him. There's a reason his hands are so nimble."

"Oh, a masturbation and a small dick joke in one." Ginny was maneuvering a topped whiskey glass through the cords and mic stands with precision. Asher knew that not one drop would touch floor or carpet.

"Ginny gets it," Tom said.

"You guys are a duo now, huh? I can dig it. *Tom and Ginny Break Down the Drums*. Live, in person. One night only."

"Oh, c'mon, Ash…" Ginny said. "Don't be an ass. We talked about this."

Asher sighed. Resigned to not make the situation worse and lose Tom's pull, he walked over and began breaking down the kit.

"Ginny, did you talk to her about getting a regular gig here?" he said.

Ginny sipped the largesse from her glass.

"I did. She said it depends. She *did* say the house has to choose the house band."

"That's a nice way of saying she's keeping her options open," Tom said. "I've heard lines like that before."

The house music came on low through speakers that were well hidden. Sam Wilson's looked like the roadhouse that stood on the edge of oblivion, but in every sonic sense, no expense was spared. Asher had to wonder if the reason she set up in Troy on a cheap lot on the banks of the muddy

Hudson was because, aside from the fact that Troy was the home of the actual Uncle Sam, aka Sam Wilson, that the spot had chosen *it*.

Screaming Jay Hawkins sang "I Put a Spell on You" and it permeated the room like it was the lobby of blues heaven.

"If we take her to Sam Wilson's grave," Ginny said. "Think Jordan would put some quarter rolls up?"

Jordan

She bobbed and weaved through the crowd to shake hands with the band. Captain Pneuma didn't disappoint. Sputnik was setting up, and if she knew Tim, the singer, which she did, he'd be figuring out a way to top the performance. That's why she had him play last. But as Jordan bobbed and dipped through bodies congregated, moving people about gently with a hand on an arm here, a few fingers tapping a shoulder there, she knew what glory felt like.

When she got to the stage, she congratulated and thanked the band.

"You guys were great," she said. "I'm so glad we were able to connect."

"Can I stay here?" Ginny said as she put her last cymbal in its soft case.

"You can stay here as long as you want, of course."

"So where do you go for breakfast, the gas station up there? Or is it better to brave the traffic and go up to the college? Mama needs eggs."

Jordan laughed. "Oh, you mean *stay here*."

"You got me. I'll make sure none of your liquor expires."

"It's cold as shit in the morning, I'm afraid," Jordan said. "You wanna bring a big old heater." She scoped out the crowd. "No guarantee your stuff won't get puked on at some point."

"So you're looking for that kind of party?" Asher said.

"No, nobody does. But before I even thought of opening, I bought as much bleach and pine cleaner as I did liquor. When you guys are ready, come on over to the bar. First drink's on me."

Jordan wandered through her patrons like the wind, keeping her ears open for mentions of the place, but closed to mentions of literally anything else. She wasn't nosy by nature, and she imagined when she'd had enough nights like this one, it'd be old hat and she'd only notice when people weren't saying anything.

She went around and checked the bathrooms, the doors to the storage areas, looking for wayward drunks, but she told herself it was overboard to expect such sloppiness on a Thursday. Eventually, she'd need to relieve the bartender who came to help her after Captain Pneuma set up, who Jordan marked in her head as a half hour late to her shift. She'd have to make up for being late. If she couldn't hack the job, Jordan wanted to know now before she started to draw regulars.

Jordan slipped back behind the bar. Her backup, Lindsey was chewing Tom Filmore's ear off. Jordan knew him from back in the day. He was a face in the crowd back then. In her absence, he must have gotten himself a name. Wasn't bad looking. She'd flirt with him if she was drunk and bored, but she wouldn't exactly send him any nudes.

"Lindsey, can you help the couple at the other end of the bar, see what they want?"

"They haven't tried to get my attention," she said. "Usually they try to get your attention when they want something."

"Yes, and usually people won't disturb someone who's having a private conversation. But they will go somewhere else to get drunk. I'd rather they stay here, you know?"

"I can take off," Tom said.

"Tom, it's cool. I'm glad you're here. I want to make sure everyone has the best time." She glanced at Lindsey. "You know, except us."

Lindsey rolled her eyes and went over to the other end of the bar.

Tom rested his elbows on the table. "Kids, right?"

"She'll break your heart, Tom."

He smiled, leaned forward and dropped his voice half an octave. "You know, for the right girl, I'll risk it."

"I'm so very much the wrong girl." She wiped the top of his head with her bar rag and walked over to meet the band, turning around with a smirk as Tom clutched his chest in mock heartbreak.

"Someone told me you were a carpetbagger," Ginny said as Jordan poured her a whisky. "I didn't say it, but Mena did. You know Mena Sherman?"

"Oh shit, yeah I do." Jordan pointed to Asher, who asked for a rum and coke. "I fooled around with her in high school. Briefly. Like, a month or two; it was a phase. We stayed friends, but she got super pissed when I went to school in New York. Said she'd never talk to me again."

"So she's full of shit then. Figures."

"She's a great girl, wears her heart on her sleeve. It's weird, 'cause if it weren't for her and her cousin Donny, and his friend Craig, I wouldn't have had the confidence to go to school for theater arts."

"You know Craig just died, right?" Ginny stirred the ice with a swizzle stick.

"Oh God, no," Jordan said. "When?"

"Wednesday night. I'll tell you 'cause you grew up with him, but—" she leaned forward "—it was an OD."

Jordan thought about two EMTs that came in the one night earlier in the week, and their debate about bourbon and an overdose.

"Holy shit, I think the EMTs who got him were here later that night. I'm not positive, but they said he was drinking shit bourbon. Does that sound right for Craig?"

"He used to like this stuff, McCall," Ginny said. "Kentucky stuff, so low on the shelf that you'd need basement access. He swore by it."

"I don't know if that was it, but they said he had a really nice study, so they didn't know why he'd drink such a shit alcohol if he was killing—"

Jordan came close enough to saying it to float it out there.

"No," Ginny said. "No way. He wouldn't have. There is no damn way Craig walks away from what he had, no matter how bad the pain was."

"He was sick? What did he have?"

"A shit job." Ginny kicked the glass and Jordan refreshed. "He had surgeries for his ligaments and muscles and nerves. Kept going back to work. No way he offed himself, but he might've worked himself to death."

"I want to go to the service. Wake or funeral? I probably can't take off from here for both." Jordan pulled out one of her business cards. "Can you let me know when?"

"Yeah," Ginny said. "Def."

"And let whoever know that if you need a reception space or anything…

Don't know if I can afford to do open bar, but I can do cost, maybe even cheaper. I owed Craig a ton."

Jordan and Ginny talked about Craig and Donny while Sputnik tried to top the energy that Captain Pneuma put out. They succeeded in the sense that people were more engaged, meaning that they were more drunk. Later on, Jordan wandered some more, yet that glorious feeling was a bit diminished, as if even Sam Wilson's was grieving some for Craig.

Chapter Eight

Danielle

She braced for another wave of congested sobs, breath caught in her throat, a mug of coffee in her grip. She couldn't keep losing it. Not if she had any hope of putting Craig's life into three paragraphs for the *Remembrances* website. Her mother-in-law would make sure that Craig's obituary made the paper on time. But it wouldn't be like the one on the website that would get passed around their circle on Facebook every time one of their comrades fell.

The *Troy Sentinel* would talk about his resume and that he liked to fish with his son, and that he was an honorary member of the Rotary. They would take the receipts of Craig Hill's life and plug them into a form as ill-fitting to his personality as the only good suit he owned pre-mortem.

Danielle would've been offended that Gloria wanted to take the helm with the official obit, if the whole damn thing wasn't so overwhelming. Earlier, she had to bring Joey and Marybeth to the funeral home—Gloria told Danielle she needed to be there if she wanted her to pay for it. Sandy couldn't watch them. That was a theme for the day, one of many decisions that Gloria had to make for her, and for Craig, because she had to pay for it.

Danielle felt eyestrain from staring at a blank white screen. The weight of the responsibility cemented her fists to the desk. She wondered if a cigarette would help her concentrate or procrastinate. Hundreds of people dropped by Craig's page with "rest in peace," "rest in power," or "gone but not forgotten," but the one person who needed to say it best couldn't say it at all.

She hopped out of the chair and blew her nose with one of the wads of tissue that had been sopping up the tear spill. She made her way out to the kitchen and slid open a squeaky drawer slowly, careful not to wake the kids, who had won a hard-fought sleep. The cigarettes were Craig's. She pulled out one of her inheritances and walked out on the back porch, outfitted in her slippers and bathrobe.

Danielle let the smoke seep out of her nostrils in the hope that it would clear up her congestion, but it just burned. The wind threw the cancerous tendrils every way like unruly spirits. It was warmer than it had been lately, and they weren't expecting snow until the night before the Victorian Stroll. That's what *Weather 12* said, skipping the "so watch out if you're planting your loved ones, might be a little slick on those cemetery roads."

Danielle and Craig, and by extension, Joey and Marybeth, were the one family they knew that dressed up for the Victorian Stroll every year. Craig dressed up as a Rag-and-Bone man straight out of Charles Dickens, with a raggedy but themed outfit and a big tray that strapped to the front of his chest. The tray would be filled with Victorian-looking junk, but mostly it would hide the stuff the rest of the family didn't feel like carrying, and of course, a silver, period flask with Irish whisky in it.

Danielle felt a pang of guilt when she thought it would've been funny to dress him in his Rag-and-Bone costume for his funeral so he could catch the last Stroll in full regalia. The guilt was short-lived because Craig would've loved it. It was Gloria who would've considered it disrespectful.

Her nicotine peace was shattered when the bush branches by the back wall rustled and groaned with a human voice.

Danielle grabbed the closest thing to her—a red metal bow rake—and held it close to her like a shepherd's staff. The door wasn't far, but she'd have to turn her back to—

Donny came forward coughing into his hand.

"Dude, you scared the shit out of me." Danielle was relieved that the light in Joey's bedroom window wasn't on. "Did you ring the bell?"

"I'm not stupid. I know not to wake the kids. I smelled the smoke."

"I almost blasted you in your face."

"I got a tough face." He reached behind his ear for a smoke he must have borrowed from someone.

"What happened to your hand? You get into a fight?"

"Nah, not really. I mean, I hit a dude, but he ain't fight me. He took a hit and bolted."

"That's a fight, Donny. Are you okay? I haven't heard anything from you in a couple days."

"Sorry, Dani, but I figure Glory Gloria would be over here twenty-four-seven, and she hates my ass."

Danielle squatted down, covering her knees with the folds of her bathrobe while she quashed her cigarette. She thought about going back in for another, but that empty screen was still up, and the clock was running down, even for *Remembrances*.

"I gotta finish writing Craig's thing for the *Remembrances* site."

"Shit, forgot all about that." Donny pulled a pack out of his pocket, probably his reserve after he ran out of dumb kids to bum off of. He pulled out two and lit them both, passing one to Danielle.

"I don't know what to write, Donny. I damn near flunked English Comp in college. I mean, I can write a report, but this is, you know, emotional, like creative writing. Remember when Rob posted what he'd written for *Remembrances* after his daughter died? I fucking cried when I read that. How am I going to write something about Craig that makes people cry?"

Drawing on his cigarette, Donny took the bow rake, spinning the handle in his palm as the rake dragged on the concrete.

"I'll do it," he said. "He was my best friend. I can write a ton of shit about him. We'll put your name on it."

"Wish I could. You know I'd never forgive myself if I didn't do this. Thanks, though."

They stood outside until the wind off the river carried the saltwater smell that came up from New York City. It wasn't cold enough to bury the stench.

"Are you okay, Don?"

Donny rubbed the band of his slashed hand. "It's life. We're all picking up pieces here. I'll make do."

Danielle reached over and put her hand on his shoulder, ignoring the fact that beneath his detachment, his bravado, and his tattoos, he was trembling.

Donny

The waiting room was thick with people, coughs and groans mixed with whispers and the practiced voice over the intercom to keep Donny on edge. He had his hand wrapped in gauze by then, but it was mostly for effect. He'd been walking around with his gashes, unattended and on full display, for two days. His wound care consisted of soaking a washcloth in moonshine and the agony of a hard scrub.

Two toddlers were crawling in and around the arms of the chair next to him like it was a jungle gym, oblivious to their mother, whose arm was guarding her stomach. She looked over at Donny with disgust. It was a look Donny often encountered, as if his entire person were the offense.

Danielle told him to go there. She'd tried to tend to the wound the other night but Donny wouldn't let her. She had enough to worry about with Craig's funeral and obituary. If Donny felt good about one thing, it was that by time he'd left her place, they had been able to hash out something pretty kickass for *Remembrances.*

He checked his phone against the clock on the wall. He felt a drop in his stomach when he thought about Danielle. He wasn't handling Craig's passing well, but Danielle had the kids, the house. Then again maybe it was for the best. Without the distraction of parenting and twelve-hour shifts, she might be the one in that waiting room with a bum hand.

His phone went off. He glanced at the receptionist, who returned a disapproving glare.

"Hey, Ginny," he said. "My favorite hippie rocker east of the river."

"Hey you, what're ya doing?"

"I'm in the ER."

"Your hand?"

"Yup."

"Should've went there yesterday. Don't fuck around with your hands. Need them shits. For crackin' the coconuts."

Donny let out a laugh. "My boss don't even have work for me till Monday.

If I'm lucky." He stopped. "You drunk?"

"You've never talked to me sober." Donny heard sipping on the other end. "Yo, we played at Sam Wilson's. It's nice."

"That the new place down in the old factory lot by the bridge?"

"That it be."

"You know, we used to go down there when we were teenagers and get wasted. Security guard would chase us around and we'd throw rocks through the factory windows." He couldn't help but laugh.

"I knew you lived down there."

"Yup, good times," he said. "Yo, this sucks so bad. I think I'm gonna bolt. Too many fucking people."

"Don't. You'll be dropping the fucking coffin 'cause your hand falls off and shit."

"Maybe you're right. You get my message to everybody?"

"Yup, and I got some goth-steampunk looking clothes that I can make for the funeral and the Stroll, too."

"Good."

"Oh, why I called," she paused, and he could hear her gasping as she held in a hit of weed. A barrage of coughs followed. "The girl from Sam Wilson's, Jordan, we were talking and I told her I wouldn't be able to stop by because of the funeral, and that we'd all probably be hitting the Stroll together. She said that she'd keep the place open after hours if we wanted to do, like, a reception. She said she knew you guys."

"I remember Jordan. I didn't know that was her place. I don't think we're friends on Facebook or anything."

"She said she wanted to go to either the wake or the funeral. Couldn't swing both. But she'd do half-offs and shit for drinks later, and dude, she's got everything."

"I don't know if people are gonna want to go all the way to there to drink. Probably stick to the city center."

"Give it a think. Hey, I gotta go."

The nurse might as well have been a meat inspector, the way she mangled his hand. It was short questions and even shorter answers and another big, long wait in a room with bedridden folks. When the doctor finally came in, he looked all rumpled, as if he'd just woken from a nap in his lab coat.

"Donny? Hi, I'm Dr. Wexler. I'd shake your hand, but…"

"The wounds."

"There's a Norovirus strain going around. Let's take a look." Dr. Wexler guided his hand under this light. The doctor had a much lighter touch than the nurse.

"How did you do this?"

"It's complicated."

"It would help me figure out how to treat you if I knew how it happened."

"Can you fix it without me telling you? It's embarrassing."

Dr. Wexler returned Donny's hand to him. "Look, I can tell you that it's infected. I can write you a script for some antibiotics and have you follow up in two weeks. That should take care of the infection.

"But there may be damage to nerves and tendons. I'd like to get you an X-ray, and maybe schedule you for an orthopedic consult."

"Aw, doc, I can't afford that stuff. I don't really have insurance, so this is out of pocket. Can't you just give me those antibiotics, something for the pain? I'll be good."

Dr. Wexler got up. "I can write the script for the antibiotics. But if you work with your hands in any way, you might find out that you can't afford not to follow up."

"Okay." Donny clenched his fist, sending a shock up his arm. "And something for the pain?"

"I can't send you out of here with anything stronger than what you can get at the store," Dr. Wexler said. "I don't know your situation, and I don't know what I'm sending you out to."

He stepped back and pulled the curtain. "If you want something for the pain," he said, "we need to talk about how you did it."

Rob

Sheila had silver stars and crystal icicles hanging from the folds of her beehive hairdo, her blond hair frosted with streaks of tinsel. To the outside, Sheila might seem too excitable to take orders at the Iron Kettle diner, but those who knew her best understood her world was a performance, and the Kettle, with its polished black-and-white checkerboard laminate floors, faux chrome, and burgundy Naugahyde booths was the perfect stage to bring the house down. The Iron Kettle: where it was never too early for the Christmas show.

Rob had swiped the paper off the counter and the classifieds were splayed out in front of him. His unemployment would run out before the holidays, which his boss hadn't thought of, or else he probably would've hung in a few weeks longer, pulled some shit jobs to keep everyone on payroll. Then again, his boss didn't make him pass up jobs because they didn't put a TIG welder in his hands.

He had it lucky. He didn't have to couch surf when Jennifer gave him his marching orders. His father had just evicted the renter who took their upstairs apartment. They didn't need the money so much as they needed someone to keep the pipes from freezing in the winter. Unfortunately, their renter spent his heat money on warming up the bottoms of spoons.

He didn't feel like he was sponging off his parents at forty. He was there at three a.m. if something happened, there with the car if his mother needed to go to a doctor's appointment in the cold and rain. He had morning coffee conversations with his dad and afternoon craft shows with mom. Their problems were never not his problems. He was their son.

Rob's newsprint hypnosis was broken by Sheila's vivacious bounce, her pad in her hand; pen, point down.

"Hey, Rob."

"Sheila, looking great today. Ready for the Stroll?"

"You have no idea."

"Have plans, I take it."

"Are you asking me out on a date, honey?" She let out a heat-seeker smile and detonated it with a wink.

"I was just—"

She put her hand on his shoulder. "You'll have to come here if you want a spot on my dance card. We have quite a show at the Kettle for tomorrow. I don't want to spoil it for you, but I will say there's a hint in the program, if you can find one."

"I'll be sure to do that," Rob said. He held up the menu. "How about a cheese omelet with some links on the side?"

"More coffee?"

Rob nodded.

Sheila clicked her tongue. "You got it, sugar."

She picked up the menu and made for the kitchen. Rob checked his watch. Terry Lewis was another regular, and he said he'd be in that day. He was good breakfast company. Moreover, he managed a temp agency, and promised Rob he'd keep his eyes open for something that didn't involve chain stores' electronics departments or being this year's mall Santa.

Then in walked the devil Rob was thinking of.

Terry shook his hand and sat down. He looked like a Texan. At least the way Texans probably saw themselves—square jawed, larger than life, sporting a western button-down shirt tucked into jeans held in place by the biggest belt buckle in Troy. Truth was Terry was born in Schenectady, and had only lived in Texas for a handful of years.

"Hey, man, I can't really stay. Got Karen pissed last night, so I'm mending fences. And she hates that I come in here."

"She doesn't like the Kettle?"

Terry braced the table with his arm and leaned over. "It's, you know, Sheila. She thinks—well, you get me."

"Did you tell her Sheila's married?"

Terry smiled. "It's cute that you think that matters."

"Did you ever cheat on her before?"

"Nah, but I'm not the only hyphen in her last name. First guy was terrible. Ruined the trust. Now, if the nuns at Saint Mike's looked as good as you-know-who, we'd never even go to church."

"Damn, it's like that?"

"Yup." Terry leaned back, arms draped over the top of the booth. "I don't care though. I can walk around in my boxers and scratch my balls all day, and so long as I'm not doing it in the front window, she don't care. That's love."

"Not to get off that topic, but have you got anything jobs-wise? I'm not seeing anything good in the paper."

"Ya ever push papers?"

"How big are the bundles?"

Terry laughed. "No, I mean like pencil-pusher stuff. Office shit-work. I know you're a trades guy, but can you do any of the office stuff?"

"I helped Ken, my old boss, with management. I had to learn all the office programs, 'cause he hated all that shit. I'm sure I could do it. I'm on Facebook enough, so it's not like I'm computer illiterate."

"Okay, good. There's an office temp job in the Continental Plaza, you know, the big glass building across from the Green Island Bridge. Ever been there?"

"Dentist appointment for Juliet." Rob stopped. "My daughter, I think I told you about her."

Terry's brow furrowed. "Are you okay with working in that building?"

"It's not a problem. How do I do it?"

Terry reached into his back pocket and pulled out a business card. He slid it across the table. "Call them and tell them I sent you. If you come to the agency, they'll test you, and you might not get first crack at it."

"Thanks, Terry. I owe you one."

Terry got up and stretched. "You know which seat is mine in here. Don't let nobody break it while I'm in time out."

Rob put the card in his wallet in time for Sheila to bring him his eggs and links. He fit it next to the card that he used to write all the funeral details for Craig. The wake was that afternoon. He smiled while he still could, and, having put some good news on to his plate, fueled himself for what was to come.

Chapter Nine

Asher

Fat flakes tumbled through the downtown like drunken revelers, destined to kiss the ground and pray for grass, since the roads and sidewalks were warm enough to soak them up. It was all squall, if the cable news channel on the lobby's flat-screen was right. Asher didn't mind. He had a full shift to wait it out, and there'd be so few cars on the road at midnight when he his time was up, he could afford to fishtail to Burgh if he had to.

Besides, the snow was pretty.

The parking lot was thick with cars. Mostly rental sedans, mostly clean. He always walked around the hotel before starting his shift to check out all the vehicles. Not that he remembered each, but cars could tell you a lot. That guest with a Dirty Harry fetish or the "420 friendly" one that's booked into a non-smoking room. It never hurt to look around, plus the barbecue joint across the street made for great air freshening.

He checked in to work with five minutes to spare. He wasn't one for punctuality, per se, but his cigarette timed out that way. A group of men and women filled the lobby, dressed in business casual, men in pastel golf shirts or short-sleeve button-downs, khakis or dress slacks, women in pantsuits and solid color blouses, most everyone with holly sprigs pinned to their chests.

Bianca was glued to the monitor behind the desk, the phone to her ear.

Asher felt his heart sink an inch. It was a far-fetched hope that they'd have a slow night on the Saturday before the Victorian Stroll in downtown Troy. It was one of the few events that united the city. Every business that could put up a display or offer a treat or bit of entertainment were running around like it was Troy's own personal Black Friday, which it was. Even more so for a place like the Fulton Square Lodge, which survived solely on city tourism.

Asher punched his time card, donned his name tag, and walked out behind the service desk to find Bianca, leaning on her hands, which were pressed on the counter. When she caught his eyes, hers rolled.

"Like that, huh?"

"Dude, all day. No idea."

"When did you get here?"

"Eight," she said. "There was a fire last night. We've got two families in from the Red Cross. That was at ten after eight."

"Didn't they buy rooms with those cards?"

"Yeah, but they were all here working with them, 'cause it was cold out and they figured it would be easier to do their paperwork in the lobby." She reached for a cup of ice water. "It wasn't a bad thing, everyone was sweet. And the kids were adorable. I felt terrible for them. But you know how it is when you get to work, you want that dead time to ease into it."

"I get ya," Asher said. "I was kind of hoping we'd have a chill night." With fingers hidden below the counter, he pointed gun-like to the lobby. "What's going on here?"

"They're from the city." she said. "You know, the *city* city. I think one of them mentioned Brooklyn when they were at the counter. I think they're developers or something. I heard that they want to develop Riverfront Park, put luxury condos there."

"You heard all that? What were you doing? Spying on them?"

"Nah, one of the guys told me after he checked in." She leaned against the workspace, away from the lobby. A sardonic smile spread over her face.

"He hid his wedding ring in his pocket. Those guys never think you see them doing it."

"Dirty dog," Asher said.

"I should tell June to watch herself on 217."

June was their maid. One of them, but the only woman on that day.

"So basically that guy's going to come down and hit on you all night. Which means you gotta do the shit work in between so I can cover you when he makes his pitches."

"Oh, fuck you, Ash. Just for that, you gotta do all shit work tonight, and for the rest of the week. In fact…" She tore off a square from a piece of printer paper and wrote "Shit Boy" in black Sharpie and tucked it in Asher's shirt pocket. She silently mouthed the word "shit boy" and got to actual work.

Ginny came in two hours after Asher clocked in. It wasn't unheard of. Ginny lived out of a room for a week one time, and that was how she met Asher. Their manager looked the other way when Ginny came in for sporadic, quick naps by the fireplace.

"What's up? I thought you were going to Craig's wake? Isn't that tonight? I thought I saw that on Facebook."

"Yes, sir." Ginny reached in her pocket and slammed down her debit card.

"A room? Seriously?"

"Yeah, dork," she said. "I'm doing the wake, then the funeral, then the Stroll, and of those things, there's only one I want to remember. Do you know how much alcohol it takes to make me forget two out of three things?"

"Not as much as it used to?"

"Point. But I don't want to have to drive back and forth to Latham. So, room please, *garçon*."

"Boy?"

"Oh, you know what that means."

Asher took her card. "I'm giving you the room by the washing machines."

"Is it by the ice machine?"

"Clear down the hall."

"C'mon, give Ginny a break, *garçon*," Bianca said as she padded his top pocket.

Asher sneered. Ginny clasped her hands and rested her forearms on the counter, not an easy feat for a girl on the losing side of the height war.

"Are you going to the funeral tomorrow?"

"I'm not sure. I mean, I only met him a couple of times. What would I even say?"

"Who says you have to say anything? Just show up and donate to the fund. You know, do your part and show support."

"There's a fund? Can I donate if I don't go?"

"Nope. Gotta go. But the fact that you want to donate means you belong there, so quit being an herb."

"*Herb*. Damn, pulled that out from the late nineties, didn't ya."

Ginny pointed at him and away, her index finger swiping the air. "It was a good vintage. So you gonna go or what?"

"Sure. I got a suit."

"Wear that frumpy, crushed-velvet thing you got. Everybody's going to the Stroll after. Dress to stroll, my man."

Asher finished punching in Ginny's details, most of which he knew already. Bianca smiled as a man with a hair product addiction and a smile too white for teeth walked by and shot her with finger guns, making Asher regret his earlier gesture. It promised to be a long night.

Jordan

The trees were small, plastic, and forlorn, with fiber-optic tips that were advertised as magical, but only served to evoke rainbow embers. Jordan spent the morning hunting for garland, candles, ornaments, and any little thing that could make someone think Christmas.

She figured she had time. She planned on crowdsourcing decorations for Sam Wilson's on the basis that nobody would think to start a tinsel drive. No one except her. She hadn't wanted to dumpster dive for people's throwaway trees earlier that year because she had other things to monopolize her time. What did that say about her business? She wasn't buying presents for all the drunks on Christmas Eve. She wasn't trying to salvage a child's sense of wonder. She figured she could wait until she'd been open a week or two and take some cash out of the register for anything she couldn't otherwise scavenge.

She hadn't planned on the Victorian Stroll. Troy was a beautiful, vibrant city, but it wasn't cheap. Events like the Stroll mirrored middle-school Christmas plays. You could tell which kids lived on the hill and which ones lived in the flats by their costumes. The society-page mothers splurged on top-dollar cosplay. The poor kids made do with PJs and homemade sewing jobs.

Jordan didn't come from the hill. But she knew how to make the most out of what she had. She decorated Sam Wilson's with enough flair to make it look like she was a minimalist fashionista. Next year, she swore to herself, she'd have a whole flotilla of red-and-green fireworks. Next time, she'd be ready.

All day she thought about Craig. About Danielle, too. She was part of the crew for a year or two. It was her and Donny, Craig and Danielle, and "Craig and Danielle" was always said as a singular thing, because she knew—everybody knew—they belonged together. At one time Jordan mused if she and Craig would make a good pair, but he wasn't who he was without Danielle. She was his other half.

She called yesterday. She was busy the night before with the bands, but as soon as she knew it was Craig, Danielle was on her speed dial. She cried, for which she felt endlessly guilty, like she couldn't hold it together while Danielle was soldiering on. But Danielle knew.

They'd kept in touch as much as anyone had kept in touch after high school. She even offered them theater tickets for a sold-out show in New York when they came down on their tenth anniversary.

What she did manage to do was assure Danielle that they would be having a private reception at Sam Wilson's for everyone who went to the funeral or the wake, after the sun set on the Stroll and people started meandering to downtown bars. They'd have to take a bus or a cab or leave their cars in the parking lot if they wanted to get ridiculously drunk for ridiculously cheap, but Danielle assured her she'd find a way to get heads to the after-party.

Jordan's phone rang and she checked the caller ID: Perry Maxwell, aka PM. Weird that he was calling before dark. His sleeping habits were what earned him his nickname.

"What do you say, PM?"

"Just woke up. I got your message. Early as fuck."

"Early for you."

"Try working third shift for a guy who thinks labor camps are inefficient."

"I'm glad you called," she said. "I need a favor."

"You always need a favor. Good thing I'm in love with you."

"No, you're not."

"I'm in love with the idea of you," he said mid-yawn. "So what do you need?"

"You remember Craig, right?"

"Yeah, that's sad shit. Fucking killed himself."

"No, he didn't."

"You know for sure?"

"Do you?"

"Nope," he said. "But the end result's the same either way."

"Now I don't know if I want to ask the favor."

"Okay, so maybe he killed himself, maybe it was an accident. Better?"

"I guess," Jordan said. "We're having the funeral reception here, after the Stroll ends. I need to book a band on the lightning tip. You and the Prophets doing anything Sunday night?"

"We're not playing, but I don't think I can't wrestle them away from downtown. I mean, it's the Stroll, all the bars got two-for-ones. I can ask, but you need bank if you're doing the funeral reception. I can't give you bank."

"See what you can do, and let me know, okay? I could always use two bands."

"Will do."

"Thanks, PM." She hung up and walked out onto the stage. Even though it was small and made a four piece with entry-level gear seem like a world tour, it was a stage. She spent hours on stages on Broadway, places that sprouted magic and lent themselves to creative interpretation. Problem solving wasn't a skill on Broadway; it was a character trait.

She picked up the phone.

"Capital Police, security office."

"Gerald, it's Jordan. Question for you."

"Shoot."

"Doc Lucian… You seen him lately?"

"Uh," he paused. "Yeah, shit, he's out there right now."

"He got his guitar still, or is it too cold?"

"He don't have it right now—"

"Shit."

"—but we have it in one of the employee lockers. We let him keep it in here when it's cold and he's our… guest, as long as he leaves the workers coming in here alone. And he does. My CO wants to just throw it out, though."

"So you got it?"

"Just said I did."

"Can you do me a favor? Can you try to keep him there for long enough for me to get over? Tell him I got a bed for him tonight, and some food. Fuck, tell him I got booze if you have to."

"You gonna take in Doc Lucian? Be careful. I mean, he's cool, but he might rob your house."

"My landlord might too." She finished pouring a cup of Rocket Fuel with one hand. "Only he'd get away with it. I'm on my way. See ya soon."

Jordan grabbed her coat off the back peg, thankful that she hadn't been open long enough for consistent hours. Soon she wouldn't have the luxury of wearing every hat in the place.

Danielle

They wrap death in rays of sunshine through arching trees in pastoral fields, babbling brooks and special, open spaces where peace floats on sparse clouds and you can hear heaven if you're quiet enough. But the reality is thick, crimson velvet drapes and dark, polished mahogany. It is walls that suck in sobs and a solemn quiet that serves only to remind everyone who walks in the door that frivolity is as dead as the body in the casket.

Danielle flicked the pile of ash off her cigarette as two black-capped chickadees sang a duet on the fence between Walsh's Funeral Home and the Italian restaurant next door. Craig used to birdwatch out on their porch in the morning, the early morning, as the sun rose for Danielle and Craig and the rest of the world was still getting ready to start its shit. Craig picked up birdwatching from a guy he worked with, a flagman who had acquired the skill on country roadwork in the outer counties.

Sandy walked around back from the parking lot, where she had stashed her phone and her cigarettes. She'd been making calls all day on Danielle's behalf, like an agent, or a manager. 'Cause death makes the survivors rock stars until the body goes to soil and the show goes to intermission. Danielle figured Sandy might be the only one who'd stick around for Act Two.

"Missy's coming," Sandy said. "And she's picking up Joe, Andy, and Keisha, but they gotta wait for Keisha to get out of work. It looks like most everyone I talked to ain't gonna be here till around six."

Danielle twirled her cigarette in her fingers. "It's only going on till seven. It's gonna be mobbed."

"Probably. But you'll have plenty of time to relax until then." Sandy wiped off the railing before leaning back so she didn't get dust and street residue on her dress, the one she bought when she was going to marry Kyle in a Goth-themed wedding, the one that she could only recently fit back into and thus found every excuse to put on. Her little black dress.

"Relax. That's funny. Did you see Gloria when you were in there?"

"She's chasing the funeral director around, it looked like."

"She thinks I'm out here smoking cigarettes because I'm shattered," Danielle said. "Not that she's wrong."

"I'm surprised your mom isn't here." Sandy lit a cigarette off Danielle's and handed it back to her. "That's gonna be fun."

"Oh, gas meets matches? I told mom I needed her to watch the kids. I do. It'll also keep her occupied, and they're not going to want to be here too long."

"Poor little turds," Sandy said. "How are they right now? Do you think they're going to be able to handle it?"

"Honestly, no. I mean, Joey knows now that his dad isn't gonna be sleeping. He was asking questions about grandma yesterday, and he was at her funeral." Danielle coughed into her hand. "So he knows. But Marybeth might act up."

"You know I'll keep 'em busy too, maybe play hide-and-seek, piss off the funeral director a little."

"I don't care. Let him add it to Gloria's tab."

Sandy ran her hands down the sides of her dress. "Is it inappropriate to pick up guys at a funeral?"

Danielle laughed. "Only if you ask the widow, you putz." She reached out and rapped Sandy with her fingers. "So what, Mark ain't getting none of that?"

Sandy waved her head side to side, giving her hair a disheveled look. "He don't want it. Believe me, if I didn't have the kids home I'd be parading around all stripper-like." She exaggerated a catwalk across the employee parking spaces. "Put little sandwiches on my tits like pasties, and he ain't gonna get a bite."

"You guys fighting?"

"I shouldn't get into it today, Dani," she said. "I mean, it's your day."

"It's Craig's day. I'm as much a spectator as everyone else. Half the people coming don't even know me. Spill. Why you guys fighting?"

"We're not fighting exactly. He's just tired every day. He goes to work, comes home, eats, and it's on the video-games. And I'm cool with it. I work too, it sucks. I wanna kick back and chill too. But I'm all about movies, and he's shooting things."

Sandy pulled her own cigarettes out of her purse. "It's like, when we started going out, he was really saving me from Kyle, who was so unpredictable. I liked the fact that I knew what to expect from Mark. It made me happy as shit. But now I'm starting to realize why I got with Kyle in the first place."

"Oh don't, please don't tell me you got that scumbag on the brain."

"Nah, never again. I learned my lesson." She lit up and waved the air around her hair. "Like Craig. He worked, came home, ate, showered, shit, shaved, all that. And the same with you. You all hardly ever saw each other, but when you did, you guys were like one goofy, funny person. I want that. I want someone to run with the shopping cart while I pretend to steer."

The reference brought the memory back to Danielle like a blooper reel. Danielle had turned her leg, and she knew the ankle was sprained. They didn't have a car at the time, and they were two miles from their house, with the nearest bus stop eight blocks away. Craig didn't want to steal a shopping cart—correction, both of them really wanted to steal a shopping cart, but Craig was the one who didn't want to get caught. Danielle didn't want to be on her feet all night at the bar, but she needed a check.

So Danielle grabbed the front of the cart and pushed it left and right and Craig, who couldn't see in front of Danielle, felt for the pressure and made the little turns that kept them from toppling over. They missed the bus, and it down-poured, but they wound up with a cart in their front yard.

"Forgot about that," Danielle said. "Shopping carts."

Sandy put her hand on Danielle's shoulder. "You okay, hon? Did I bring back bad memories?"

Danielle balled up her fist and pressed into her eye socket. "No. The bad ones are easier."

Danielle got up and flicked her cigarette into the flowerbed, which was well seeded with butts.

"They're not going to bring him out here," she said. "About time we went in."

Chapter Ten

Donny

Craig was in his study napping, a white ruffled sheet around him.

That was Donny's first thought when he cleared the foyer and made his way into the main showroom. The casket was gloss walnut.

Gloria's money was all over the wake. Donny could guess that his last piece of furniture cost thousands.

Danielle never would've spent the kind of money. How could she? She had kids to feed. Donny knew Craig had been barely holding on with the house and car payments. If he'd been on Easy Street, Craig wouldn't have shut up about it, which was a game they played since they'd been a crew.

Donny remembered the game well. If he got new sneakers, Craig would never hear the end of it until he got a paper route, or mowed lawns or shoveled sidewalks and bought the next better pair. Then he'd be the braggart until Donny could hustle enough kids at the South Troy Pool or the Atrium or wherever he decided the action was, and he'd show up with a video game system. They'd truce long enough to try all the games it came with. Then it was bragging rights for new games.

Pride. Damn straight it was pride. It wasn't what you were taught. You had to be humble, and quiet about the shit you had because God was watching and blessed were the meek, but Donny and Craig noticed that the people who talked that shit the most seemed to have a whole lot more stuff to be humble about than they did.

The place was packed. He separated the room in his mind by fam, who milled about, friends who were huddled in tight circles like Craig was DJing a prom, and people he didn't know or barely knew, who were either seated or playing wallflower in the corners. Danielle and the kids were sitting too, probably the only people, in his opinion, that had the right to sit.

He walked over toward the casket, brushing Danielle's shoulder with the back of his hand on the way. He worried that he wouldn't be able to talk to her after seeing his best friend molded, stitched, and painted over like a Beverly Hills whore, but he swore he'd sit with Craig in the boat to Hades and make change for the ferryman before he'd abandon him.

He put his hand on Craig's hand and there wasn't any backstage trickery that could impart the illusion that Donny was touching something other than room temp. He withdrew his hand slowly, so as not to disturb the kids. Their Uncle Donny wasn't afraid of anything. They needed that in their life; a new superhero to pick up Craig's cape.

Not that Donny had designs on Danielle, since his feelings for her over the years had settled, but he knew she'd need him to be a better man. Someone had to protect them, protect her, and Craig wouldn't have trusted anyone else. He backed away, gave the sign of the cross in the non-church out of superstition and drifted over to Danielle.

"Thanks for coming," she said. She was carrying a crumpled tissue, and the skin around her eyes was pink and puffy from her eyelids to her cheekbones. She swiped her nose absently.

"You know I wouldn't miss it." He knelt on his better knee. "Hey Jo-Jo, hey, Bethy. Come give Uncle Donny a hug."

Joey was wrapped around the chairs, crawling up and down them. Marybeth was grabbing onto Danielle's leg. Instead of going to Donny, she clutched tighter.

Danielle tapped Joey on the back. "Go say hi to your Uncle Donny," she said. "It's not you, Don. The kids have been getting hugs and pokes all night. I want to kill some people."

"It's okay," Donny said. "I'll give you a hug then." He leaned over and hugged her. He smelled lilacs. He wasn't used to smelling scents on Danielle. She rarely wore perfume. She once told Craig to bring some back that he'd gotten her, saying that since she never knew when she'd get called in to the hospital, or who would be allergic to what, she'd never wear it. Donny also knew that Craig had her keep it for special occasions. Maybe that's what he smelled.

Danielle smelled something entirely different. "Really?" she whispered. "Weed? Really Donny? You gotta quit that shit."

"What? It's what I told him I'd do, and he was gonna do the same for me. It's not just weed."

"It doesn't smell like just weed."

"I got hash from Amsterdam about five years ago. Me and Craig were gonna smoke it when he either quit his job or got fired or retired. That way he didn't have to worry about a piss test. So, I mean, he's not working anymore."

"You got it five years ago, it's probably dried-out dust, isn't it?"

"Damn near," Donny said. "I really didn't even get that high. Dani, I did it for Craig. I wouldn't have came here fucked up, you know that."

"It's cool," Dani said. "I wish I could smoke weed. They piss test me too. But promise me you won't be high or drunk or anything tomorrow at the funeral, okay?"

"Sure."

"You can be a little drunk. I think everyone is gonna be a little drunk, with the Stroll."

"I'll take a shot of absinthe then. That's Victorian, right?"

Danielle smiled. "You're sharing."

Donny made the rounds and pressed the flesh, taking on the mantle of First Friend. Danielle didn't try to stop him, and he put it in his mind that he was doing it for her, but he had to be the center of attention for a little while. He was a part of Craig that everyone there, to a person, assumed was just how he was on his own.

He saw Rob and Ginny. They eventually settled down with Danielle in the corner behind the viewing area and talked about the funeral and making sure they had enough pallbearers, to which Ginny told him that she had a guitar player who she'd convinced to show up and help. They also took a guess at what the numbers might be based on Facebook's count of RSVPs. Danielle's eyes got wide when the figure ended up north of five hundred.

"Jesus," she said. "What are we going to do with five hundred people after the funeral? We should've ordered a hall and a caterer and—"

"Everyone's going to the Stroll afterward," Ginny said. "So as far as ordering something … you might as well have ordered a whole city."

Rob

Children's caskets are a shock to the eye. They don't fit any funeral home, and there's not a whole lot to make the little container blend into the occasion, however solemn. When Juliet was in that viewing room, that same one, they tried to fill the extra space with bright rainbow-colored carnations and stuffed animals, some hers, some bought for the wake. Rob saw the ticket booth to a macabre circus.

He stayed till the end of the wake, hanging out with Donny and his friend Ginny. No one stayed behind during Juliet's wake, not even his wife. Jennifer couldn't handle being there after the first wave of consolation, after the common expressions of comfort had been exhausted and had become repetitive.

She ran out of the funeral home and went home. Rob had to stay through the main push of mourners and tell them why Jennifer wasn't there in a way that didn't make her seem weak or cold. Because he still believed right then that they were in love and you protect the ones you loved. He had the notion that, having lost their daughter, they wouldn't run headlong away from each other. But even then, deep down he hated her for leaving him there alone.

Danielle's mom took the kids, who had been good through the whole three hours. They were hurting just as bad, but they grieved their own way because society hadn't taught them to be solemn and wear their tears right. But they were tired, and Danielle's mother offered a welcome respite.

All total, they guessed that two hundred people came to the wake. It wasn't bad for a Saturday night. Danielle was wiped out, but she told Rob she skipped dinner, and she knew if she didn't eat, she wouldn't sleep. When they were outside smoking, Rob suggested they go out for a quick bite at the Kettle, which was open twenty-four hours, and had a not-terrible evening menu.

"I can't go in there," Donny said. "Can we go to the Trojan Diner down by the jail? I got credit there."

"I'm not going that far," Danielle said. "Why can't you go to the Kettle?"

"I beat up the owner's kid."

"Mike Miller?" Rob said. "What he do?"

"He's a douchebag. I won't go in there no more. But you know, you do you. I won't fault you or anything."

Danielle tapped the tip of her cigarette, making it snow. "He probably tried to kick you out, didn't he?"

Donny groaned. "If you all must know, his wife got with me. A few times. And he lost his shit, called me a scumbag."

"You were fucking his wife, I don't blame him," Ginny said. "Control your meat, dude."

"Yo, I didn't know she was his wife." Donny was talking with his hands. "She comes up to me, slides into the booth one night and slides her hand up my thigh. How many married women you know do that?"

"Too many," Danielle said.

"Okay, so we can't go to the Kettle, and we don't want to go to the Trojan," Rob said. "Where's that leave? There's fifty places to catch a meal in Troy."

"Do the Kettle," Donny said. "I should go home anyway, get my suit ready for tomorrow."

"It's cool, man. We'll go somewhere else…"

"No, seriously. Grab that grub. Dani needs to be ready for tomorrow. Just if you use the shitter—miss all over that motherfucker."

Ginny bailed as well. Since she had a room at the hotel, and she had a sub waiting for her in the mini fridge. Rob and Danielle drove down to Third Street, to the heart of the city, and lucked out on a parking spot that wouldn't force them to navigate the crack dealers and random drunken frat goblins.

The Kettle sat kitty-corner to the second biggest bus stop in Troy, the one that took its passengers to all points south. Namely, Albany. Behind the stop was a restaurant, at one time a chain fast-food oasis, now a perennial rotation of Chinese take-out or chicken joint. There was a day the two businesses used to compete.

The county office building and the courthouse were imposing granite monuments to the fact that Troy was the county seat. Rob had been a regular in the county clerk's office when he got DBAs for one of his boss's many side businesses. He stopped when he learned his boss tried to use his Social Security number and tax information in another county.

They sat at the counter with coffees. He didn't know the night shift, but the waitress was scratching off a stack of Money Magic tickets, a game Rob never had the patience for.

"How did you do it, Rob?"

Rob shook his head. "It was different," he said. "I mean, I'm sure it's always different, but…" He sipped his coffee. "In some ways, you're worse off than I was, and that's really hard for me to say, but it's true. Craig wasn't just somebody you loved. He brought money into the house.

"Juliet was my world, and I shattered. I'm sure you remember, you and Craig were there for me. I was lost. I absorbed into work, and so did Jennifer. So we were bringing in money, and we didn't have to worry about how we were going to make ends meet."

"I know what you mean," Danielle said. "I'm spending every minute that I'm not working or doing something else trying to put Craig's financial papers together."

She sipped her coffee and pulled a napkin out of the dispenser to wipe the ring off the counter. "He paid the bills. He was good at keeping up with it. He'd tell me my share and I'd give it to him, no second thought about it. Now, I don't know if my one job can cover everything."

"I can help you with that if you want," Rob said. "I've had to do it for my boss before I got laid off. I can at least figure out what's due when, and what you can afford to put off."

"You, Rob, are a saint," Danielle said. "I will owe you a home-cooked dinner."

"That's okay. You don't have to cook me anything."

She leaned over and bumped Rob. "Oh honey, I never said I'd cook it."

Asher

Two fully decorated trees stood at each side of the front door and combined with the pale-blue net of lights suspended from the ceiling, the strategic placement of wreaths and, of course, the enclosed fireplace, made the Fulton Square Lodge look like a private four-star chalet, not the chain hotel it actually was. But in a few ways, there was a personal touch that set it apart even in the off season.

The manager, Cherie, had a big sway over how the place looked on the inside, since her father was a bigwig in the national company, and she got Fulton Square Lodge as a test of her management skills, a well-adorned career stepping-stone. She wasn't a bad manager. In fact, she got a lot of things for the staff that the other hotels were envious of, like better pay and a great discount on stays to any hotel in the chain.

One thing she didn't get was a TV for behind the counter. The lobby screen was, by design, set apart from view as well. Asher didn't blame her, because he knew himself and he knew Bianca and during the dead hours, when busy work waited in dark hallways to pounce, they easily would've figured out how to watch movies.

The clock was in view, and it was slow torture. Bianca left at ten, an hour ago. She would've accompanied him to the midnight hour, but she asked for an early leave to get a jump on a weekend trip to Poughkeepsie. Why she needed time off to drive two hours south was beyond him. She was mum about the trip, and he didn't ask. They were married the moment they walked in the door and divorced amicably the moment one of them clocked out.

Asher pulled the lever and watched the water level recede on the refreshment table. One of his minor duties was to fill two plastic containers with ice, water, and citrus wedges, whatever they had, and to keep it full as guests came down and filled tiny cups from the spigot on the bottom. It was not his duty to drink it when he was bored.

He watched the clock, then the one screen he did have at his disposal—the surveillance cameras in the hallways. Working in hospitality taught

Asher that if you wanted to cheat on your wife, deal drugs for a weekend, plan a mob hit or hide out from the cops, a chain hotel was not the place to do it. Or, if you were going to, tip well.

They respected your privacy enough not to film your room, but you didn't need to film people's rooms if you could see who was coming or going. When it was slow, like that night, Asher watched the hallways and made up stories of the people going back and forth. Made it only slightly embarrassing when they'd come down to chat.

The Stroll was coming; he'd worked last year the night before and the night of, and there was an energy in the air, like it was the night before Halloween and the stores had mysteriously sold out of eggs. It wasn't malice, though; instead it was exuberance. People were coming in from the bars flushed and laughing. Asher was even invited up to a woman's room, which was far less appealing than it sounded, considering the strict prohibition against the thing.

It started to pick up in the hallways, as it was gearing toward party time on a Saturday night, a call even strange travelers couldn't resist. He noticed the man who tried to impress Bianca was waiting for the elevator on the third floor. Asher watched him get on, ignoring a gaggle of college girls in the lobby by the fireplace trying on each other's scarves.

The man came down and poured himself some lemon water and grabbed a cookie from the tray in front of the dispensers.

"This stuff's great," he said—maybe he was talking to Asher, maybe himself. "I gotta get one of these for the office."

"I don't know where they sell the dispensers, but it's just ice water and lemon and lime wedges."

"It's clean. Wipes the palate." He walked over to the desk and extended his hand. "I'm Harley."

"Like the bike?"

"Yeah, like the bike," he said, his smile bright as the fluorescents overhead. "My parents used to ride. They told me I was delivered at a Sturgis, but I don't know about that."

"That's cool." He extended his own hand. "Asher. Mine's biblical, I think."

Harley held up his small cup. "To funny names."

"So where ya coming from?"

"I live in Manhattan, but I'm coming up here soon. We're here to check out the Stroll this weekend. Then a meeting with the EDC on Monday, then back to the rat maze."

"What's the EDC?"

"The Economic Development Council," he said. "It's like a board that oversees economic development in the city. We're working with the Riverfront Renewal Project. Have you heard of that?"

"Nah, man. Don't take offense, I sort of live under a rock."

Harley laughed. "That's fine. We're trying to create a pedestrian path all the way to the end of South Troy, and have it open up into a park around the bridge down there."

"That sounds cool, but how's that economic development?"

Harley put his forearms on the counter and folded them, splaying his hand out to talk with it.

"South Troy is huge," he said, "but it's mostly forgotten. It's residential, sure, but there's a lot of room for business growth. But—and I hate to say it—no one's got money in South Troy." He coughed in his hand. "You want to get the money there, you need the college kids. You get the college kids, you get the business owners. You get them, and you start getting ideas on where you can buy out houses and create little business strips here and there. You can really breathe life into it."

Asher considered what he was saying. He checked the lobby for anything that needed his attention, and, seeing nothing, continued the conversation.

"What if people don't want to sell?" he said.

"Most of South Troy is slumlords," Harley said. "Or seniors who would sell their souls for a retirement community in Florida. Despite what people tell the world, they'll sell." He took out his phone and pulled up a picture. He slid it over the counter.

"That's what the park on the riverfront might look like," he said. "Cool, right?"

Asher spread out his fingers to enlarge the pick and dragged it around on the screen.

"There's a club there right now," he said. "It's called Sam Wilson's. My band played there the other night. Man, she just opened, and it looks like the club would be in the middle of your park."

"Huh. Didn't know that," Harley said. "I'll have to check it out."

"It's a nice club. You should work with her."

Harley nodded. "I'm sure something could be arranged."

Chapter Eleven

Jordan

Driving up State Street from Broadway, Jordan could see the lights and decorations as she neared the split at the state capitol building. They must've just gone up; Albany didn't have any specific city-wide event before First Night and the fireworks on New Year's Eve. The streets were dead, and few people would believe that the capital city of the behemoth New York State could be so dead that a hundred people could jaywalk on a Saturday night, and not a one would score even a honk from an inconvenienced driver.

She stopped at a Wilbur's and picked up an Italian sub with double meat, which sat in the passenger seat. A two-liter of lemon-lime soda was in the back, and a pint of rum was in the glove box, in case extreme bribery was needed. Some people might think that the promise of a meal and a warm bed would naturally coax a person off the street, but a hard-living man like Doc Lucian might not so easily be appeased.

In fact, the thing that would probably get Doc Lucian to accept her hospitality was the fact that she needed him to do work. People like Doc didn't see themselves as accepting charity, even when they panhandled, figuring it wasn't easy to brave hypothermia for pocket change.

Half the time she knew Doc, which was a very long time, all the way back to his much younger years in Troy, he'd take a job over a handout.

People saw him, they assumed him incapable of doing much but collecting pocket lint. What they didn't know was that Doc Lucian was older than dirt, and his guitar was the history of the blues.

The legend was that Doc Lucian was the one that introduced Robert Johnson to the devil at the crossroads. There were a lot of stories like that, how he helped Howlin' Wolf get his name, and how he was the inspiration for Screamin' Jay Hawkins' "I Put a Spell on You." Jordan knew, from hanging out with him, that he didn't start practicing hoodoo until the seventies, when the Black Panthers were celebrating everything black. In a mostly white Capital Region, he found his niche, his own personal rebellion.

All of that was beside the point. Doc Lucian could get his guitar and play some of the best Delta Blues for days with only piss and liquor breaks. And he preferred it that way.

Jordan had to park blocks away from the security office in the concourse, a massive underground hall that extended from the capital, across the Empire State Plaza and terminating at the New York State Library. Parking anywhere in Albany was a black-tie affair. She locked up and started her journey to go get her long-lost friend.

Gerald was watching surveillance screens like a moviegoer missing popcorn. Jordan walked up to the front door and tapped on the glass. He was slightly spooked, but he hid it well.

"Jordan, homegirl," he said. "He's still here. Down by the far end of the reflecting pool."

"You mean the skating rink?" she said.

"Is it winter yet?" He glanced at the calendar. "Close enough."

"I'll go see if he's game to help me. We can get his guitar, right?"

"Yeah, just have him come with you. Don't want him to say anything. Not that you aren't trustworthy, but you know him. He'll say it was the principle of the thing."

"Sure, sure. I'll be back soon."

Jordan walked the streaked-marble ground of the plaza, with the Egg, so called for the performance theater's shape, and the plaza office buildings looming overhead. There were art installations that she remembered from her time before New York City that were still standing. A few were new. As she got to the far side of the reflecting pool-slash-skating rink, she saw an elderly man, wrinkled and liver spotted, with intense dark eyes partially obscured by a newsboy cap. He was dressed in tattered leather and torn blue jeans, and his guitar case was out, though all he had was a harmonica.

"Doc," she said.

"I know you?"

"I'm Jordan. You probably don't remember me. I'm from Troy."

He looked up and smiled. "I'd sure like to."

"Hey, you wanna earn some money?"

"I ain't do curses no more."

"Curses? Oh no. You were doing curses?"

"A little. It ain't good though. I do mojo hands now. You want me to do mojo hands?"

"If you want to. I'll pay, but I need a musician."

"Oh, I can do that. It's gonna rain tomorrow. Are we gonna be outside? 'Cause I try to hide from the rain. I'm not superstitious or nothin', but I'm an old man, and I can't hustle good with a sneeze or a cough."

"No, Doc, it's all indoors. I own a music club, and my act split on me. I need a solid left hand."

Doc laughed. "I got a solid left hand. Got a solid right one too."

"So I got a sub sandwich and some soda in the car. Are you good for now? Can you come with me?"

Doc looked into his guitar case. "I don't know, can I get a couple more folks? I want to get just a nip, 'cause it's cold, you know. Just a little nip from the store down the bottom of the hill."

Jordan smiled. She forgot how much she loved Doc Lucian. "Buddy, I got a good nip in the car too." She thought quick. "Rum. But it'll have to come out of your pay."

"You got it," he searched for her name. "Jordan."

"You remembered."

"There's a river named Jordan. It's in the Good Book."

"That's what I was named after," she said. "Now let's get you picked up. He can get your guitar out of the security office and we'll go to my place. Get you cleaned up. I'll see if I have any clothes anyone left behind that will fit you."

"Oh, I can't be a bother," he said.

"Are you kidding? You're a lifesaver."

They walked to the security office, and Gerald retrieved Doc Lucian's guitar. Jordan wished he'd let her have it restrung, but then she realized that would be like replacing a magician's wand, and she thought better of it.

They were driving down the interstate toward Troy, toward her apartment. She wasn't going to leave Doc Lucian in a bar full of liquor by himself. She turned to him when he'd finished his sub and was wiping his lips with a napkin.

"On second thought," she said, "I'd love it if you made me a mojo hand. For my club."

Danielle

Craig's mug could keep a coffee warm until lunch, if he would ever have spared enough coffee to test that out. It was a twenty-two-ounce steel mug with a stylized bull's head on it. Danielle got it for him for Christmas last year, after his favorite regular mug slipped out of his hands one morning and shattered on the kitchen floor. He swore he knocked it into the edge of the kitchen sink, but his hands had started having muscle spasms.

It was dark. The little hand on the wall clock passed the five, and the only hand on the window thermometer was close to forty. She checked the forecast on her phone before she went out on the porch, and it looked like there would be snow squalls. Love of snow was something she and Craig had shared. Maybe a squall would greet the graveside ceremony.

The door squealed in protest of its being opened. Danielle prayed it wasn't the kids up already. Her eyes followed the sound and they met her mother, in a bathrobe, with her own mug of steaming coffee.

"I hate it when it's dark like this so late," she said.

"It's only five o'clock."

"I know." She moved over to the other seat, the one with Craig's ass-print worn into it. "I wish we could catch the sunrise today."

"Why can't we? This window is east."

"It won't be up for another hour and a half," she said. "We'll be wrangling the kids into their church clothes."

"We're not leaving here until nine. I was hoping we could get them dressed after breakfast."

Her mother picked up a pack of Craig's cigarettes on the table between the chairs. She flipped it open and pulled out one of the two remaining.

"I might want both of those, Mom."

"Stop. Mine are in the car." She picked up the matches and bent one around, over the matchbook to the friction strip and flicked it with one hand, bringing it to life and taking it to the tip of her cigarette.

"I don't think you all should go to the Stroll afterward."

"Mom, we're going," Danielle said. "Joey looks forward to dressing up like Tiny Tim, and last year might possibly have been Beth's first memory with her dad, at the Stroll, 'cause it's one of the few things we do as a family."

"But the kids are going to be surrounded by people at the funeral, then they're going to go out and be surrounded by strangers on River Street. They're going to be worn out, and then they'll get cranky and start acting out and then they remember today as a day they were acting up." Her mother took a drag. "Why don't you all just come up to our house and watch Christmas movies or something?"

"C'mon, you know we're not going to do that. Why don't you come with us? If you see them starting to act up, you can bring them to the house and make Christmas cookies."

"You mean while you go out drinking with your buddies."

"If I didn't have my kids, what's wrong with that?"

"Maybe you have to think about the kids right now."

"I think of the kids every day. I might want to have a little time to breathe myself after this. My original plan was to take the kids out for the day and bring them over to Sandy's tonight and go actually have a good time for once. You want to take the kids to your house? Fine. I'd be pleased as punch, but not if it's gonna be a guilt trip. I've been raising the kids just fine for eight years."

Danielle's mother nudged the ash off her cigarette into the ashtray. "You had Craig backing you up before. I'm trying to prepare you, is all."

Danielle groaned, got up, and went into the kitchen.

"Mommy, I don't wanna wear church clothes," Marybeth said.

"Honey, I know," Danielle said as she pulled at the plaid dress to catch the best fit. Marybeth was growing, and she was rarely ahead of that curve. Marybeth's curly blond ringlets had the wispy look of bed hair despite the fact that she just washed it. Her usual wiggle-worm nature was subdued, and Danielle would've assumed it was because it was so early, but it was something else too.

"Mommy, will Daddy be able to see the f'runeral?"

"I'm sure he's watching down from heaven."

"Why can't he watch from his box? Like yesterday."

"The box is going to be closed, honey. It's not the same as last night."

"Why couldn't God let him wake up to say 'bye?'"

"I don't know, honey," Danielle said. "No one knows."

"He's dead, Beth," Joey said. "It's just a body, like in that movie I let you watch. The one about the shopping mall."

"You let her watch a zombie movie? When?"

"Halloween."

"Mommy, is Daddy a zombie?" Marybeth's face crinkled in and her brow furrowed. Her sole front tooth laid claim to her bottom lip.

"No! Jesus, Joey, you aren't supposed to watch those movies. How did you even get past the parental lock?"

"Dad let us watch it 'cause we didn't get a lot of candy."

"Figures." She sighed. "Daddy's not a zombie. He's…" Danielle realized that there was no way to talk about death that bridged the understanding of both an eight-year-old and a five-year-old.

"He's in heaven," she said. "It's like a dream, only it's the best dream ever. And you can see the people you love, you can watch over them, but we can only see him when we're asleep in our own dreams."

Marybeth yawned. "I'm tired. I want to go back to sleep and see Daddy."

"We have to say goodbye to his body first," Danielle said. Joey was playing airplane with the scrambled eggs on the tip of his fork. If he didn't buy Danielle's explanation, he was doing a great job at not showing it.

"I'm not hungry," Joey said. "Can I just have stuff on the Stroll today?"

"You're not loading up with crap all day. Eat your breakfast, and we'll stop at the Sweet River Candy Shop for *one* thing."

She finished dressing Marybeth and got her a plate and a promise to try to finish everything, but she knew that was a tall order. Danielle darted around the house, putting her formal black dress on. Even though it was encouraged that people who went to the funeral dress up for the Stroll later if they were going, she couldn't do that herself, even though Craig would've loved it so much he might have popped the casket just to sit up and clap.

She gathered up her black Victorian cuirasse bodice and a black-and-purple pleated bustle skirt to put on later. She had it tailored so that she wouldn't need a corset, since she went to the Stroll to have a good time, not to give herself a gastric bypass. She wasn't a heavy girl by any means, but she did have access to food in the twenty-first century. So no on the corset.

She dipped back out on the porch to smoke her last cigarette. She needed to pick some up before they got to the church. If she didn't smoke them all on the Stroll, she was fairly sure that they'd be hanging with a few cigarette bums, and she wanted good times for all that day.

"You look nice," her mother said. Danielle turned around and said the same.

"What you said to the kids," she said. "About Craig, about death ... pretty good stuff. I wouldn't have come up with anything better."

"I guess I believe it, but who knows?"

Her mother let out a laugh. "I didn't know what to say to you when your grandfather died 'cause I was a wreck myself." She opened the empty pack, inspected it and threw it out in the wastepaper basket. "Good a guess as any."

Donny

The coffee wasn't cutting it, but he knew it wouldn't. All of his joints and muscles were throwing Molotov cocktails at the cop cars and the castle gates, full riot. His head was screaming and his nose was running, but even wiping the snot away meant touching his head, which wasn't great idea. He got up and went to the living room and set himself gently on the couch.

He spent last night with Craig. First at the wake, but later on in McEntyre's, and then the Rooster, ending up at the Barn Owl, which is what took over the Yarrow. That one was weird, as it was a complete hipster joint and everyone knew it, but he was only there to hang out with memories, so fuck them. Fuck everyone.

The coke was too much. He was shitfaced and high as fuck by the time he got to the Barn Owl, which should've been fine. He was even having a good time, hustling pool with two kids that he knew sure as shit weren't twenty-one. But he'd been going into bars since he was seventeen, when he had a beard growing contest and reached the top pocket of his T-shirt within a month. Craig said it didn't count, because he had to stretch his stragglers out to hit the top pocket, but it sure as hell counted when he walked out of Hudson Market with a case of the cheapest beer they had.

So he hustled the kids but ended up a hundred bucks poorer, with a punished body and about two thin lines of shit so stomped he had to wonder why the baby aspirin wasn't helping his headache. He didn't want to be there, like that, on Craig's last big day.

They talked about going to the Stroll after, and Donny was all up in it, but truth be told, fuck the Stroll. It wasn't for the true Troy kids. It was a tourist trap, selling out the city's history to a bunch of people who think they would've survived in late nineteenth-century Troy. Welcome to the collar factories, ladies. Welcome to the ironworks, jerkoffs.

Donny was doing his best to fool himself. Craig loved the Stroll, but Craig had Danielle and the kids. It was a family thing for them. They'd only been going dressed up for five years. Before that, Craig's mom would watch

Joey and they'd hang out at Jurica's sixth-floor apartment in Monument Square, getting plastered and making fun of the people freezing below. Then they'd hit all the bar specials later.

But it wasn't right, like life can fucking go on that easy. Sorry Craig, too bad you'll miss the costume party this year. We'll visit you sometime when the spring flowers come up in the graveyard.

The phone rang. Loudly. Donny winced and reached over, narrowly avoiding the baggie and grabbed the phone.

"Whattup?"

"You getting ready?" Ginny said.

"Who's this?"

"Ginny," she said. "Jesus, dude, you get wrecked last night or what?"

"A little." He held his hand out and looked at the time on the phone. "Oh crap, I didn't realize it was so late."

"I'm dressed up. I mean, I don't go to the Stroll, so really I just tried to find something that was brownish. And a dress, 'cause women didn't wear jeans back then. I think I'm good though."

"I'm gonna have to wear a good shirt and my slacks. The Stroll was always Craig's thing."

"Spoilsport. I'll be over in about twenty minutes, a half hour maybe. Don't go back to sleep."

"I wasn't sleeping, swear to God."

"Whatever. See ya."

Donny rummaged through his closet and found an actual suit, still in the plastic. He pulled it out and stared at it for long enough to realize that he was drawing a blank as to exactly why he had it. Then it hit him—it was the suit he wore to Craig and Danielle's wedding.

He sat on the kitchen table, holding the suit in his hands by the hanger poking out of the upper slit in the dry cleaner's plastic. Craig and Danielle had celebrated their tenth anniversary in August. The suit was ten years old. He knew it would fit him, that wasn't in question. One of the benefits of working with your hands and living hard was that, if you could keep your clothes from getting torn, tarred, painted on, or burnt by cigarettes, you could still fit in them.

What really got him was that in ten years, it sat in plastic. Not one occasion where he needed to dress up in a decade. If anyone had brought that up before Tuesday, or rather, before he'd found out what happened Tuesday, he would've laughed about it.

But sitting there with such an unused thing in his hand, such a symbol of the absolute insignificance of his past ten years—and even the ten before it, because let's face it, the suit was for someone else's achievement—any high left in him pooled in his bladder to be pissed out.

After relieving his night's party in the toilet, he walked out and tried on the shirt and slacks. As he guessed, they fit, though the slacks needed a belt. He felt odd using his paracord work belt, but the coat covered it. It came back to him that he'd had the thing tailored but ran out of cash that day, so he had to put the belt back.

When he was all dressed, he walked over and checked himself out in the full-length mirror. Maybe it wasn't custom tailored anymore, but he was downright dapper. Maybe, if he played his cards right, he'd get to make up an excuse to some eligible bachelorette as to why his house was a mess. Loneliness meant never having to say you were sorry.

He picked up his phone and stared at the baggie longer than it should've taken. He needed a little rail to pick him up. The comedown would put him in the dirt. He was also about to join a collection of hundreds of the most likely people in Troy to have better coke than the shit he had on the table. He'd be doing a fat line on a headstone by the time he was low again.

Craig would probably look down on him from his new perch. But Donny put Saint Craig on the shelf for a moment while he decongested his nostril.

Chapter Twelve

Rob

His smile fell a bit when he walked in, fully dressed for the service, and his dad walked out of the dining room with his finger to his lips. It only happened on two occasions: when he was on the phone, which he was not, and when his mother was in bed with a migraine. Rob got dressed a half hour early to accommodate the fact that she took longer to get herself dressed, so he wasn't going to be late. But he realized he wouldn't be late, because he knew he was going alone.

He backed out of the front door into the hallway that he shared with his parents, and his dad, dressed in a Southeast conference football sweater and pajama bottoms decorated in old fifties gas pumps, pressed his feet in a pair of brown slippers and followed Rob out.

"She's real bad, kid."

"How long was she up last night?" Rob asked.

"All night. Off and on. She got sick a few times."

"Did she drink anything this morning, like water, tea, anything?"

"A sip of water," his father said. "She just wants to rest."

Rob's dad chipped at the flaky paint on the door trim, a leftover from at least five years ago, before they bought the house.

"She just needs to rest, pal."

"Is there anything I can go get her?"

His dad scratched his elbow. "We have ginger ale in the fridge," he said. "She did a lot yesterday. She probably shouldn't have sewn that costume. She tries to do so much, you know how it is."

"I told her she didn't have to do it. She would've been more than welcome at the church no matter what she wore. It's not like she would've spent any real time at the Stroll, with all that walking."

"You know your mother. She wants to do something. She won't let anything stop her … better or worse."

Rob pulled his phone out of his pocket and checked the time. "You up for a cup of coffee? I got a few minutes."

They sat in the living room with the news channel on mute. His dad sat in the recliner, his coffee resting next to a Himalayan salt lamp shaped like a pyramid. Rob was on the couch trying to keep his outfit uncrumpled, though his guess was that his chimney sweep get-up could stand a few wrinkles for authenticity. It wasn't imaginative, just the closest late nineteen-century profession that matched the rag clothing he already had in his closet.

"Dad, at some point we gotta talk about the surgery. I'm not saying now, but sometime soon. We can't keep seeing her like this."

"I know, kid. I think about it all the time. Believe me. But what money?"

"I'm gonna be getting a job. Maybe I can—"

"You just paid off your school loans," his father said. "We can't see you go into debt again."

"Mom doesn't have to know."

"She's not stupid. She'll figure it out. And she might refuse."

Rob opened his laptop's browser to Facebook by habit and scrolled down his timeline. "I won't let her refuse."

His father sat there, quiet, which was hard for Rob because he didn't know if he was thinking about it or thinking about the best way to quash the idea.

"We'll see. But right now, go to your friend's funeral." He took a sip of coffee and held the mug in his hands. "She just needs rest, kiddo. I'm sure by lunch, she'll be up and finishing that scarf she's working on."

"We will talk though, dad, right? Promise me?"

His father wrung out a coffee-stained strand of his beard.

Rob met Donny and Ginny at the Fourth Street Diner, an economy version of the Kettle, but one in which Donny was not a *persona non grata*. Every bit of the place was a story out of a pulp fiction magazine, where the coffee told tall tales and the eggs and hash browns were honest.

They were entirely overdressed for the Fourth Street Diner, but the beauty of such a hole in the wall was that nobody gave anyone a second look. Donny had a piece of toast, untouched, on the plate. Ginny was staring down a short stack with a syrup drip that mimicked pop art.

"You aren't gonna drop the casket on me 'cause you're fucked up, are you Donny?"

"I'm not fucked up."

"You drank a pint in my car on the way over here."

"Yeah. A pint. That's it. I put a pint in my thermos every morning before I go to work. I don't drop roofing tiles or two-by-fours."

"They ain't a big thousand-pound casket, are they?"

"That casket isn't a thousand pounds," Rob said. "I wouldn't put it past three hundred. Plus you figure Craig was probably a buck eighty, maybe? So, five hundred pounds. How many guys we got?"

Ginny counted on her hands. "Eight pallbearers."

"Shit, I could carry sixty pounds on crack," Donny said.

"I figure you could probably carry a thousand pounds if you're on crack," Rob said.

"If you want to blow your ticker."

Rob chewed on a burnt link. "Anyone talk to Danielle this morning?" Donny and Ginny shook their heads. Donny straightened up, sucked down his coffee and pulled out his phone. He tapped enough to let Rob know he didn't have her number on speed dial. Rob could hear the ringing, then the pick-up of voicemail.

"Hey, babe, it's Donny. We're at the Fourth Street Diner. We'll be on our way to Saint Patrick's soon. Call me back so we know where we gotta be."

He put the phone down. "She'll call. We'll meet her and Craig—"

Donny sat back enough to distance himself from his words. It was the first time Rob saw the loss from inside Donny's eyes. He had to wonder, among all the people they'd see that day, how many would be pregaming the Stroll alongside Craig with the not-yet-cemented reality that he'd be parting ways by the turnoff to Oakwood Cemetery.

Asher

Twinkling lights and plump snowflakes were not what Asher wanted to see when he walked out his door clad in brown cotton frock coat and matching vest, white button-down and a sand-colored tweed newsboy cap. That, and the garland strewn across the street at the beginning and end of the block, read, "Police Line, Do Not Cross."

The cops were blocking off traffic, parked at a slant with the twinklers decorating the oak trees lining the street in blue and red. Parked within the barrier, and completely blocking his exit, were a fire truck and an ambulance, and two other cop cars. A group of officers in bulletproof vests were congregated in a circle, and past each barrier, the bystanders.

If the neighborhood lurkers knew what Asher knew, they would've stayed indoors. It was Seventy-Three. It was always Seventy-Three. Every street had their problem address, and that was theirs. If he didn't have a funeral to go to, Asher would've lifted up the blinds, seen the lights and gone back to sleep. God help him if there was an actual emergency.

Asher didn't know his name. When he wasn't having the week's meltdown, he didn't mix. There were plenty of people going in and out of the apartment, and if he cared, Asher probably could've figured out the guy's life story from all the threats and taunts his guests threw at him when he'd get home in the middle of the night. Drugs? Sure. Crazy? No doubt. Evicted? Never.

Carl hopped out on the porch in sweats and frayed jean shorts.

"Andy Andy's at it again. Shame," Carl said. "Ooh, you going out to the Stroll?"

"Yeah, but I'm going to Craig's funeral first."

"Good luck with that." Carl pulled a lollipop out of his pocket, a substitute for him when he was too lazy to go buy another pack.

"His name's Andy Andy, for real?"

"Andrew Andrews. Not lying."

"What fucking parent would name their kid that?"

"Oh my dude, that family tree is a Giant Hogweed."

"Giant what?"

"It's this poisonous— oh, never mind. Bad seed, that kid."

Asher wiped off the railing. He wanted to keep his costume clean in case he could still go.

"What's his deal?" Asher said. "I don't give a shit, but he's killing my time right now."

Carl took out his lollipop and twirled it, pointing it down toward Seventy-Three. "It ain't his fault, man. Like I said, bad family tree. He got a brain injury when his daddy slammed the car door on his head."

"That sucks," Asher said. "I feel bad now, but seriously, I got to go. How long you think they're going to keep us from being able to get out of here?"

Carl pointed to the corner. A cop was walking toward them up the street tapping his walkie-talkie. "Go ask him."

Asher walked over and tried to catch the cop's attention without spooking him, 'cause he didn't know if it was a skittish cop and if taser points could go through all his layers. He waved, putting his hand halfway up like he was in middle school.

The cop put his finger up and kept listening to the chirps and garbled utterances coming out of the box on his shoulder. When he was done, he turned toward Asher.

"Sir, I have a funeral to go to." He pointed to his house, then his car. "I live right here. How do I get out?"

"I'm sure we'll be out of here soon. Sit tight."

"The funeral's in twenty minutes. I can't really show up late."

"Where is it?" The cop said.

"It's at Saint Patrick's," Asher said. "It's down the street."

"You can catch the bus down there. Runs all day today. If you need to get down there, it's the most guaranteed way right now."

"Thanks," Asher said. "Merry Christmas."

The cop started walking again.

Asher needed to call someone, but everyone would either be on the way to the church, or they were there already. He knew he didn't really have to go. It wasn't like he and Craig were close buds. Certain things drove people to connect, moments, things that would form the basis of the friendships of the next ten or fifteen years. This was one of them. It was practically dues if you were Troy born and raised to see the fallen Good out the door.

"Fuck," Asher said, back to Carl. "Asshole tells me to take the bus."

"You need to get there, huh."

"I don't want to miss this shit. I mean, not just the costume, but there's a vibe through the old town about it. We see Craig off, and go strolling, celebrate life, get drunk, make great memories we can forget tomorrow. And 'cause of Andy Andy, I'm stuck here."

"No, you ain't," Carl said. "My car's in the alley. I'm not dressed for shit, but I can drop you off at the church. But do me a favor."

"Anything."

Carl put his hand out in the universal sign of *got a smoke*? Asher pulled his pack out and handed it to him—small price to pay. He took the pack, pulled out one cigarette, and handed the pack back to him.

"I'm good," Carl said. "No, the favor is, when you see Danielle, tell her I couldn't go because I was helping a friend through a rough time."

"Okay," Asher said. "Are you, by the way?"

Carl looked down the street. They were pulling a man, likely Andy Andy, out on a stretcher, strapped in.

"I'll probably go to the hospital," Carl said. "Make sure they don't fry his melon."

Asher and Carl finished a cigarette on the front porch before they left, it only being ten minutes to the church, and Asher exaggerated the hurry to the cop by an extra ten minutes. The snow was coming down in a squall, at least Asher hoped. He was going to have to hike, hitchhike, or bum rides all day.

Jordan

It was his insistence. In fact, it was his time-honored spot. It was a spot where he played for change even when Jordan was a high-school girl waiting to catch the bus up Hoosick Street. It wasn't the most highly trafficked area in terms of people who had folding money, but pretty much everybody that rolled through Hoosick and River under the Collar City bridge had a few dimes to pitch.

She offered to let Doc Lucian stay at her place while she went to the funeral. She'd pick him up to work the Stroll after she got back, but he insisted on earning some coin before she paid him for playing Sam Wilson's. And despite her offering him an advance, he still insisted. She knew arguing with such a seasoned musician would be pointless, so she made him promise to wear a leather bomber jacket with a hood that an old boyfriend forfeited while she ran his clothes through the wash.

"I'll try not to be long," she said as he got his guitar case out of the back seat.

He chuckled. "You can't rush a funeral, honey," he said. "They don't work like that."

"You know what I mean. I won't stay around. I'll get you as soon as possible. So please don't go anywhere."

"It's here, the morgue or the drunk tank."

"Don't say that."

He smiled, showing a row of teeth like soldiers coming out of a heated battle. "You don't worry, I'll sing my songs. Man gotta practice, you know. Might as well earn some jingle jangle."

She took off, Doc Lucian in her periphery until she made the turn on Sixth Avenue and he disappeared, his form swallowed up by the graffiti mural on the bridge support.

When they got to her apartment the night before, he was all set to empty the pint of rum and sleep off the cold, clothes and all. Jordan felt bad about putting her foot down and didn't do it until she knew she had clothes that fit him. It was good luck that the same boyfriend who forfeited his hooded bomber also forfeited about a suitcase worth's of other clothes.

She made Doc shower and change and threw his clothes in the wash, which, were it entirely her decision, would've been incinerated. But Doc was a man of intense superstition. He wasn't sentimental, or superstitious, about the clothes themselves, but he picked them up at a homeless shelter that shut down the year before, so he told it when she was washing them.

"My clothes are the only thing left of them," he said. "So it ain't past until the threads wear out and they fall apart. I carry the spirit of the place on my back."

"Is that a Hoodoo thing?"

"That's a Doc thing," he said. "We all bring our own selves to hoodoo. That's my part."

"You know you gotta wash them, or they'll fall apart faster."

He looked at her with a raised eyebrow. "You think?"

"I'm sure. You gotta wash clothes."

"I know that. But it don't make 'em last longer. I don't roll around in my clothes like they in a washing machine. I think that makes them wear and tear more than sitting on my back."

Jordan realized arguing would be an exercise in splitting hairs.

"Okay, Doc. You gotta be presentable for the gig."

"All right then. I can dig that." He got up and went toward the bathroom, turning back to say, "I get that rum when I get back, right?"

All in all, Doc Lucian cleaned up nice. And thanks to having an ex-boyfriend that worked in midtown Manhattan, even the casual wear he left behind looked like finely tailored stage wear. If not for his teeth and the permanent red that ringed his corneas, Doc Lucian would've fit into a Big Band club with a trombone or a saxophone.

She got to the church with ten minutes to spare. She would've liked to have more, but she spent longer on her Victorian Stroll costume than she thought she'd need. Plus arguing with Doc about staying at the apartment.

But slightly early was far better than slightly late. She was glad she used to hang out in North Troy, because only true locals would've known how to navigate streets with stuffed parking spaces to find a spot that wasn't two miles away.

They were mourners, the extra cars. She could tell by the river of black-clothed jaywalkers interspersed with costumed jaywalkers. It was going to be a packed house. Jordan wondered what Saint Patrick's would do if they hit capacity. Did they have a megaphone outside? Considering she hadn't been in a church since she was twelve, an outdoor funeral might be preferable to walking in and catching everything on fire when she burst into flames.

She found a spot by the river on a side street. She'd have to double-time it to get to the church on time. Ordinarily, a start time was an estimation, a time for people without lives to show up, until the people with better things to do decided to grace the event with their presence. But this was church, whose rules, strictures, and start times were enforced with nuns and rulers. Last thing she wanted to do was be the heathen that strolled in and disturbed Craig's last moment in the stained-glass-filtered sun.

She walked around the corner onto Fifth Avenue, and the crowd had nearly blocked off the road. Had she not known better, she might've assumed that Saint Patrick's was having a Stroll event. And technically, they were. The solid oak doors were wide open and people were filing in the wide steps. Small groups were standing around, talking, smoking cigarettes.

She saw Ginny talking to a man with short hair and a goatee, seemingly struggling to stand right in a good but ill-fitting suit. As she walked over, a car pulled up and Asher popped out in full Victorian regalia. She didn't picture him for the festive type.

Ginny flagged her over and made the introduction.

"Thought I was going to be late," Jordan said. "When are they going to—"

The heavy brass bells atop the steeples clanged in syncopation, letting the assembled know that death and the church waited for no one.

Chapter Thirteen

Danielle

Saint Patrick's pipe organ belted "Nearer My God to Me" as the pallbearers—a motley crew that would've looked completely alien in their mix of cobbled-together costumery, were they not in a building that was born in Victorian Troy—wheeled Craig's body up the center aisle.

Danielle could practically feel the air from the pipes wash through her. It wasn't bought by the church. Not entirely. Danielle remembered the field trip she took to the church when she was in middle school. The church was only going to buy a simple organ, because the diocese decided to direct all funds to the downtown church, St. Francis.

But North Troy, which back then had been a strong, close, working-class neighborhood, took it upon themselves, through street festivals and good old-fashioned door-to-door goading, to raise the money for a pipe organ that rivaled only the cathedral in Albany. The alderman at the time was reported to have said that "North Troy would be heard."

The church was packed, standing room only. Danielle seemed to know everyone. And those she didn't looked vaguely familiar. Perhaps they were Facebook friends, or people she'd taken care of at the hospital. Or maybe they were people that would come home with Craig after a light workday for a few beers. She didn't know whether to feel relieved at the support or terrified that she'd lose it in front of everyone that ever meant something to her.

Craig's casket was before the chancel, and Father DeGeorgio sprinkled holy water from a polished brass aspergillum in a quick, jerking motion, as if he was shooing something away. Danielle could smell the trace of alcohol on a few breaths. She felt angry, but only a little, because she knew the draw of showing up drunk at Craig's funeral was too irresistible, helping pad the head count. And as much as she hated to admit it, she needed them.

Her mom and his mom nearly came to blows over putting a donation box in the vestibule. Danielle figured that the tie would be broken by Father DeGeorgio, and the rules of church decorum, but he didn't seem to care. The church was closed, the basket-bearers were home, and he was glad to play for a packed house again. But her mom won out, and there was a big glass jar that had fattened up.

Father DeGeorgio ascended to the lectern, opening his Bible and adjusting the purple silk ribbon that acted as a bookmark.

"In life, Craig cherished the Gospel of Christ," he said. "May Christ now greet him with these words of eternal life." He picked up ruby rosary beads in his hand. "In life he prayed the mystery through the rosary. May Christ now welcome him to the throne of grace."

The crowd mumbled, all reading from the pamphlet they'd picked up in the vestibule. Danielle almost laughed at the thought of Craig picking up a rosary. In the time she knew him, the only cross Craig had any contact with was the one on his arm, which he got senior year in the back of the library when Donny stole a tattoo gun and was bound and determined to learn a trade.

Father DeGeorgio continued with the service, praising Craig's good Christian life. It was laughable in a way; Craig, if he could, would've popped out of the casket and, fake cutaway suit sliding off his naked ass, walked over to Father DeGeorgio and shook his hand for such a performance.

But Danielle looked around at the people gathered there, and true, some were there for the simple chance to get tanked and have a Stroll story to tell for the ages. But she knew at least half of the people were getting this story in trade for a story that began with them in trouble and ended with Craig coming through. Craig would have laughed at the pageantry of his life, but no one could argue the truth of him. Or so she thought.

"As we say goodbye to Craig, let us pray," Father DeGeorgio said. "His suffering has ended. And we will never know what storms may have tested the waters of his soul before such a tragic event. But we know that, in Christ, he has found the peace that may have eluded him in his last days. We must not burden ourselves for what we could not know. We can only go on in the understanding that he showed all of us the best part of him."

The organ seemed to creep up on the crowd like the waterline of a flood. What did he mean, *What we could not have known?* But Danielle knew exactly what he meant. Which was what Craig's mom alluded to before they went in when she said, "We couldn't bury him in St. Peter's cemetery, because it's a Catholic cemetery." The assumption of a fact not in evidence. A fact, the truth of which would throw her life and all her memories into reverse.

He didn't know what he was doing that night, she thought. He'd never do that to us.

"Mommy," Marybeth said. "I'm tired."

Danielle patted her head. "I know, honey. It's almost over."

"I wanna go to sleep like Daddy."

"No you do not, Marybeth," Danielle said. "You just sit here."

"Why can't I go sleep with Daddy?"

"Honey, he's not going to wake up, and you are."

Marybeth calmed down, or what passes for calm with a five-year-old. Joey was buried in the hymnal. He hadn't said more than ten words all morning, and all of them involved telling Marybeth to shut up. She moved in and out of the understanding that she'd never see her father again, but Joey understood the concept of death. Any notions that he had of seeing his dad again were moments when his young mind allowed him to forget what had just happened.

Danielle wondered if the kids would need to talk to someone. Which caused her to wonder how she could arrange that while working enough to cover the bills. But such thoughts were a snowball down the mountain. What they could live without; what she didn't think they could live without. Who she'd have to rely on, and which of the devils in her life she'd have to bargain with to keep what she took for granted a week ago.

Father DeGeorgio and his altar boys blessed the casket, before folding the cloth that covered it. It was time to move Craig out of the church for the hearse. Then on to Oakwood Cemetery, and the committal service at the graveside. She didn't imagine as many people would be at the graveside except friends and family.

Donny, Rob and Ginny, Terry and Ollie, Ginny's last minute pallbearer pick Asher, her cousin Willy—and someone she only recognized from Hill family gatherings—got up and took their places alongside the casket. Four took each side. The organ cranked up, and, as Father DeGeorgio motioned them, they started to wheel the casket down the aisle before they'd have to pick it up once they got outside.

"Daddy, Daddy, wake up!" Danielle had only looked away for a second. She turned to see Marybeth running down the aisle in a desperate attempt to catch up to the pallbearers. Her little shoes echoed off the aisle of the nave, then stopped when she tripped and fell on her stomach and her purple princess dress, the only one she had, splayed out on the marble. The church reverberated with the sound of her cries.

Donny

His hands were trembling. The slashed-up one was worse. Unfortunately, that was the hand he needed to grasp the handle. He could've asked to be on the other side, but he decided the pain would suffice as his last offering. He'd forgotten to pour a drop of his pint out for his best friend. The pain was penance.

For Donny, being drunk meant noticing things two times: once, when they happened; and twice, when he realized the significance. He won lots of street fights because he didn't realize his broken nose till a half hour after he threw the last punch. But he missed things too. Like the fact that Marybeth was face-first on the ground, crying her head off.

He didn't notice until Rob had abandoned his spot on the other side and was rushing over to her. Rob knelt and picked her up, wiped off her nose without any hesitation, like she was his own daughter. She still cried, and she tried to wiggle out of his arms, but not enough to break free. Danielle was hurrying over, and it was she who caught Donny's eye, not Marybeth.

People made a show of getting up out of concern, but what do you do for a kid? They had to make it look like they were ready to act. Donny didn't try. He couldn't. That should've been him to rush to his de facto niece's aid, to swallow her up in his big arms and absorb her young nightmare, but he couldn't keep himself from being coked up and drunk. He knew Craig would forgive him, but Craig ran a side business of forgiving him. Donny was carrying that forgiveness out the door with his body.

The church organ came to back to life with the classic "On Eagles Wings." Donny wondered if they had to request it or if it was such a standard that you'd have to request anything else. Rob returned with a quick apology for the delay and they continued toward the vestibule. Donny's hand ached, and he focused on the razor-edged sting.

He imagined it as a gift to his friend, a paycheck he was putting in that vase, 'cause the ten he threw in there was pathetic and he was fortunate to able to cross the threshold alone. His perverse hope was that he could reopen his wounds and bleed all over the handle. At least then, a part of him would go into the ground with his friend.

"Donny, you okay with that hand?" Rob said.

"Never better," Donny said. "Thanks for catching Marybeth. I was readjusting my grip. I didn't even see her until it was too late."

"I used to have to keep Juliet from electrocuting herself with any metal thing she could find," Rob said. "She had a thing for light sockets. I had to keep one eye on her for years."

They went through the doorway. The hearse sat, gray and freshly waxed with a floral spray between the part where the casket went and the front seats.

"Thanks. She's like my niece."

"I feel for you, man," Rob said. "You guys were best friends. I don't even have a best friend right now. I couldn't imagine losing one."

One of Craig's cousins, Zed, an Albany county sheriff, and not a great pal of Donny's, took it upon himself to coordinate the movement down the stairs, which were mercifully few and wide. Donny caught two kids, maybe early twenties, walking down the street in down jackets and hoodies, with earbuds in their ears and not a care in the world or a seeming thought that they were going to walk in between them and the hearse. Donny felt himself getting ready to hop off of casket duty to take care of any problems. But they looked up at the last minute and swerved out to cross the street.

"Hey, Ginny, can I get a ride to the cemetery?" Asher said.

Donny barely knew him, and at first, he wasn't pleased that a stranger was going to be carrying Craig. But then again, only one of his family was carrying him—the rest wrote him off long ago—if Ginny's friend was willing to take a morning out and be there for someone he didn't even know, he couldn't be too bad.

"Sorry, bud," Ginny said. "I got a full car. You should've called it before we went in."

"I'm sure someone will give you a ride," Rob said. "I mean, half the city's going up there."

"Yeah, buddy. You're a pallbearer," Donny said. "People will recognize you."

They worked their way to the hearse, and Donny struggled to grip the rail. His hand may well have ripped open, or maybe it was sweat born of liquor and stress. They slid the casket in on the rollers, and Donny hooked the thumb of his carrying hand into the pocket of his slacks and pressed into the fabric. When he took his hand away, he looked for a bloodstain. He didn't know whether to be happy or sad when he didn't see one.

The priest was out of the top step, shaking hands and firing volleys of inspiration at the people coming out. Half of the people were dressed in standard funeral fare, half may well have stepped out of a time machine. Donny wandered back in to find Danielle, and it comforted him a little to smell alcohol floating around the vestibule. He hadn't been the only one.

Danielle was talking to Craig's mother. Joey was with his uncle. Marty, Danielle's brother, was the only person more prone to waking up in gutters than he used to be. Marybeth was sleeping in Danielle's mom's arms. That was maybe the best blessing so far that day. He waited for Danielle to be free of parents, because her mom barely knew him, and Craig's mom knew too much of him and would've barred him from the church had he not almost singlehandedly brought the funeral party.

There was a pause in the conversation, when everyone seemed to be looking off in the distance.

"Dani," he said. "I should've grabbed Marybeth. I'm sorry."

"It's fine," she said. She wrapped herself up in her arms. "We should be getting her home. She's tired."

"I'm her uncle, I should've handled it."

"I'm sure there will be plenty of times she'll need her uncle. I'm just glad you all got Craig in the hearse. You guys did get him in the hearse, right?"

"Yeah, he's good."

Danielle walked out into the center of the now empty aisle. "Everybody was drunk."

"That's how we got them here, remember?"

"I figured people might have more respect."

"Are you mad at me for drinking?"

She shook her head. "Nah, you're always drunk. I wouldn't want to see you here sober."

Donny would've seen that as high praise a week ago. "I'm not that bad."

"You're fine," she said. "And thank you for getting everybody here. I couldn't have gotten through this without you."

"You know, I'm here for you." He stepped to the center aisle, genuflected the empty altar and made double-time to get his ride to Oakwood.

Rob

The shortcut to Oakwood Cemetery wasn't shorter. But bypassing the funeral procession afforded a stop at the Troy Mini Mart on the corner of 110th and Second Avenue to pick up cigarettes. Rob wasn't much of a smoker, limiting the habit to social situations or long car rides. He had quit twice, when two things happened in close proximity. First, his mother was diagnosed with pancreatic cancer. Then his wife announced that she was pregnant with Juliet.

Rob pulled out of the three-car parking lot that could just have easily been the convenience store's front yard. Donny was in the passenger seat, lighting up as he clicked at the window release.

"There's a trick to it," Rob said. "You gotta fuck with it."

"I'll get it." A few seconds of jiggling and they were tasting the fresh cold air. Rob didn't mind. At a red light, he grabbed a cigarette of his own and punched the car lighter, but Donny flicked his lighter and cupped his hand over it to give Rob flame and obstruct his view.

"I got it man, I can't see."

"Aw, c'mon dude, there's nothing coming. Live a little."

Rob puffed his cigarette into life with his foot off the gas. They turned to go up 114th Street, where they'd go straight up the hill and catch Oakwood Avenue from the north end and drive south to meet up with the procession. Ginny was keeping tabs on the assembled masses through her phone in the backseat.

"Did you say that Asher kid needed a ride?" Rob asked.

"He's fine." Donny tipped his cig out the slit in his window and let the air flow take his ashes. "There's like two hundred people at that church."

"Yeah, but he's a pallbearer." Rob stopped on a stop sign and waved the oncoming lane through the turn they were planning. "Do you guys have some kind of beef or something?"

"Nah, he's just new to the crew, you know? It's his initiation."

"He's your guitar player, right, Ginny?"

"Yeah. Let him walk."

"Damn, you all are cold," Rob said.

"He's okay," Ginny said. "But Donny's right. He's new. He doesn't get a pass to ride VIP yet."

They passed through Sixth and when they hit Gurley Avenue, a back road that climbed Diamond Rock, the ride was punctuated only with the occasional cough, sniff or sigh. Rob went through his cigarette faster than he realized, lighting another with the embers of the first. He figured they'd arrive at Oakwood Cemetery before the procession. Even with all lights in their favor, it still had to navigate Hoosick Street on the Sunday of the Stroll.

The funeral broke Rob's heart. Marybeth, the fear and anger on her little face, her hair matted in her mouth as she looked up from the floor of the church. Her daddy, her rock, one of the two pillars that held up her universe, was sleeping and dreaming and going away from her forever. He knew she only half-understood what was happening, but that half propelled her forward faster than her little feet could keep up.

When he held her up, he was holding Juliet when she first got stung by a bee. He wiped the hair back on Marybeth's face like he did Juliet's when she wouldn't stop crying during one of his and Jennifer's many fights. The love of a parent for their kid is universal, like a lens that knows not one child for another, but one hurt for another, one joyous wonder for the next. People without kids wouldn't know how transferrable that love truly is. And they definitely wouldn't know that the heartache of losing your daughter would become an endless reflection in those still living.

They rounded the corner, and, in his head, Rob was at the Empire State Plaza, ice skating with Juliet who was brave enough to get back on the ice after falling on her butt.

But in real life a man in a jean jacket and camouflage pants stepped off the curb in front of their car.

"Dude, watch out!" Donny put his hand up in front of him. Rob slammed on the brake, lurching forward to the screams of his tires as the car came so close to the guy that he had to put his hands on the hood. He pounded on the hood with one fist and kept walking.

"Pull over."

"No, Donny," Rob said, "we got to go."

"Let it go, man," Ginny said. "The guy's some rando."

"Pull. The. Fuck. Over."

Rob went to turn up Northern Drive, but Donny grabbed the steering wheel, jerking it to the side.

"I'm not kidding." To emphasize that point, he opened the door while the car was in drive and slammed the door, possibly fucking the car up more than the guy who pounded on it.

Donny raised his arms, making himself a human Y. "You got a fucking problem?" he said. "You gonna pound on people's cars, you scumbag?"

"Fuck you, asshole." The man kept walking.

Donny was out of the car while he was still talking.

Rushing toward the guy, his good arm dragging low like a bowler in midstride, Donny found a crusty brown glass bottle and hooked it in his hand. Rob shouted his name, like he might recognize it through the blood rushing his ears. Donny righted himself as he launched the bottle toward the guy.

It hit the guy in the side of the head. The blow spun him sideways, but he kept walking, pushing off with his hands as if to say he wanted none of Donny. Too late.

"Donny," Rob shouted, "we got a funeral to go to. You're a pallbearer! You fucking dick."

Donny turned around. "You got a problem now?"

"Will it get you back in the car? Fine, beat the shit out of me once we get Craig off-loaded."

Donny looked at the man, who, by that point, was about a half-block away. He turned to Rob, and shook his head, his eyes rolled back and he walked back.

"Craig ain't freight," Donny said as he passed Rob toward the passenger door.

They started driving again. Ginny sighed.

"And I thought estrogen was a hell of a drug," she said. "Bottle your shit up and sell it to the college kids downtown."

Donny had his arms folded, and they connected onto Oakwood Avenue in silence. Rob picked up speed, going beyond the forty-five miles per hour that was rarely ever enforced on that road, seeing as how the only people who used it had to know it was there, and that limited the traffic to locals.

"Don't ever call me a dick, dude," Donny said. "That ain't cool."

"Sorry, Donny, I didn't know how to get you to go back in the car. Figured I'd get you pissed at me. No offense."

Rob could spot the glow of car headlights as they got to the entrance to Oakwood. Apparently traffic was kind to the procession. They slipped in at the end and, once again, they separated from the main party, since Juliet was buried there and Rob held fast to the assumption that his best parking space was by her row.

Donny ran his hand over the hood when they got out. Rob could see the man's fist had made a minor impression.

"Should've let me beat on him," Donny said.

Chapter Fourteen

Asher

She had on black suede gloves. Asher would've given anything to reach out and hold her hand, feel the squeeze of her fingers against the backs of his as they stood over the gaping hole that swallowed death, or rather, the earthly remains of Craig Hill. But the closeness between them was of circumstance, not of the insistence of their two hearts.

Jordan's jet-black hair was held up in crowned braids, and the sun bounced off them like they were made of oiled satin. She was dressed in a black corset with a gothic dress. Steampunk? Asher's knowledge of women's clothing styles was limited to all that he could pick up in the celebrity magazines at the hotel. That, plus the bored bridesmaids who would trawl the lobby in search of "random encounters," for which he was never considered.

He didn't see Jordan at Sam Wilson's. He saw a regular gig, maybe. Moreover, he saw a woman who had to have a boyfriend, or a fiancée, maybe even a husband down in Brooklyn waiting to come up. But he had to see her as something else that day: his savior.

Donny was wrong. Being one of the pallbearers didn't grant Asher instant fame with that group, nor did it help get him to the cemetery. This was mainly because he didn't know how to be a loudmouth like half the other people filing out of the church. Only one of the spirits in the church was of the holy variety; the rest came in bottles with warning labels.

He found the ridiculousness of his position unnerving. He knew some of the people, sure—was hard to be in a Troy crowd and not know somebody—but he couldn't get up the nerve to talk more or ask for a ride. The problem is, he tried every day to stay away from people. He liked being the mysterious loner. Which didn't help in times when you needed others.

So he'd all but decided that he'd go home, hoping they could find some other loudmouth to take up his handle, content knowing he did his part. He remembered the donation vase in the vestibule and went in to wedge a twenty in the stuffed glass. And his fingers slid up against a hand wrapped in black suede.

"Hey, Asher." He looked over to see Jordan wipe away a rogue curl of hair. She smiled and he almost forgot her name.

"Hi, Jordan. Did you know Craig?"

"Yeah," she said. "We were friends in high school. You weren't in our high school, were you?"

"No. I did Catholic in Albany," he said. "I'm kind of a transplant."

They walked out to the top step. The priest was talking to a woman whose daughter had run out in the middle of the aisle when they were carrying Craig. He knew she was his widow but forgot her name.

Jordan stepped to the sidewalk. "So how did you know Craig?"

"Ginny knew him more than me. I agreed to help with being a pallbearer." He looked down the street. "But I didn't drive here."

"I'll give you a ride to the cemetery."

Jordan's car was a VW Microbus. Baby blue with white trim. She said she got it when she was working set design on Broadway. It smelled of turpentine and plywood and the seats were upholstered in a patchwork of materials.

"Yes, I have lived out of here for a time."

"I don't blame you," Asher said. "You could go anywhere with this."

They caught up with the funeral procession before they hit the intersection of Sixth Avenue and Hoosick Street, and Jordan leaned over Asher as they got to the corner. He almost leaned into her, but thought better of it. *If she was putting the moves on him, she'd have to beat him over the head.*

"Sorry," she said. "My entertainment for the evening, I left him right there to play. He's not there."

"What's he look like?"

"Black guy, older, bomber jacket and blue jeans … but he'd be playing guitar. Shit—"

"You mean that guy right there?" Asher pointed to a man on the kitty-corner matching the description Jordan gave.

"Thank God."

"I think you're going to lose the—"

Jordan blasted through a long yellow and sped up to catch the tail of the procession before it got to the mouth of the Collar City Bridge, where Alternate Route Seven fed into Hoosick.

"Never mind."

Jordan looked him over. While he liked the attention, he would rather she watched the road. "Hey," she said. "You're going out with everyone to the Stroll today."

Asher scratched his nose. "I didn't get any kind of specific invite, but yeah, I guess so."

"You're not dressed like you 'guess so.'"

"Okay, I'm going." He laughed. "And you look like you're going."

"For a little while," she said. "The reception is tonight. You're coming to that, right?"

"Am I invited?"

Jordan laughed and put her hand on Asher's shoulder. "Asher, hon, you really gotta stop thinking you're gonna get an invitation to life. This is Troy. You get invited fifteen minutes after you show up."

The wind kicked up as the priest reached the crescendo of the committal.

The other pallbearers had walked over to stand by the widow, whose name was Danielle, he learned from Jordan. After they carried Craig's casket to the rollers on top of the grave, he chose to walk over to where Jordan was standing and joined her for the service, creating his own invitation.

Jordan

Fresh snow was falling on the pile of dirt, along with the rest of Oakwood, when Jordan walked over and grabbed a small handful. Everyone remaining took flowers out of the spray that came along with the hearse, but Jordan wanted Craig to remember her contribution. Her father told her the Jewish custom was three shovelfuls, to represent the three parts of the spirit. He did so at her grandfather's funeral. But her mother was Methodist, so that made her Methodist. Later, she made herself agnostic.

Soon, Craig would be a name on a stone and a silent listener to Danielle and the kids when they'd visit, less and less frequently over the years. And they'd always bring flowers. He'd have enough flowers. She walked over to the casket and, along with the dirt, placed the only thing she had from when they ran the streets together—her old Troy High ID card, the best picture she had of youth.

Asher was standing by the edge of the folding chairs, fascinated by nothing on the ground. She thought he was going to try to hold her hand when he walked over from carrying the casket. She might've let him—at least she wouldn't have started a scene to stop him. He wasn't a bad guy, but his lack of confidence shaved a few points off. How he got invited to carry Craig was a mystery.

"I take it you want a ride to the Stroll, then?"

"I do have a car," he said. "My neighbor was losing his shit, and they had the street blocked off."

"Where do you live?"

He tugged at his collar and swiped his hand to scratch the back of his neck. "I live in Burgh, around 118th Street."

"You must be swimming in hookers," she said.

Asher laughed, his hand travelling up to pick at his hair. "My downstairs neighbor is, not me."

She punched him in the arm, enough to push in his coat sleeve. "I bet you sample the two-tooth special."

"Please," he said. "I work at the hotel. Much better class of prostitute."

Jordan opened her eyes and smiled. "Oh boy, there you go."

"Kidding," he said. Jordan started walking down the hill, wondering if Asher would stand there until he had an inch of snow in his pockets, but he took the hint and caught up with her.

"I'm not kidding about hotel hookers, Jordan. They're real. I don't screw with them."

"You probably can't."

"Well, no…" he said. "But I know myself. I could never pay some woman to have sex with me. I can barely ask a girl out who's not a hooker."

Jordan side-stepped the indentations in the ground that she knew were caused by the decay of coffins past.

"You know, I never would have thought he'd be the first of my close friends to go," Jordan said. "Did you know him at all?"

"Mostly by reputation. I knew he would always set up benefit shows, but I don't even know what band he was in." Asher slid on the growing slick of the grass and caught himself.

"He used to play his big fat mouth," Jordan said. "He sang in a band back in the early nineties, when we were kids. It was called Ignus." They made it to the main path, and they walked its edge, as cars were driving by. Jordan's car was at the end, in front of her favorite mausoleum in Oakwood.

"Three years," she said. "They mostly played at Prospect Park and the Community Centers, you know, Italian, Polish, Irish, and the one that used to be on Fourth Street. It was a real neighborhood thing, before the hardcore scene in Troy got to be so well-known in the area."

They got to her car, where she pulled out her keys. "By then, Craig was working every day, Danielle was in Rhode Island for design school … and I was taking theater arts in Oneonta."

She never locked the doors, so Asher hopped in and slid his seat belt on. Jordan grabbed a rag and wiped the snow off all of the windows to cover for what her one working wiper couldn't. By the time Asher realized what she was doing, any attempt to help would have been a firefighter putting out embers.

She got back in and tossed the rag at Asher. He jerked. She laughed and started the engine.

"You know Troy—or maybe you don't," she said. "You get a name when you're young, your name don't wear out. Good or bad, really."

They drove slowly, down the rutted paths, to the few paved versions of roads the cemetery had. They threaded into the traffic on the way out, emerging from the leaf-barren branches and twigs to see the main crematorium, a gothic structure that resembled a fortress or a church, complete with gargoyles watching from on high.

"Jordan, I forgot to mention it," Asher said. "I was talking about the hotel, which reminds me. There was this guy in the hotel last night. Name's Harley, like the bike. Anyway, he was talking about that stupid bike path they're trying to ram down our throats. Through your club."

"I heard about it," Jordan said. "I'm trying to find out more from the city. You know, nice of them to mention it."

"Take it seriously, yo." Asher pulled out his pack of cigarettes, waving them at Jordan like a question. Jordan grabbed them and took one, then tossed them back as an answer. "I've seen these developer assholes. They're always coming and staying in the hotel. They sit in the lobby half the time, cutting up the city like it's manifest destiny and they're a fucking conquistador."

"Conquistador. Someone paid attention in history class."

"I'm not fucking around," Asher said. "I like Sam Wilson's. I like you—I don't want to see you get screwed over by that dick."

They were flying down Oakwood behind a car in the funeral procession with a bumper sticker that had "Coexist" with an alien invasion background, flyer saucers shooting little laser beams at the letters. Jordan took a slow drag, scrunched her face, and aimed her exhale at a singular, solitary point in the windshield in front of her.

"Don't you worry," she said. "I'm Montezuma, bitch." She was so proud of her comeback that she didn't want to admit to herself that Montezuma was killed.

Danielle

The flakes came down from the spotless white sky like paratroopers, blanketing the top floor of the parking garage and filling the air with the feel of winter. The real calendar winter wouldn't hit for another three weeks, but by that time most years, they had already had a pre-coating. Danielle allowed herself to be transfixed by the fledgling maelstrom as the frantic day tucked itself into the folds of her subconscious.

The kids were chasing each other around the row of handicapped parking spaces, the only open space that wasn't a driving lane.

"Watch the road," she said. "I'm not going to tell you again. You don't stop chasing each other, you go home with Grandma."

Danielle had a temporary peace, but a mother's peace, prepared at any moment to spring into action to pull the kids from the brink of their own foolishness.

"We can find your friends down there," her mother said. "The kids are gonna get in trouble up here."

"The kids can get in trouble just as easy down there." Danielle glanced over the ledge at the crowds of revelers, only some of whom were in anything resembling a costume.

"I think the pallbearers are here." Her mom pointed, and Danielle followed her finger to see Donny, Rob, and Ginny walking up. Donny was the only one who looked like a pallbearer—Rob and Ginny had found a way to play the part. Ginny had been slightly dressed up at the funeral but must've had the rest of her emerald ballgown in the trunk of the car. Rob looked out of place by over a century.

"Ginny, love the gown," Danielle said before turning around to catch mischief. "Marybeth. Go hang out with grandma. That's it for you being on your own today." Marybeth whined with alligator tears.

"Can't wait to get this kicked off," Ginny said. "I can smell the fried dough up here."

Rob's nose crinkled. "I smell cloves."

"I smoke cloves sometimes." Ginny lifted her dress to reveal a pack from inside a black-lace garter belt. "I'm immune to it."

"Watch out now," Danielle said. "You'll give poor Rob a heart attack here." She smirked at Rob, who blushed through the cold winds.

Rob spun around and shielded his view with his hand. "Isn't that the van that was behind us in the procession? The VW Microbus?"

Danielle saw it parked in the back corner, not quite sure how she missed it. "Nice save, lover boy."

Danielle checked on the kids, happy her mom was stepping up. She was going to take them home after one stroll, their usual, River to Broadway, up to Second, down to State, before circling back to River. When Craig was with them, they'd have found a spot on the grass of Monument Square to watch the crowds and the merry mayhem.

She walked over to the kids. They had kept their costumes remarkably clean, considering they'd had candy—and Marybeth tasting the marble floor of Saint Patrick's.

"Okay, guys, I got a treat for you." Danielle reached into her purse and pulled out disposable cameras, a lucky find in the thrift store. She'd found four and hoped that they could start a new family tradition.

"Beth, you remember these, right?"

Marybeth smiled and went to grab one, but Danielle held them back.

"You don't grab," she said. "You ask."

"Mom, do I have to use this?" Joey said. "I have a phone."

"That phone is for emergencies only," Danielle said. "When I was your age—"

"When you were their age, all the phones had rotary dials." Danielle looked up to see a familiar face: Jordan Wilson.

"That was you."

"Guilty," Jordan said.

"I'm glad you came," Danielle said. "And thank you so much for agreeing to hold the reception at your club. It's called Sam Wilson's, right?"

"Yup." Jordan moved aside to reveal two people standing behind her.

One was dressed up and their age. The other, an older gentleman, was dressed up too, but not in a way that would blend in with the nineteenth century.

"You met Asher," Jordan said. "He was a pallbearer."

Danielle shook his hand and thanked him.

"And this is Doc Lucian. He'll be jamming out at the reception tonight."

"Please to meet you," he smiled and extended his hand. "I know this is quite a time for you. You have my good spirits today, you and the li'l ones."

Danielle wanted to say thank you but was afraid she'd cry.

After hashing out their plans to conquer the city, the crew assembled at the corner of the parking garage that overlooked River Street while vendors set up shop on the blocked-off street and crowds began to spill through the barricades beneath falling snow.

"Let's take a picture," Danielle said.

They all lined up, and Danielle moved everyone to capture the height differences. She made everyone stand there while she went to her mother's car and dug into the props that she'd brought just in case, coming back with a foot-high top hat.

"Here, Donny. You're going to be Mr. Hyde." Danielle fitted the hat on him and chuckled when it listed about ten degrees.

"No, leave it like that," she said. "Now, who will take the picture?"

Chapter Fifteen

Donny

The street looked brighter than normal. It wasn't the snow, but that did help. So did the bright colors of the banners advertising food that wasn't even a thought in the Victorian era and arts and crafts like cellphone cases with Charles Dickens scenes painted on them. Well, not painted, at least not painted by anyone's hand. Still, it was beautiful, and the sounds of children running around and giggling stirred the peace Donny kept close to his heart.

He'd have to buy more of that shit as soon as he got back to work.

Hopefully it was going around because the guy just came up to him in the second level of the garage while he lagged behind the rest of the crowd. His tipped hat must've been a signal to any dealer that he needed to get high. Or maybe he was simply the one out of a hundred the guy propositioned who didn't say no.

Danielle wasn't happy when he caught back up. She knew him well enough to know all the tricks he used to cover up being high, like the magic coughing fit he'd fake to mask his sniffles, that cold that magically went away in a half hour.

Danielle didn't mind when they'd drink, and she didn't give a shit when they used to smoke weed, as long as they didn't do it in the house with their kids around. That was understandable. But she hated it when Donny did coke, not that she gave a fuck about Donny. Her job was protecting Craig. And sometimes that meant protecting Craig from *Donny*.

But Craig was in the dirt. Donny had put the flower on top of the casket, and a bud he scrounged off the coffee table before he left his house. Craig was as set as he was ever gonna be. He didn't need to be protected from Donny anymore.

They passed the old porno theater, never a welcomed guest in the city. It was nothing but a conversation piece, devoid of any trace of what it once was. If it wasn't connected to all of the other buildings on River Street, the good people in the city council would've gladly razed it.

"They should do something with that," Donny said. "Turn it into one of those artsy theaters that show films with subtitles."

Danielle turned her head. "You'd actually go to one of those?"

"No. But it beats sitting there vacant, attracting river rats."

"Hell no," Ginny said. "You'd get pregnant touching the rafters in that place."

"They could douche it out, you know, bleach, industrial whatever. These hipsters wouldn't even know."

"They spend enough money building up downtown," Jordan said. "They should aim that cash hose at South Troy."

As they walked on, the circus that is the Stroll began to swell with the size of the crowd. There were, historically, two types of Stroll attendees: people who spent the year preparing to get their pictures taken a hundred times; and the casual attendee, the post-Stroll hooligans. For all those who wouldn't dream of waking up before noon, the night of the stroll belonged to them.

The coke felt like a kilo in Donny's pocket. As the warmth and the fuzz in his mind settled, he became a walking mathematician, calculating how to stretch the remains, which was actually a half-gram, long enough to get him to the reception. Because he had to go there. That was his last duty. After that, he knew he and Danielle would drift, and his face would grow stranger to Marybeth and Tommy, until eventually they would move on and forget all about him.

Donny grabbed a smoke, shaking the empty pack. "Shit, I need more smokes."

"The news store is open," Rob said. "If you're going, I could use some for later. Or do you want us to go with?"

Donny smirked at Rob saying "us," like he was directing their little parade. "Nah, man. Just give me ten bucks." Donny held out his hand. "You trust me, right?"

Rob laughed. "Of course, is ten enough?"

"If it isn't, I'll steal them." Donny caught a little too much deadpan. "Kidding. C'mon, guys, it's the Stroll. Been a long day, let's remember the good times a little."

Rob handed him a ten spot. Danielle passed a twenty for a pack of her own.

Donny didn't mind running errands. He was the provider. They needed to be happy, and if he spent the whole day taking care of everybody, getting them what they needed, he was doing that.

Truth be told, he needed to get away from everybody. He saw Craig everywhere, but it wasn't Craig. Craig was a wake-up call, and he hadn't gone to bed yet. Donny was going through the last of his bill money and, yeah, he had a name, but that name wore the shit stain of every couch he'd surfed.

Fourth Street News was in a corner building whose front door was in the rounded edge. The building made him think of pictures of the Flatiron Building in the city that his dad showed him, one of the few times he was home. It was only five stories, a popular look, and Donny wondered whether Flatiron was the inspiration or the inspired.

He walked in and stood in line behind a kid. Couldn't have been more than eighteen, trying to get a forty. He'd get it, too, guys there didn't give a shit. He pulled out his bills and smoothed them out.

"Yo, Donny," Donny turned around to see Easy, his nose taped up and his eyes still harsh from being blackened.

"C'mon, man. Don't fuck with me today," he said. "I ain't in the mood."

"Nah, we all right," he said. "I didn't know y'all were that close. We cool. I know half your crew out in the streets today. I ain't stupid."

Donny got up to the counter and made a calm request. The cashier, a big, brawny Korean, gave him a look, a look he probably had to give every Friday night. The look that said he had a .45 under the counter and a pistol permit.

"Yo, if you ain't fucked up about shit still, I do got some good shit."

"Up or down?"

"Both. But for you, I got some shit that'll put you out your skin." Donny checked the cigarettes in his hand. Danielle would be jonesing once they got to the food vendors.

"I ain't got long," he said. "Let's go."

Rob

The edges of their blue-and-gray gospel robes caught waves of the pulsing breeze coming off the river as they danced and clapped on their rests, cleaving out the parts of "O Come, Emmanuel." They smiled at each other and at the crowd, which had gathered by the entrance to the baby parking lot where they'd picked to sing, probably because the space between buildings made for a natural amplifier. People shot video on their phones that would likely find their way to social media by the time the gospel choir broke for a drink of water.

The kids were over by the curb, petting a Great Dane. Rob didn't know the historic significance of bringing your interesting pet to the Victorian Stroll, but then again, they were selling chili dogs and overstuffed burritos down the road. He was glad, and not at all worried that the Great Dane could probably eat Marybeth and not be full.

"C'mon, Joey, c'mon, Beth," Danielle said. "We're going to get some food."

Marybeth, surprisingly, listened, and walked over. "He slobbers."

"He's a dog," Rob said. "that's what they do."

"He licked my whole head." She pressed the sides of her head with her hands and slid them up for effect, succeeding in mussing up her hair.

Danielle picked at the newly liberated tufts from her ponytail. "Oh child," she said. "Try to keep clean, okay? Grandma's going to be back in a little while. Let's not give her something to bitch about."

"Ooh, mom, that's a bad word," Joey said.

Rob remembered that kids were recording devices. He had gotten used to it when he had Juliet, but her absence had spawned bad habits.

They kept walking down River Street, weaving in and out of waves of revelers. They'd come upon a trio of women in tight corsets and generous hoop skirts with lace flounces, their heads topped with heavily ornamented bonnets. They'd been standing, posed for a hipster couple, while various and sundry partygoers photobombed them and shattered the illusion.

Three times Rob and Danielle were asked if they could have their picture taken. It was an accepted custom to be agreeable to all-comers in this regard, but it was also an accepted custom for cellphone shutterbugs to ask first. If they counted people snapping shots at random, they'd probably had enough pictures of them to capture all sides, good and bad.

Rob kept an eye on Joey, who was weaving in and out of the crowd with his camera. If anyone casually glanced at him, he was a happy kid enjoying a little leeway from trusting parents. But not thirty seconds ticked by that Rob didn't catch the fear in his eyes. Rob didn't have to imagine having his security stolen in the middle of the night by an ambulance.

The snow came down, light and not sticking to the road, the air spiked with the sounds of Christmas, chimes and the carols given seven-part harmonies by the South Troy Baptist Gospel Choir. Rob felt excitement spread through his gut into his spine and his extremities. He felt at home, even if it wasn't with Jennifer. He felt unattached to the weights he carried in his mind.

It was funny that the Victorian Stroll, in all its frivolity and sentimentality, celebrated a time in Troy's history that, despite its incredible successes, was hard on people. Really hard. As much as every woman looked like a debutante and every man a captain of industry, most of the people who lived in Troy back then could never have afforded the outfits they wore.

Danielle searched her purse and pulled out two twenties. "Hopefully this covers us," she said. "Joey, get over here. We're getting something to eat."

"Ya' know, I can help, I still have some money left." Rob reached for his back pocket but felt Danielle's slight grip on his arm.

"No way," she said. "We gotta be able to do this on our own. We're not gonna have someone there to, you know…"

"Okay. But I do still need my wallet." He smiled, and Danielle let go.

"Sorry," she said. "But you're not paying for shit today. You were a pallbearer. Least I can do is get you lunch." And before Rob could object: "If you reach for your wallet, I swear I will throw it in the construction site."

The site she was referring to was encased by chain link in front of the former city hall, which, after a long battle with time and asbestos, had been torn down, leaving a gaping crater in the River Street landscape.

They made their way through the Victorian Stroll's "Cholesterol Alley," a tight grouping of food trucks, motors running, high octane, dirty-burning human-fuel. It wasn't that the Stroll didn't have healthy food—the Stroll was taking place over the whole city; even the vegan bakeries were getting in on the action. But if you wanted that deep fried, you had to go to River Street.

"I want a doughnut," Joey said, pointing to the picture on a red truck decorated P.T. Barnum styling.

"No way," Danielle said. "You'll get the powdered sugar all over yourself. They have cheeseburgers over here. You're getting candy later. We'll get cheeseburgers now."

"I want fried dough too," Marybeth said.

"Honey, you just want it because Joey wants it. You threw it up at the baseball game we went to." Danielle turned to Rob. "What do you want?"

"How about a…" He gauged the cheapest.

"Don't you dare look at the prices," she said.

"Cheeseburger, then."

They found a spot on the marble barrier separating the sidewalk from the monument from which Monument Square got its name. Marybeth was in Danielle's lap, playing with her pickles. Danielle offered no resistance, as she had wiped them off first.

"Twenty-seven-thousand. Wow. And they won't cover it at all?"

"Nope," Rob said. "It's like that term, *embarrassment of riches*. I think it's that. She has so much wrong with her, because of the cancer, the falls, and she's always had migraines—so much that they can't guarantee the surgery will help, even though it probably will. And they're all about results, and since they can't guarantee a result, they won't cover it."

"That is so wrong," Danielle said. "Your mom's been on my floor a few times. I swear every time she shows up, it's like she's making rounds on us." She wiped ketchup off her mouth. "Does she still bake? Those cookies and brownies were fought over."

"She just does the crafts now," Rob said. "I mean, she cooks, but she, I don't know, maybe wants to give people something more permanent."

"I love her stuff," Danielle said. She covered Marybeth's ears. "I might need it, when they take my house away."

"Oh, stop."

"I haven't opened his drawer yet," she said. "It's stuffed with all the financials. I told him to put it on a spreadsheet, but he was lucky he could post pictures of dickhead drivers from his work onto Facebook."

"I told you, I'll help."

"I know." She pulled out a napkin and wiped Marybeth's fingers. "I wish we could help each other."

Asher

The hustle and bustle of early afternoon Troy felt boundless. It was the holiday spirit of whimsy locked in brownstone and granite, concrete and glass etched in initialed business names, released for one day only, to haunt the historic streets and possess the young and the old, the happy and the sad.

Asher didn't know whether to feel happy or sad. Ginny and Jordan were as drunk as two women could be with just one shot. They stopped at Diamond's, a bar in the basement of one of the oldest buildings of Troy's historic district, which was undersized due to the city's love affair with sweeping fires.

When they left Diamond's, Asher pointed out the wall, partially visible because the building had a floor up on its neighbors.

"See those bricks?" he said.

"I see bricks," Ginny said. Jordan snickered.

"The ones that look off, like they don't belong there. Different color."

"Yeah, okay." Jordan pointed them out to Ginny, who was way past her first shot.

"Sam Wilson had a plot of land up by Mount Ida, where the clay was good for bricks. He made bricks. Those are actual, historical Samuel Wilson bricks."

"They're Uncle Sam bricks," Jordan said.

"I thought he was a meatpacker." Ginny started giggling and Jordan nudged her.

"He was. But he was also a brickmaker."

Asher was surprised that in a neighborhood filled with so much crowd noise, his neat thing could catch dead air. He wished he hadn't brought it up. He also wished he'd had more than one shot.

"We have to get you laid, Asher," Ginny said.

"Shut up, Ginny. Trying to show you all something interesting. Just forget it."

"Leave him alone," Jordan said. "It was a cool story. Now I know that, and every time I come by here, I'll know those are Uncle Sam bricks. I'll wait for one to fall off and put it in my club in a glass case."

"Your charity is unnecessary."

"Come on now," Jordan said. She closed the space between him and planted a kiss on his cheek and wiped her black lipstick off. "We love you. But you really should lighten up."

Nobody understood why Asher was so introverted. When he was onstage, he owned it. He was animated, shredding with the grace of a skateboarder doing the same thing, pausing for the split second here and there to catch the flash of a camera he'd see lining up a shot. His voice was smooth, and he teased the audience, made them his friend. That all stopped the moment he hopped offstage.

His fans, the few that there were, didn't realize that in most venues, the stage lights shone in his eyes so much, he could barely catch shapes. He was usually playing to the audience he imagined was there. When he first started up Captain Pneuma, he sat and played until Ginny told him she was the only one allowed to sit.

Ginny and Jordan were posed for a group of college kids and young couples with cellphone cameras and one man with a DSLR. They leaned into each other cheek to cheek, one leg bent in pose. Asher felt like taking a picture himself. And he did.

"Asher," Jordan said. "Get over here!"

"Are you sure? I don't want to ruin the shots."

"We're not asking twice," Ginny said. Asher walked closer, and Jordan grabbed him and put him in between them. They weren't cheek to cheek, but they made use of having a third person to wrap around. They hooked their arms through his and made him skip along with them down Second Street.

As they approached the corner of Second and State Streets, they hit Monument Square. The crowds were dense, and as the crowd size grew, the less it looked like a quaint reenactment of a bygone era, and the more it resembled downtown Albany after a pop show let out of the Arena.

He also noticed that as the crowd became less and less Victorian, the people who did dress up, like Ginny, Jordan, and himself, were more of an attraction to shutterbugs. Jordan and Ginny danced with the crowd and would probably be in all the newspapers at least once. Asher also realized that Ginny had brought her diamond-plated flask and was sharing it on the sly with Jordan.

Asher saw many of the people from the funeral, but he didn't know them well enough to change buses for another ride through the neighborhood. He did, however, find a friend.

"Hey, Ash." Bianca was dressed in her hotel uniform, a black pinstripe pantsuit with two faint holes where her name tag hooked in, which only Asher would've recognized. Her wavy hair was up in a bun, which she was loath to do at work.

"You on your break?"

"Lunch. I am taking next year off."

"I'll work the Stroll next year," Asher said.

"I'm taking the whole year off."

"For real?"

"I wish. My landlord already wants to kick me out. He'll slap on some new paint, flip it to a luxury apartment 'cause you can see the Green Island sewer pipe across the river from my bathroom."

"That's riverfront property right there."

Bianca checked her watch. "So you had that funeral, right?"

"Yup, glad it's over."

"That sucks." Asher caught Ginny's and Jordan's approach from the corner of his eye.

"Come to join us, Bianca?" Ginny asked.

"Lunch break. You coming back to the hotel?"

"Not until long after you're off your shift." Ginny slipped, and Asher caught her taking a nip. "But I got a bottle of Irish whisky in my room. Make sure you get some."

Bianca laughed. "I'll try," she said. She patted Asher's arm with the back of her hand. "I get off at midnight, if you're looking for somewhere to go." She waved goodbye to Ginny and Jordan and made her way to the food trucks.

"Why can't you get with her, Asher? She's so sweet."

"I work with her," Asher said. "There's like a video about all that stuff."

"That's your problem," Ginny said. "You're so much about the rule book—you couldn't put a toy train together if it didn't come with a manual."

Asher laughed. "What? What did that even mean?"

"Whatever," Ginny said. "I'm hungry. Drunk hungry. Let's go get me some deep-fried jalapenos."

Asher glanced at Jordan, who returned the glance and shook her head. Ginny would get more fun as the night went on. Surprisingly, her fun drunk never turned mean. Obnoxious, sure. But never mean.

Despite Ginny's mission, they didn't move far from the corner of Second and State. Asher bought Jordan a sprig of evergreen with red ribbon and holly sprigs. She grabbed him and Ginny and, as if by some Gothic winter magic, drew a small crowd of photographers. Asher decided to make the most of it, posing like he was onstage, arms wrapped around Ginny and Jordan, eyes in the sky like it was the stage light, and the digital sound of flashes seeped through the air. One man was taking pictures with a large DSLR with a long lens. He put down the camera and smiled. A smile too bright for teeth that chewed food.

"Hi everybody," he said. "Hi ... Asher, right?" He extended his hand. I'm Harley Morris, over at the hotel, from the EDC."

Chapter Sixteen

Jordan

When you work in the drinking industry, it is an unwritten rule that you are paid in crinkly bills for your silence. If Susie tells you she's fucking the pool boy when the bar's dead and she comes in for aperitif before going out to eat, you don't tell hubby Roger when he comes in for the nightcap. And his late-night romps with Fourth Street heroin whores are his business and his business alone.

Bartenders have whole books full of stories in them, and Jordan was friends with a few authors that cashed in on the seediness of people once they were one beer past sober. Change names, call it fiction. No, it's not an omerta, but it is a take-home that you need to keep, and it's not a bad job if you're not a big mouth.

Asher worked in a hotel, and he had similar unwritten rules, which he broke when he told her about Harley and his plans for the city. It wasn't exactly a tryst, but he might be fucking the city. And he might be fucking her, and not in any way she'd like. Still, he was a charmer.

"I gotta tell you," Harley said, "all of you, you look great. You do this every year?"

"I haven't been back in a while," Jordan said. "So not me."

"We're in a band," Ginny said, pointing to Asher. "We got to play a

Christmas set one year." She pointed to a makeshift metal stage that had speakers on it. "Right over there."

"I'm really surprised that there are so many people dressed up," Harley said. "I expected to see a couple groups here or there. Nothing like this."

"It's usually cold as shit when the Stroll is on." Asher pulled his frock coat tighter to him, folding one side over the other. "Today, it's just snow."

"I saw your coworker out here. Bianca, right?"

"You remembered."

He pulled out a red flip notebook with a golf pencil in the spiral-bound. "I make sure to write down the names of people I may need to know in the future. You and Bianca made the list."

Jordan wondered if Asher told him her name, or if it would be the next entry in his notebook. She also wondered if she even wanted in on that contact list. She could see what Asher meant about the conquistador thing. He didn't seem like a bad guy. More like the kind of guy that could afford to come across with a smile because he had his games won before he started playing. She would've hated a guy like him before she opened up a business. Now she had to admit, she wanted the secrets behind that confidence, that too-white smile.

"You want to see something neat?" Harley asked.

"I was actually going to hit up the Beat Shop down the street," Asher said."

"Please, you're at the Beat Shop every day," Ginny said. "Jimmy's playing music outside, like he does every weekend. I can hear it from here. C'mon, let's go see something neat."

"I don't want to break up the group—"

Asher shrugged. It was clear he didn't like Harley. But it was more than that. She knew Asher had something for her, however misguided it was. She probably should've laid it to him straight, but who the hell lays down the law on a day like that? He stepped up to the plate on a day his friends needed him most. That was admirable.

Jordan took Asher's hand, granting Harley his chance to impress. They got to the end of Second Street and crossed River, through the vendors and food trucks, and walked up to a building that Jordan always thought defined Monument Square, as much as the Monument and the Cannon Building on the other side.

They walked in the front doors of the building, which must've had a name—all the old buildings in Troy did—but Jordan didn't know what it was.

A massive glass front extended to a wide arch, all framed in a marble façade. There was a Christmas installation in the window, on the ledge, as the main floor was a wide stairwell that went down into the floors below River Street. Jordan went to take those steps, but Harley tapped her on the shoulder and pointed to a small set of stairs to the upper floors, which they followed. She gripped the wrought-iron handrail tight, because the stairs were steep, and she was wearing heels higher than her normal ones.

The stairs emptied into a small, cluttered hall. Through a thick hardwood door, the hallway emptied out into a large loft, barren except for boxes of paper reams, disassembled cubicle architecture strewn about, and framed Art Deco pictures leaning against the walls.

"What is this place?"

"This," Harley said, "is the future home of the Economic Development Council. When it's set up, it's going to be part EDC, part small business incubator, part meeting space. We are even going to set up a coffee shop on the first floor." He walked into the office graveyard and rolled out two chairs. "Ladies first."

"Thank God, my feet are killing me," Ginny said. "You have no idea how hard it is to walk in these when you're drunk."

"Only when you're drunk?" Jordan laughed. They pulled up a seat to what must be the main draw, the "neat thing" Harley was talking about: a completely unobstructed view of all of Monument Square. Crowds waited at the food trucks. Parents sat by the Monument with their kids. Drummers set up by the stage on State Street as the throng in their Victorian costumes posed for the masses.

It was hard to tell just how many people were taking part in the Stroll. It was the whole downtown, even though the heart of the activity was Monument Square and River Street. Jordan wondered what they were missing.

Harley leaned over Jordan's shoulder to flick a switch, and a display of multicolored lights shone bright in the window. Bright, colorful, and festive enough for people to look up. Ginny waved. After a second, so did Jordan. A few returned the gesture.

"We have big plans for this city," Harley said. "You guys aren't going to believe it."

"You have a pond going directly where my club is in South Troy. You've probably heard of it, Sam Wilson's?"

"Did you talk to Asher? We were talking about it last night."

"I saw it on an artist's map I came across," she lied, not wanting to get Asher in trouble. "Is it true?"

"It's just an artist's conception," Harley said. "We've gotten grant money for a bike trail, and it has to end somewhere before the 378 Bridge. A nice park in those oilfields would be a good addition to the city, you have to admit. Especially if we're getting money to clean them up."

"Except your dream jams a fountain up my ass."

"It's not finalized. Troy takes care of its businesses, I've learned."

"Since when?" Jordan said. "Maybe here, with the college kids running around. You need to go back to school though, if you're talking about any other part of the city."

Harley walked away. Jordan thought she'd offended him, but he came back with a bottle of champagne and, with a deft move, probably brought about by many successful real estate deals, he popped it.

"I'll tell you what," he said. "Let's enjoy this now. Later I'll come and check out Sam Wilson's. That's why they're called negotiations. A venue called Sam Wilson's in the middle of the park? Might be a selling point."

"We're having a reception tonight," Jordan said. "There'll be a bunch of people there. I'll show you why Sam Wilson's ain't going nowhere."

Harley passed around glasses. Asher refused, instead leaning up against the window, obviously miserable. She wished she wasn't the one making him that way, but it was only a day for him. This was her life.

She saw a minor commotion out of the corner of her eye. Wouldn't have been a big deal. Except the cops were involved, and the man in the middle was wearing clothes she'd lent him. This evening's entertainment.

Danielle

Her mother brought candy canes when she met Danielle at the Kettle to pick up the kids for the night. It was like bringing a cup of coffee to a meth house at noon. Marybeth was sleeping in Danielle's arms and Joey was occupied blowing bubbles in his chocolate milk through a straw.

She didn't stay long. She wasn't much for Troy anything, and Danielle hoped she had a good time while roaming the streets, but it turned out she just went to a restaurant, and then the Beanery afterward, to kill time until she had to meet up with them.

Like nearly every other business in Troy that day, the Kettle had its own seasonal offering. The waitress, whose name was Sheila, Rob told her, was dressed like Mrs. Claus, and she sang Christmas carols as she took orders. She was amazing. Sprigs of holly, tiny crystal ornaments, and even a small string of LED lights were woven into her frosted blond beehive hairdo, and her costume blended Santa's workshop with classic seventies New York diner.

Rob smiled as she strolled by and tapped him on the shoulder. "Seriously, I think she puts enough into this Stroll for everybody."

"I think she likes you, bud."

"Nah, she's married."

"That matters these days."

Rob shook his head. "If he fucks up and she throws him papers, hell, I'll sign them for him, but till then, I'm not with it."

Danielle smiled. "Such a gentleman."

"Nah," Rob said. "Before me and Jennifer signed the papers, she was, um, *sampling the next course.*"

"Ew."

"Glad I'm not the only one to think that." Rob ordered stuffed French toast, because he said he was still hungry, and he could get away with paying for his own food there. "I blamed him, you know. I mean, I still do, but then I was like, it was all his fault. I couldn't let go of her yet, even if all

I was holding on to were memories of when it was better."

"I don't know how it's going to be for me," Danielle said. "I don't know how this is to people, but I'll say it to you, 'cause you might understand." She sipped soda and grasped a napkin in her hand.

"Part of me is married. I mean, like, married right now, like Craig's on a business trip and I'm at home watching the kids."

"It's denial," Rob said. "Totally common."

"No, but the other thing is," she lowered her voice and leaned over the table. "I feel single too. And I don't even mean lonely, I'm not lonely. Like today. I could just feel guys looking at me. I come to this thing every year, wear the same outfit, but I never felt guys looking at me.

"And I'm not saying it like I was creeped out. But I get these waves of guilt."

Rob stroked his chin. "You're going from 'Danielle, wife and mother' to 'Danielle, single mother.' Nothing in grief is a straight line." Rob chewed a corner of his stuffed French toast, talking as he chewed. "They tell you the five stages of grief—denial, anger, bargaining, all that—but they weave in and out of each other. It's why people think they're done grieving, only to get hit with it even harder later."

"When does it go away?"

Rob laughed. "I'll let you know."

They traded marriage war stories while Rob finished his second lunch. She never realized how good—how terribly guilty—she'd feel about dishing on Craig. Death made him the immortal Good Guy, but he was just a guy. They fought. He did stupid shit, and so did she. And she'd grown tired of being the rock that all her friends saw, part of the stable marriage who dispenses advice with her right hand and hard truths with her left.

Her phone rang and she took it out of her purse. Jordan. She put the number in her contacts when they were on top of the parking garage.

"Hey Jordan, where are you guys?"

"Monument Square. My friend almost got arrested."

"Who, Asher?"

"No. Doc Lucian, our entertainment. I gotta go and take him with me. I'm going to go back to Sam Wilson's. I kinda need to bus it. Ginny's here, she's a bad influence. Where are you?"

"The Kettle," Danielle said. "If you guys can walk up here, we'll go to the Third Street bus stop and join you. I'd rather pick my car up at the garage tomorrow if I'm gonna drink at Sam Wilson's."

"You're gonna drink at Sam Wilson's," Jordan said.

Donny

He had his appendix taken out when he was eighteen, and he remembered how he woke up in the intensive care unit. When they call it "coming to," they ain't kidding. He didn't open his eyes to reality—they were opened to some form of unreality, and slowly the gurney, the machinery hooked up to him, and even the hospital itself came into his focus, like he was a video camera laying on the ground that had been picked up and turned on.

That's exactly how Donny felt when he came to in a puddle of rancid puke, streaked dark with what he thought was tar. But that didn't make as much sense once he pressed on his temple and his hand nearly slid off his hair. He righted himself as much as the throbbing aches and the stinging and ripping of lacerations let him. He wasn't a doctor, but he grew up in the projects enough to diagnose an ass whooping.

Easy. That motherfucker. He didn't remember much after they hopped in the alley behind Fourth Street News and found a spot to light up, between a dumpster behind the shit bar on Fourth and a parked van. They smoked. It couldn't have been just weed; they didn't grow weed that could make him forget being beaten. And Easy wouldn't have oversold just weed to a pro smoker like Donny; reputations were on the line.

He wished he could've sussed out what Easy gave him besides some serious payback. He got up and went into the bathroom to get a look in the mirror. He prayed it wasn't the face, but he was still so numb he couldn't feel his dick. Maybe he should check that, too.

The mirror was the friend he needed that day, but not the one he wanted. He was bashed. He half-entertained the idea to go through his room and see if his ex-girlfriend left any makeup, but he'd never make himself up unless it was Halloween. He had a bashed nose, and his eyes were puffing up. They'd be blue-black by that night, at least the right eye. There was crusted blood on his chin, and he had to admit that on Halloween, he would've been a great vampire.

He shook his head at great personal expense. It wasn't a proud beatdown.

There were such things. You couldn't be soft in the world, because no one gave a fuck if you lived or died except you, and if someone got in your way, you could only be nice about it once. He laughed at the peaceful people. They turned being pussies into a strength. They talked high and called people like Donny when other people like Donny didn't respect their principles.

So he fought. He beat people's asses, and he got beat. But he always felt good about it, even if he knew he'd be making a pit stop at the ER. Because they were good fights. But Easy, and whoever he had gang up on Donny, because he was sure that motherfucker couldn't do it alone, had beat Donny like he was a puppet. He didn't know if he even fought back, or if he put his hands over his face and curled up in a ball.

He inspected his clothes, and all in all, they weren't as bad as they could've been. Easy seemed to only have it out for Donny's head. He almost forgot to check his wallet, but as soon as he thought about it, it was priority number one. Be sure that piece of shit didn't rob him too. He pulled out his wallet. Good sign. He opened it to see the edges of dollar bills. Another good sign.

The bad sign was that the two bills were twenties, and that was all that remained of the knot. He wanted to think that Easy stole the rest, because the other explanation was that he blew the fuck out of his rent money, and he didn't know if Meyer was going to give him work the next day. Even if he did, rent was due, and the landlord had blank eviction notices by his nightstand.

He could hear the crowds outside walking by. Music was playing off in the distance, and as he checked out the window, it was snowing. It was supposed to be a fun day. How the hell did he manage to fuck it up like this?

He checked the clock, and figured that Danielle, Ginny, and Rob would be getting ready to go to Sam Wilson's. He needed to catch the bus, but he had to get their cigarettes first. He couldn't tell if they got stolen, or he spent the money, and he was sure they'd bought other packs in his absence, but it would be a long, drink-filled night, and he could at least show some heroics at the last minutes by showing up with the cancer cavalry.

He called Danielle's cell to make sure they were still going.

"Hey, you," she said.

"Hey, Dani, sorry. Got held up."

"Like, you got robbed?"

Donny hesitated, but caught the save. "Nah, found one of my cousins. I had to go visit my aunt, and you know how Italian families are, food upon food. I'm stuffed. I have yours and Rob's cigarettes. Sorry about that."

"We got some at the news store," she said. "We're going to Sam Wilson's," she said. "We're taking the bus. We're at the corner of Third and Ferry, you know the stop. How fast can you get here?"

"Probably not fast enough," Donny said. "I have a couple small errands to run. I'll catch a later bus and meet you guys there."

"Okay, hon. We'll see you."

"Wait," Donny said. "Is Rob there?"

"Yeah, you want to talk to him?"

"Nah, just let him know I have his cigarettes too, and I'll bring them."

"Okay," Danielle said. "That's the bus. Talk to ya." She hung up.

Donny tossed the phone on the couch. Then he realized that he forgot what brand Rob smoked. His top hat, the one Danielle gave him to wear, was on the ottoman he got from Craig when he and Danielle moved to the house from their old apartment. He picked it up, moved the brim around in his hands, and threw it down the hall like a frisbee.

Oddly enough, Donny did see his cousin. He was on Third, across from the parking garage at the Fourth and Fulton Street bus stop, where the statue of Uncle Sam shone in weathered aluminum. It was easier to blend into the crowds than Donny thought; the face scrubbing, however painful, seemed to get rid of the spectacle that had borne witness to his loss. Or maybe people turned their eyes away from the losers. But as he was getting on the bus, waiting in line behind the mostly regular riders he saw every day, he heard his name called. He turned to see his cousin, the only person in the family in worse shape than he was.

Chapter Seventeen

Rob

When he was growing up, the breadth of Rob's domain was typed in small print on over thirty tri-folded bus schedules. The magic spot was the museum, where a display held them all. It was like a doorway to Albany, Schenectady, Troy, and every village and town that formed the cushions between them. Towns you couldn't get to with a bus and two transfer tickets was the frontier.

Every weekend, he and his dad would go to Albany on the twenty-two bus and he hogged the window seat, staring out as the bus made its stops and to watch all the poor souls walking and on bikes, assuming that they did so because they couldn't afford a bus ticket. It was funny that, since he had a car, he now looked at people in the bus shelters with the same sense of pity.

Danielle was sitting next to him but had turned around to talk to Ginny and Jordan. Asher was also on the bus. He was across the aisle with an older gentleman, Doc Lucian, whom they'd had to rescue from the cops. All he was doing was playing guitar, busking, which was perfectly legal every day except the day the whole city was doing it. Then you needed a permit.

The bus cruised through South Troy, and when it hit the end, it would turn up the hill and drive to the community college and then back down, a fast route since Third Street in South Troy might as well have been a country road with a handful of stop signs.

The hydraulics let out a hiss and the bus lowered. A man got on. If it hadn't been the Victorian Stroll, Rob would've openly laughed at him. He was dressed as a cartoonish version of Uncle Sam, sporting a top hat you'd buy off a carnie at a county fair. Every part of the costume—flimsy blazer, balloon pants, a tie, and no shirt—looked equally low rent.

The driver glared at him. The man paid with a handful of change before getting on the bus and swinging from pole to pole to get to a seat in front of them. He then opened up a pint of low shelf whisky and pulled off it. Rob noticed the bus driver glowering in the rearview.

"Sorry, sir." The man tucked the pint in the inside pocket of his construction paper blazer.

"One more, I'll throw you off," the bus driver said.

They didn't get much beyond the canal that bisected South Troy before Shabby Uncle Sam, without warning, got up and took a surfer's stance, legs parted, arms out in front and behind as he yelled in time to the bumps in the road, "My balls, my balls, my balls."

In all of Rob's time of riding, he'd never felt a bus pull over that fast. The driver yanked the lever to open the doors and got up. Their decorated passenger shouted, "Whoo!" and ran out the back door.

"Sorry, folks." The driver chuckled as best he could, taking his seat.

"I'm surprised we didn't see him at the Stroll," Danielle said. "He would've stood out."

"He strolls the dumpsters between Third and Fourth," Ginny said. "He's a vacuum."

"A vacuum?" Rob said.

"Sucks up anything in front of him," she said as they passed the convergence of Third and Fourth. The stop nearest Sam Wilson's was coming up. "Heroin, coke, crack, meth, and when he can't panhandle people or steal enough change from parked cars, he vacuums dicks in the parking garages."

"That's gross."

"Life is gross." Ginny dipped her head down to take another nip from her flask. Rob could smell the peppermint liqueur.

"How do you even know this stuff?"

"Me and Donny went to school with him. He wasn't always like that. Honor student, nerd-type. Damn respectable back then."

"What happened?"

"I don't think anything happened," she said. "His folks are still around. They're actually rich. Like, Albany-rich. Like, Loudonville-rich. If he could get his fucking head right, they'd probably put him in some rehab with pillow mints and rosewater baths."

"That's sad as hell," Rob said.

"I don't have any sympathy," Danielle said. "I know who he is, too. One of Craig's friends OD'd on fentanyl. Guy sat in the room the whole day, shooting up while the body got cold."

The bus caught the light at the five-way intersection that pinched all the north-south streets in South Troy into Burden Avenue. The road that went down off Burden Avenue to the oilfields, and to Sam Wilson's, the next stop.

"My balls, my balls, my balls…" Rob said.

"Don't you start," Danielle said. "He'll throw you off the bus too."

"He won't have far to go," Jordan said. She reached over to the plastic strip that lined the top of the windows. *Stop Requested* lit up. "C'mon guys, we're here." She shooed Ginny up out of her seat.

Ginny grabbed Rob's shoulder as she tried to right herself. "Ooh, head rush."

"Take it easy now," he said.

They exited the back door about a block away from the access road.

"I really gotta talk to the bus company about relocating the stop in front of the bar."

Rob didn't question it; he knew they never would. Bus stops were like emergency exits: people depended on them being at a certain place.

They began the trek to the bar, Danielle giggling with Ginny and Jordan. As he walked between them and Asher, the nice man they called Doc Lucian behind him, he felt like he was in the only place he needed to be.

Asher

Walking around a gas station, throwing snacks into a big paper bag felt a lot like shoplifting to Asher, but few gas stations put baskets by the door, reserving that space for holiday favorites like ice-melters and car scrapers. They were nice enough about it when he told them he needed to spend about two hundred dollars for junk food. They even gave him the bag. He tried not to dwell on the fact that, even on his day off, even during the Stroll, he was doing shit-boy work, stuck comparing the weight ratio of cheese puffs to honey barbeque potato chips to caramels, while Jordan, Ginny, and everyone else was getting drunk off Sam Wilson's drink card, which Jordan assured them all was handed out to them and only them.

Asher didn't mind helping out. Sometimes he amazed himself with how much of a sour fuck he was, because he really loved people. He got misty when he saw commercials of kids holding threadbare, mangy stuffed toys with their ribs nearly bursting through their skin. He even "adopted" a kid once, until he changed jobs and had to tighten up expenses.

He grew up in a hard house, and as much time as he spent rebelling from the string of cold, shrewd aphorisms that his dad offered in place of any actual nurturing, Asher knew it wasn't his fault. He was a trucker, born of a trucker, all the way back to when there were no roads and his great great great grandfathers drove the wagons on the Oregon Trail. His father was a man that they based shaving cream commercials off of; a rough guy with a rough way and he was a little boy whose eyes trembled when he saw sad puppies on the shelter commercials.

Jesus, he had to get out of his head, but shit work was shit work. Jordan hadn't planned on snacks for the reception. She could have gone up to the Hudson Market on the top of the hill, where they had real snacks. Except she was too drunk to drive and had been forced to abandon her bus downtown.

He filled the bag as best he could and brought it to the front counter. The clerk smiled. The woman behind him, who looked like she lived to speak with the manager, tapped her feet. And he would have let her go ahead of him, but Asher was tired of being pushed over.

The clerk rang everything up. All said and done, he's only spent eighty-five bucks.

"Thanks," Asher said as he walked out. The snow had been falling all day, off and on, but it was pretty snow. Looked nice in the air, didn't stick to anything. He made his way across the street and checked with his feet for traction as he walked to the access road to Sam Wilson's, which was steep enough to be treacherous when it had a coat of ice on it.

He saw Ginny and Rob smoking outside with Doc Lucian. He walked over and extracted two packs, a request on top of the candy and snacks.

"You are awesome," Ginny said. "A literal prince."

"Thanks, Asher," Rob said.

Asher tossed a pack of generics to Doc Lucian. "I didn't leave you out."

"I'm okay. I got to save my pennies."

"On me," Rob said. "We're all having fun tonight."

Doc Lucian considered it. "Well all right. But I owe you," he said. "Maybe I'll make you a mojo hand."

"Sure," Asher said, and he meant it. He'd need all the help he could get.

Asher entered the bar to Blind Faith's "Can't Find My Way Home." Walking over to the bar, he found Jordan turned around, rearranging liquor bottles, facing them.

She saw him in the mirror, spinning around. "You really are the best. Did you have enough?"

"I still have over a hundred," he said. "I damn near wiped them out of all the stuff you'd actually have in a bar. I didn't buy sticky buns or mini doughnuts."

"You could've," Jordan said.

"Look, I have a better idea," he said. "How about I go down to Hudson Market for you? While I'm there I can pick up your bus and bring it back."

"You'd have to go all the way downtown."

"That's fine. I'm not drinking."

"You gonna get an Uber?"

"I was thinking bus, but that's even better, sure."

"Okay, I guess. Take it out of the hundred, the fare."

"I have money—"

Jordan held up a hand. "Least I can do for fetching my bus." She rummaged through the bag.

Asher took a seat at the bar and pulled a small stick of beef jerky out of the bag. "I always feel better at stuff like this if I have something to do. I know it sounds weird."

"Not at all." Jordan dug through her purse for her keys.

"Before you go out of your way to do this," she said. "I want to make sure we're clear about something."

Asher braced for whatever soul crushing thing she was about to say.

"I hired you not too long ago," she said. "I don't mix business with pleasure—"

"I'm not trying—"

"I just don't want you to think there's something going on between us. That's not about you. It's how I arrange the books in my head."

"I get it."

"You still want to go downtown?"

"Of course," he said.

She gave him the keys, and he saluted and walked out. The salute was awkward as hell, but what else can do when the girl you're crushing on lays you out as a business decision? He wasn't mad, but awkwardness and anger were cousins.

Jordan

The storage room in the back of Sam Wilson's was where the building's former role as an industrial tool and die shop couldn't be hidden. Jordan stepped around steel braces bolted to the ground to search for extra chairs. She meant to have them all lined up, stacked at the far wall of the main room, so that anyone who got tired of tearing up the place could park it. But there was so much to do every day, even when the only people there were day dwellers catching the paper with coffee and store-bought boxes of doughnuts.

She picked up her hoodie and threw it over her corset, an Envied print of a hellspawn Cupid on the back and a life-sized human heart design on the front that she picked up at a metal expo in Knoxville. She had a thing for guerilla clothing lines.

Jordan needed to hire at least four people to get the club into fighting shape. She didn't have the resources to do that yet. Friends helped with stuff like moving, but it wasn't like it was when they were young, when they were the South Troy Street Team and worked their asses off for an all-access pass to every party and show in the area code.

Now the only one willing to work for the good of the party was the guy she preemptively shot down. She felt guilty about what she'd said to Asher and she didn't know why. It's not like she owed him anything, and if the debt for a vehicle retrieval was eternal love, she'd hate to see the interest rate for another small business loan. He was a good guy, and cute enough, but she couldn't get with him. She didn't have the heart to tell him the truth: he wasn't her type. Best blame it on the business.

She gathered up chairs three at a time. She had Danielle, Rob, and Ginny out at the bar and stage area, and Laura, a bartender she hired for the night through one of her friends in Albany, who was serving the first handful of funeral goers that had started to come in. Christmas music blasted on the CD player, a rock-and-metal cover compilation. She figured it would be a big hit when she found it online. They'd switch on and off between that and Doc Lucian jamming out of his guitar, miked up. And before midnight, a CD of Craig's favorite songs that Danielle gave her. By then the acquaintances would have left, and Craig's true-blue friends would be left to give him his last call.

"Yo, Jordan!" Ginny shouted. "What you doing? C'mon, girl, get out here."

Jordan approached with a stack of three chairs.

"Don't worry about those," Ginny said. "Nobody's coming here to be wallflower. Well, except Asher."

"Is he really that bad?"

"He will literally hug the wall all night, unless someone gets him talking about one of maybe three subjects."

"Which ones?"

"Music, history, and ghosts." Ginny poked a stirrer through the maraschino cherry of her drink and sipped. "It's weird. He's an encyclopedia about those topics. Ask him about the latest movie out in theaters, or where all the lady parts are, he couldn't tell you."

"My God, really?"

"No. Not the lady parts thing. Jesus, I'd never ask him about that. Gross."

"You said it."

"I'm drunk. You're my filter." She jostled Jordan's shoulders. "Work, damn you."

"I told him that nothing could ever happen between us," Jordan said. "I said I didn't mix business and pleasure."

"And he's business?"

"Sort of. You guys play here."

"There you go," Ginny said. Her tone carried a tinge of disappointment.

Jordan moved the chairs around and pointed across the floor, like she was measuring with her fingertip. Really, she was trying to look engaged. "Is he going to be okay with that?"

"You'll never hear another word about it."

"Doesn't really answer the question though."

Ginny set her drink down. "If I had to guess, he's sad. By now he's done being mad at you and now he's hating himself." She grabbed the drink and picked it back up. "The beauty of somebody that keeps everything in is that you don't have to deal with it."

"I don't want to hurt him."

"He hurts himself. C'mon, I can help you stop feeling so heartbroken." She grabbed Jordan's hand and dragged her toward the glass sliding door she'd had installed to allow people access to the jetty.

Ginny pulled out a joint the size of Jordan's pinky.

"I don't usually smoke," she said. "Just special occasions. It makes me metaphysical, and before I know it, my keys are in the freezer and I'm trying to start my car with telepathy."

"You mean psychokinesis," Jordan said. "That's moving stuff with your mind. Telepathy is mindreading."

"Yeah, sourpuss corrected me on that shit before. Maybe you two do belong together."

They found a spot next to the vent where a thrash version of "Good King Wenceslaus" came out crystal clear, and they power-huffed the joint. Jordan wasn't as heavy a smoker as she used to be. In the theater scene, most potheads she worked with couldn't do the fucking job. But that night, with Ginny, it felt like a part of the job that had to be done.

"You really gotta blow this shit up," Ginny said. She pointed outside. "Like the river. Imagine if you had a sound setup right here, and you set up the—" she pointed to the jetty "—whatever that is, and you fill it with snacks and T-shirts and shit, drinks…" She opened her fingers like a burst. "And face it all out to the water. Boaters could get crowds of people and dock here, and you could have the live show for them so they can buy snacks and merch, and you can also have the show on the inside… All you need is soundproofing."

"That's a little … really fucking cool, actually." Jordan pictured Ginny's idea like it had, in fact, been telepathy. "Holy shit, that could be the game plan. If they wanna make a park here, we could totally do that. Like South

Troy could have the hottest spot with Sam Wilson's on the river."

"It was my idea," Ginny said. "I want to design the T-Shirts."

"Done."

They stayed out a few minutes more, their grand ideas filtering down to nice little touches, things that Jordan could do right away. It was good to have someone to talk shop with who wasn't trying to sell her something or get in her pants. They got up to rejoin the crowd before it blocked the doors.

Chapter Eighteen

Danielle

A punk band crooned to a hard-banging version of "Jingle Bell Rock" as Danielle drifted from circle to circle, each group sharing their best Craig stories. They were in open competition, each person claiming their connection to Craig with their own story of that time when they went on a bone cruise and that thing happened, or why some mean or lecherous fuck was cruising the streets of Albany or Schenectady and not Troy, or exactly how many shots Craig had held down when he got arrested for shitting on the Bantham Club's polished maple bar during the one and only hardcore show they'd ever had.

Only Danielle knew the right answer to that last question: it was nine. She knew because it was her working the bar that night. It was the first time she ever saw his bare ass. How would she have ever guessed that years later she'd be charged with checking it for rashes and cleaning his shit willingly when he didn't get a clean flush?

She gagged a little as Sean Bollard, a tiny little scrapper from the Yarrow days was giving up his offering.

"Me and Craig went to Woodstock," he said before he saw Danielle. "It was the twenty-fifth anniversary. And it wasn't the big commercial, shitty one—it was on the farm, the original farm."

He took a gulp of something that looked like black coffee, but knowing

Sean, it was probably grain alcohol mixed with tattooing ink. "We took off that morning with two pounds of weed in the car, Canadian schwag. It would probably be dirt today, but we were fucking banging. Walked in with it in a tent bag. Walked right by the state troopers. We figured they wouldn't have dogs or anything 'cause they'd fuckin' go nuts or get contact highs and the cops would have to retire them or something."

Sean took another sip. Bobby Tallman tried to launch in with his own tale, but Sean put his hand out.

"Ain't finished, man. So we're sitting on the side of the road, which is really just a dirt path in the farm, and we got two lawn chairs from this old hippie couple, hairy, ain't shaved since they was at the first one, and that's the wife too." Sean holds out his hands. "So we're sitting there, I'm selling weed in one chair, and Craig got a sign that said 'Looking for Uncle Sid' in the other. And the Staties walk by, and they say, swear to Christ, 'Let us know when you find him, we're looking for him too.' They didn't even give a fuck. I had a scale in my lap."

Sean doubled over laughing and Danielle really wanted to know what was in his drink.

"What is that?" she said.

"It's that coffee 'Rocket Fuel' that they got behind the bar," he said. "Mixed with grain, which they also got behind the bar."

"Jesus, you're gonna kill yourself with that shit, Seanie."

He got quiet and his eyes found some new territory away from Danielle's. All of theirs did. She knew it as soon as she said it, but she hoped they skip over it and move on, like a Lansingburgh pothole.

"Speaking of," Sean said. "Did you know? Like, did he leave a note?" Danielle forgot that Sean's personality was a rim-bender.

"He didn't kill himself, Seanie."

"Dude, chill the fuck out, man," Bobby said to assuage his own guilt at thinking it too.

"Sorry, but we were his friends too. Shit don't go away 'cause you don't talk about it."

"Craig loved Marybeth and Joey so much, he worked sixty hours a week, busted his ass, so that those kids could have everything he never did. You think he's gonna take the one thing they need most away from them without clawing and scratching at it and fighting it tooth and nail?"

Danielle walked over to the stereo, hoping to draw them to it and cover up the talk, lest it overtake the evening. "If he was like that he would've reached out," she said. "You all saw the tough guy, Mr. Big Balls, but I saw the guy that put on a princess hat and a frilly curtain gown-type thing to have tea with Marybeth every Sunday morning."

A death metal version of "Hark, the Herald Angels Sing" wasn't distracting anyone. Doc Lucian was setting up onstage. Hopefully when he started playing people might pay attention and stop speculating about Craig's final minutes.

Thankfully, the bathroom was close to the stage, allowing Danielle to gracefully remove herself. She couldn't lock the door, and she didn't know how to sob controllably, so she prayed to a God she barely believed in that the music was loud enough to drown out her cries. Just get through the night, one more sunset-to-sunrise, pass another day like every one since Tuesday. But she wasn't sure she'd make it. She felt good in the midst of her bad, and bad in the midst of her good. It was just like Rob said, the stages of grief weaving in and out of her, phase to phase, stripping nerves bare.

Danielle stuffed up her nose and the pressure in her sinuses told her to get it together. She washed up and walked out of the bathroom, meaning to go down the narrow hall into the bar area and avoid the stage. Instead she walked directly into Rob, who braced the impact by holding onto her.

His eyes had no guile, only compassion. But more than compassion. She never saw his eyes that deep. Then again, she'd never looked into them so intensely.

"Are you okay?" His voice trailed off. She let herself fall into him, her lips embraced by his, soft flesh to soft flesh, and the tension she'd contorted herself into fell apart and reformed with him inside the coils.

And then it was over, and one became two again, sharing the shock.

Donny

It didn't feel right bragging about beating an ass that actually beat yours. He didn't tell anyone about Easy being the one who stamped a map of the Adirondacks across his face. They would've given him some ribbing for losing a fight but losing to a Black dude somehow didn't gel. Sure, they had black friends in the scene, and maybe catching a beating from one of them would be just another fight, but there was a Black scene and a white scene in Troy, and the two scenes kept a wary and mutual distance from each other.

No, the story was: he beat up a pedophile that was chasing after his little cousin. And the creep only got some shots in because Donny was high as fuck, which everybody believed. No one would ask his cousin shit; she was sixteen. And only Danielle knew who she was.

There was a Black man playing guitar on the stage. It wasn't Donny's music. It was acoustic for one, and full of that fingers sliding on and off strings. The guy tapped on the body, and the whole thing sounded like how he imagined an old steam train would pulling off the track. He hung back on the wall and let the melody bring him away from Troy for a second. Maybe he didn't like the music, but he could enjoy the effect.

He watched as everybody that could've narrated his and Craig's life tell the story of one brother short. He heard the echoes of outrageous adventures that he had with his best friend, all the bravado and macho shit, and he wanted to talk about the flip side of it all, about how many times Craig shit his pants when he was hiding from the cops in the back alleys between Sixth and Seventh Avenue, or about how he almost cried when the kids at the South Troy Pool picked on him for being poorer than them, and how Donny punched him in the arm to keep him from marking himself a coward.

Craig wasn't the toughest guy he knew, but he became the strongest person he'd ever known, and Donny had played a role in that transformation. And it was Craig's time—in fact, it was his last time—but Donny fumed walking through Sam Wilson's relegated to sidekick whose hero rode into the sunset.

He felt in his pocket for the cigarettes. He remembered Danielle's brand through the many times he'd had to bum one, and he bought Rob a pack that he wouldn't mind smoking if Rob turned them down.

Donny walked over to the bar, pulled out a five-dollar bill and hoped that all the talk of drink deals would put a beer in his hand with enough to leave a little tip. He didn't need Jordan looking at him like a charity case. She hadn't been back long enough for him to burn her out like the rest of his friends.

"Do you know where Danielle and Rob are?" he asked Jordan, who had her back turned, lifting liquor bottles to the shelves from the floor.

"I haven't seen Rob, but I think Danielle went out to hang by the river."

"Okay, thanks." Donny would try to find Danielle first. Hopefully he'd let enough time pass that Rob would've figured out a way to get more smokes and forget about him, and he'd get a bonus pack. As he walked out, he tried to shake off the prickly heat in his face that he got when he knew he was being a scumbag.

It was dark out. The oilfields weren't completely unfamiliar territory for Donny, and in an ironic way, it was fitting that the reception be at a club built on top of them. The South Troy kids inherited the oilfields in the nineties through neglect; nobody wanted it, nobody cared. When they were younger, Sam Wilson's was a factory, albeit a small one. It had workers, a security guard too. By the nineties it was out of business, and not even worth the cost to raze everything. They couldn't have given the youth more if they'd gifted the deed to the Troy High senior class.

It was theirs, and back then he could have run around the place high as shit, and he often did. But neglect changes the landscape as much as attention, and he couldn't find a few yards in front of his face. The lights of Menands across the river didn't help, as there were so few, and the jetty looked deserted.

He called out for Danielle.

He found Rob in the hallway to the bathroom as he went back in to take a piss.

"Dude, I got your cigarettes," Donny said as he pulled out the pack. "I hope it's your brand. I forgot."

"You look like hell, man."

"I got in a fight with a scumbag. Don't worry. He spit a few teeth out."

Rob had a closed-off posture. Donny didn't know him that well, but his attitude seemed weird.

"You cool, man?" Donny said. "Something go down?"

"I'm cool." Rob walked toward the opening where the hall emptied out to the stage. He stopped, looked, and turned around and came back.

"Dude, I did something bad," he said.

Donny sighed. "Join the club. What did you do, kill somebody?"

"No, nothing like that."

"I was fucking with you, of course nothing like that. You've been with Danielle—" He caught Rob wince. It was slight, but it was there.

"What did you do to Danielle?" Donny asked, knowing there were very few answers he'd accept without a blood donation.

"We, oh man, we didn't mean to—"

"So it's 'we' then."

"Look, we kissed. I wasn't trying to, and she wasn't—"

Donny couldn't hear the rest. Then again, when he punched Rob in the mouth, Rob couldn't say the rest.

Rob

He knew his lip was fat as he staggered on the dance floor. He'd had enough bourbon to numb it, but not enough to lose track of his features. He didn't fall, but that was less about his ability to take a punch and more about providence, though he questioned why any force would be on his side in this. Maybe he should've bounced off the hardwood. But Donny was advancing, and he was looking to make it happen.

Rob backed up, righted himself and wiped his lip, checking for blood. "Look, man, let's talk about this."

"We need to talk about this? That's you're go-to now? Talking? Maybe if you thought that a couple minutes ago I wouldn't be about to knock your fuckin' teeth out."

Rob put his hands up. He didn't want to fight Donny but when a man comes at another man, he either gets his legs under him or he gets them swept out from under him. It was instinct, fight or flight, a part of the brain disconnected from guilt or knowing what's due. He knew how to fight. He grew up all over the Hudson Valley, jumping neighborhoods and schools, and he'd handled enough bullies.

"Just take the ass whooping, man," Donny said. He was bouncing on the balls of his feet. People were gathered around for the spectacle, and it took Jordan and Danielle to keep the cops away.

Jordan grabbed Rob by the shoulders, and Danielle tried to grab Donny, but he dodged and landed a shot at Rob's ear, which rang out. He tried to back up and regroup, but Jordan kept him in her grip.

"I will start throwing people out," she said, and it was clear she was talking to both of them. "I don't know if the city's gonna try to fuck me. I'm not giving them a reason to turn my stage into a goddamn geese pond."

"You, too," Danielle said. "What happened, happened. It was a quick moment, we're over it. You think you're doing something, you're just keeping it a thing. You want that? You want me and Rob to be a thing? Keep at it, Donny."

"What the fuck would Craig think?"

"He wouldn't go tearing after Rob half-cocked," Danielle said. "You knew him best. Better than me. You think I'm having an easy time? We're all living in his shadow, and I feel like I just failed him. He was the father of my kids."

"Fine. You got an excuse," Donny said. "What's his excuse?"

Rob knew there wasn't an answer to that question that Danielle could give. There really wasn't much of one that he could give. All he had was the feeling at the Stroll, that oneness that he had when he walked with her, with the kids, like it was what he was made for.

Danielle completed him. But he knew it wasn't real. She was grasping for a normalcy that she'd had just days ago, and he was grasping for one that he never had. She was grieving and he was lonely. He could've given her space even if she ran toward him. He should've. Donny had every reason to bash him except one: he knew if Rob took a beating over her, she'd never leave his side. And some small part of Rob thought it wouldn't be a bad thing.

"It's not going to happen again, Donny," he said. "Everybody here can witness that. If you want to beat my ass, we can take it outside. That way, Jordan doesn't have to get the cops and everybody can still have a good time."

"Dude," Bobby Tallman said. "If you guys take it outside, then the party's going with you." He looked over to Jordan. "No offense."

"Nobody is fighting anybody tonight," Jordan said. "Donny, where were you today? You were in the parking garage, then nobody sees you all day. They were hanging out today, with the kids, by themselves, and you were off doing whatever. You don't get to walk in here and lay down the law if you're not going to be a part of shit otherwise.

"I know you got a lot of heart, and I also know you loved Craig dearly. I remember. There ain't nothing you wouldn't do for him, but you're not doing him any favors by making Danielle go puke, which she's in the bathroom doing right now."

Donny had his hands down. He wasn't calm, but it was clear to everyone the fight was over. Jordan turned to Rob.

"And you," she said. "You better know what you started, or ended, whichever one it is. Danielle's a good girl, and I'm only stopping this fight out of self-interest. You have to deal with whatever it is led you to do that, 'cause she is not ready for anything like that."

Donny walked out the sliding back door, probably to go out to the river's edge. At least that's what Rob would've done if Donny didn't beat him out there. The crowd had spread out, and Jordan's friend started playing, wailing out a song about a man who was chasing another man's woman. Rob couldn't help but think the song was the best he had in his repertoire for the situation.

Danielle came out of the hallway, pulling her hair back in a ponytail. He wasn't sure if he should go over and talk to her given all that just went down. There were groups of people looking at both of them and any words shared between them, no matter what words they'd be, would be further grist for the rumor mill.

Rob passed her with a "hey," which she returned. Sam Wilson's had two bathrooms, but only one was unoccupied. Neither was labeled a Men's or Women's. He opened the door to the other bathroom, the one no one seemed to be using that night, and he went to the mirror to have a look.

Donny hadn't really done a lot of damage. Maybe he'd worn himself out beating on his cousin's pervert stalker. That made Rob feel even worse knowing that Donny was walking around thinking his day was filled with punching scumbags.

Rob felt like a scumbag, but he wasn't as deserving of Donny's wrath as he wanted to be. Danielle kissed him, too. And Jordan was right. Where the fuck was Donny all day? If he had been walking with them, maybe the connection would've been broken, or maybe not made so strong.

And maybe that was ignoring the way she made him feel when they were together, joking around, talking about kids, medicine, and life. Maybe he was wrong for kissing her. Maybe. But he wasn't some leech trying to take advantage of a widow. If anything, he was a guy that got too close to a hurting friend.

He rearranged his culpability while he threw up bourbon and stuffed French toast in the trashcan.

Chapter Nineteen

Asher

The second wave of Strollers darted in and out of the retreating traffic. They weren't costumed in anything but the red faces they got as they hit all the bars early. They could at least see the traffic they were taunting. Asher knew by the time the third wave hit, about midnight, the streets would be theirs.

He saw a cop car fly by in the oncoming lane as he pushed forward down Third Street. Aside from the mobile command center set up on River Street to manage the crowd earlier, he hadn't seen much of Troy's finest. The Victorian Stroll was a big event in downtown Troy, and it got the most column inches in all the local papers, but Troy, to anyone outside of it, wasn't known for period celebrations. It was known for police tape and scrubby pictures in six-by-two boxes under headlines like *Shooting, Robbery Ring or Prostitution Sting* like they were trophy shots from the county fair.

Asher stopped for the light by the liquor store next to the homeless shelter. He got why people like Harley came into the Fulton Square Lodge with an appetite, and why they bought buildings with bountiful prosceniums that looked out over the quaint architecture of the Hudson Mohawk confluence. They weren't the first, and it was a good bet that a hundred years ago, men dressed like Asher and his friends walked around the dirt farmers and the children at labor with soot-streaked faces and staked out Troy's future in dinners and on ledger sheets.

The street opened to where it was only stop signs for a mile, and Asher was tempted to open Jordan's carburetor up and fly. It was his sin, speeding. But he knew Jordan would see a ticket as revenge for rebuffing advances that Asher hadn't known he made. At first he was pissed, but on the way to get the bus, he made his peace. Jordan didn't owe him. He'd had girls come up to him after shows that he didn't want; it didn't make them bad. Asher would be an employee. He'd offer to play as many times as she needed him to.

He hit the last light before the turnoff to Sam Wilson's when he realized he'd probably be the one called upon to go to Hudson Market for snacks. He couldn't for the life of him figure out why he thought Jordan would be doing that. On a night like this, she'd have to delegate, and he was business. But didn't you pay business?

He caught the image of Bianca writing *Shit Boy* on that slip of paper and putting it in his pocket. He'd miss most of the reception, and it was all his choice. He offered to be a gopher, tagged himself the errand boy, and he wished he could say he did it to support Craig's family, or the community, or even to squeeze out an offhand reconsideration from Jordan, but it wasn't any of that. He was hugging the wall.

He was a pallbearer because he felt like a stranger to the community's grief. He had to scramble to find a ride to the cemetery, even at the expense of being one man short moving Craig's casket because who was he to tell Donny he needed to be in the main car as much as Donny did? Getting snacks, getting Jordan's bus, everything to avoid standing there in Sam Wilson's and having some Old Guard name come up to him and ask him, "Who are you?"

He pulled the bus down the roadway, feeling the wheels slide half an inch on the small accumulation of snow. The lights were on, of course, and the big neon red-white-and-blue form of Uncle Sam tipping his top hat was on a pole about twenty feet tall. It looked great as he drove down, but it would look even greater on Burden Avenue, where actual drivers would see it. The parking lot was nearly packed, and it was big enough to move big trucks around, because, according to Jordan, that was part of the day's work at the old factory. He found a spot on the side, in front of the dumpsters, and parked.

He thought he hit something. His heart jumped. Then he hit something else, but he was already parked. Then he realized he hadn't hit anything at all when a silhouette swung something and a spider fracture pattern spread across the windshield. He jumped out of the car with no particular plan on what he'd do, or any idea who hated Jordan enough to bash her ride.

"Get out of here, dude," Donny said.

"What are you doing? What the hell happened?"

"Ain't about you. You did good today. Don't fuck nobody in here."

Don't fuck nobody? So whatever was going on was already in progress. As Donny slumped over and rested the tip of the pipe he had on the ground, tried to catch his breath, he looked like he was going to have a heart attack. Was he high? He looked like he got into it with someone inside—couldn't have been Jordan, not unless she took a few MMA courses in Brooklyn. But was this about fucking someone?

"Get the fuck out of here, Donny," Jordan said as she rushed out the front door. "You owe me every penny for this shit."

"I ain't done yet." By then, more people were outside. In fact, there may have been more party outside than in. "Call the fuckin' cops."

"That's what you want? Get locked up? You need a fucking detox or something."

Donny squeezed his temples with his balled fists, one still holding the pipe, and he flexed out, launching the pipe into the side of the building, where it chipped off some splinters and sprayed dirt.

They may have been waiting for Donny to say something else, maybe that's why they didn't say a word as he walked up the access road to Burden Avenue. By the time he was a stick man under a streetlamp, Danielle had come out.

"God," she said. "This day won't fucking end."

Asher handed Jordan the keys. "Do I want to know what that was all about?"

"Hope not," Danielle said. "'Cause I sure don't feel like talking about it."

Jordan walked over to the bus and opened the back. She rifled through what passed for a trunk in a VW Microbus, and she came up with a flashlight. A few passes around the car showed a tragedy for anyone who liked old classic hippie wagons, or a test case for restoration specialists. Donny knew where to hit to destroy both body and glass.

"You have to call the cops." Asher turned around to see his favorite guy that week, Harley, who must've been in attendance, because he didn't just drive down.

"I can't call the cops on Donny," she said.

"I'm sure he'd call the cops on you if you did this to his car."

"No. He wouldn't. He'd have his buddies fix it and talk shit about it on Facebook."

"Unless you share the same buddies, you're looking at a couple thousand dollars in damage there. Insurance is going to want a police report."

Asher knew enough to know Jordan didn't turn on friends. She wasn't a pushover, or afraid; she knew the value of loyalty. But she also couldn't live without rubber on the road. She turned to Danielle.

"My phone's behind the bar," she said.

Jordan

The lightshow in the Sam Wilson's parking lot wasn't much of a draw to the crowd, who by then had gone back inside to rekindle the good times with shots of whiskey and two-dollar drafts. Jordan stood by her vehicle with her arms wrapped up in case she had the impulse to finish breaking out the windows for aesthetic principle. The two cops were young, and one looked like a slightly grown-up version of the kid she babysat when she was sixteen.

"So do you know who did it?"

Jordan planned it in her head, how to get Donny to look like someone in need of help, not a vandal in need of a three-hots stay a quarter mile down the road. The plan in her head dissolved as it hit her lips.

"I don't think so. It was dark out here."

The cop she hadn't babysat shined his flashlight in the window. "What did he look like? It was a he, right?"

"I guess so," Jordan said. "He had short hair, like a shaved head, maybe? Beard? He had a canvas work jacket, jeans. Again, it was dark."

The other cop's name was Nelson, and he must have gone and poked his head in Sam Wilson's earlier. "Short hair, beard, work clothes. There are a few of them here."

"Are you sure they aren't still here?" The babysat cop, Ianocca, said.

Jordan backed up from the bus and walked over to the front awning to get out of the snow, which was in full squall.

"I'm sure it's no one in there," she said.

"How can you be sure if you didn't really see him that good?"

Jordan pointed to the top of the hill. "We watched him walk up there when he was done."

"And he didn't say anything?" Ianocca said. "You didn't?"

"Listen. We're holding a reception inside for a friend who just died. Not exactly thinking of chasing down vandals. It's South Troy." Jordan knew that answer should get them off her back.

Officers Nelson and Ianocca huddled in the parking lot, swinging their flashlights across the abandoned oil storage area behind the club and over Jordan's Microbus. Danielle, Rob and Asher stood by the smoky-glass window. Harley walked up with her coat. She took it from him, lest he try to put it on her shoulders and start a new war with Asher. The cops came back, Nelson swinging his flashlight so the beam would fall on the one thing Jordan forgot about.

"Can we check the footage for those?"

"They're not working right now."

"Are they dummies? Because they're lit up."

"No, they're real," Jordan said. She hated to do what she was about to do. Donny fucking owed her for more than the Microbus.

"Ever since I got in here, it's been one thing after another," she said before she unleashed a litany of misfortunes that made Job seem mildly inconvenienced.

Nelson kept shining his flashlight on the camera. "It's a shame. You'd have the guy dead to rights. You should definitely get the camera situation fixed."

Jordan sat on a stool behind the bar as the crowds were thinning out. Danielle had left, saying she needed to go pick up the kids. Rob too, with a similar story about checking on his mother. Neither of them had said much since they kissed. Asher was talking to Doc Lucian, who apparently had decided to make Asher a mojo hand. Jordan hoped Asher didn't give him a lock of her hair.

"All in all," Harley said, "most lively funeral reception I've ever been invited to."

"Thanks," she said. "We didn't try."

"It'll be remembered."

"It might be remembered longer than this place, if you all get your way."

Harley leaned his back on the table, a local microbrew in his hand.

"It really doesn't have to be like that," Harley said. "Do you think I'd come here, meet all of you and drink your beer if I wanted to send a bulldozer in?" He took a swig and belched in his hand. "The music's not that good."

"What's wrong with the music?"

"For one, you got a homeless guy playing blues in between metal CDs. I'm assuming this was a last-minute thing."

"Craig died Tuesday, so, yeah."

"Imagine if you had a stable of bands at the ready, like you could order off a list when you had an event? That's the game I'm playing."

Jordan laughed. "What, local band promoter?"

"Not only that." Harley turned around and grabbed a stool. "When you see Troy, you probably see memories, you know, this place people used to hang, that event, these bands that were 'in.' All the architecture, the cool lights, tree lines, things that, if you took all the crap out of the city, would make Troy a place where even people like us would want to vacation—people who live here tend to forget the potential the place has for the future."

"What do you mean, *people like us*?"

"You're from Brooklyn, I'm from Manhattan."

"I'm from five blocks away. I only lived in Brooklyn."

"I'm just saying."

"You're saying stuff that doesn't make me feel like I'm going to keep my club."

Harley sighed. "Okay, I'll be honest. The EDC will want changes. Overall, they like the Sam Wilson's vibe. I pitched it to them."

"You pitched my club to other people? How chivalrous of you."

"Look, I'm trying to help. Do you want to hear what they had to say?"

Jordan motioned him to talk.

"They like the groove, the feel. But they want the place to be able to expand. Now, I've been looking around tonight, and I'll submit a report to them. They'll make recommendations, and we'll work to get you an EDC grant to make the changes. You just have to agree to it."

"You want me to agree to something before I see it?" Jordan said. "You're either dumb or you think I am, and that would make you an asshole."

"Neither, and neither," Harley said. "You'll get something in the mail from the EDC. This is all you." He slid the empty beer bottle forward and pulled out a ten-dollar bill.

"I'm the devil you know, Jordan," he said, before walking away.

Danielle

Mr. Walters honked as he drove by, and Danielle waved from the front porch. A cigarette burned in the big crystal ashtray beside her on the top step where she was sitting. The drizzle was gentle, but pervasive, and the knees of her black leggings were starting to get soaked. It was two weeks before Christmas, and it might as well have been a cold April morning.

Over the past week, Mr. Walters been over more times than in all the time they'd lived next door, even offering to help her make sense of the bills Craig left behind. She had originally planned to have Rob help her, but the idea of being alone with him, kids or no kids, wasn't something she was ready to process.

She spent the days since the party vacillating between blaming him for taking advantage of her grief and remembering that she was the one who initiated the kiss. He hadn't called. She didn't know whether to feel good or bad about that.

Soon, she'd have to get her scrubs on to get ready for a night shift. Her mother offered to babysit while she worked, which included Christmas Day. Danielle would have to celebrate with the kids on Christmas Eve this year.

Gloria Hill wasn't happy about Christmas, and Danielle knew she hadn't heard the end of it. Gloria was coming to terms with the possibility that maybe Craig didn't kill himself. That started happening when she came over to help Danielle organize and took on the bathroom. Seeing all of the icy heat creams, lidocaine patches, pain relievers, and Craig's fanatical collection of elbow and knee braces didn't hide how much pain Craig had been in. So she stopped dropping hints that Danielle drove him to overdose, expecting too much, working him too hard.

But Gloria was still helpful in the aftermath. Danielle had to admit, when it came to organization, her mother-in-law was Craig's polar opposite. She arranged his mess of receipts, invoices, and bills into cohesive order. Danielle declined any additional help with as much politeness as she could muster. Because she knew that they were in it deep. It wouldn't be her life if there wasn't a ticking time bomb in the paper pile, and while she found it great that her mother-in-law was trying to lend a hand, she knew Gloria was helping the kids, not her.

Every bill, a whole table piled an inch thick, was distilled down to two pieces of paper which Danielle had in a red, pocketed folder. One, Craig's life insurance policy. Fifty thousand dollars, if Mr. Walter understood the policy as well as he thought. That was the angel standing guard over the pit of hell, which was paper number two: a final notice from NT Bank.

Their mortgage payment was due on January first. Final notice. Not a big deal in the course of paying off the house. They'd sent a few final notices before, and they didn't come to take the house if they weren't paid up right away, so long as it got paid. But this *final notice* came joined with a notice of foreclosure.

Craig handled the bills. Not because he was the man or because he was better at it, but because they did a division of labor in the household, and Craig had a better chance of staying on top of deadlines.

Danielle took another cigarette out of her pack and lit it, while the other first burned itself down to the filter. She pulled her phone out of the oversized sweater she got for Christmas last year. The insurance company's number for cashing in a policy was in small print on the back; the number to pay was much bigger and on the front. She squinted as she typed in the digits.

The call center agent was friendly, overly so. They were probably trained to handle grieving people that were waiting for an excuse to unleash hell on somebody.

"Okay," the agent said, "it seems like the policy is in review."

"What does that mean, review?"

Danielle heard clacking.

"It could mean anything, but they're reviewing the policy."

"So we paid all these years for a policy, and they're not going to pay out when they're supposed to? Is that what you're saying?"

"No, not at all," the woman said. "They could be sending you a check tomorrow. Some cases, they have to review the policy to make sure the conditions warrant the payment."

"You know, that still sounds like they're deciding if they want to pay it."

"If everything fits the policy, they'd have to pay it, or you could sue them, and they'd have to pay out even more." The agent covered the foam mouthpiece and uncovered it. "Let me talk to my supervisor. Maybe we can get you a number to someone that can give you a little bit more specific information, okay?"

The agent put her on hold and a sad classical piece played through a tin can.

"Hi, my name is Gene. Is this Danielle?"

"Yes, it's me."

"Sorry about that. I'm looking at your policy." He paused. "It looks like you were paid up, so that's not a problem. I know this is tough, but may I ask how he passed?"

"He accidentally overdosed. He was in pain from work, and he didn't realize that he took too many Vicodins."

"And how do you know that? Did he almost do it before then?"

"I know him." Danielle took a drag away from the phone. "If you're thinking he killed himself or something, he didn't. He wasn't like that."

Gene let out a breath. "I'm sure you're right, Danielle. You knew him best, but with the opioid epidemic, it's caught the whole insurance industry off kilter. When it comes to opioid deaths, we've got to investigate them further. So I'm guessing that's why the payment's being held up. They go fast, the investigations. We send someone out to ask friends and family questions. And if you want to tell us who to question, it'll help us make a determination more quickly."

"I really need the money now. I might lose my house."

"Maybe you can go to the bank and get a loan in anticipation of the payment? They sometimes do that. I'm not sure what else I can tell you."

Danielle gave him a few names and thanked him. She opened the folder and picked up the third paper, a court paper. A judgment against Craig Hill for nonpayment of a loan for twenty thousand dollars.

Chapter Twenty

Donny

The line was silent. It was the sound of a coward having another coward try to explain why two grown-ass men couldn't scrape up one bit of backbone and tell Donny they didn't need him anymore on the job. Donny ran his finger along his head from front to back, trying to keep the rage on the inside his hairline.

Meyer had been playing the game with him for the past week, not being around at first, then being busy when he realized Donny was going to call, passing the calls off to Harry. Donny felt it in Harry's voice that he was going to start leaving his phone in the truck.

Word must've gotten out. It wasn't a big area, and with contracting, not everybody could do the work and withstand the hours and temperatures in the winter, so that list was short too. He saw at least four people he worked with at that party when he lost his shit. Any one of them could've gone back to tell Meyer, and that was assuming it wasn't just the window he broke on site that made Meyer so apprehensive.

Donny had his shit boxed up in the living room. It wasn't much, just his work clothes, the suit he wore to the Stroll, and a canvas backpack whose most valuable articles were a fireproof envelope filled with his important papers and every bit of paraphernalia and scrap of drug he could squeeze from couch cushions, ashtrays, and empty kitchen cabinets.

The rest of it—the furniture, TV, stereo, appliances—were right where they'd always been, and they'd stay there when he left later that night. He put the eviction notice under a magnet on the fridge, and the deadline was three days after he got it. That was a week ago. The landlord was already threatening to call the sheriff's department. Donny didn't need the grief, even though he could've squeezed an extra two weeks out of the eviction process.

He didn't want to become homeless on Christmas. It wasn't about 'tis the season or the Christmas spirit or depression—it was about everyone celebrating at their own homes, with their girlfriends or boyfriends, husband, wives, kids—no matter what people said about being charitable on the holidays, no one was opening their spare rooms on Christmas.

He watched the clock because the cable had been turned off, and the prime time for him would consist of the "Front Street" contest at McEntyre's, where he was going to plan his second-round resurgence. He was dressed in his baggiest clothes, the overalls he wore when he did some jobs that required him to have boundless pockets. The half hour he spent grooming his beard and dashing himself with aftershave, cologne, and body spray would hopefully come in handy when he had to sweet talk Lisa behind the bar for an extension on his tab.

The buzz was ground-level and muted in McEntyre's, the bar stocked with regulars and a few college kids that were a few years shy of legal with IDs that wouldn't have fooled the people who printed them up. They were playing Irish music, flutes and fiddles that spoke of rough shores meeting verdant hills. The lights were dim, not that that was unusual, but it made what he was there to do even shadier.

"Lisa, hey," Donny said.

"Hey, guy." Lisa slung her towel over her shoulder. "You look like shit."

"I am what I look like." He smiled. Lisa whipped him with the towel.

"Stop." She grabbed a beer and lifted it. "This one, right?"

"Actually, do I still have my tab? I don't get paid till Friday."

Lisa dug in her pockets. "I got you. Mack's trying to square up debts before New Year's, 'cause he does that Jubilee thing."

"What's that? He wipes out debts, right?"

"Yup, but he's not letting anyone load up." Lisa slid the beer over. Donny didn't want to take it, but if it went well tonight, he figured he would come in and buy a round and the tips would square him.

"Thanks, babe."

He walked over to the back booth, like they'd arranged. He knew it was the only spot in the bar that was invisible to the cameras. It was dark and faced the back wall. It was also near the door to the patio, so it was an easy getaway should the cops come in for a sting.

Lenin wasn't his name. They called him Lenin because he looked like Lenin, with his sharp features and his small, round wireframe glasses, and more so for the fact that he dressed like the Russian revolutionary. He normally carried a suitcase around with the things most people put in a backpack, except for one thing he very rarely had on him. Which would be the one thing he'd have that night.

"Hey, Lenin, thanks for coming, man."

Lenin folded the newspaper he was reading, a gesture surely performed for his benefit. "Don, I've got reservations," he said. "There was talk recently. You on the up and up right now?"

"Yeah, bro, fine."

"You have a place to go? Enough to eat, all that?"

Where was he going with this? "Lenin, I'm fine. I got nothing going on that selling a little bit of my overhead wouldn't cure. I mean, I appreciate the concern."

"I'm not concerned about you." Lenin was drinking a cup of coffee in a small round cup with a saucer. He sipped, and Donny waited for a pinky stuck out.

"I wouldn't fuck you."

"Everybody who starts out says that, but people still get fucked, so you can see my apprehension." Donny would've got his ire up and laid down the law, but he wasn't in possession of the sacred tablets at that point. Having an ego cost money.

"What do I have to do to prove I can handle this?"

"You can handle this, Don," Lenin said. "You have half this town as a connection. I don't see you having a problem distributing it. But you have to have a safe place to store it, or you're going to be spending all your profits on a nightly motel-rate. And then why would you be doing it?"

"So you know I got evicted," Donny said.

"I sell to your landlord."

"No shit." Donny swigged his beer. "I can flip whatever you got in there, go to him tomorrow and square right up. He's not mad, he just wants money."

Lenin gazed into his coffee, as if Donny's fate was in the swirls of creamer as a form of divination.

"Okay," he said. "I usually start people out small, but I know you'll move the stuff fast, and I don't want to keep meeting. It's a kilo."

He slid a cloth bag under the table and Donny picked it up.

"I know you do coke normally, but all I could get was H," Lenin said. "It's okay, though. There's no fentanyl. It's downright therapeutic."

Rob

His cubicle was unassuming, not like Mary's cubicle across the aisle. She had keepsakes like waiters at family restaurants showcased tokens on their suspenders. She'd only been there for a few months longer than Rob, but she'd spent her whole working life surrounded by walls that could be rearranged on a whim.

By contrast, his faux walls were decorated only in instructions, scripts, and code sheets, so that he could know what he was doing at a glance. He had a thermos full of home-brewed coffee, a holdover from his days out on site. It was a thermos his mother bought him last Christmas. It was red-and-green tartan patterned on the case and didn't pick up a smell no matter how long coffee or soup sat in it.

His mom said she laid on the charm with the store owner, playing the everybody's kindly grandma role to get the seventy-dollar one for the price of the fifty-dollar one when he told her she spent too much. He didn't know if she played the owner or was playing him because she didn't care how much it cost. Her patron saint was Robin Hood.

His mother was up and knitting on the rocking chair when he left that morning. He made it a habit to go downstairs and check on her before going out. He'd been on the job for two weeks. She usually wasn't up so early, but it was a rough night.

"I think I got two hours last night," she said. "My buddies were running around poking me."

Her "buddies" were the neurons misfiring along her spine.

"Toe-Joe and Jimmer-Jammer were on my toes, up my leg and down. I don't hurt from it or anything but made it hard to sleep."

"I'm sorry, Ma. Anything I can get you on my way home from work?"

"A new back?"

"You gotta get some sleep, though. And please don't drive anywhere today."

"I'm not driving anywhere." She looped the yarn around the needle.

"Don't know what they'll tear down this time."

The day after the Stroll, his mom came home after a trip to her outpatient appointment in tears, as the house she'd shown him every time they drove down Second Avenue and the pub where she spent her youth were nothing but a pile of rubble with construction fencing surrounding them.

Fifteen thousand dollars. Rob had time to make calls and send faxes and emails since he was working out of an office. He could get a loan for everything he needed for her surgery except fifteen thousand dollars. Two weeks ago, during the party, he would've seen that as a slightly lower, but still impossible, bill. But by the time he got through orientation, he hit the phones with a twenty-four-ounce thermos full of hope.

Commissions. That was the name of the game in the top floor of the Continental Building on Fourth and Federal, where the Green Island Bridge flowed into the division between the downtown and North Troy. They worked on percentages of sales. They weren't selling anything.

The company bought properties, similar to the outfits that advertised on telephone poles, the kind where "J-U-N-K" might be part of the phone number. But they didn't buy scrap houses. They bought houses that developers wanted and tried to get them to accept a slight premium on their properties. They even had the power to offer ten percent more than what was listed on their sheet.

There was a downside, though, as Rob found out. Carrots that came with many sticks. Mainly the fact that the developers were usually working with their city governments, and if they couldn't get the sale, they'd go through eminent domain and take the properties. But it was a lengthy and drawn-out court battle. It was cheaper to offer above-market value. Either way, they won.

He wished he hadn't seen the name Jordan Wilson on his sheets. He wouldn't have recognized the address of 1 Warren Drive, because he didn't know that sloping access road that led to Sam Wilson's actually had a name. But there it was, a property on a list of properties, a name on a spreadsheet, last name, first name. The breath he let out was the wind out of his sails.

He picked up the phone, preparing to claim ignorance at the rule he was breaking.

"Mitchell Realty, this is Jennifer."

"Jen, it's Rob."

"Rob, where are you calling me from?"

"I'm at work. I need your help."

"You have some nerve. Why don't you have Danielle help you?"

"You too? Does everybody know about that?"

"I was there, remember?"

"I don't remember much, trying to forget what I do remember. I need your help as a realtor. If you were there, at the party, then do it for Jordan. She's the owner, and it's to help her out."

Dead air. Then: "Go ahead. We are not making this a habit."

Rob explained his job, read off the address for Sam Wilson's and gave her the "premium" amount they would offer her to sell.

"Okay, hold on," she said. Rob could hear clacking. "So you like her?"

"Who? Jordan?"

"Danielle."

"Not like that. We're friends."

"I have to say you two looked cute together, however inappropriate that roller coaster would be." She stopped clacking, then some more dead air.

"That's slightly above what it's worth," she said. "I like the place, but if she was smart, she'd take it and go buy a dance club in Albany or something."

"Damn. All right, thanks, Jen. Sorry I was a dick."

"Whatever. Last time I help. Normally I make money when I work." She hung up.

He glanced through the details of the purchase request. The requestor was the Troy Economic Development Agency, which made sense given that they had designs on the oilfields. That man Harley told Jordan that they would work with her. He was staring at the lie, and short of losing his only way of paying for the surgery, he was helpless to stop it. He didn't have long before he heard a rapping on the felt of his cubicle wall.

"Hey, can I talk to you for a second?"

Rob turned to see Harley, smiling like he was trying to sneak a wary dog a pill.

Asher

December wasn't the banner month for the Fulton Square Lodge. After the Stroll and the EDC convention left, they were on lean times. True that it was never empty so long as there were in-laws in town, or trysts or fires that sent the victims out in need of a place to regroup. Of course, there were the permanent travelers and the homeless people who lucked out on a coupon from a shelter, and there were always drug dealers, hookers and johns, but not as many as some other places outside of the city. It was too expensive to be profitable for those who made their pay on human degeneracy.

Asher wore his new tag with ironic pride, because really he took on a bunch of extra responsibilities for an extra ten cents an hour and the ability to write Assistant Manager on his resume. He didn't earn the honor; the previous assistant manager, Dale, left for the branch in Albany, and Bianca was going to college for a job that would be impressive enough to be her entire resume.

Basically, he was a certified Shit Boy now. He still worked the front desk, and he had not one underling to boss around. He could suggest that Bianca do stuff, and she would recommend he lick the ashtray out front.

He did have to pay more attention to the big picture stuff. Cherie was training her replacement, and she told him he'd get nasty jobs because management means making sure ten jobs are done, even if only five people show up. So in between the extra work, responsibilities, and the outside coffee he could now afford, he was learning the business.

They had three weddings booked the week before Christmas, plus another EDC meeting. That week promised to be an overtime week for everyone. He would get to make the schedule, which he thought was great at first, until he realized that most workers had plans. Meaning, those extra hours would be his hours. He'd likely be ordering pizza on Christmas Eve.

But he wasn't getting pizza today. He was at Dom's Subs, waiting for Rob Paulson, who he'd met at Craig's funeral party a week ago. Rob told him he was working at the building across the street, and they'd been grabbing lunch since he started. They mostly hit Troy Legends, a famous counter lunch shop or the Kettle, which Asher hadn't been to, odd since it was fairly close. The past week they were playing pin-the-tail-on-the-phonebook, and the tail landed on Dom's.

In a sad way, Rob was a reminder of Jordan, like the scent of her perfume or a song that played on her stereo. Asher wasn't pining for her, not anymore. He didn't think he'd see her until at least summer, when she might have shows over at Sam Wilson's. It's not like she had any reason to reach out to him. Ginny was her contact with the band now. And when she met Harley, he knew there was something. She didn't mix business and pleasure, but everybody says that until they find a way to redefine the words.

It was brisk as he made his way down Third Street. Dom's was on State Street, on the block that emptied into Monument Square. It, like the cross streets, were tree-lined and populated with brownstones and old brick rowhouses, painted in light blues, slate grays, maroons, and darker trims. Dom's was the converted basement of one of the rowhouses, with a large ground-floor window, neon sign illuminating the Dom's logo and the word *Open*.

Asher walked in. Rob was already seated, which was usually the case. It wasn't because of the nature of their respective jobs; Rob was punctual.

"Hey, man, sorry I'm late."

"It's cool." Rob handed him a wrapped sub. It smelled like an Italian mixed, the one he bragged to Rob about when they were figuring out lunch. "I grabbed you a sub, in case you had to go early."

"That's nice of you, how much?"

Rob wiped his mouth with the corner of his napkin. "We're even."

"Nah, I'll pay," Asher said. "You're saving for your mom."

Rob put his palms on his knees as he looked up out the window. "I need a favor, so that's my payment."

Asher sat down and unrolled the wax paper. Dom's was glorious in that they put double meat on their subs, assuming that real people would be the ones eating them. The lettuce was crisp, the banana peppers and the tomatoes were succulent and juicy like they should be, and they glued everything together. Even the pickle that came with it was better than what he could find in the store.

"I'm assuming it's an actual favor, with a bribe like this."

"It's Jordan, remember her? Sam Wilson's?"

"Of course," Asher said. "What's going on?"

"They're trying to buy her out." Rob reached into a satchel he had slung to the back of his chair and pulled out a piece of paper. He put it on the table and pointed.

"That's her entry," he said. "I told you they pay me to try to get people to sell their properties. She's on my list."

"She doesn't want to sell Sam Wilson's, that's her baby."

"I know. And these guys I work for are all, 'Take the honey or we'll force feed you the poison.' And it's a good offer, according to my ex-wife."

Asher looked at him funny.

"She's a realtor. I got in serious shit for calling her about it. They're checking on me. That guy Harley smiled his way through reading me the Riot Act about contacting Jordan."

"What do you need me to do?"

"I could probably sneak a call to her, but I have to call her and try to do my job. If they're listening, and we talked, they'll know. They might fire me, or they might give her name to someone else. Either way, she needs to know, and I'm not the best person right now."

Asher chewed through a quarter of his sub, not realizing that being an assistant manager built up an appetite. Or maybe he wanted to eat as much as he could before turning Rob down.

"Dude, she likes Harley," he said. "And she kind of thinks I'm a scrub that has a thing for her. If I tell her this, she's not going to believe me."

"At least she'll know."

"But what I'm saying is, she will tell Harley if I tell her this, and he'll know she got warned, and that'll fall back on you."

"Just tell her not to tell him."

"She's not going to listen to me. She'll call him. She doesn't trust me, I don't think, and she does trust him."

"Try. Or at least pay attention in that hotel. They have standing rooms, the people I work for. Keep your ears open. Maybe you'll hear something we can use."

Chapter Twenty-One

Jordan

It came in an overstuffed manila envelope, addressed to Jordan at Sam Wilson's. She'd gotten plenty of mail for printing and marketing services, sending her samples of their work like pens and mousepads, notebooks, even a mug that she used to keep golf pencils in by the cash register. They were always generic, with the Sam Wilson's name, not the logo, and a price sheet. And if this envelope hadn't had the Troy Economic Development Council name and logo on the corner where the sender's address usually went, she would've dismissed it.

The brochures and flyers showed a menagerie of photographs, a testament to the glory of a city that marched into the industrial revolution from the front of the pack, a city that was so successful, that at one time, it had more millionaires than any other city in America. Jordan didn't know that, but there was lots of arcana about the city that lay buried in the historical archives for Easter-egg hunters to uncover on social media.

They were clever in the fact that they mixed the history with the drawings, at the turn of the century, of what Troy would look like currently, and conceptual art of what modern Troy may look like over the next twenty years. Jordan wished she could afford to hire the designer who did it.

The flyers were strewn about the bar, the radio at quarter volume. Jordan picked the packet apart to the three pages that were specifically for her. Harley had told her he'd look around Sam Wilson's during the party a week ago, inspecting it for the EDC so that he could get back to her with what they wanted changed. If it was minor, she could fix it herself, through a small loan, barter, or the old classic, beg, borrow, and steal. She'd set aside pride to save the place she was living in more than her apartment.

But it was decidedly not minor, cosmetic stuff. It looked like Harley had inspected it to determine how ready it was to be a full bar and restaurant, and Jordan's kitchen was little more than a fridge, counter, pantry, and the centerpiece of a commercial two-basket fryer. A fryer that, according to Harley's itemized list of fixes, would have to be replaced.

Doc Lucian had taken a temporary residence at Sam Wilson's and began assuming the role of night security and handyman, payable with food, a cot in the back room, and dibs on the liquor she kept in the basement, which was the elevation it deserved. Doc cared not.

"Okay, Jordan? You look like a mean dog bit ya," he said as his sweeping crossed the section where the stage area narrowed to the bar area.

"If you want to call the city a mean dog, yeah." She took the calculator off the shelf by the mug. "Hell, they could tear the place down and rebuild it with the amount of money they'll have to give me to fix it."

"Maybe that's what they aiming to do."

Doc stopped sweeping and rested his hands on top of the broomstick, and his chin on top of his hands.

"You need people in here, honey," he said. "I'm not a guy for city politics, grants and loans and all that, but I know restaurants. Ran a few in New Orleans, good ones. What made them good wasn't the food, not when you were running it, no. You could sell slop to a thousand people a day and you could sell high cuisine to ten people."

Jordan held her head in her hands. "It's winter, though. I figured I'd have at least half a year to line some stuff up. I'm gonna have to pull out all the stops, I guess." Jordan bounced her train of thought off the tracks in search of a few more stops, but one was straight ahead.

"Can you watch the place? I have to talk to this guy real quick, run downtown."

Doc rested the broom against the bar and wiped his brow. "Go git 'em."

The building they were in a week ago was now a full office with a coffee bar on the ground floor. Jordan took the elevator up this time, grabbing a view of the Hudson River as she went up to the second floor, where a secretary had Jordan wait for Harley. It was strange, because she could see his office, if one could call it that, with its white modern desk, large screen monitor, and ergonomic leather desk chair, set apart in style, and probably cost, from the other chairs throughout the second-floor half-cubicles.

She was not the only one to need Harley's ear that day. She could gauge his gravitas in the EDC by the body language people used when they approached him. He was friendly and courteous in his expressions, but also forceful, like he wanted people to be comfortable or fake it. He was a person she knew a thousand times over on Broadway, a power player, the star that defines the constellation.

"Miss Wilson?" the receptionist said. "You can go ahead."

Jordan walked over to Harley, who by then had turned his back, forcing her to call his name. He turned around, and those brilliant white teeth could damn near reflect the street below.

"Hi, Harley, I got your packet."

"Have a seat, Jordan." He motioned to another desk chair.

Jordan sat down as she pulled out the papers.

"You were … well, you were thorough," she said. "This is a lot right here."

"It is, but if you could imagine what it'll be when it's done. Sam Wilson's will be one of the places they take pictures of when they advertise Troy."

"That's great and I could use it, but I was spit-balling the costs of what you said—"

"Don't shoot the messenger. I just reported what the EDC said."

"Either way, it's a lot of money. I need to know how I go about applying for the grant."

Harley swung around and grabbed a business card off his desk. "Do you like Thai? There's a great little restaurant. It's on Fifteenth Street, if you can believe it."

Jordan pulled the papers closer to her. "It's dark in there."

"That's a problem?"

"It's too dark to fill out paperwork," Jordan said. "I like to read the fine print."

"We're just talking. Assess some options."

Jordan got up and walked to the proscenium. The square was desolate.

"My landlord in Brooklyn," she said. "He also owned a restaurant off Broadway. Freshest fish in New York, really, you can look him up."

"Jordan—"

"He got the fish from the biggest supplier at the Fulton Fish Market. And he got it out of the guy's truck. Do you know how many dinners it took to get that deal?"

Harley kept his smile, but his eyes were soaking up carpet.

"Just send me the application," she said as she walked away. "If you deliver it, we'll have a beer. My treat."

Danielle

Swallowed pride tasted like three-day-old coffee. But there wasn't enough change in the change drawer to get a new cup from Tollsby's.

A week ago, Danielle learned that absent some form of divine intervention, she'd lose her house in the new year. Craig owed too much—*she* owed too much. She couldn't scrape together the three thousand dollars she would need just to pay the mortgage, not when she was closer to twenty thousand in debt to various lending institutions. Craig never once mentioned taking out a loan, and Danielle, despite being at the mailbox half the time, never saw an envelope from a bank. She never even heard from a debt collector until two days ago, when they started calling her at work.

Danielle was stopped at the light at the intersection of Hoosick and River Streets, under the overpass. A man in a puffy purple jacket and what looked like pajama bottoms bounced across the street, moving in a way that, at five a.m. meant his day was winding down. She plucked a cigarette butt out of her ashtray, one of the many she would leave in there when she didn't have time to smoke a whole one. She didn't normally pick them back up, but her newfound poverty demanded tribute.

Her eyes still hurt from the night before, from the tears that she thought were done and gone, the well shut after so many hours facing the loss of her best friend. But her mother had all the elbow grease she needed to unclog the well.

Danielle was in the kitchen when she made the call, feeling some comfort in the hum of the refrigerator, which was an odd thing, like the ticking clock you give a lonely puppy to make it think there's something there. She was on the landline so that her cellphone could charge.

"Mom, I really need you to just be a mom and help. No judgment, okay?"

"No judgment," her mom said. "But Dani, I'm going to give you my opinion. I love you. I'm not going to smile and tell you everything's going to be all right if it's not. You have your friends to do that for you."

"I need your help. I don't know where to turn, and my friends can't help me here, not with this."

"You need money, is what you're saying."

Danielle sighed. Leave it to her mother to reduce everything she was going through to its simplest terms. "Yes, I need money."

"Dani, you and Craig couldn't afford that life, that house... the car, maybe. But not that house. I'm not surprised he took out a loan. But if he owed twenty thousand on the loan, and you guys were thousands behind on mortgage payments, how did you not know? How did they not kick you out before now?"

"I don't know," Danielle said. "I don't know any of it. But I can keep the house if I pick up extra hours. I can sell the car and buy something cheaper, or lease something. I'm a single mother now. I'll be able to get some help."

"You're not going to sit in the welfare office," her mother said. "No daughter of mine is going for a handout."

"Jesus, what is it with you and that? It's like the homeless shelter you guys are fighting."

"I didn't move to this neighborhood to share the sidewalk with alcoholics and nutcases, and I didn't help put you through school to see you break out the food stamps when we go shopping."

"So we starve."

"So you move," her mother said. "You move up here."

"And pull the kids out of school, away from their friends."

"That's cute, you think you can afford the Academy. You'll have to pull them out, anyway."

Danielle pulled a mug out of the dish strainer. "I can't just give up like this," she said. "Craig would turn in his grave if I yanked the kids out of Troy."

"If he left you abundant options, you wouldn't be calling me."

"I'll have to think about it. Let me try some stuff."

"That's fine," her mother said. "But if you sign up for welfare, in any form, and I find out about it, don't call here looking for a place to stay. I'm serious."

Danielle hung up, and the well her mother loosened began to spurt.

She made the turn into the hospital parking garage. It was new, and she would have ordinarily asked the valets to park for her. But it wasn't their job to park for hospital staff. They did it as a favor. She decided to cut out all unnecessary favors to save up for the oncoming slew of necessary ones.

The hospital was mercifully quiet, decked out in pine wreaths, polished brass bells, red velvet ribbon, and synthetic jolly. Everything said Happy Holidays, even though Grace was a Christian hospital. Not that any of that mattered to Danielle, as long as there were presents and eggnog. But it did remind her that Christmas was a little over a week away, and she'd only begun shopping before Craig passed.

She saw Marjorie, head nurse of the sixth floor, and her boss, for lack of a better term. She was hoping to run into her after she'd done a few rounds and got her flow, but it wouldn't change the ask.

Danielle explained her situation, and what she needed, for each of two cases.

"Hon, I will do everything to get you as many hours as I can, but you know it doesn't work like that. I can't find something salaried for you, not now. And you know they just approved the hospital consolidation. That's three hospitals. I actually could get you hours if you want to commute throughout the Capital District for them, but you'll spend more in gas than you'll make in pay."

"What about adjusting my schedule for a commute from Saratoga?"

Marjorie shook her head. "Again, I can try, but I can't promise. And I think you're looking for promises."

"I kind of am," Danielle said. "And Saratoga's a last resort."

Marjorie hugged her shoulders. "Have you considered working in Saratoga?"

"I'm trying not to."

Donny

Selling heroin was different than selling coke or weed, which Donny had experience doing. Cutting it was different, sure. One of the things Donny left in his apartment was milk sugar, which was great for cutting coke. But heroin was going up veins. And he didn't want to leave a trail of bodies behind. Fuck them, they make their choices, but dead customers stop buying.

It had been a week since he got the satchel and the kilo. Lenin was right to have faith in him, because he had the man paid off in three days. Donny owned a little black book of every addicted creature in the five-one-eight area code. More than that, he knew the functional people—the lawyers, the forklift operators who had a clean piss sample at the ready. And he knew the girls that could barter for drug money, and the very few he'd invite to his motel room to barter for a taste.

Donny made enough to pay his landlord and move back into his place, but since he found his stuff out in the cold on the front curb not even two days after he was evicted, he wouldn't give that son of a bitch a penny. He was fine where he was, at a small, twenty-room motel on Congress Street, going up the hill, past where the old county jail was. It was fitting that all of the drugs and prostitution that Troy had to offer had sprouted in the sight of the old bars, like weeds coming up through a new concrete sidewalk.

He was cold. His coat looked warm, but it was hollowed out to fit his business interests. He waited for the bus with people going to work nine-to-fives, keeping to himself that he was already working the twenty-four-seven. He felt powerful and alone, with a pocketful of fifties and nowhere to call home.

He wanted to call Danielle, or Ginny, or even Rob, if it came to that. He wanted to pay Jordan back for what he did to her Microbus, but the cops had shown up. She actually called the cops. And if she did that, could she even be trusted to take his money, or would she sound sweet on the phone and lay a trap for him? He felt like he was on the other side of the mirror.

Why did he care if Danielle kissed Rob? What if she fucked him in one of the bathroom stalls, what would it matter? Craig left. He took the fuck off. He was frolicking in the old neighborhoods of heaven or getting a heating pad shoved up his ass in hell. Either way, he wasn't tuned into the reality channel. If he cared about what happened here, he wouldn't have chased pills with liquor. So Danielle had a moment, so what?

So what if it wasn't with him?

Donny's hurt had wrapped itself around Danielle, but since he'd become homeless, he wrapped it around the Troy version of sex, drugs, and rock-and-roll. He had money. He was able to buy an old hardcore CD from the Beat Shop downtown, and he went to one of his few remaining friends to get it put onto his phone. He still had a phone, which was good. He was able to barter for coke, weed, and he even tried the product, which was a time-honored no-no, but he did it anyway, and it was glorious. And he had girls any time he felt like making a call—it was harder to order chicken wings.

He left the hotel after last night. That was when the clouds cleared under the tightrope he was walking, and he got a glimpse of the ground.

Sandra was five-foot-six and compact, like she used to be a gymnast. She wasn't like the other girls that came to see him. She had curves and muscle tone. Her tattoos—they all had tattoos—were professionally done. And she wore black glasses.

She was quiet when she came to the motel. Her first time, she had money. The second time, she wanted a front, and Donny knew better than to front to a heroin user, no matter how well put together. So she bartered, and it was so good, Donny told her that she wouldn't need money if she brought that to the motel every time. He didn't see that he was paying for sex, 'cause dope wasn't money and if she didn't like him already, she wouldn't have gone down on him, right?

Last night, she sucked him off and fucked him. He hooked her up, and he heard the sound of a baby crying coming from her purse.

"What the fuck is that?"

"It's my little girl. I'm keeping tabs on her with my baby monitor."

"I didn't know you had a…" Donny said. "Wait, how can you be monitoring her? Those baby monitors have a range."

She pulled her jeans up and buttoned them. "The other part's plugged into the car ashtray."

"The fuck do you mean the car ashtray? Is your kid in the fucking car?"

"I can bring her in," she said. "I didn't think you'd want her in here when we were, you know, working out a payment."

"You left your fucking kid in the car? A baby? Right now, in the car?"

"Look, I'll just get out of here. You're freaking out, dude."

"Don't come back," Donny said. He got up and grabbed all of her stuff, which consisted of her purse and her coat, opened the front door, and dumped it on the walkway.

"Asshole," she said as she knelt down to pick up her stuff. Donny had half a mind to knee her in the head, but he knew it would only keep that baby in a cold car longer. He shut the door and paced the motel room. Child Protective Services wouldn't be any help in saving a baby if her mother's heroin dealer was the one who called.

He wished it was warmer where he went after the motel. He couldn't stay there. It was a mirror that reflected a scumbag. And he didn't know if Sandra was the vindictive type. This new place might be hell, in every sense of the word, but he'll be reminded every minute of where he is. No more rock-star dreams. Just business. Just living for himself. It was very "back to nature."

He walked up 114th Street and turned off on Third Avenue. At that hour, the sun was barely poking through the hills in the distant sky visible beneath the clouds. Most people weren't going to work yet; they were showering, or pounding *Snooze* on their alarm clocks.

He turned into the yard that had a No Trespassing sign on it, a sign he quickly ignored as he made his way to the slate-blue Queen Anne. It has an ample yard surrounded by a gate, and it had something else, the reason for the sign—a decayed, fallen roof and a large square placard with a reflective orange X on the front doorway, marking it as condemned.

Donny had found the perfect place to camp out, a fellow disaster waiting to happen.

Chapter Twenty-Two

Rob

The sound of a cash register signaled another round of Pink Floyd's "Money," which the company Rob worked for had. They'd pump these motivational anthems through the speakers in the ceiling at elevator muzak levels. Others included "Eye of the Tiger" and "We Will Rock You," but Pink Floyd was up every time Rob noticed the music track.

Maybe the bosses missed the irony, but goddamn, was it effective. Over the past week, Rob got three people to agree to sell their properties, even if the people he got were called "dumpers"—people who were only holding on to their houses or businesses because no one wanted to buy their shit for more than the cost to tear it down. A fair market offer was manna from heaven.

Rob made a percentage based on how low he could get them to sell below the dollar amount on his screen. If he offered the full amount, he'd get twenty-five dollars, which wasn't worth the screen burn on his eyes. He'd done far better by working out a fair amount for him and them and standing his ground as he made the case. At least he could sleep at night.

He was on a second call with an elderly gentleman named Earl Miller. He'd made an offer last week, and Earl needed time to think. Rather than pressure him into making a quick decision, like a few of his cubicle mates,

Rob took his number down and promised to call him back.

"I thought about what you told me," Earl said. "About this street, how we're going to be looking. I still don't know."

"Do you need more time, Earl? I have your number. I can always call you in a week."

"I doubt your boss would be too happy about that."

"Eh," Rob grabbed the pen off his desk and spun it between his fingers. He adjusted the mouthpiece and the earphone. "I've been here two weeks. How long have you been in your house?"

"Forty-five years."

"Right, so if you need time to think, you get time to think," Rob said. "I wouldn't try to get in the way of that. It's a big move."

The line was quiet for a moment.

"Is that Pink Floyd I hear?"

"Damn, you've got good ears."

"Everything else is shit," Earl said. "God, fate, whatever … gotta leave something. I saw them when they were first in the country. It was down in the city. July, '68, if I remember right. They weren't as big as they got, but I had a blast."

Rob chuckled. "They're playing all kinds of classic rock to pump us up. I like the songs, don't get me wrong, but they can be distracting. Hard to concentrate."

"What did you used to do?" Earl asked. "I can tell this wasn't your out-of-high-school job," Earl said. "So what'd you do before?"

"Union welder."

"Tradesman." Earl shuffled papers in the background. "Figured we were kindred spirits. I used to be a longshoreman at the Port of Albany. Union too. Fucked my back up, but you know how it is."

"I was lucky. I just got burn scars all over my arms."

Again, the line went quiet. Rob could hear Earl breathing. He wondered if he was strapped to an oxygen tank.

"I lived here forty-five years," he said. "Raised my kids, had my first granddaughter piss on me when I was dumb enough to change her on this chair I'm sittin' in." He chuckled. "Now my kids are trying to get me into a retirement community, said they could put me up on Diamond Rock, like it's still in Troy, so it isn't what it actually is. But they're struggling, too."

"Everybody's so underwater, makes you wonder who's left in the boats."

"But you see my dilemma, right?" Earl said.

"I do," Rob said. "If you don't want to sell, I will leave you alone. I get it, and I'll tell them something so that they take you off the list. But they want the property, and if even if you keep the place for its memories, you might be opening your front door to a parking garage or something."

Earl was quiet again. Rob could only imagine the weight of what he was asking, what an old man was trying to hold on to while questioning the reason, the weight of one decision.

"Tell me you get something for this," Earl said.

"If I offer you the total, I get twenty-five bucks," Rob said. "If I lowball you, I get..." He checked his chart. "Hmm. Five grand. Something between the two, then."

"You really suck as a salesman."

Rob leaned forward in his chair to crack his back, something he never had to do when he worked with his muscles. "I'm a union welder."

"Send me the paperwork, kid."

Rob spent his lunch break in the break room. Earl Miller agreed to take the lowest offer, and that left Rob with the entire commission. It also got Rob a pizza of his choosing as an office bonus, hence his time in the breakroom. He decided to share it with Vanessa Hawley, a punk girl with the sides of her pink hair shaved down. She was the youngest person working there, and so far had proven herself to be a better office snoop than a salesperson.

"Thanks for getting just cheese," she said as she folded a slice. "I could've picked meat off it."

"Their cheese pies are good. I'm not picky. I didn't pay for it."

They chowed a slice in relative silence, punctuated only by the perfunctory compliments about the food. Vanessa wiped her mouth with a napkin.

"So you got the big score," she said. "What'd you have to tell him?"

"I just talked to him," Rob said. "Made the case."

"You know, you can lie to them."

"You can't, no."

"Yes, you 'can't,'" she said. Trust me. I was 'coached' to make up housing statistics if they asked. And that was by our boss's boss, that guy Harley."

"You've been lying to people?" Rob set down his pizza.

"Not me," she said. "I haven't sold shit. I'm just working here long enough to get my guitar fixed. It's not worth the bad karma to actually sell something here." She smiled and pulled off another piece. "No offense," she added.

Asher

The weather people were gathered around a graphic on the floor, a virtual-reality model of the snowstorm that was heading their way. They had a few days, which meant that Asher could practice his walkway shoveling and ice-spilling moves before he needed them, in time for the forecast to change into rain. If he was lucky, he'd get to use the snowblower they had in the garage, a two-stage number that they bought to replace an electric version that could only reach the front walks surrounding the porte cochere.

"AM, that's all you, that walkway," Bianca said. "They aren't paying me enough."

"They're paying me ten cents more, and AM? Really with this?"

"Sorry, Mister Assistant Manager, sir."

"Can't it be just Asher?"

"Nope," Bianca said. "You are now crowned AM for eternity."

"Whatever." Asher would've loved to say that Bianca was giving him a hard time because she was jealous, but there was not a person in Fulton Square Lodge that envied Asher in the least bit.

"Oh, my keepers," Ginny's voice was an unmistakable, yet welcome, addition to the dead quiet of the empty lobby.

"Hey, Ginny," Asher said.

Bianca performed a minor courtly bow. "Guinevere…"

"I'll take it," Ginny said. "Okay, it's five o'clock somewhere. Time to pack my belly before I go out. Where we ordering from?"

"When was the last time we got something from Johnny Conk's?" Asher glanced out the window at the barbeque restaurant, which was a burgeoning local chain, and had an outer look not totally different than Sam Wilson's, with its darkened, weathered wood exterior and neon signage. Asher liked their pork ribs and smoked brisket.

"Are they quick?" Ginny said.

"Quick as any pizza joint around here."

Ginny pulled out her wallet and flipped through a stack of bills heavy in twenties and tens. She nodded to Bianca.

"Find me something good, and yours is on me."

"Deal."

"What about mine?" Asher asked.

"You got a promotion," Ginny said. "And Bianca's going to need money for textbooks soon."

"Fine." Asher walked over to the front vestibule to stare out the windows. "A damn dime and everybody thinks I'm a one-percenter."

He couldn't get mad at Ginny, not just because she was his drummer. She was in and out of the hotel, claiming she booked it every time she wanted to drink downtown, but that wasn't the truth, not the whole truth. Despite her overflowing personality, Ginny was lonely. Unlike Asher, she didn't cherish her solitude, so she reached out place to place to find somewhere to belong. And her room wasn't just rented by the night.

Asher's phone rang. He almost didn't recognize the number at first, because it was new to his phone. Most of the time, Rob called him to grab lunch from his work phone.

"Hey, Rob, what's going on?"

"Not much, man. I got a fat commission today. Five grand."

"Damn, lunches are on you the rest of the week."

"Nah, it's earmarked for Ma. Look man, I had to skip over Jordan today in the calls. What did she say when you told her?"

Asher wished that he could tell Rob he got over himself and called her.

"I didn't yet," Asher said. "I'm trying to find the right time. I might go down there."

"Asher, man, listen, call her. I mean tonight," Rob said. "Look, I was talking to this girl that works here today. We had lunch, that's why I never called. This place, the EDC, all this renew Troy shit, is going to happen. They don't give a fuck if they tell people the truth or lie to them, and they're only buying shit up to tear it down." Asher could hear a TV in the background. "If they're telling Jordan they can make a deal, they're screwing with her. She was cool to us. She didn't have to do that for Danielle."

"Then why not have Danielle call her?"

The line was silent. "I think you know why."

"She'd listen to Danielle."

"C'mon, Asher, play through whatever you got going on about her. Tell her what I told you. If she believes you, she does. If not, you tried. That's all I'm asking. Five-minute call, if that."

Asher turned his head to see Ginny dancing and Bianca waving her finger around from behind the counter like a conductor.

"All right. I'll get over my shit. But you need to take your own advice with Danielle." Asher hung up, not trying to come across as pissed, but if Rob hadn't made life weird with Danielle, he wouldn't be looking up his contacts for Sam Wilson's.

"Good evening, Sam Wilson's, this is Jordan."

"Hey Jordan, this is Asher. You remember me, right?"

"Of course I remember you, Asher. What's up?"

Asher wasn't one for flowery language, and he couldn't sell crack on Fourth Street at 3 a.m. without a script, but he laid out what Rob told him in as simple terms as he could; they were trying to buy her out, so they could turn Sam Wilson's into something much less vertical.

"Why would they give me a chance to fix the place? They're sending me a grant application."

"Who? Harley? I wouldn't trust him. He's a part of their thing. Look, Jordan, we care about you. I care about you."

"How long have you known this?"

"Is that important?"

"A little bit. It sounds like you've been sitting on this."

Asher didn't want to lie to her. He realized how important it was for her to believe him, even if it made her hate him. Even if it caused him a little heartache.

"Jordan, I know you don't—can't see me the way I see you, but I was worried that you wouldn't believe me. I assumed you'd go to Harley about it and he'd smile and say some sweet shit and then go fire Rob."

Jordan was quiet, and Asher knew that storm clouds stood still before they poured.

"I just have one question and I'll let you go." Jordan's voice was quiet, flat. "You say you care about me, how you have feelings for me. But how can you have feelings for someone that you have so low an opinion of? You need to find someone better. Or maybe be someone better yourself."

Jordan

She wanted to slam the phone, but she was on her cell, and the force she'd use would blow the screen to bits. Instead, she ran her hand across the papers on the bar and flung them to the floor in a flurry of curled corners. Her hand still hurt from filling out the grant application, which had arrived the day before. Now a waste, if Jordan believed Asher.

The problem was, she believed Asher. She hated him, his self-absorption, his decision to withhold the truth because he assumed she was some bimbo who was stupid enough to have a schoolyard crush on a guy who could fuck her in all the wrong ways. Asher decided to put her behind the eight ball, and she wouldn't forget that.

But as she looked around at the empty club, whose last customers were the morning breakfast crew that she never built the place for, that had to bring the breakfast from the gas station and only got their coffee from her.

Doc Lucian was gone. He had everything he needed except a thing she couldn't give him, a freedom that found him when two shopping carts and a sheet of murky plastic housed him and he held court at the Empire State Plaza. He didn't want to be taken care of.

She walked around looking for something to do. Doc was good, and she'd miss the work. She started Sam Wilson's on a napkin in a bar in Brooklyn, after watching them take thirty at the door for the privilege of sitting at an overcrowded bar to drink overpriced drinks and go home and brag about the aesthetic of a business that was a pastiche of a nineteen-twenties speakeasy.

When she looked close—because she had time between shows—she realized that everything they had, everything that created a multimillion dollar operation, was obtainable through the same sources she used when she designed theater sets.

She knew she never could've opened in Brooklyn, and yes, she knew opening in the Capital Region ran the risk of being an empty house, but she had the spirit to do it. She made it her mission as she found the property, going and even sleeping weekends at the very hotel her would-be friend worked.

She didn't just walk into a bank and apply for a loan; she became a lay expert in the process, creating a business plan that, had she located in Brooklyn, would have her franchising by then. The loan officer even asked her if he could use her plan, censored, of course, to teach their new hires. It was that good.

She found a commercial antique dealer in Albany that made their business going into historic buildings and pulling out frames and fixtures before they were torn down. Every part of Sam Wilson's was born of the history of the Capital Region that stretched back more than two hundred years. In fact, if she had known that thing about Samuel Wilson's bricks earlier, she would've had one.

Chalk that up to another thing Asher told her that was too late to do any good. That's why she was so pissed. If he had told her last week, she would've known it when she went to see Harley. Maybe she could've confronted him, or maybe she could've watched his eyes, but she would've known. Rob couldn't tell her without risking his job, and she got that. Rob had talked to her for a half hour during the party. If he could pay for his mother's surgery, he couldn't be asked to give that up. He was a saint in her eyes for even risking it enough to tell Asher. Hell, she wouldn't have blamed him for withholding it from her. At least he had a reason.

She picked up the papers. Someone could still walk in and want to get their five o'clock on a little late. And she needed it because scratched into the margins on the three-page itemized list was the amount also listed in the grant proposal: a hair over a hundred thousand dollars.

And that was the last bullet point on her list of eternal grievances. Despite Asher, despite Harley, despite a slow winter, which she pretty much expected, it all boiled down to a hundred thousand dollars. Make that, and they'd have no reason to shut her down, or at least no easy excuse. Not make it, and they'd likely descend on her passion like it was a fire sale.

She made a call that she was hoping to never make.

"Yo," the voice said.

"Charlie, it's Jordan."

"Whattup, kid?"

Jordan took a deep breath. "I need your help."

"Told you, you would," he said.

"Shut up."

"What do you need help with? I'm guessing it has to do with your spot, or you wouldn't be calling me."

"You were right, and I hate you for having to say it."

"You're not closing already, are you?"

Jordan explained it to Charlie, the EDC, the plan for the oilfields and the itemized list. She didn't want to, but she told him the figure she came up with.

"Wow, good luck with that. A hundred-fucking-grand, that's nuts."

"Tell me about it. I want to raise the money, like, crowdsource it, and do a benefit at Sam Wilson's, so we can raise money and show it off to people."

"You had a party there a couple weeks ago, right? Craig Hill, his thing?"

"Yeah, but no one's really come back."

Charlie yawned. "Sorry, not you," he said. "Yo, look, that EDC shit, they're bastards. They're trying to turn Troy into New Brooklyn. I don't even recognize half the people in my neighborhood anymore. So I'm in, anything to stick it in their eye. But Jordan, yo, a hundred-thou, I don't know if we can get there."

"Let me worry about that," she said. "Can you get Headcase to play?"

"When?"

"I want to do it the day before Christmas Eve."

"That's like a week from now," Charlie said. "You're not serious."

"As serious as it gets," Jordan said. "You're all still in bands, so you all can play, don't tell me you're out of practice."

"We're out of practice as a group, though. Why not at least wait till New Year's, or after the first of the year?"

"Need the money quicker than that, Charlie."

"You still have to set it up and invite people. It's a big undertaking."

"I got five hundred people to show up at Prospect Park when you guys played that Halloween show back in what … ninety-three?"

Charlie coughed. "Look, Jordan, I'll get the band together. Fuck it and fuck that EDC. But, and I'm not trying to be an asshole here, you know if you can grab even three hundred people on a week's notice to show up for a concert, they probably wouldn't be trying to take your shit." He coughed even harder. "It ain't like it was."

Chapter Twenty-Three

Danielle

The fireplace was empty as the snow fell outside, adding to the eight inches that fell overnight. Danielle did manage a roaring fire, however, on the fifty-two-inch flat-screen that was affixed to the wall above. A fifties Christmas crooner belted out the classics, and she felt comfort in scratching vinyl.

She held cocoa in her hands while she sat, dressed, under a red blanket Craig bought. It was bright out, even without the sun. They predicted a few inches, and she'd covered her car with a nylon sheet. Now the sheet was buried. She'd have to call into work, not because of the car, but because Marybeth and Joey both had snow days.

Joey bounced in the room with a foam football and pounced on Danielle's lap, nearly tipping her mug over. "Mom, do we have to be inside all day?"

"What are you gonna do, play catch with Beth? Good luck."

"Teddy's mom is taking him to the park to go sledding," he said. "I want to go, too."

"How do you know that? Did you get on the computer again?"

"No, mom. He came to my window."

"If I find a scratch from another rock—"

"He just yelled."

"He better just yell. Or come to the door like a normal child." Danielle took a sip of her cocoa, made from the packets, but with milk and half-and-half and her own multicolored marshmallows.

"I can't let you go and not Marybeth," she said. "I'll take you two out."

"I want to go with Teddy. Please-please-please…"

"We'll see," she said. Joey drifted, his eyes on the flames in the screen. "Bud?"

He turned to her.

"I went by your room last night, I wanted to check the smoke alarm in the hallway, I heard you."

"I was faking it, mom," Joey said. "You're supposed to do it, and I don't know how."

"You never have to smile or frown … or cry, if you don't feel like it. But you're my kid. I know all your fake tears. That's not what I heard."

Joey ran his hand along the arm rest.

"I don't want to cry," he said. "When I cut my knee, Dad said real men don't cry."

"Your dad cried at the end of *Bambi*," Danielle said. "And you laughed. You go ahead and cry, kid. Any time and place you want. Don't worry about anything."

"Why don't you cry?"

"God, I cry every day," Danielle said, her eyes tingling at the mention of more tears. "But I don't do it around you and your sister because I don't want you guys to cry."

"You said it was okay to cry. Why isn't it okay for you to cry around us?"

Danielle's mom liked to say *out of the mouths of babes* every time either of the two said something clever. She let out a laugh.

"I have no good answer for you." *My insightful son…*

She swept her blanket off her shoulder. "I'll go over and talk to Jane and see where they're going. I'll see if she wants to double-up. Don't say a word to your sister yet. I don't want her screaming about it."

Joey mimed zipping his mouth closed, hopped up out of Danielle's lap, and ran off into the hallway.

Jane had been her neighbor for five years, which was enough time to have watched Marybeth grow up. She was blessed with two things: ten-year-old fraternal twin boys and an abundance of patience. She was able to stay at home to watch them, which wasn't as nice and privileged as it sounded because she had a home job doing data entry for a medical firm.

They drove out to Frear Park. It was the gathering place that day for kids with their sleds and parents with coffees from every gas station and convenience store in north Troy and Lansingburgh. It was still snowing, but it was slowing down, the flakes getting finer. The road, slick when they arrived, had a layer of salt and sand down, and the center of the road everybody was parked on was brown and slushy.

Danielle and Jane stood on top of the hill their kids were sledding on, Jane on her phone and Danielle smoking while she could.

"You ready for Christmas?"

"Not even close," Danielle said.

"Shit, I shouldn't even have asked. You know, small talk."

"No, it's coming. I mean, they just lost their dad, I don't want them to lose out this year under the tree. They'll end up hating Christmas every year."

"You mean they'll be like us?"

Danielle laughed. "I don't hate Christmas. This one sucked big, but…"

"If you need help this year, no one will blame you for reaching out."

"Their grandparents on both sides are planning on spoiling them," Danielle said. "They'll have presents. Maybe not from me, but I'll be happy if I can keep a roof over our head. That's goal one right now."

"Is it that bad?"

Danielle took a drag and waved to Joey as he was coming up for another run.

"You gonna keep the house?" Jane said. "I'd hate to have to break someone new in."

Danielle flicked the ember of her cigarette into the snow. She turned and smiled, trying to hide the weight of the bills on her kitchen table. "Shit, I broke you in," she said.

They sat at the counter of Collar City Eats, a combination burger joint and ice cream shop that was renowned for serving a burger and fries that were full grease and no nonsense, and ice cream cones all year round. Why Joey wanted ice cream after immersing himself in wet snow for a whole morning was a mystery. Why Marybeth wanted the same thing was not— she loved her brother.

"Grandma said we were going to move to Sarah's toga."

"You mean Saratoga?"

Joey sounded it out. "Saratoga. Are we going to move away from my friends?"

"Honey, I hope not," Danielle said. "Your grandma needs to talk to me first before she tells you stuff like that."

"If it's true, I won't get to see Mrs. Pix have her babies."

"Who's Mrs. Pix?"

"The gerbil in Miss Rafferty's room," he said. "She's got a big ol' belly, and she might give babies before Christmas. I want one. If we move, they'll all go to Mr. Barnes's pet shop, and Billy said they'll get fed to a snake."

"Joey, if, and I do mean *if* we have to move, I'll talk to your teacher and make sure you get one of the babies."

Their food showed up on patriotic-themed paper plates with a flood of napkins, all of which she knew would be used. She knew because when she was sledding, or swimming in the South Troy Pool when she was eight years old, and her mother brought her there to eat, they gave just as many napkins out, because through the decades of her life, Mr. and Mrs. Kowalczyk were growing older together with every patty, dog, and grease-soaking bun. Because it was Troy and its institutions didn't leave.

She watched her children beginning their memories, and she realized she had to be an institution, too.

Donny

A rip in the arm of his jacket was what turned Donny's downfall into a freefall.

It wasn't a monstrous rip; he'd worn out better clothes at his job, when he had one. But he couldn't fix it, and he didn't go up Hoosick Street to go buy another coat. And, in truth, it wasn't just the coat. It was his shirts, his pants, and his shoes. He was a drug dealer who was living like one of his worst-off customers, and now he was starting to look like it.

He woke up to a face full of snow yesterday morning. He had to move himself into the basement to get dry, but then he was sharing the space with furry, shitting, pissing things, and even he could smell it on him. It would all be unbearable if he wasn't digging himself out of a depression with a burnt spoon.

The freefall, in all its glory, came at the third-floor balcony of the Atrium, the closest thing Troy had to a mall. It housed mostly state workers, and while it did sometimes hold events and saw foot traffic, it was almost as much a shell of itself as Donny's current squat was. It was the dead nature of the place that drew Lenin to discuss business up there when McEntyre's was closed.

Lenin was dressed in a black leather coat and jeans and a red plaid deer hunter hat. He had the picnic table cleared off, and sat in front of two coffees, one of which he handed to Donny.

"I don't really do coffee," he said.

"Today you do," Lenin said. "You look like shit."

Donny didn't want to argue with his supplier. He took the coffee and upon his first sip realized that it was something he needed.

"Lenin, I'm a hair short, like fifty bucks," he said. "But Christmas is coming, and business always picks up on Christmas."

"Lots of family drama to escape from, I get it." Lenin removed the lid and blew on the black magic, kicking up a cumulus cloud of steam into the cold tight air. "But I can't give you any more."

"I need it to pay you back. Are we not cool?"

"We're fine, but I'm worried about you." Lenin took a sip, holding his hand under his lips to catch any dribbles. "I don't really give a shit about clothes, styles, and whatnot. I got mine, other people got theirs. But I care when people that are moving thousands in product can't keep at least decent clothes on their back.

"It's bad for business, but more than that," he said. "If you're dressed like a junkie, how do I know you're not doing junkie shit when no one's looking? I can't have that."

"I ain't a junkie, man."

"I hope not, but I can't take the chance. I started moving weight 'cause I got tired of seeing that junkie look on people's faces. You got that look right now. Like you want to beat the shit out of me, but you're too shelled out to do it." He got up. "We're square on the fifty," he said. "Christmas bonus, we'll call it. But if you want more, I need it up front. Build yourself up. Clean yourself up."

For Donny, freefall smelled like lighter fluid and felt like the pure prick of the last needle in the pack he'd bought at the pharmacy on Sixth Avenue, where all the junkies went, at least the ones who cared about having their own needles. But downfall was the realization, after he came to later that day, that he'd have to sell at least some of the dope he pinched to buy food. And that meant going out into the city.

He didn't know how he ended up in front of the Kettle, scoping out the lunch crowd, looking for panhandlers who had a good take. But there he was, and he was cold and alone, and wishing he had never shot his hand through that window and got himself kicked off the crew. He wanted his apartment back. He wanted his life back. He needed a friend to pull him back like he'd done so many times before, a friend whose grave he visited two nights before to smoke a joint.

When Rob tapped him on the shoulder, he nearly flinched. Of course

Rob would pick now to blast him in the face and get some payback. Donny couldn't do anything except applaud his initiative at this point. But he wasn't expecting a hand presented to him.

"Donny, if you're not pissed at me, you want to join me for lunch?" He said. "My treat. I owe you."

Donny went in with him, because if he had it in him to fight, he'd have knocked Lenin's teeth out for cutting him off. Also, he was hungry as hell.

The owner wasn't there, which was good, but Rob was a regular, apparently, and he said he'd take care of it. They ordered off the breakfast menu, and Donny saw a western omelet that caught his eye.

"Why you treating me to breakfast, man?" Donny said. "I mean, I hit you in the face last time we saw each other."

"I deserved worse than that, truth be told." Rob unfolded a cloth napkin and set it on his lap. "You were looking out for your friend."

"Are you trying to fuck her? Answer me honestly."

"Donny, I haven't talked to her since. So no."

"But you want to, though, right?"

Rob picked up a butter knife and tapped it on the table.

"I'll say this, if I met Danielle, and I never knew Craig, and it had been a while since he passed away, I'd probably want to get with her."

"You had a daughter before."

"Yeah," Rob said. His eyes took in the table. "It felt comfortable, man, being with her and the kids at the Stroll. It felt right like I hadn't felt since Juliet and all that went down with me and Jennifer.

"I know it looked like I was taking liberties at Sam Wilson's, but when I saw her crying, it felt like I had to hold her. I just, for like a second, completely lost my place and the situation. Do you see what I'm saying?"

Donny nodded. A waitress came over to take their order, Rob called her Sheila. She had high hair and Donny thought he saw her play in a band at McEntyre's one time. He asked, and she admitted to moonlighting in a cover band.

They drank coffee and watched the noon crowd come in and get seated.

"I get you, man," Donny said. "I'm not going to apologize for punching you, but I misjudged things."

They got their food, and Donny inhaled it like a dog in a shelter with a trough it had to share.

Rob's phone rang. "Hey, Dad." His face crinkled and his eyes got big. "Is she okay? How?"

"What's up, dude?" Donny mouthed the words.

"I'll ask at the reception desk once I get there." He hung up. Then he made another call.

"Harley, I need to take the afternoon off," he said. "My mother fell. She's in the hospital."

Rob

The parking garage at Grace hospital was new, a four-story structure taking the place of a parking lot that held a lifetime of memories. They never thought of stuff like that when they were drunk on the prospect of progress. He remembered once having to kiss the parking lot ground before Juliet would get out. It was because they watched a comedy where a guy got out of a plane and kissed the ground theatrically, and she had a hysterical laughing fit. She died a few years later. So it was their joke, a joke that was in chunks of asphalt in a pile somewhere.

A rug did it, according to his father. She snagged her foot against the corner of the rug on the landing. He said she was conscious and could wiggle her toes. In fact, he said she fought him about going to the hospital in the first place, and only agreed after his father threatened to take her car keys, an impossibility for anyone who knew her.

"I'm gonna stop at the gift shop on my way there," Donny said, who decided to tag along with Rob to the ER. "What's her name, so I can find her?"

"It's Theresa," Rob said. "That's cool, man. You don't have to get her something."

"Everybody likes a little teddy bear when they're hurting, even dudes."

Rob laughed. "Even dudes?"

"You should try it, next time you're sick. I mean injured, not sick with the flu."

They exited the garage and were halfway to the emergency room entrance. Donny held his hand for a second.

"Maybe you should get that fist checked out."

"You think I hurt it on your head?"

"Didn't you put it through glass? That thing could be infected, and you don't want that."

Donny shoved his hands in his pockets. "I was here a couple weeks ago. They gave me the antibiotics. I'm good."

The walked through the automatic doors. Donny split off for the gift shop and Rob followed a small corridor to the waiting area. It was dense with the sick and all who loved them. There were coughs and sniffles, and the smell of vomit competed with the smell of disinfectant in a death match.

Rob walked up to the counter, where the receptionist was protected behind Plexiglas, her back turned to him. He waited patiently, his only course of action.

"Are you here to be seen?"

"No, my mother was brought in."

"Name?"

"Theresa Paulson."

She ran her fingers over the keyboard and the light from the computer screen reflected in her glasses. "She's in there. Have a seat and someone will come out shortly."

Rob sat in the back corner, holding a seat for Donny and one for his dad, who he assumed was in there. Grace was notorious for its long waits. If his mother hadn't been taken there in an ambulance, she could've broken her neck and been made to wait ten hours to be declared paralyzed. The thought of it, paralysis, not the wait, punched Rob in the gut.

He ran through all the mental moves he always did when she fell. It was her fault. She wasn't watching where she was going, always in such a damn hurry. But then he'd think of how he saw her raise her feet to avoid the rug when she didn't think anyone was looking. She didn't want him and his father seeing her be cautious.

It was the rugs, these goddamn rugs today that they don't make with even a thought to people that might get caught up. Why does a rug have to be a half-inch thick? Can't they make a good, gripping rug that's thinner? But of course they could, they did, and his parents had nothing but safe rugs.

Then it was the meds. They gave her meds for her migraines, meds for her pain, and they expected her not to be dizzy and woozy when she stood up? Couldn't they kill pain without fumigating a person's equilibrium?

He created reasons that his mom fell, and battled each one, and in the end his heart deflated when he realized that, even if he found a culprit, even if they could solve the problem this time, there would be a next.

Fifteen thousand dollars separated them from hope, from peace of mind. Ten, he should say, now that he got that commission. But how many could he get? How long would he have to work there? They were racing against the clock.

Donny walked in with a small brown bear as the door opened and a nurse called out, "Theresa Paulson."

Rob got up. "That's my mother."

"Come on in."

He followed through the groans and whispers masked behind long white curtains threaded through hooks and grooves in the ceiling. He listened around the corner for a louder, jovial, familiar voice, and found his mother, sitting up in the bed, curtain wide open, his father standing next to her. She was joking with a nurse, which was about what he expected.

"You okay?" Rob said. "Jesus."

"Lord's name, watch it," she said. She turned to the nurse. "This is my loving son, Rob." The nurse introduced herself, then went on her business.

"Mom, what happened?"

"She tried to get—"

"Hugh, my dear, he asked me." She picked up a cup of apple juice and fiddled with the straw.

"I was trying to get out the last of the Christmas decorations from the back," she said. "And there's a lip in the doorway to the kitchen. I caught it with my toe."

"We gotta fix that," Rob told his father. "Mom, Dad, this is Donny, a friend of mine."

"I bought you a teddy bear." He handed it over.

"I love it," she said. "You didn't have to, honey."

Rob looked at his mother's face. "Looks like you got beat up, ma."

"You should see the floor."

Donny laughed.

"There's got to be something we can do," Rob said.

"I just need that surgery," she said. "I'll rob a bank if I have to."

Chapter Twenty-Four

Asher

He looked over his work from the night the snow fell, when he had the misfortune of catching the overnight shift. They hired a truck to come in and handle the parking lot, but they couldn't rightly tell the guests to move their cars out until the plow had a chance to come through, so tons of cars got plowed in. That meant that a slow trickle of guests that were late-night bar-bound would come in and ask if they could get plowed out. Asher could've asked Benjamin, the other night worker, to do it, but Benjamin was a sixty-five-year-old man who complained every time he was asked to take the trash out.

Truth was, Asher didn't mind. He considered it acts of penance, or time out to think about the hole he'd dug for himself with Jordan. She was right. He had her too high on a pedestal there wasn't room for an opinion; he held her so high he could never touch her, and he'd fashioned her to be delicate ivory when he was learning she was more diamond plate.

Why would she go to Harley if he gave her a heads up? All he had to say was not to, or to keep it between themselves. She would've been armed against that douche.

He pulled an extra cigarette out of his pack and lit it up. Bianca was working and, oddly, she was taking it easy on him. Maybe she felt bad that he had to use the shovel and snowblower all night. More likely, Christmas was coming, and based on the bells coming off her ears, and the plush reindeer antlers clipped to her head, she was tipsy with holiday spirit.

His Christmas spirit was kept in a bottle on his dresser, where it stood since last Christmas, when he replaced the one before. Christmas was over for him decades ago, when his mom brought Chad home and his dad tried his hardest to act like Chad was a new family friend with a skateboard wrapped up in Noel paper, not the guy who was fucking his mom while he was in school. They were separated on New Year's Eve, and he was living in two homes soon after.

He flicked the butt into one of the snowbanks, knowing he'd be the one that would have to pick it up when the snow melted. He had trust in the cosmic law that decreed him to be eternally screwed. He had trust issues when it came to Jordan. He had trust issues that any loose thread on his sweater could unravel. But he kept hitting a wall when her name came into his head.

She didn't want him. He might as well have been a customer in her bar. Why should she have been at the mercy of his trust issues? He knew the deal when Rob asked him to warn her. He wasn't sharing a secret with a love interest; he was on a CB radio, telling an oncoming trucker about Smokey.

Asher walked into the hotel and saw Harley talking to Bianca. What the hell was he doing there?

"Hey, Asher, right?" he said. "Long time, no see."

"You staying here? I thought you guys were only here for the weekend of the Stroll."

Harley pointed his finger around. "I work nearby. Got a loft. We're having a meeting this week, a few people from New York, a few people from here. We've booked out the ballroom across the street."

He pointed to a pin on his shirt of an Uncle Sam top hat with the outline of New York state in relief. "If you see anyone with these on, can you direct them over to the ballroom? Oh, and you know, be nice to them, of course."

He smiled chlorine and patted Asher's shoulder on his way out the door.

"That guy's a scrub," Asher said.

Bianca gave him a muted raspberry. "I like him," she said. "He's respectful, which is more than I can say for half our guests."

"Con artists are respectful until you check your wallet."

"How is he a con artist?"

Asher told Bianca about Harley's and the EDC's plans to buy out properties and steamroll over them, including Sam Wilson's.

"So you're saying he's giving people money to get the hell out of Troy, and they're gonna bulldoze the buildings and put cool stuff in?"

"You're making it sound better than it is."

"It sounds like some people are going to really hate them. I'm sorry for your friend and her business, that is foul, but ... Troy needs it."

"I can't believe you're okay with gentrification."

"I can barely afford to live in Troy right now, and for someone my age, there isn't shit to do. I have to go to Albany to party, and there isn't shit to do there either. Look, I love the history, and they should be preserving it. But I'm tired of seeing houses with those orange Xs on them."

"It's not fair, you work your ass off for something, and they can take it from you, treat you like you gotta beg them to keep what you earned."

"That's every tax time," Bianca said. "What I'm really hearing is you like that Jordan girl, and this is pissing you off because it affects her. 'Cause the Asher I worked with a month ago didn't even read the paper."

Bianca had just left when Asher got a call he would never have expected at that point. The Call ID read Sam Wilson's.

"Jordan?"

"Hey, Asher. I got a favor to ask, I know you might not want to help, but it's small."

"No, Jordan, whatever it is."

"I need to talk to Rob, but I don't want to message him on Facebook. I know you two hang out at lunchtimes, right?"

"I'll see him tomorrow."

"Can you have him call me here, then?" Jordan said. "I'll stick around."

Asher cupped his back pocket. "I have his number somewhere in my wallet. Do you want that instead?"

"If you got it, thanks."

Asher pulled out his wallet and flipped through cards until he found the business card that Rob gave him for the contractor he used to work for. His number was scrawled on the back. Asher read off the number.

"Got it," Jordan said. "Thanks."

"Jordan, I want to say I'm sorry. You were right. I have issues, I know, and they have nothing to do with you. But I made them about you when I didn't do the right thing. I'm sorry."

Jordan was quiet. Asher was going to sum it up with a goodbye when she said, "You know it's not you, right?"

"What's not me?"

"Go online tomorrow, on my page. I'm calling on everyone, and I wouldn't mind if you were one of the 'ones.'"

Jordan

Sam Wilson's was closed early. All the lights were off except for the flames from a handful of Saint candles she got at the behest of Doc Lucian, before the funeral reception. Jordan sat behind the bar wondering if they were really bringing the kind of mojo that Doc claimed.

She had her laptop open to a word processing program, and she'd filled three pages with meandering text. She wouldn't use it and would likely delete it by the end of the night, lest someone get a hold of her laptop and sneak a peek at her innermost thoughts.

She opened the browser tab that had her new CrowdPool campaign. She felt bad. Most people used CrowdPool to cover medical expenses and memorial funds. She used to laugh when brides tried to raise money for a Tahiti wedding, or people used CrowdPool to cover their cable bills. Now it was time for someone else to laugh at her.

Charlie called her earlier. His news was mixed.

"I got the band to play," he said. "But we went through the set list we used to have, and seriously, these guys only remember about twelve songs. You might want to scrape together some more bands."

"Do you think any of the old South Troy bands can come out?"

"I actually tried. I thought of the four bands were used to play with all the time. Trigger Mortis is all split up in other bands, and only one of those bands is still in the area. And they said they couldn't. Scarry Night, fuck them, they're crackheads now. Deform said they could play next year, which doesn't help. That leaves Strike, and even I remember shit wasn't cool between you and them."

"No, it wasn't. I wouldn't even care now, except that Dillon still hates me, I'm sure."

"He's a dog with a bone, so I'd say so." She could hear the bubbling of Charlie's bong. He gasped, then coughed. "I still don't get why you want the show to be the day before Christmas Eve. Why not New Year's Eve? It would give us more time."

"Personal reasons," she said. "They might not be smart, but they're real. Besides, it's a charity concert. Christmas is the most charitable time of the year. After Christmas, the giving spirit wears off and people start thinking of that bill coming in January."

"Then you should've started earlier."

"I called you when I realized how bad it was. And I have money. Just not enough to fight off the city if they want to steal my shit."

"Well, sister," Charlie said. "I got your back. I'm sharing the shit out of your CrowdPool. Shaming motherfuckers, so you should see some cashflow."

There was about a hundred dollars in there currently. It was a start. Jordan stared at her phone. She only had a few minutes before eight o'clock, when she announced on her page that she would be doing a live post about the future of Sam Wilson's. She pegged out ten minutes in her mind for what she'd have to say, but ten minutes could've been five minutes or an hour once she was actually talking.

She watched the clock on the far wall until showtime. Pulling up her phone's camera, she hit "record."

"Hey, everybody. Jordan Wilson here. I have a lot that I want to say, and a few things that I don't, but I'm going to say them anyway."

She cleared her throat. "I grew up in South Troy, right off the canal, actually, on a second-floor apartment on Fourth Street. It really is 'us against the world,' and even though I left after high school, South Troy never left me.

"I went to school for theater arts in Oneonta and I've spent twenty years down in the city working on and off Broadway—hey, my theater peeps." She smiled and waved, and noticed people commenting words of encouragement.

"I recently came home to start my own business, a bar, concert venue, called Sam Wilson's, and that's kinda why I'm here right now."

She grabbed her cigarette and took a drag.

"Some of you, only a handful of you, know about my childhood, what I had to go through, and if I have to tell you all that, expose it to the public to keep this place, I'm tempted to. And that says a lot, if you're one who knows. But I want to say that if you grow up rough, you learn not to take anything for granted. You learn to fight. You learn that the high road was made for people who had the luxury of being born up there. We're not all so blessed.

"I have a pretty damn great place here. A sweet stage and enough room for about five hundred people to dance, we're right on the river, and I'll get you any brand of liquor that is your favorite.

"But the city doesn't think it's good enough. They want me to pump a hundred thousand dollars into the place so that it meets their definition of worthwhile. In fact, they don't think South Troy's good enough for the rest of Troy either. That's why they're trying to change it. They don't want my club wrecking their nice little reflecting pond. They want me to sell, and if I can't raise that money pretty quickly, I might have to."

"I'm not good at doing this," she said. "Asking for help, rallying the troops. I used to be a one-woman army posting flyers back when they were drawings on paper, but the game was all about telling hundreds of people where to go. Now, it's getting even twenty people *to come*." Jordan adjusted her phone. I'm rambling because I put my heart in South Troy and City Hall's got me on the table for an open bypass. I don't want to lose this place, and if you come to the benefit on the twenty-third, the day before Christmas Eve, even if we can't save it, we'll have a helluva goodbye party that'll be legendary. Did I mention Headcase will be playing?"

"Come down, or donate to the CrowdPool," Jordan said. "Before you unwrap your presents, consider dropping me—and South Troy—one."

Danielle

She woke up twice, to two phone calls. The first was her mother, who knew Danielle had the day off and called at six a.m. sharp. Danielle hoped to never be so naturally a morning person.

"What are your plans for Christmas, with the kids?" she said, her first words after "hello."

"It's six in the morning, Ma."

"I have a bus coming to take me to the casino today."

"You also have a cell phone."

"You're awake," she said. "Do you not know what you are doing for Christmas?"

"You know I have to work Christmas Day," Danielle said. She yawned. "You're getting them, right?"

"Yes, yes. I was worried that you might not have much under the tree for them this year, considering."

She was guessing the right situation at exactly the wrong time.

"I didn't lavish on them, but I did get them stuff, don't worry." Danielle didn't dare tell her that most of her shopping was done at the five-dollar store.

"I have a mountain of stuff for them here," her mother said.

"Are you going to spoil them now so they don't think about their dad? It won't really work. He used to play with their toys more than they did."

"I'm thinking that maybe I can pick them up on Christmas Eve, so they wake up on Christmas Day with presents."

"So I don't get to see my own kids on Christmas, Eve or Day."

"I wasn't saying that…"

"Call me when you win at slots, Mother." She hung up.

Her second wake-up call was at eight, which was respectable business hours, since she'd already seen Marybeth and Joey off for their last day of school before Christmas break.

"Danielle, it's Gloria. Your mother-in-law."

"I didn't forget you, Gloria."

"I wasn't sure," she said. "I haven't heard from you. I assumed we'd be able to see the kids sometime on Christmas Eve or Christmas Day."

Shit. For once, Gloria had a right to be offended.

"Sorry, Gloria, I wanted to see what my mother had planned. She wants them on Christmas Day. I'm keeping them on Christmas Eve, since I have the day off." She got back out of bed. "Tell you what, let me have you coordinate with my mother. That way you can both get them on the actual day."

"I don't mind visiting them on Christmas Eve, if you'd rather."

"That's okay. Christmas Eve was something that me and Craig did with them, it's a whole little thing. I want to keep that going. I'll give you my mother's cell. Tell her I asked you to call. She's up now."

Danielle rattled off her mother's number.

"Thank you, Danielle," Gloria said. "Can I ask you something personal?"

"Sure," Danielle said, for lack of a better option.

"I heard some things," she said. "I know I can't tell you how to live your life, or how to move on, but the kids are young. I heard you and someone … had a moment … at the reception after I left. Are you planning to bring him around the kids so soon?"

Rob. "Gloria, it was a weak moment. A mistake. We're both sorry it happened. So, to answer your question, no," Danielle said. "But someday I am going to meet someone. Craig wouldn't want me to raise the kids alone. And then, you're going to have to be okay with it."

"I know," Gloria said. "It was just soon, is all. I'll call your mother."

Gloria hung up. Danielle tossed the phone on the bed before tossing herself back on it.

Danielle wrung the pine oil out of the mop and slapped it down on the dance floor. She was impressed by Jordan's video the night before. She was more impressed that Jordan was so generous to Craig's reception, seeing as how she needed so much money to keep the lights on. Sam Wilson's was scrappy and warm, like the garage when your parents told you that if you cleaned it, you could make it your clubhouse.

The floor didn't need a bath. Danielle needed somewhere to go, and the kids were occupied, so she was off. She used to relish solitude, but since Craig died, he was in every shadow, a benign but indifferent presence. She found herself needing to get out of her headspace. It didn't help that Gloria threw the net of suspicion on her over Rob. Maybe scrubbing the floor was returning to the scene.

"Do you need more soap?" Jordan called out from the back room.

"I don't think I need this much," Danielle said. "This floor is spotless."

Jordan came out with a bucket full of rags. "That's not the compliment you think it is. This floor is only clean 'cause no one's stomping on it."

"That's gonna change tomorrow."

"Hope so. Or this place is gonna wind up at the bottom of a pond."

"Then we'll be neighbors," Danielle said.

"What do you mean?"

Danielle balanced the mop handle and walked over to the bar, where her root beer waited for her. "I'm about to lose my house."

"What? When? And why?"

"Gonna have to move, first of the month, foreclosure."

"Don't you have insurance, like Craig? Life insurance?"

"They won't pay. They think he killed himself. And if I didn't know him better, I'd almost believe that. The finances were his job, and we're so in debt I'd need ten grand just to be in respectable debt that I could pay on."

"Jesus, I could've helped you if you came to me," Jordan said.

"You're struggling, too," Danielle said. "I feel good being able to tell someone other than my mom, so swear you're not going to tell anyone, okay?"

"Sure, fine." Jordan poured herself a soda from the soda gun. "But what are you going to do?"

"I'm going to have to live with my mother in Saratoga, yank the kids out of school. Maybe get another job."

They shared cigarettes and sodas as they talked about the state of things like two old friends enjoying a nice view from a porch on two wicker rocking chairs.

"You know, you talked about your childhood in that video, or started to. If you ever really want to talk, I'm here. It feels good to let things out. I'm figuring that out now."

"I will," Jordan said. "But I gotta be iron for a while longer."

Chapter Twenty-Five

Donny

Craig didn't mean to die. Donny knew that, even when the lead-weighted murmurs beneath his daily hustle told him that his best friend had cashed in his chips. That his depressions were more than just the blues that everyone got when they ground their bones into dust for some paper with disappearing ink. But he'd never leave his kids. Pain or not, Craig didn't mean to die.

Donny didn't mean to die either, in the bathroom of the Tollsby's on Sixth Avenue, his concrete legs having kicked open the front door just enough to rest his shit-kickers in the corridor alongside the ATM and the magazine rack. He didn't mean to die but there he was, his breath on vacation, heart beaten and not beating and his head propping open the door to the only stall.

Donny didn't mean to die when he shot up the last of Lenin's shit, but he did mean to get high as fuck. Maybe he did mean to kill himself but couldn't admit to it. He was sleeping in a house that was owned by rats. He was in homeless clothes, and he was far past "roughing it;" he was just "rough."

Whether he meant to die or not, he found out quickly that he was going to hell. It started the moment his eyes opened to a fat man standing over him in a leather jacket, holding something between his two fingers and his thumb. He knew what it was because he knew things. Too many things.

His haze, his blissfully fluffy high was erased. He felt himself crashing into his body, into every itch and pain receptor at once and his skin was trying to morph into an insectoid creature out of a B-movie while he was trapped in it. He was dizzy and his mouth was dry and he was furious that he was there and he had teeth trying to rip themselves out of his mouth.

"Whoa, fella. You just overdosed," the man said. "I think you died. We called 911, just sit tight."

"Who the fuck are you, man?"

"I saved your life." He checked his watch. Did he have somewhere to go?

"I ain't need your help," Donny said. "I was just chilling out. What the fuck was that stuff?"

"Naloxone, and you were dead," The man said. "For almost two minutes. How do you feel?"

Donny started to get up, and the all-out assault on his joints and muscles opened up new fronts.

A girl in a Tollsby's uniform and matching black cotton visor walked over with a cordless phone in her hand. "Is he okay?"

"Yeah, but he's trying to get up."

"I'm right here, asshole," Donny said as he managed to get to his feet. The dizziness and the twitching, itching, consciousness-smearing pain competed for his attention, as did the do-gooder and the store worker, who by then had backed off a few feet.

The worker turned and mumbled something into the phone. The do-gooder looked at his Narcan sprayer and put it back in his pocket. "Look, man, an ambulance is on its way. That dose isn't gonna last—"

"Shouldn't have wasted it then," Donny said. He felt for his cigarettes, the last drug he had on him, and walked past the do-gooder toward the side door.

"You're welcome," the man said.

"Didn't fucking ask you, dude." Donny walked out with his middle finger aimed behind him.

The night bus that ran from Lansingburgh to downtown Troy would seldom finish its route without picking up a twitch case, a crack whore with a sparkling personality and a street merchant who left shit-stains on the seats. Donny made up that rule one night when he, Craig and Danielle would bus to the Yarrow on nights when driving promised not only to be illegal, but impossible. Now Donny sat in the back, twitching as the Naloxone continued to work on his opioid receptors.

He didn't understand how the spray took his high away. He didn't even remember getting the spray; he just knew it from what the guy had in his hands and all the articles and videos online. He used to say they should let those junkie losers fucking die rather than waste medication on them. Sitting there in a cold fever, he wasn't altogether sure his view had changed.

He got off in front of McEntyre's. He wasn't planning on going in, not from the front. He owed Mack, and looking like he did right then, he'd never even get a seltzer for fear he might decide to drink it there. He walked over to the corner and tried to gain some composure as he walked up Ferry Street and hooked through the alley.

The street layout in downtown Troy let one look down even the most crooked of alleys, see all the way to where it terminated at the Atrium. He could see a van's headlights coming down from at least four blocks away, and he could hear people talking in the patio behind McEntyre's. He followed the sound, which was earsplitting to him in his present state.

"Oh, shit, look who it is." Easy was sitting there, sharing a blunt with three of the guys in his crew. It was both Donny's hope and his fear.

"I ain't here to fight you," Donny said.

"I'd say so," Easy pointed to him with the blunt. "You ain't looking to be fighting anything right now. You looked wrecked, son."

"I need a favor, and we're square."

Easy's one friend said something, and his other friends laughed, but Donny couldn't hear it. He was furious, but desperate, and only one emotion could animate his frame at a time.

"I need a little bit, man. Even some Vicodin will help."

"Damn, you turned yourself into a regular, generic dope fiend," Easy said. "You suckin' dick yet?"

"Yo, fuck you, dude."

"So not yet. But you will." Easy reached into his pocket and pulled out a pill bottle and an empty pack of cigarettes. He tapped out two pills and put them in the pack. He walked over to Donny, who reached out his hand.

"Thank you, bro," Donny said. Easy placed the pack in Donny's hand but didn't let go. He leaned in and whispered in Donny's ear.

"You punched me in the motherfuckin' face 'cause I offered this shit to you not even a month ago and here you are, 'bout to lick my boots for the shit. That's a long fall, my friend. What you best do, if you're smart, is take these, even yourself the fuck out, and go march your pathetic ass into one of those twelve-step programs, 'cause you're so low right now I can't even diss you."

Donny took the pack and he tried to straighten himself up to make a graceful exit. Their laughter showed it to be a hasty retreat.

Rob

The back alleys of downtown Troy were a dicey proposition if you were trying to go clear across town, but if you were selective, and you knew the city through years of living and miles of driving, you could make it from the Continental Building where Rob worked to Sam Wilson's in less than ten minutes.

Odd thing was that he could've sworn he saw a guy who looked liked Donny, even dressed kind of like him, but unless Donny had hit the dirt faster than the speed limit on the highway, it had to be someone else. Donny left the hospital soon after giving Rob's mother the teddy bear that day. He'd have to give him a call or text message him after work.

His mom was still bruised, and it tore Rob up that he could still be grateful, if only because she didn't break anything or bend any pins.

Anyone that knew him would think he was as independent as a man could get. He was married before. He had, and lost, a child. He'd held a steady job for almost long enough to retire with a full pension, if he'd worked for a company with a better union contract, or any union contract longer than a square of paper towels. He was one paid-off house away from being perfect on paper. Except for Juliet, it was nothing if his mom and dad weren't able to share it.

They went everywhere together when he was growing up. They were both travelers who'd settled down, his mother, the late sixties vagabond of the Troy party scene, his father a continental hippie hitchhiker. When they had Rob, his mother often told him, they made a promise to show him everything that was out there and teach him to make his own sense of things. As he did when he had Juliet. That's what parents do: they sacrifice for their kids. Sometimes it worked the other way too.

Rob shook off these thoughts as rounded the bend and Sam Wilson's came into view. After Jordan's video, which he, and probably most of Troy, saw, she'd called him and asked him if he could meet her to discuss a private matter. He didn't question it, even if he did have questions. He pulled up in the parking lot and let out a sigh as he saw Danielle's car parked near the old loading area.

Rob walked in to see Jordan and Danielle at the bar, laughing at something on a laptop.

"Am I interrupting?"

"Not at all," Jordan said. Rob could smell the cigarette smoke from the entrance.

"Hey, Danielle."

"Hey, Rob."

"Cut it with a knife, you two." Jordan pulled the ashtray back out from under the bar. "I hope you all can deal with your business by the show."

"Won't be a problem. Just here because you called."

"And I really do have to go," Danielle said. She got up from her seat and pulled at the jacket upon which she was sitting. "How's your mom?"

"Resting," Rob said. "Thanks for asking."

"Tell her I'm using one of her scarves."

"She'll like that." Rob had brought one of his mother's scarves to the reception. Now he knew where it went. "Say hi to the kids for me."

Danielle smiled, and he could see the embarrassment in her cheeks. He was glad there would be a crowd at the party.

"Catch you at the party, my love," she said to Jordan. She backed toward the door in a dancing motion, hands waving. Then she was out.

"You two crack me up," Jordan said.

"I'm glad someone finds us funny."

"She didn't cheat on her husband with you, that makes her better than half the women out there."

"There's that, I guess," Rob said.

Jordan pulled a carafe off the coffee pot and filled up a mug, which she slid toward Rob. "I assume you're not drinking, since you're on the clock."

Rob held up the coffee before lowering it to his lips.

"You want to talk."

"I do, but Danielle said something about your mom. Is she okay?"

"She fell." Rob reached for a napkin to wipe his face. "She's in a ton of pain, she's got to take meds and a combination of things, she falls sometimes. But, she's okay."

"Is there anything they can do for her?"

Rob hesitated. Jordan had her own problems. "There's a surgery that can help stabilize the … stuff … that is causing her so much pain. It's not a cure-all, but it could help a lot. But it's twenty seven grand, and the insurance company are bastards, 'cause they think it's chasing good money after bad. A doctor actually told me that. I got it knocked down to ten grand, but still, ten grand's not exactly gas money."

Jordan sunk her cheek into her fist, arm propping her up on the bar counter. "That really sucks, man."

"She's an angel too, like a 'fills the food pantries' kind of angel."

"When do good people get a break?"

"Speaking of good people getting breaks, it looks like you got a ton of views on your video."

"I saw that," Jordan said. "I'm thankful that people tuned in, but the CrowdPool campaign is less than five thousand, and that's outstanding. But if everybody and their brother shows up to the show, and they all donate twenty bucks at the door, *and* add extra to the campaign, I still probably won't break ten thousand here."

"And you need a hundred, right?"

"Yes and no," Jordan said. "Grand total would be a hundred thousand, but I was researching the Riverfront Renewal grant, and they could theoretically cover half of that."

"Half is good."

"They're the reason I have to do any of it in the first place. You know they're gonna hardball the fuck out of me."

"What do you need me to do?"

"I may have to sell," she said. "There's a chance this is all for naught. If I'm going to cave to these assholes, I want them to pay through the nose, and I want you to get something out of it."

Asher

World music, with its flutes and soft drums and atmospheric sound that always seems to include falling rain, must be in a soundtrack CD delivered to every trendy coffee shop. Asher hit the Beanery before clocking into work. It was too late for the lunch crowd and too early for the after-work crowd, and the place was bare except for the respectably dressed homeless kids that could pass for college writers and, to Asher's surprise, his friend Mena.

She was oblivious to everything, her face buried in one of the circulars that the Beanery carried. She had a biscotti and a large coffee, still steaming, and her tablet had the background of a New York City night skyline.

"Hey, you."

"Asher. You look thin. Are you eating right?"

"Are you actually concerned, or are you fucking with me?"

"What do you think?" Her eyes returned to the paper.

"Since you're here, can I ask you something?"

"Are you getting coffee?"

"Uh, yeah," he said.

She handed him her cup. "It's the bold mix. I asked for the regular mix. Get me my order and we can talk." He took her cup and started for the counter. "A pumpkin muffin, too," she added.

Asher got his order, corrected and added to Mena's, and returned with the treasure. Mena set down her paper, elbows on her knees, interlaced fingers rested on her chin. Her yellow-dyed ponytail fell at the side of her face.

"So, Mr. Asher. What troubles your young mind?"

"If you're not going to be serious—"

"Chill out," she said. "What's going on? Is someone dead?"

"No, well, Craig died, but this isn't about him."

"What has you twisted?"

"There's this girl."

"Always."

Asher leaned back and rubbed his face. "Aw, c'mon…"

"Dude, with you, it's always a girl."

"Do you want me to go on, or do you have a diagnosis already?"

"Wow," Mena said. "She's really got you twisted. What's her name?"

"Jordan."

"Jordan Wilson," Mena said. "Stop right there."

"What?" Asher liked Mena's bluntness, but she was treating his hangnail with dull shears.

"Jordan is…" Mena said, "…and I'm going by how she used to be … *she's driven.*"

"So what?"

"You're not." Mena bit into her biscotti, holding her hand under her mouth to catch the crumbs. "She's the kind of girl, well, not a girl anymore, a woman, that needs movement in her life. She's gotta be piloting a ship in some destination. And you, my feathered friend … you're not any of those things.

"Don't get me wrong, Asher, you are a great guy when someone gets to know you. But you are okay doing the same thing, in the same band, at the same job, forever. If she even wants a man in her life right now, it's gonna be the kind of guy that makes big moves."

"So I need to make big moves," he said.

"No, you need to realize that she's not for you."

"Harsh."

"You bought me a pumpkin muffin, I figured I owed you the truth." She set down her coffee. "You want to try something? She's about to lose that place, if what she said on that video is true. Do something for her, as big or as little as you want, but do it knowing that she's never going to want you because of it. Do it because she's a cool person and could use the help. If you can do that, well, you won't get her, but you'll be doing a good thing."

"So do a nice thing without expecting anything in return," he said. "I do stuff like that all the time."

"Not when it comes to women that you like." Mena winked. "Gotta work on that."

Asher had finished making rounds in the lobby and on the grounds. The place wasn't dead, but it may well have been. The hotel may've been at capacity, but residents didn't have family members visiting over the Christmas holiday. Those remaining were the people who were on their last night of the Riverfront Renewal Project seminar, identifiable by their lapel pins, but also by the fact that they all looked, to a person, like the upmarket creatives that posed poor and shopped in boutique grocery stores.

Beyond envy, Asher tried to get mad at Harley and his crew, but he ran up against the wall of his lack of knowledge about what they were actually doing. But Rob, working in the boiler room next door, wasn't so naïve, and over their lunches, Rob had been fueling a fury in him.

These neo-yuppies were selling the college kids and the city council members a utopia, with new bells and whistles, capitalizing on the picturesque history of Troy, and it was great. Everybody would love the way it looked. All that room for those new stores that sell high-value products to high-value people. And if a few people were conned into selling their homes, their dreams, their institutions, what was the big deal? You couldn't live in the past and survive.

But everywhere Asher drove, he saw the construction of luxury condos and the destruction of the affordable stuff. They were bringing the stores in that sold twenty-dollar water and there wasn't any money in the coffers for the supermarket that sold three-dollar milk. They were attracting the talent from Brooklyn and Manhattan and letting the public schools hit the floor until they, too, would be torn down and remade in a richer image.

"Excuse me, sir." A man with a red plaid shirt and a bushy, oiled beard was standing in front of him with a lapel pin, a Riverfront Revival guest.

"How can I help you?"

"I got locked out of the Fulton Square Ballroom," he said. "I was wondering if you had a key."

Asher patted his shirt pocket. He was about to give him the key but thought elsewise.

"I can't give you the key, but I can go over with you, let you in."

The man adjusted his round, black plastic glasses. "That'll be great."

Asher found Benjamin and told him to man the fort, and they walked across Fourth Street.

"You know, we could use a local perspective tonight," the man said. "Would you mind hearing a little and telling us what you think?"

Asher smiled. "You know, I'd love to."

Chapter Twenty-Six

Jordan

Prayers were never answered in the real world, not by some angel floating down from the sky like snow to light upon the bills, or a sick relative, not in Jordan's experience. Unlike many of the people she knew, she did believe in God, but believed that He was indifferent to the plight of His creation, like a man who farts in an elevator and walks off. But it didn't stop her from praying the morning of the show; even if the lottery's a sham, you still buy a ticket once and again.

She opened at nine in the morning, knowing that no one would show up, but certain that there was nothing further she could do to get the place ready. And in true form, Troy pulled the unexpected.

Jordan had a small breakfast crowd by ten, mostly the crew of the Third Street firehouse, who chose her over the diner up the road, maybe only for that day. In her favor, she was able to serve them muffins, bagels, and hot coffee because she had stocked the kitchen the night before.

Doc Lucian had also shown up at her door, which was incredible, seeing as how he couldn't have seen her video. Turned out, he left a root bag in her back room, and he was fond enough of it to panhandle the bus fare to get over to Troy. She offered him a job that day. He took the job but waived his fee.

"You lookin' like you need every penny, Jordan," he said. "You been good. We're good."

In addition to the fire crew and Doc, Danielle showed up, Joey and Marybeth in her arms. Jordan found orange and grapefruit juice for the kids and fed them cookies.

"Obviously, I'm not going to be able to come today," Danielle said.

Jordan wiped the counter. "You're here now, that's what counts."

"I can't have anybody watch them. My neighbor has her in-laws over, and my girlfriend Sandy is away with her boyfriend and the kids to Florida."

"I could never do Florida at Christmas time," Jordan said.

"We did it last year. We had a choice, that, or a drone for Joey. Turned out he forgot about the drone once we got there. He liked the beach, though."

They made small talk, reminiscing on days of high school abandon and roaming the streets like they laid the asphalt, before the needs of adult life was placed on their shoulders. Joey chatted it up with the firefighters and Marybeth danced with Doc Lucian. Soon she, and everyone else, save Doc, left, and Jordan and Doc made busy work until noon, when the first trickle of people came in, including the members of Headcase.

Charlie brought in his PA system through the back, unnecessary since Jordan's was top of the line.

"We brought three more," he said. "They can use our shit. They didn't want to bring their own."

"Three what? Bands?"

"Shit Pot, Cyanide Lines, and Censored. That cool?"

Jordan hugged him. "You are a god, dude."

"Good, you can sacrifice beers to my belly."

By two, Sam Wilson's was as packed as it was at the height of Craig's funeral reception, and Headcase didn't go on until three. It was a weekday, and Jordan had decided to set the show from three until eight, even when she had one act. Now that she had three, she still didn't want to up it much past ten.

By four, an hour into the show and nearing the conclusion of Headcase's set, Sam Wilson's was packed. By then, both Rob and Asher were there. She put them to work. They used Charlie's PA, with his reluctant permission, to pump the show into the back, through the sliding-glass doors, into an area which was dug out as much as there was concrete, which gave Jordan enough room to handle the overflow, but barely. Every step she made was to keep the fire department from shutting the party down due to occupancy. It was a tidal wave that soaked the drought.

Things were chaotic, and there was moshing, but Jordan was shocked that no one broke anything substantial, not even each other. She would have some blood drips to mop up the next day along with the slush tracked in from outside. The bands rocked out with a fury she didn't expect for a Christmas show on such short notice. They were standing up for something bigger than her.

Charlie retired to the bar when his set was over.

"Hey, Jordan," he said. "If you don't make it—if you don't raise enough, don't give the money back to anybody."

"I'd kind of have to."

"Nah, you don't." Charlie downed a shot. "Are you giving up on Troy?"

"Hell no, fuck that," she said. "I'll buy a garage in a back alley if I have to."

"Then keep that whole shit, no matter what happens."

"Your vote of confidence is comforting."

"I know the city, *proper*, are bastards. Don't ever do this shit for them. Do it for you. And us, all of us."

"Run for city council, you dick, maybe I'll get a better shake."

Charlie looked around the room. "Run for city council yourself, Jordan."

One last unexpected person came in: Donny. He looked like dogshit. Doc was dressed with more care, and he was homeless, which made Jordan wonder just how rough the past couple of weeks had been.

"Donny, you're not here to cause trouble, are you? I still haven't got my Microbus totally fixed."

"I have to pay you back," Donny said. "It's been bad for me. I'm not holding it together. I wanted to come and tell you I'm sorry. I know it don't mean much, but I want to do something. Anything at all, put me to work."

"Donny, you don't have to—"

"Please," Donny's hard eyes bore into her. "I pay my debts, even when I don't have a dime. Let me help."

Jordan thought about it. "Okay, go in the back room, there's a shovel," she said. "We need to clear out more snow from the back patio."

Donny went off and Jordan hoped she wasn't giving him something to swing around.

The show trickled out around two a.m., something Jordan hadn't anticipated. She had nearly run out of liquor, and mostly did run out of beer by the end. The tills were fantastic, but as she shut the door, she knew she'd have to count the take from the door and the money on the CrowdPool and see if she could meet the balance of a hundred thousand dollars.

She locked up, letting Doc stay behind. She locked herself in her office and counted bills while the Doors played and Jim Morrison sang, *This is the end*—a somber choice for the task. She counted three times, to check for bills stuck to bills, or perhaps a hundred or two that were counted as twenties, but her count was accurate.

She was staring at five thousand dollars. Checking on the CrowdPool site, she had an extra ten thousand, which was amazing, but fifteen thousand wasn't close to what she needed to stop a costly, and ultimately futile, battle with the Riverfront Renewal Project.

She got damp in the eyes, but she pressed in with her palms. No. She wasn't going to do that. It wasn't what she was all about, or what Troy was all about. Troy's history was one of monstrous conflagrations that charred whole blocks and neighborhoods, but it always rose again, and stronger. And so would she. They wanted to take her right there? Fine. She'd rebuild right next door to City Hall and blast music into the mayor's office every day. She'd get a spot right on River Street somewhere and make for herself the iconic venue that Harley promised with his bullshit words.

She'd been smacked in the face and it stung, but life taught her to swing back, and she would.

"Did you do it, honey?" Doc said as she walked out.

"Not quite."

"I'm sorry, business is tough. But you don't give up, though. Don't give it an inch."

"I don't plan on it." Jordan got out her checkbook. She was wiped and might have to postdate some checks, but there were bills she had to pay. And some she wanted to.

Danielle

The tree glistened in the living room, multicolor lights twinkling in tiny plastic faux-candle tapered casings. Tinsel caught the lights and shot them through her children's eyes into her own, and it felt like a rekindling of everything she cherished. But there, in between the lights, in the places she and Craig left unadorned, lay the shadows where Danielle felt his presence watching over them in their loneliness.

She had an actual fire going in the fireplace. She bought a package of wood at Tollsby's, which would've made Craig laugh his face off. When they first got the house, Craig went off with his uncle to their family land up in Essex County, near Lake Champlain. They spent a whole weekend out there, chopping down a white oak and fashioning a cord of firewood, which took up their whole backyard.

When they realized they weren't going to be a wood burning family, Craig spent a year selling the wood off to the neighborhood for summer firepits, and he spent too many afternoons chopping it down into smaller sections. But it was Craig, never one to throw his hands up and leave something half done. The maker of lemonade.

Joey and Marybeth were allowed to stay awake until ten that night, much to the protest of both grandmothers. Marybeth would never make it until ten, but Joey would. Danielle planned on loading him up with sugar until about six, so that by nine he'd be crashing. It was sad to know your kids' drug habits.

"Mom?"

"Yes, my son." Joey hopped on her lap, wearing the superhero pajamas that were supposed to be a Christmas present until Danielle ran out of laundry detergent the other day.

Joey started playing with her ponytail.

"Is Santa coming tonight?"

"I'm sure he is, honey."

"Will you see him?"

"Maybe," Danielle said. "But he's already got his list, so you can't ask for anything else. The elves are done for the year."

"I'm on the nice list?"

"Why wouldn't you be?"

Joey wouldn't look her in the eyes. He wasn't much for hiding things, so she stroked his hair.

"What's on your mind, Buggy?"

Joey down put her ponytail. "What if Santa can't find us when we move to Grandma's?"

"Why wouldn't he be able to?" Danielle didn't have it in her to try to convince him they weren't going to have to move, a thing she couldn't even convince herself of. "Santa knows where all the nice little boys and girls are, even the naughty ones."

"But you said Grandma's a B-I-T-C-H sometimes, so does that mean she's on Santa's naughty list?"

Shit. "Okay, one, never say that to your grandmother. And two, I didn't mean it when I said that. I was mad. It has nothing to do with you."

"Is Santa Claus real?"

"Of course he is," Danielle said. "Why are you asking?"

Joey touched the fingers of his one hand with the fingers of his other hand. "'Cause Mike Bartoli is a mean butt-wipe, and he got a Module 10, and we don't even have our dad anymore, and it's not fair. If I'm not a naughty kid and Marybeth isn't, then why is Santa giving Mike Bartoli stuff and taking stuff away from us?"

"Santa didn't take your dad, Joey. You know that, right?"

"It's not fair." Joey buried his face in her sweater. She put her hand on his head.

"Buggy, I know it's not fair. But we'll all get through it. And it's not your fault, or Marybeth's fault, or Santa's fault."

Joey fell asleep with his face buried in her chest, and she let him sit there, her hand rubbing his little back, until he woke back up and, without a word, crawled off to go play in his room. Marybeth poked her head in and out all morning, mostly to eye the candy jar, her single-minded purpose being utter sugar annihilation.

Danielle heard the mail slot open and shut while she was holding Joey, and she found it odd, being Christmas Eve, because she didn't think there was mail delivery that day. But after she could get herself free and go into the kitchen for a mid-morning snack, she opened the door and checked the mail.

The box was bare, except for one envelope. Danielle picked it up and noticed that it didn't have a stamp on it. It was hand-delivered.

And inside was check from the business account of Sam Wilson's.

"God, Jordan, what the hell…" she murmured as she looked at the amount. Ten thousand dollars.

Danielle grabbed her phone and found Jordan's contact.

"Merry Christmas," Jordan said.

"Jordan, tell me you got enough to keep Sam Wilson's open."

"I can't tell you that. But I can tell you that the check is from a donation that came in late last night. I told them I couldn't take it, and they said they wouldn't take it back. So you get to stay in Troy, and I get to go out to dinner one night."

"You pimped yourself out for me. That's so sweet."

"I'm such a cheap date."

"You know the guy's gonna want a taste," she said.

Jordan laughed.

"I'll buy him a whore with what's left over," she said. "Win-win."

"God, Jesus, I can't accept this," Danielle said. "What are you even going to do?"

Jordan let out a slow breath. "I don't know yet. I'm still flushed that so many people showed up yesterday. Real roller-coaster week."

"I bet."

"Hey listen," Jordan said. "If you can, if you don't have the kids, come over tomorrow. I want to have a few of you over to hang out. I might close shop early this year to get a jump on whatever I'm planning on."

Danielle agreed. "So I just cash this?"

"Wait until after the first," Jordan said. "I postdated it."

Donny

The coffee pot was on its third rotation as people gathered around it to fill up, some grabbing a Styrofoam cup from the plastic-sheathed stack on the table, some using their own cups and mugs they brought. Donny had to use a Styrofoam cup, but if all went well, he'd be shopping for something distinctive, with a lid.

They were a hodge-podge of people. Some were rough, even rougher than him, wearing stuff that the thrift stores couldn't resuscitate. Others were dressed in two-hundred-dollar shoes and thousand-dollar jackets, but those people were few. It made him not feel so bad, and he imagined it made everyone there not feel so bad.

The urge to use, to transform yourself chemically, whether to escape your problems, or to take shortcuts in solving them, only to create more. This time bomb ticked in everyone's minds, and each day they needed the timer reset to keep it from exploding. Because when his exploded, Donny was on the floor of a Tollsby's, a dead sack that his sober self would've walked past with a feeling of disgust. That's what addiction made you.

Allen was talking to two of the other attendees. He was the one who ran into him yesterday outside of St. Benedict's Church, where they had a meeting and Donny had an idea that it was a spot he could get food money. It was actually food money, which he thought was why Allen took an interest in him. Because as much as he'd like to think Allen introduced him to the meeting, it was what Easy said to him the other night that took the needle out of his hand.

Allen walked the two over. "Donny, this is Bernie and Gail. Guys, this is Donny. He's brand new here."

Bernie and Gail shook his hand. Their hands were warm, sweaty, but full of life. He could only imagine how his felt.

"Nice to meet you," he said.

"Are you going to talk today?" Gail said.

"I'm not sure anyone wants to hear from me," Donny said. "I'm a little rough. I might trigger people to go use again."

"Don't think that," Bernie said. "Whatever you're going through right now, someone here is considering putting themselves back on that path. You might be the one that stops them."

Donny hadn't thought of that. "So I could be, like, a cautionary tale?"

"We're all cautionary tales," Allen said. "I hope I'm a cautionary tale to you, too."

Donny smiled, but he was feeling his guts rearrange themselves. He was a day without dope, and over the past night, he started feeling like shit. He felt like he had the flu. He couldn't imagine what long-term users felt after they had to go off dope or couldn't score. His drug of choice, until recently, was coke. Heroin wasn't even on his radar until that fuckface Lenin threw him the first kilo to sell.

Yet here he was. As shitty as he felt, he should've been thankful. The addiction in him was a demon that had grown weary of the half-hearted exorcisms. Donny was sick and tired of being sick and tired, and fed up with his own bullshit and broken promises.

Allen patted Donny's shoulder. He looked up at the clock. Time for the meeting. Donny was happy to take a break from the introspection.

Allen led the meeting. Donny didn't know if he always did, or how the groups were organized; he had no sense of protocol. He always saw the people who went there as weak people. It didn't take long being on the other side to realize they were the strong ones.

After handling the housekeeping stuff—announcements, rules, and the like—Allen had the new people introduce themselves. Donny surprised himself by speaking up. They all welcomed him in. Then there was a man who, it was pointed out to him, was the key speaker. Maury was small and thin and dressed like a man you would expect to be coaching a high-school basketball team.

Soccer. Not far off. His story wasn't Donny's story, but they shared the main points, starting with an affinity for coke, which the speaker started using in college to get his schoolwork done. Donny used it to get through twelve-hour days of contracting work. Both used it as a means to an end. Neither of them bought into the whole mystique of drugs. But each had let down those they loved.

Eventually, the key speaker sat down, and Allen asked around the room. Donny expected Allen to call on him, but apparently it didn't work that way. Eventually, Donny stood up, if for no other reason than that the bugs under his skin, which he knew weren't there, made sitting still a bitch.

"Hi, I'm Donny," he said.

Everyone said hello in unison.

"I died yesterday," he said. "I died in the Tollsby's on Sixth Avenue. Dead, hanging out the bathroom with a needle by my side, dead. Two minutes. The only reason I'm here is because someone had that Naloxone shit and sprayed it up my nose. And I flipped the guy off."

"I came here because a dealer told me to clean myself up." He glanced around and was amazed to find not one judgmental stare. Just curiosity, understanding, even. "He was a dealer who had beaten me up, and belittled me, and laughed at my face in front of his buddies. But I was begging for pills, so what could I do?"

Nods around the room, by people who'd begged and done worse.

"A month ago, I beat his ass for offering me those same pills. See, my friend, best friend, Craig, he died from mixing pills and alcohol. I don't think he meant to do that, but I was furious at the dealer. I was maybe furious at my friend, too, for being stupid. But I'm here right now, and I got dope sickness going on, and mostly I'm furious at myself."

Donny sat back down. Allen thanked him for sharing, and the room was filled with the sounds of approval that he knew came from experience.

Others told stories like his, like his near death tore open a topic that too many of them had been familiar with. After the meeting, Donny waited for Allen in the vestibule of the church.

"You did great, Donny," Allen said. "Really good first meeting."

"I got a lot more."

Allen smiled. "We're not going anywhere."

Chapter Twenty-Seven

Rob

They watched the *Twilight Zone* this year as they sat around the tree, presents wrapped beneath like foothills of pine needle and holly wrapping paper. The eggnog was in a white ceramic bowl with a matching ladle, the pair of them older, by a few years, than Rob was. Their manger was new on the sideboard, but the figurines beneath it had set the nativity scene for his great-grandparents on his mother's side. His father's side, though not against it, had no interest in Catholic iconography.

His mom sat in her rocking chair with a skein of yarn, knitting the end of a blanket for Rob's younger cousin, who was living in Manhattan working for a brokerage. The wind was whipping at the front window, but the heat blew up from the floor through a large vent, and it made the wind and the chill outside seem so distant.

"Okay, we're going to get set," his father said. "Theresa, are you ready for the presents?"

She put the skein and the blanket down carefully. "I want Rob to open up his first. Then you, then me."

"Ma, I'm fine however we do it," Rob said.

"I want to see the look on your face with this one thing," she said. "I saw it and thought of you. It wasn't expensive, but I know you're going to love it."

"You got it for me," he said. "Of course I'll love it."

His mother smiled wide. Rob sat down with his legs crossed and sorted the pile for his goodies. He told his parents not to get him anything beyond some body wash, boxer shorts, and other personal care items.

But he didn't hold himself to that standard. When he was laid off, one of the first things he did was go Christmas shopping. He was in a low place then, and his friends were all in the club that exchanged phone calls instead of gifts. So it was Mom and Dad on the shopping list, and he poured his heart into his shopping spree, short as it was.

The key, for as long as he'd shopped for Christmases or birthdays, or whatever special day they had, was for his gift to reflect how well he knew them. It wasn't about the money. It was the thought that counted.

He unwrapped his first gift, and it was a perfect example of his parents knowing him. A smoke detector. As he turned it over, he noticed that it had a convenient button to press when he was cooking bacon. The damn stupid one he had upstairs wouldn't stop going off.

"Thank you, guys," he said. "This is awesome." As he unwrapped his other gifts, there couldn't have been more than a hundred dollars' worth of stuff there, but each gift was going to be thoroughly used and treasured. That's why Christmas was always such a welcome time in the Paulson household.

Rob unwrapped his last gift, and the one his mother couldn't wait to for him to see. It was a towel set, gray and deep blue, emblazoned with wolves howling in the desert by the crescent moon. Strange as it sounded, Rob needed new towels that could handle all he put them through. He felt the towels and smiled.

"I'm actually going to put in a hand towel rail in the bathroom for these." He motioned to the hand towels. "I can't believe you found these."

"Like I said, I saw them, and thought of you."

Rob surprised his father with a new pocket watch. His dad was still an aficionado. Rob also got him a few artifacts from Troy's industrial history and a few very old newspapers, preserved in plastic sheets. He bought his mother a shawl, like the one she wore when he was young but could no longer find. He also bought her a porcelain angel with fiber-optic wings, a warm, relaxing pad for her car seat, and a handful of knitting books.

What he didn't wrap up was a Christmas card he bought for them both. Inside of it was a check, with a blank amount. It would be filled in as soon as he knew how much he could put on it, but it would be made out to a specific surgeon's office in Albany. He intended to give the gift of the surgery, as it was a gift given him, but at best it could be considered bittersweet.

Jordan and he worked out a plan for her to sell the property that Sam Wilson's sat on to the Troy EDC, but it was hardly a plan. More a statement of inevitable intent. She would get more than she paid for it, even with Rob getting a commission. She'd have enough to move on, and Rob would have almost enough to cover the surgery. A few more commissions, and he'd be there.

But a call from Asher earlier that morning changed the game.

"I got Harley on video saying they were getting PILOT programs from the city in exchange for buying out the people who live on development sites."

"I didn't know about the PILOT programs, but I've been telling you about the buyouts. What does this mean specifically?"

"You know, not much by itself," Asher said. "But when I went apeshit last night and told them my friend was getting screwed because of it and I thought The Sentinel would be interested in the video, Harley was shook."

"Jordan was going to sell. I hope this doesn't screw her up."

"They had a huge set piece with that park smack dab. They're planning a full neighborhood revitalization thing, man, no one's going to recognize that place when it's done. They're going to want her to sell bad. And now, they won't be able to just bulldoze her."

Rob was quiet for a second. "And you have the video."

"Yup."

"You should tell Jordan what you did."

Asher laughed. "Actually, just tell her you got leverage. Leave me out of it."

"Are you afraid you're going to get fired?" Rob said.

He could hear Asher inhaling, and he had to assume Asher was enjoying himself a little green Christmas.

"Not worried at all," he said. "I already got fired. Merry Christmas, dude."

Asher

It sat there, in his cupboard, since October, when Ginny thought it was hilarious to get Asher a Christmas dinner in a can. So there it was, on his first morning without a job in eight years, a shiny silver-wrapped can, all the way from the U.K. containing everything he would need to enjoy a feast of legends on a cold and lonely but cheery day.

He dished out the layers of his dinner, wishing he had the dexterity or the patience to take a knife to it and slide it out, like cranberry sauce, which was one of the layers. All in all, it was not the worst smelling stuff he'd ever pulled out of a tin can.

He turned on the television as he warmed his bounty in the microwave. He didn't expect there to be anything on the news, but he would've loved to see that smug asshole Harley being carried out in cuffs. That was never going to happen. Harley wasn't a criminal to anyone except the people not caught in his shiny window dreams. Guys like him got everything they wanted in the end. But Asher didn't care, because he wouldn't get it for free.

Asher debated going to the paper with the video, which even he had to admit would only make what they were doing politically unpopular and more expensive, but he figured it wasn't his fight. He was a frog who leapt the night before last. He liked his ponds, and the inertia of calm water.

It was the fight of people like Jordan, who could rally Troy with her voice and the heart she wore on her sleeve. Even if she sold, she'd take Harley, and the EDC, to the cleaners. They'd get their centerpiece, but Jordan would end up stronger than ever. And they had all next year to plan the comeback.

He played with his dinner on the TV table as the TV played "*Miracle on 34th Street*," as Kris Kringle sat in the courtroom and the mailbags came in, letters after letters.

He lit up the half-joint in his ashtray and felt the sweet kick in his lungs. He wasn't much of a smoker, not nearly as much as his downstairs neighbor, but he always kept a joint or two for Christmas and New Year's Eve, on the rare occasion that he didn't have to work. This qualified.

His manager fired him over the phone. As he looked back at it, he probably could've been arrested for extortion, except that he only threatened to release the video. In his odd fury, he hadn't given a thought to demands. That was Harley's mind at work. A guy couldn't get arrested for getting someone to extort themselves, could they? He'd find out, and he'd find out high.

The phone rang. *Black Betty*. Ginny's ringtone.

"'Yello,"

"Whoa, you're home. Ha."

"Yeah, why, what's up?"

"Bianca told me you got canned. True?"

Asher exhaled. "That is true."

"Weird, I'd expect you to be bugging out. What the hell did you do?"

"You know," he said. "Asshole customer, finally had it, blew up on him. The hotel business isn't really a long-term deal."

"Says the guy that's been there for eight years."

He stared at the joint's cherry. "We all gotta move around once in a while. Guess it was my time."

"Are you too fucked up to go to Sam Wilson's? Annette and I were going to go over and jam. Christmas Day is boring when you do the family thing the night before. You in?"

"Sure, fuck it. Why not?"

"You need a ride, Mr. Bake Boy?"

"That noticeable?"

"You're not bugging out right now, you've got to be pretty toasted."

Asher coughed out a big, steamy hit. "Pick me up then."

The snow was falling by the time they got to Sam Wilson's, and a light trace was on the ground, enough to cover the dirty piles from the previous storm in soft white. The front door was open, and Jordan was leaning back on it, arms folded. If Asher had just met her, he'd say she looked upset, but he'd gotten to know her well enough to see her posture as the stance of someone forever ready to engage the world.

"You guys cool to catch a cab home later, my treat?" Ginny said as they got out of the car. "I wanna drink a li'l…"

"I'll give you all a ride home if you're staying a while," Jordan said.

She welcomed them inside with hand gestures and followed them. Asher missed the party, and his contribution to the cause was going to the grave with him, so he was slightly in a bind over how to act. Ginny helped to make it even more tense.

"Hey, Jordan, Asher got shit-canned, day before Christmas. Nice of them, right?"

"Really, dude? What happened?"

"This guy, he was just, you know, shitting all over everything and everyone, not literally, but you know, we get the type. I had it, and I told him to get out or I'd toss his shit-stains out the window for everyone to see."

Jordan laughed and her eyes lit up. It was so pure. "Really?"

Asher mustered up a smirky face. "I'm paraphrasing."

"So you got shit-canned," Jordan said. "I wouldn't imagine you going off on somebody. You don't seem the type."

"I guess I was properly motivated."

Asher hated drinking before playing. Nobody kept time well when they were drinking. People missed changes, and everybody thought they weren't loud enough. The number one biggest thing Captain Pneuma fought about was not set lists or gigs or even who got to do what in the band aside from playing; it was whether Ginny could—or should—drink before they played.

But on Christmas Day, high as he was going to get till the next year, he added some proof to his belly and got up to jam. He let loose, not caring if he was too loud or too soft, playing through odd times and finding it a blast to do so. They made changes on the fly, and Asher would've liked to say he was doing it because suddenly he saw the merits of alcohol, but he knew it was freedom. Freedom from his job. Also, more importantly, freedom from himself.

They took a break, and Ginny and Annette sat offstage, talking about some new songs they had been working on. Asher sat at the bar, readying himself for another vodka martini.

"I just want to say," Asher said, his hand clamped down on the bar surface.

"Careful, bud," she said. "I can tell you don't drink much."

"I know." He took his hand away. "I want to say that I hope you do well, whatever you do. You deserve it. I hope that you're a part of the scene, that's all."

Jordan's features softened. "I'll be here," she said. "Maybe I'll hire you."

"I don't mix business with pleasure," Asher gave her an exaggerated wink.

She laughed. "Dork."

Jordan

She grabbed her bomber jacket off the table and put it on. It was a McPride design, green and black, with the diamond-plated sole of a work boot kicking out of a shamrock at the breast. She bought it off a guy that showed up at the club selling everything out of his truck. What she saw was a guy like her. Hell, dressed like her, daring to swim against the river so he could carve out his own tributary. That was when Jordan knew the idea she had for Sam Wilson's would be her own little tributary on the east bank of the Hudson.

Jordan wandered through the bar and the stage area, out into the main dance floor. In the past month, she'd seen it dismal and a deluge, placid and violent, with tears of laughter and of loss. She'd won. Whether she could keep the place or not, she'd succeeded in creating her own stream, that of words shot around shows in Clifton Park and Albany, at the people who, in their cups, would reminisce that "If only Sam Wilson's had gotten a better shot..."

She sat at one of the tables and stared at the empty stage. It was weird. Not once in the year she'd been setting up, had she ever just sat at one of the tables. Plenty of times she sat there with napkins and math scribbles, using geometry lessons everybody forgot from high school, trying to figure out the best placement of chairs, of lights, even double guessing the professionals she went to for help. She had never invested as much of herself in anything as this.

But then again, she wouldn't be there next year.

She considered asking a few people to come over and help her close up shop. She knew she was rushing it, that there was absolutely no hurry for her to get anything in order. She and Rob had an arrangement; she'd call him the next day, and ask for fifty thousand more than he would be allowed to offer her, the amount of which she knew. She felt bad that what they were doing was probably illegal, but what was being done to her, and to everyone else, was only legal because the crooks could afford to rewrite the laws as they went along. So no, she didn't feel as bad as her character urged her to be.

Her phone rang. It was Danielle. For the third time.

"Hey, hon. Sorry I didn't answer. Taking care of some stuff."

"That's okay. Are you sure? With this check? Aren't you trying to save Sam Wilson's? I don't want to—"

"Danielle, even with it, I'm not gonna be able to keep the place," Jordan said. "I'm just happy I can do something good with it."

"So wait, that's it?"

"I'm not really sure right now. I'm going back and forth between tucking in and packing up."

"You better get back up and running," Danielle said. "Look, we don't have anything around here anymore. This city sees us as a bad investment, all of us. We have tattoos, we drink; most of all, we remember when Troy didn't need luxury everything to be great. And they fear that."

"What happens when they go after the next place I buy?"

"We'll do the research. We'll find a place they'd have a hard time touching, and we go hard."

"You don't know how hard this was to set this all up."

"Then I'll find out when I help you set up the next one."

"I'm not saying I won't. I'm a little bummed right now."

Danielle was quiet. "I just want you to know that I didn't even really remember you, and you did more for me and my family than Craig's best friend did," she said. "And I know Donny's fucked up, but that's saying a lot. Don't give up on this shit. Two days ago, Troy, the real Troy, showed you it's not giving up on you.

"And one more thing," she said. "If you're really planning on giving up, I don't want this check. If Troy's not good enough for you, it's not good enough for me."

"You're not going to pull your kids out of school over it, are you?"

"No," Danielle said. "But this will be blood money."

Jordan sat at the only place at Sam Wilson's where she didn't feel the pressure of all that was on her, a spot on the jetty that Donny had shoveled off. She picked at her hoodie, realizing that she was completely decked out in underground design. She thought of asking the artists to work together to make a zombie version of Uncle Sam, complete with moth-eaten top hat. It would be great for a window decal when she opened the new Sam Wilson's.

She didn't realize she was planning for a Sam Wilson's Two until she started searching her recollections for possible sites. A smile escaped her impending sense of doom. She jogged back inside.

Her laptop was filled with stickers of things that were wrong; her favorites were deconstructed cartoon mascots and trick package advertisements. She flipped it up and pulled a flash drive out of her top pocket. She opened up her video recorder, adjusted her hair, and reached behind her to turn on the bar mood lighting.

"Hey, everyone, Jordan here." She ran her finger under her nose to catch an itch. "I want to thank you all for coming to the benefit, and to those who donated to the CrowdPool. I wish I could say that we pulled it off, but we came up a bit short. Well, more than a bit.

"I never thought, even when I opened this, that Troy would come out in force to try to save my ass. Truth be told, it's because I didn't think my ass would need saving, not so soon anyway.

"If I had known that they were going to develop this neighborhood and buy me out, it would be easy to say I wouldn't have fought, that I would've sat on an empty property, but I really don't think I would have.

"I was just thinking to myself that based on the people I met, and the times we had, though they were few, we all had a 'win' here. And I want to believe that, because it's easier to give up after a win.

"But now that I think about it, it wasn't a win. I didn't win, and more than that, we didn't win. I bought this place to give the old Troy a place to go. A community center for the rejects, no offense, since I consider myself one. So no, this wasn't a win. The new, prettier, touristy Troy won."

Jordan reached back and grabbed a bottle of whiskey. She pulled off the cap and took a slug.

"They're buying us up," she said. "Every day I see businesses that I grew up with having 'For Sale' signs in their windows long enough to reopen as a kale bar or a spa for little yapper dogs.

"I got money from you all, and it would be hard to return it all. It would also be unfair, to you, not to me. You all paid to save Sam Wilson's, so come the beginning of next year, I'm going to be looking for a new and improved Sam Wilson's somewhere else in the city, and I'll need your help then, too."

She took one last slug off the bottle, set it down, and pulled her jacket up over her shoulders.

"Oh, and Harley … if you want to buy me out, buy us out for your little candyfied Troy, you're gonna have to buy the whole goddamn city, 'cause we ain't gonna give it up without a fight."

New Year's Eve

When she was a little girl, Danielle's dad held her up on his shoulders and she pretended she was a hawk suspended in midflight, determined, with its magnificent eyes focused on the turbulence of the Hudson River and the fish that, unaware, went about their nights beneath the rippling waves.

She had Joey up, but it wasn't the same, thanks to the twelve feet of chain-link fence that was installed when one too many hapless people jumped off the bridge. They were all pressed against it to let passersby through the walkway, and they weren't the only ones on the bridge that night.

"Which one is going to start first, you think?" Jordan said. She sat on the railing that kept them from being a traffic hazard. Rob was standing next to her, trying to read a First Night program. She didn't know if it was for Albany's First Night or Troy's.

"My bet is Troy's," she said. "I'm guessing we're gonna blow our load first."

"Oh, Troy," Jordan said. Rob looked up.

"Huh?" Danielle and Jordan giggled.

Asher and Ginny were on the other side of the bridge, making whooping noises every few seconds. Asher turned his head over and made a megaphone out of his hand.

"What the hell are you doing?"

Asher turned around and, looking twice, hopped the guardrails and crossed the roadway.

"We're watching the boaters down under the bridge," he said. "One of them is playing with fire."

Jordan shook her head. "Then maybe you guys shouldn't be watching them."

"No, it's cool. They have a stick. It's a professional act, it looks like."

"Tell them to come over here, so we can see them."

"They can't hear us," Asher said. "Ginny's communicating by flashing her tits to them."

"Hey, kids," Danielle said. "Mouth."

Asher covered his mouth even though neither the kids nor Danielle were watching him. "Sorry."

Jordan laughed. "It's nice to see you in such a good mood, Ash."

Asher blew into his hands and rubbed them as if it was ten degrees below the balmy twenty-eight degrees that it was.

"I like my new job a lot," he said.

After he was fired, Asher wasted no time in finding another job. Jordan was proud of him, regardless of the fact that he didn't have a choice if he enjoyed food and a ceiling.

"So they're treating you good?"

"Every day I go in, and it's like I'm in the casting room for a time machine."

Asher's love of history met its match with A.J. Harris, where Jordan had gone to get all the historical decorations for Sam Wilson's. As she had to break stuff down, she called upon Danielle, Asher, and the others to help her sell off the things she couldn't store. Danielle and Asher walked into A.J. Harris with their arms full of materials Jordan had just purchased the year before, and Asher got even more back than Jordan paid with his historical knowledge, not to mention some salesmanship no one knew he had.

Asher had something for Jordan that he showed Danielle when they were waiting in Jordan's mostly empty club.

"Do you think she'll be weird about it?" he'd asked.

"Absolutely," Danielle said. "Do it anyway."

Joey was getting heavy. She eased him down. Rob tapped her shoulder and offered to lift him back up. Joey shook his head so hard Danielle had to hand him over to relax her muscles.

"New Year's Eve," Rob said. "New Year, new you? Got anything?"

"Like resolutions? Nah. Don't believe in 'em. You?"

"Maybe lose five pounds."

Danielle smiled. "You? Vain? Who would've thought?"

"My belt's a little tight," he said.

"So you trying to look good for someone?"

Rob glanced over. "I don't know, I kinda have a star-crossed lovers thing going on…"

Danielle inched closer as Joey went arms out, body straight like an airplane.

"Stars might be crossed for a while," she said. "Think you can handle that?"

"Got my telescope."

Danielle laughed. "Nerd."

The pop and sizzle came from the south. By then, Ginny had crossed the street to join them, and Donny, who'd been on the phone with Rob every day for the past week, was there, showing Ginny a coin that he kept on him to commemorate one week's sobriety, until he could earn his one-month coin. The night sky erupted in a yellow, blue, and red-purple glow as white streaks of sparks trailed out like wayward comet tails. It was smaller than the Troy lights would be, but soon they had fireworks coming from the north as well.

Danielle tugged at Rob's sleeve. "Look at Asher," she said. "Pray for that kid."

Asher unwrapped a box. Jordan didn't know how to react. It was way too big for a ring, and a little too big for a necklace. She had hoped that she wouldn't have to turn Asher down again, not on New Year's. She was starting to feel a little bit mad at being put on the spot, till she saw that Asher was holding a brick.

"It's one of Uncle Sam's bricks," he said. "They got it in at work. I'm gonna pay off on it a little. You do not pay me back. This is for Sam Wilson's Two. Build it with a real damn brick, even if we have to knock one out to put it in. Like a corner—"

Jordan grabbed him by the front of the shirt and kissed him as the Albany fireworks started their crescendo and the Troy fireworks started to pick up, grabbing the brick as she did so, because she knew that, in shock, he'd drop it on the walkway. She let him go.

"I'm not going to go out with you," she said.

He smiled.

She mouthed the words *Thank you*.

Acknowledgements

This book would not be possible without the following people: My mother, Mary Anne Sweeny, my family, Jim, Sophia, Michael, and Kayleen, Art Fredette, my brothers in arms Joe Clifford and Gabino Iglesias, for the edits that made this possible.

I would further like to thank Renee Fahey and the Street Soldiers crew, Dannielle Hille and A Block at a Time, Stephanie Bartik, Niki Chaos, Rob Smittix, Janet Stark, Jessica Von Guiness, Mike Tripodi, Juli Ersfeld, Josh Moskowitz, Tommy Smith and all the volunteers at the Eastern New York Red Cross not mentioned, Breanne, Val, and Kristen, who continue to make Troy interesting, and all my creative subjects at *Xperience Monthly*.

This book would not have been possible without the hard work and dedication of the Bronzeville Books crew; Danny Gardner, Allison Davis and Erin Mitchell.

Lastly, I'd like to acknowledge whatever pissed off person I forgot and now regret it, and Henry Lyman.

www.ingramcontent.com/pod-product-compliance
Lightning Source LLC
Chambersburg PA
CBHW072117020726
47501CB00003B/863